Amen Corner

Amen Corner

Rick Shefchik

Poisoned Pen Press

Copyright © 2007 by Rick Shefchik

First Trade Paperback Edition 2007

10 9 8 7 6 5 4 3 2 1

Library of Congress Catalog Card Number: 2006932882

ISBN: 978-1-59058-479-8 Trade Paperback

Poisoned Pen Press
6962 E. First Ave., Ste. 103
Scottsdale, AZ 85251
www.poisonedpenpress.com
info@poisonedpenpress.com

Printed in the United States of America

For Barbara

Acknowledgments

Thanks to John Camp for suggesting the idea and for gener-ously providing his expertise and encouragement.

Thanks to Dan Kelly for his editing skills, suggestions, enthusiasm and friendship.

Thanks to George Eskola for the hospitality.

Prologue

Saturday, April 5

The thick-necked, small-mouthed guard named Dewey opened the door to Lee Doggett's prison cell at 8:01 a.m.

"Big day for you, Doggett," Dewey said. "Eight years, huh? C'mon, grab your stuff. Warden wants to say so long."

"You're late," Doggett said, glowering at the apathetic state employee who'd just stolen another minute of his freedom. Doggett was tempted to sink his fingers into the soft, stubbly flesh of Dewey's neck and snap his spinal cord like a celery stalk, then haul the guard's gelatinous bulk to the back of the cell and smash his face to pulp on the rim of the steel toilet. He could do it, easily; he'd worked out in the prison weight room from the day he arrived at Reidsville, with the sole purpose of turning himself into an executioner. But he wouldn't waste his talents on Dewey, even though the lazy pig had forced him to spend 60 extra seconds in the 6-by-12-foot box that had been his home for the past 2,848 terrifying, humiliating, rage-filled days and nights.

"Aw, so what?" Dewey said. "Like you got plans or somethin'?"

The same plans I've had from the day they sent me to this urinal eight years ago, Doggett was tempted to scream at him. *I'm going to Augusta to kill my father.*

◇◇◇

There was no one to meet Doggett when he walked out the main entrance of the Georgia State Penitentiary at Reidsville. His mother was dead, his wife and kid long gone—off to Florida, last he'd heard. He put the nylon gym bag he'd arrived with eight years ago over his shoulder, refusing to turn around and look at the bleached-white walls, barred windows, and cyclone fences of the prison he was leaving behind. It didn't matter where he'd been. All that mattered was where he was going.

The Masters would begin in less than a week. His father was always in Augusta for the Masters.

The April sun had already pushed the temperature into the sixties. Sweat began trickling down the small of his back as he walked the quarter-mile to the state highway that led into Reidsville. The sun felt warm and strange on his face—there was something different about the way the sun shone and the wind blew when you were outside the confines of the prison yard. It felt good, but it felt loose and wild, too—like no one could tell nature what to do. That's the way he felt, too.

Traffic was light, maybe three or four cars per minute. No one would be crazy enough to pick up a hitchhiker that close to a state prison, but Doggett hung out his thumb anyway as he walked along, thinking about his route: North into Reidsville, northeast on U.S. 280 to Claxton, then north on U.S. 25 through Statesboro to Augusta. He'd memorized the route from maps in the prison library, since he'd never been to Reidsville before the judge had sentenced him there for printing and selling counterfeit Masters badges and possession of a controlled substance with intent to sell. His idiot public defender had assured him that trafficking in bogus passes to a sporting event normally got you three-to-five, at most. The dumb son of a bitch apparently didn't realize that normal rules don't apply to Augusta National.

Someone at the club put pressure on the Richmond County police and the district attorney. The D.A. pressed for the maximum and the judge threw the book at him: 15 years, no parole. A year later, the Georgia Sentence Review Panel agreed that Doggett's sentence was extreme and cut it to eight, with credit for time served while waiting for his trial.

The drug charge was the part they couldn't ignore, but it was pure bullshit; the cops planted the cocaine in his house. And he knew why: His father wanted to see Doggett in prison—with luck, to die there. He was a big man at Augusta National, and the cops would be glad to do him a favor.

They'd wish they hadn't.

In addition to the weight room, Doggett killed a lot of time in the prison library. You could learn a lot just thumbing through the magazines and newspapers. You could learn, for instance, that there was a women's group raising hell about Augusta National still not having a woman member. There were going to be protests again this year; the media and the TV networks were going to make a big deal about it. The chairman of Augusta National, some corporate button-down named David Porter, kept telling the world that the club would admit a woman when the time was right, not when they were told to do it. But now some of the members were talking to the press, saying the time might be right.

Everybody was pissed off. Perfect cover.

You could learn a lot from the guys you met in prison, too. Like Bernard Pettibone. The guy was a certifiable lunatic, but he knew more about bombs than an Al Qaeda terrorist. Mailbox bombs, letter bombs, car bombs, fertilizer bombs, shoe bombs, pipe bombs—if something or someone needed blowing up, Pettibone knew how to do it, with the cheapest materials.

"Ain't no trick to makin' things explode," Pettibone told Doggett one night in the mess hall. "It's basic chemistry."

Pettibone was doing thirty to life for maiming a county judge with a mailbox bomb. The judge had ordered Pettibone to clean up the junk around his farmhouse, and Pettibone had taken exception to the infringement on his property rights. The judge lost his left arm up to the elbow, and the left side of his face. Pettibone would have gotten away with it if he hadn't decided to leave another one for the county sheriff. It went off on the front seat of Pettibone's car while he was parked in front of the sheriff's house. Pettibone was luckier than the judge; he lost only two fingers on his right hand, a chunk of his thigh, and all the hair on the right side of his head. With his wispy blond hair hanging lank on the other side of his pale, scarred skull, he looked like a baseball with the stuffing coming out.

"See, explosions is just a increase in volume from oxidation, causin' a violent release of hot gas," Pettibone told him. "You just need your fuel, your accelerant, your container, and a spark. The spark gets the oxidation goin', and when the container can't hold the pressure no more, you got your explosion. Get me?"

Doggett understood chemistry—he'd understood all that school shit, but he knew he was never going to college, so why work at it?

Pettibone seemed to think further explanation was necessary.

"Here's your fuel."

He scooped up a spoonful of mashed potatoes from his plate.

"Here's your container."

He spooned the potatoes into the empty apple juice carton.

"Here's your accelerant."

He poured a few drops of water from a plastic cup onto a piece of napkin and placed it in the carton, on top of the potatoes.

"Then alls you need is a fuse—" he twisted up a paper napkin and stuffed it into the carton— "and a spark."

He pretended to light the napkin, and stared it for several seconds with a kind of intensity that suggested he was watching a real fuse burn down. Doggett had seen it all in prison, but this guy still gave him the creeps. Then Pettibone brought his fist down hard on top of the carton, splitting the sides and sending mashed potatoes spurting onto them and all the nearby inmates.

"Godammit, Pettibone, you fuckin' psycho!" one of the spattered prisoners yelled, diving across the table at him while

Pettibone bayed with delight like a hound dog. The guards rushed to the table and hauled Pettibone off to solitary.

The lesson had not been lost on Doggett. If a total nutjob like Pettibone could make a bomb, he could, too.

◇◇◇

He walked through Reidsville, a typical Georgia town with a few gas stations, feed stores and restaurants, and began hitch-hiking again north of town. He was halfway to Bellville when a farmer in a powder blue Chevy pickup eased over onto the dirt shoulder and pushed the passenger side door open.

"Gettin' too hot to walk," the farmer said. "Hop in."

"Thanks," Doggett said.

"Where y'all headed?" the farmer asked.

He had a weather-beaten face and wore a greasy green seed cap with a plastic adjustable strap in back, a denim work shirt, newer Levis with the cuffs rolled up, and a pair of battered brown work boots. He looked briefly at Doggett, but didn't seem to give much thought to why a man wearing a denim shirt, jeans, and carrying a gym bag would be hitch-hiking on this road. Doggett slid into the front seat and the farmer pulled back onto the highway. George Jones was on the radio, wailing about getting drunk; Christ, Doggett thought, isn't that guy dead yet?

"Augusta," Doggett answered.

"Ain't goin' that far," the farmer said, "Just headin' back to my place north of Claxton. I had to run down to Reidsville for some fertilizer."

He gestured over his shoulder to the bed of his pickup, where Doggett saw dozens of 25-pound sacks of fertilizer stacked to the back window.

"What are you growing?"

"Corn, mostly."

"Planting kind of late, aren't you?"

"Crop's already in. I'm just stocking up for next year. Sale at the co-op this week. You farm?"

"No," Doggett said. "I used to work on the grounds crew at a golf course."

"Uhm," the farmer said, unimpressed.

Doggett took a good look at the farmer. He wasn't particularly big, but he was wiry, the kind who had ropes for muscles from working with farm supplies and equipment every day of the year. His kids would be grown now, most likely gone. There would be a wife, though.

"You want some help with those bags?" Doggett asked.

"Naw," the farmer said.

"Least I can do for the ride," Doggett said.

"You ain't gotta be someplace?"

"Not today."

"Wife's in Atlanta this weekend," the farmer said after a while. "I guess I wouldn't mind a hand."

◇◇◇

By the time they got to the farm, an 80-acre spread on the northwest side of Claxton with a neat white clapboard farmhouse and a pole barn, Doggett found out that Don Robey's kids had moved away right after high school, passing up farming for the lights of Atlanta. His wife Marge was visiting them, and wasn't due back home until Wednesday night.

By the time he'd carried the first sack of fertilizer into the pole barn, Doggett had spotted the axe.

He stayed in the barn and waited until Robey had a sack of fertilizer over his shoulder, about to drop it on the pile with the others. Doggett came up behind him and swung the blunt part of the axe like a baseball bat, catching the farmer flush on the back of the head with a crunching thud and sending him sprawling onto the fertilizer bags. He was prepared to start hacking at Robey, but he didn't need to. The first blow had killed him.

He waited until just after the sun set and buried Robey and the axe a good 75 yards out in the cornfield, making the grave look exactly like the furrows around it.

He returned to the farmhouse and wandered through, looking for anything that might prove useful. He found a pair of work gloves, a loaded Smith & Wesson revolver, a box of bullets and a good, sharp hunting knife in the basement; upstairs, in an unused bedroom with a dusty Dominique Wilkins poster on the wall, he found $6,700 in a cigar box in a desk drawer.

He fried up some hamburger in the kitchen, drank a couple of beers, and watched TV until nearly midnight, then drove Robey's pickup into Statesboro. He found an unlighted football practice field on the campus of Georgia Southern University and parked on the street next to the small wood and metal grandstand. He filled an old metal watering can he'd found in Robey's pole barn with fertilizer from the bag he'd left in the truck bed. He doused one of Robey's pit-stained undershirts with gasoline and put it in the watering can, on top of the fertilizer. Then he rolled up a full sheet of newspaper into a cylinder, unscrewed the broad, perforated metal cap on the watering can's spout and stuffed the newspaper into the spout until it touched the gas-soaked shirt.

Doggett took one more look around. No one in sight. *Okay, Pettibone—let's see if you knew what the fuck you were talking about.*

He walked under the grandstand and placed the can beneath the fourth row of the six-tiered structure. He lit the newspaper with a kitchen match and ran to the idling truck. He was a block down the street when the can blew up with a boom that could have been heard on the other side of the campus—maybe the other side of town. He could see sheared-off wooden planks and twisted chunks of metal railing strewn around the smoky field as lights began turning on in the nearby dorms.

Pettibone, you sick, beautiful bastard.

Doggett drove north on U.S. 25 through downtown Statesboro, grinning and smacking the steering wheel with his open palms. He hadn't been this elated since—when? Not in the last eight years, that was for sure.

It was 80 miles to Augusta.

See you soon—Dad…

Chapter One

Sunday, April 6

Sam Skarda sat on the front porch of his South Minneapolis bungalow and waited for his cab to arrive. It was a cool morning in early April, but the sunshine felt warm on his face through the budding branches of the towering elm trees that lined the street. A pair of robins hopped across the mottled lawn.

Next to him on the porch was his golf bag, zipped into a travel cover, and his suitcase, packed with everything he thought he'd need, even in the unlikely event that he made the cut in the Masters: seven golf shirts, three of them new; five pairs of pressed cotton pants in assorted shades of khaki; two pairs of shorts and two t-shirts for lounging between rounds; a summer-weight suit, an oxford shirt, and a striped tie; enough socks and underwear for a week; three new golf gloves; a golf hat bearing the U.S. Publinx logo; two pairs of golf shoes—one that was almost new—and a polished pair of loafers; a rain jacket; a cotton sweater; his favorite pair of blue jeans; his overnight shaving kit; a 200-count bottle of ibuprofen; his shoulder holster and his .40 millimeter Glock handgun.

Sam wasn't an active-duty cop anymore, but he still had a permit to carry. After ten years on the force, he felt naked without his gun. He couldn't imagine why he'd need it at Augusta National, but packing it was a long-ingrained habit.

He took his invitation out of his jacket pocket and read it again:

The Board of Governors of the Augusta National Golf Club
cordially invites you to participate in the Masters Tournament
to be held at Augusta, Georgia, the 10th, 11th, 12th, and
13th of April. David Porter, Chairman. RSVP

He'd earned the invitation by winning the previous summer's U.S. Public Links tournament, open to any low-handicap amateur with no private course affiliation. If it had been held anywhere else but at Rush Creek Golf Club, 20 minutes from his house, he never would have entered. But when he made it into the match play rounds and started beating the college hot-shots, it occurred to him that he had as good a chance as anyone to win the tournament.

He'd been shot in the left knee while on duty as a Minneapolis police detective two years ago. The surgery had been complicated; he'd needed almost a year to rehab. His orthopedic surgeon ordered him to walk as much as possible. To Sam, that meant golf. He practiced and played every day until he could no longer stand, then got up the next morning, swallowed a handful of Advils, and did it all over again.

By the time the Publinx came to town, he was walking well and playing even better—much better than his days on the varsity at Dartmouth, when he'd actually harbored some thoughts about turning professional. But that had been a decade ago, before he chose law enforcement over the living-out-of-the-trunk-of-your-car lifestyle of an aspiring tour pro.

One guy on his college golf team had chosen to chase the dream, and made it happen. Shane Rockingham had been all-Ivy. He was also a case of squandered potential who would rather get drunk than go to bed the night before a big tournament, and a campus playboy who went through girlfriends the way he went through range balls. Sam had lost touch with him during Rockingham's years of scuffling on the Asian, Hooters, and

Nationwide tours, but he was in all the papers and magazines now, a muscle-bound basher with good looks, a swollen bank account, and two divorces, with a third on the way.

Thanks to the pairings committee at Augusta National, Sam was going to reunite with Rockingham soon. They were scheduled to play their first two rounds together at the Masters.

He put the invitation back in his jacket pocket and pulled out the two badges he was carrying with him to Augusta: the laminated Masters participant badge that had been mailed to him several weeks earlier; and the silver Minneapolis Police Department badge that he rarely carried with him anymore.

The Masters badge had his picture on the front: short, sandy-blond hair, still kept at police trim; pale blue eyes that an old girlfriend had once described as the color of a lake on a cloudy day; a slight crook in the bridge of his nose from running into a fence in a high school baseball game; and a clean-shaven face that showed the hint of a golfer's tan, with the cheeks, nose, and chin darker than the forehead.

The silver-plated police badge was heavier. An eagle spread its wings above the engraved words *Minneapolis Police*; his badge number was engraved below the seal of the city. He was still entitled to carry it, but he didn't know if he wanted to anymore. He'd discovered during his layoff that there was more to life than putting assholes in jail.

Sam had spent much of the previous year filling his 60-gig iPod with thousands of songs from his CD collection. He put each track into a playlist from the month and year the song was released, going all the way back to the '50s. He preferred older music—pure escapism into long-gone eras that seemed more innocent than they probably were—and he hated to listen to songs out of season. "Hot Fun in the Summertime" sounded as ridiculous to him in January as "The Christmas Song" did in July.

He put in his earbuds and dialed up the playlist for April, 1969, the month and year that George Archer won the Masters. The first song was "Will You Be Staying After Sunday" by the Peppermint Rainbow. Sam's goal this week was just to stay *until* Sunday.

A coffee-colored sedan accelerated up his block, too fast for the neighborhood; Sam was about to get up and yell at the driver to slow down when the car pulled to the curb in front of his house. It was an unmarked squad car, and Sam knew the driver: deputy chief Doug Stensrud, head of the investigations bureau.

"I'm glad I caught you before you left, Sam," Stensrud said as he got out of the car.

He was a broad-shouldered man with a dark moustache and thick, black hair that was turning white from the center of his forehead outward. He'd been Sam's partner for a couple of years after Sam was promoted to detective. Then Stensrud made deputy chief, and became his boss. There was still a bond between them, but the relentless paperwork and pressure from the chief, the city council, and the mayor had taken a toll on Stensrud's sociability.

"What's up, Doug?"

"I just wanted to wish you good luck at the Masters," Stensrud said, laboring up the concrete steps to the porch. He'd put on about thirty pounds since he and Sam had been partners.

"You could have sent flowers and balloons like everybody else."

Stensrud eased himself into the Adirondack chair next to Sam's and wiped his damp forehead with the sleeve of his sport coat.

"Weather's finally warming up," he said.

Sam knew what was on Stensrud's mind.

"Might as well spill it, Doug."

"Sam, it's been almost two years since you got shot and took medical leave. Don't you think that's long enough?"

"No," Sam said. "I still have things I want to do."

"Like what?"

"Climb Mount Everest."

"You've had time," Stensrud said, looking at him out of the corner of his eye, without turning his shoulders. He returned his gaze to the sidewalk, where a mother pushed a stroller over the cracks in the concrete. "Look, we need you back. We've got eight unsolved homicides since the first of the year, and you know the gang killings are about to start piling up. Now, it's great that you're getting a chance to play in the Masters. We're all thrilled beyond words. But I gotta tell you, your odds of making it on the pro tour are between zero and dick."

Sam laughed. Nobody knew better than he did that this was not only his first major championship, but his last.

"I'm not turning pro, Doug."

"Then it's time for you to get serious about your job. I'd like you to come back to work after Augusta."

A passenger jet rumbled overhead, low to the South Minneapolis rooftops in its landing pattern. Sam waited till the noise abated. He wasn't sure if Stensrud was asking or ordering. Technically, his leave of absence was good for one year. The department could extend it if he asked, but they didn't have to.

"What if I don't?" he finally asked.

Stensrud now shifted around in his wooden chair to stare at Sam.

"We want you, but we need a body," Stensrud said. "You're one of the best detectives I've ever worked with, but you're useless to me if you're not working. I've got cases to clear. If you don't come in after next week, I'll hire somebody else. I've got a stack of resumes to choose from. Some of them look pretty good."

Sam was surprised to feel a brief pang of concern. It was like seeing another guy dating the woman you broke up with.

"I'm not ready," Sam said.

"Sam, I know it sucks to get shot. I've become a fucking blimp since I took that one in the hip ten years ago. But I went back to the streets. I had to—I'm a cop. And cops get shot sometimes."

Sam had gone through all of that with the department psychologist that Stensrud had insisted he see. He'd told the doctor that he wasn't worried about getting shot again—although he also wanted to ask the condescending prick if he'd ever taken a bullet. He just didn't feel the same way about the job that he did when he first made detective. He was tired of chasing scumbags, tired of working for civil servant wages, and tired of taking shit from the good people of Minneapolis for doing the work they wanted done but were too lazy, scared, or morally superior to do themselves.

The months away from the job had been the most stress-free time he'd had since college. He wanted more of it. In fact, Sam wanted to tell Stensrud he would turn in his badge and his gun as soon as he got back from Augusta. But he couldn't do it. He'd gone through his savings and needed to start cashing paychecks again. Maybe it would have to be cop paychecks.

"I told you I'd make a decision after the Masters, Doug."

"I need your answer a week from Monday," Stensrud said. "I can't hold your job open any longer. I need a cop, whether it's you or somebody else. In or out, Sam—it's time to make a decision."

A maroon airport taxi pulled up next to Stensrud's squad car and sounded its horn.

"There's my limo," Sam said, getting up from his chair.

"Need a hand?" Stensrud asked.

"Think you can handle a golf bag?"

They walked down to the street as the cabbie opened the trunk for the bags.

"You'd make a good caddie," Sam said to the deputy chief, who easily slung the bag off his shoulder and into the trunk.

"I'm a cop," Stensrud said. "So are you. Call me as soon as you get back."

Chapter Two

Lorraine Stanwick sat in front of the mirror in the bedroom of the Firestone Cabin and fiddled with the clasp of her pearl necklace for several minutes before deciding she had to ask her husband for help.

"Ralph, could you come in here a minute," she called toward the living room. "I can't get this fastened."

Ralph Stanwick was sitting in a padded armchair, alternately watching television and looking at the golf course through the living room window. He never got tired of the view of the 10th fairway, even during Masters Week when tens of thousands of ordinary golf fans traipsed up and down the hills, some within just a few feet of the cabin, leaving their footprints, their trash, and their common taint on his beloved Augusta National.

Stanwick got up from his chair with a muttered curse and walked into the bedroom. The one-story house with white wooden siding and a gray roof was located next door to the Jones cabin and just east of the clubhouse, facing the 10th tee. The central living room was decorated modestly with framed photos of the National's early years, and furnished with casual, comfortable arm chairs, a leather sofa, and a dining table off the kitchen. The bedrooms were located on either side of the living area. Due to their membership seniority and Ralph's position on the club's governing board, the Stanwicks had stayed in the Firestone Cabin during Masters Week for many years.

"What is it now?" Stanwick asked.

"This necklace," Lorraine said. "Can you do the clasp?"

She turned her back to her husband and held the two ends behind her neck.

"I need my glasses," said Stanwick, a tall, trim man who was mostly bald, with gray hair at the temples and eyebrows. His wife was five years younger, carried no extra weight, applied just the right amount of makeup to deal with her aging skin, and was wearing a tasteful Oscar de la Renta spring skirt and blouse combination. Stanwick thought his wife was shapeless, bland, and dressed like an old woman.

Stanwick returned to the living room to find his reading glasses, and stopped in front of the TV to watch a local news reporter talking about the annual influx of golf fans that would hit town Monday morning. The reporter mentioned—as reporters always did, because the club requested them to—that police would be looking for scalpers and counterfeiters along Washington Road all week.

"Richmond County Sheriff Leonard Garver said that his department confiscates as many as a dozen bogus badges each year," the reporter said. "Augusta National won't comment, but sources say a four-day badge can sell for up to $10,000 on the street..."

Stanwick couldn't help thinking back to the trial. He hadn't been there, of course, but he'd gotten the verdict he wanted—or so he thought. Sixteen years would have been just about enough. Enough for Lee Doggett to get killed by an inmate, or maybe kill one himself. Even if he did make it to the end of his original sentence, Stanwick would either have been dead or too old for Doggett to bother with.

But Stanwick didn't dare attempt to influence the Sentence Review Panel. As a resident of Connecticut, he knew no one on the panel, and didn't have enough pull with anyone who did. The new sentence—eight years—had not been long enough, and the eight years were up. Doggett was out now.

"Ralph?" his wife called from the bedroom. "Did you get lost?"

Stanwick picked up his reading glasses and returned to the bedroom.

"You are so distracted lately," Lorraine said, turning her back to him again with the ends of the necklace in her hands. "Is something wrong?"

"Nothing's wrong," he said. He put on the glasses and began the aggravating task of trying to fasten the tiny clasp. He fumbled the little lever that opened the hook several times, and finally gave up in disgust.

"Wear something else," he said.

"We're having dinner with Harmon and Annabelle tonight, and I want to look nice," Lorraine said. "I'll bet you don't even remember when you bought this string for me."

He didn't. He knew it had probably been a gift some years back to cover up for something else he'd bought at their usual Manhattan jewelry store for one of his girlfriends. How could he be expected to remember which girlfriend, or when it was?

Stanwick returned to the living room and sat down again, his mind returning to the subject that had worried him ever since he and Lorraine had left Connecticut for their annual trip to the Masters. He had no doubt that Doggett knew he had been behind the planted drugs and the excessive sentence, and he had no doubt what Doggett would do to him if they were somehow to meet. He glanced at the date window on his watch. April 6. Doggett had been out for a full day. Where was he now? Would he dare come back to Augusta? Even if he did, could he somehow get inside the gates and find me? Not likely…but not impossible. Masters Week, after all, was the one week of the year that the club opened its gates to the outside world. Stanwick was vulnerable—and the green jacket that members wore when they were on club grounds would make him that much easier to identify.

He didn't dare call the police. That might stir up old business that was best left forgotten. They'd want to know why he'd be afraid of a former groundskeeper who'd served his time. Best to just get through the week, be wary, and get out of town as soon as the Masters was over. Maybe Doggett wouldn't come back.

By next year, things could be different. There were ways to have Doggett taken care of permanently.

Stanwick hated Lee Doggett for ruining springtime in Augusta—a time and a place he loved best in the world. More than winter in Palm Beach. More than summer in the Hamptons. More than autumn on Wall Street.

He loved the sincere, "Hello, Mr. Stanwick! How was your winter?" that he received from nearly every employee on the grounds, from the locker room attendants to the waiters to the pro shop crew to club manager Bill Woodley. He loved seeing his friends from around the country, the captains of industry, finance, and government who forgot about business at the National, and instead just played cards, smoked cigars, drank good scotch, told filthy stories, and played golf on the finest and most coveted course in America. Most of all, Stanwick loved the looks of envy he received from gawkers on Washington Road every time he made the turn onto Magnolia Lane.

Now, he was afraid to look at those gawkers. One of them could be Doggett.

It was the one mistake Stanwick wished he could go back and fix. That first year as a member, he was so enthralled with the sense of power and privilege that came with the green jacket that he felt he could do anything. When that maid caught his eye, coming in to clean his cabin as he was leaving for a round of golf, he got the stupid idea that, with Lorraine back in Connecticut, this was just another easy opportunity.

He had stayed in bed the next morning, pretending to be sick. He told the boys he might catch up with them on the back nine. When the maid came in   Laverne Evans, according to her name badge—she saw him in bed and said she'd come back later. He asked her not to go; he asked her to come into the bedroom and feel his forehead. Stanwick was young then, almost handsome—and with more hair. He was obviously well-off financially—how was a cleaning woman supposed to resist that combination? Besides, technically he was her boss—the employees were told they worked for the club members.

She had been nervous, but she came into the bedroom. He put her hand up to his forehead, and she said he didn't feel warm. She tried to take her hand away, but he held it, kissed it, ran his hand up her arm, told her she was beautiful, eventually drew her down to the bed with him and began unbuttoning her maid uniform. He could tell she didn't want it to happen, but she didn't pull away, either.

When he saw her the following year at the club, her name badge said Laverne Doggett, and she would not look at him. In fact, they didn't speak a word to each other for another 19 years, until the day she stopped him as he was getting into his car behind the Firestone Cabin and told him they had a son named Lee who desperately needed a job. Stanwick laughed at her, but she showed him a picture of Lee. It could have been Stanwick's picture from his prep school yearbook.

"I'll make you take a blood test if I have to," Laverne had said, her voice shaking, yet iron determination mixed with the fear in her eyes.

That would be a disaster, Stanwick realized. He wasn't as worried about Lorraine's reaction as he was about being booted from the club if it became known he'd fathered a bastard child with one of the maids.

"Does he know?" Stanwick asked her.

"No. He thinks his real daddy's dead."

"Don't tell him. I'll take care of it. But don't ever—ever— speak to me again. If any of this gets out, you know you'll be fired immediately."

I should have found a way to be rid of both of them right there, Stanwick had told himself many times since then. Instead, he arranged an interview for Doggett with Jimmy Fowler, the club's superintendent.

Doggett was hired as a greenskeeper, seemed to do a good job, and never gave any indication that he knew who Stanwick was the few times they passed each other on the grounds. Laverne, petrified of losing her job, avoided Stanwick from that point on.

Then came the counterfeiting arrest. Stanwick couldn't believe Doggett would be stupid enough to risk one of the best jobs in Augusta for a few thousand bucks. There was something wrong with that kid. He'd had his chance. Now it was time to get rid of him.

It had been easy enough to find a friendly cop who was willing to plant drugs in Doggett's house in return for some political favors with his higher-ups, and the judge—in return for a couple of extra Masters badges—was amenable to using Doggett as an example for those who thought they could rip off Augusta's most important fixture.

If only that sentence had stuck…

"In other state news, authorities are investigating the disappearance of a farmer from rural Claxton, Georgia," the news anchor said. "Sixty-one-year-old Don Robey has not been seen since Saturday afternoon, and Tattnall County authorities report evidence of a robbery at his farmhouse…"

The locator map on the screen showed Claxton about 50 miles west of Savannah—and about 100 miles south of Augusta. Not that far from Reidsville.

"Ralph, are you going to put your tie on?" Lorraine said, now standing next to him. "We're supposed to meet the Ashbys on the veranda in five minutes."

"Aren't we spending enough time with them already?" Stanwick said. "Let's just order something from the kitchen."

"Ralph, what's gotten into you?" Lorraine said. She was used to being shut out of her husband's business dealings, and she wasn't naïve enough to believe he didn't have his little flings now and then. But when she was with him at Augusta National, he was usually compliant with her social requests. Dinners at the clubhouse with the other members were their special times together.

"Ashby should have kept his mouth shut when that reporter talked to him last week," Stanwick said. "If he wants women to join this club, that's nobody's business but his."

Stanwick turned his back on his wife and re-knotted his tie while he watched the newscast.

"Also last night, an unexplained explosion rocked the Georgia Southern campus in Statesboro," the anchor continued. The news footage showed the charred remains of a small wooden grandstand; then a new locator map came up behind the anchor, showing Statesboro to be 80 miles south of Augusta. "No one was injured in the blast that occurred at approximately 1:30 a.m., though Georgia Bureau of Investigation authorities estimate the apparently homemade device could easily have injured or killed dozens, had the grandstand been occupied. University officials and Statesboro police have turned up no motive for the blast..."

"Ralph, are you listening to me?" Lorraine said. "We have to go. Harmon and Annabelle are waiting."

Stanwick turned off the TV and put on his green jacket. Yes, he thought, feeling a chill that seemed to begin between his shoulder blades and descend down his spine to the pit of his stomach. We should go.

The phone rang as they were heading out the back door.

"Let it ring," Stanwick said.

But Lorraine waved him off and went back into the living room to answer the phone. She said hello, then called to her husband.

"Ralph, it's for you," she said.

"Who is it?"

"I don't know."

Stanwick took the phone and said hello. The line was dead.

It couldn't be Doggett. How would he know where to call? Then again, he worked at the National for five years. Maybe he did know...

"Who was it?" Lorraine asked.

"No one," Stanwick said. "They hung up. Come on, we're late for dinner."

Chapter Three

It was a few minutes before midnight when Lee Doggett parked the blue pickup truck in front of the playground on West Vineland Road and turned off the ignition. The playground—sparsely equipped with a plastic climbing structure, a swing set, and a couple of benches—and the houses on either side of it were separated from the densely wooded eastern boundary of the Augusta National property by a six-foot chain-link fence.

There were no lights on at any of the neatly kept brick houses up and down the street. Nevertheless, Doggett remained in the cab, making sure there was no one moving in the middle class neighborhood. Doggett knew there were security guards patrolling the grounds, but at night they tended to stay close to the clubhouse. He would avoid them by going in over the playground fence. He'd be finished in a few hours, and he'd be back at the truck long before the newspapers were delivered along West Vineland.

He put the Smith & Wesson and a small flashlight that he'd stolen from the farmer into the pockets of his windbreaker, got out of the cab, closed the door softly, and walked through the deserted playground to the back fence. Glancing over his shoulder a final time to be sure he wasn't being watched, Doggett put his toe into one of the metal holes and hoisted himself up and over the fence.

It's good to be back at the National. Did anybody miss me?

Eight years had done little to impair his sense of the club's geography, and the moon filtering through the tops of the towering loblolly pines provided all the light he needed. He set out westward through the woods and soon came to the large parking area for the television production trailers, surrounded by trees and positioned well away from the golf course. The public never saw this area, even though it was less than 100 yards from the eastern edge of the par 3 course that wrapped around Ike's Pond.

There were still lights burning in the one-story wooden cabin that was used as CBS' production headquarters. A Securitas guard—wearing the company's standard-issue dark windbreaker, black pants and black baseball cap—walked leisurely across the lot, keeping an eye on the mobile production trailers and satellite trucks with their millions of dollars' worth of broadcast and editing equipment. Doggett stayed well back in the trees as he skirted the TV compound to the south, eventually finding the dirt service road that led to the golf course. He passed through an area so thick with trees that even the moon could barely penetrate, crossed a bridge over a creek, and came up a steep hill to a clearing in the woods. The open-ended auxiliary storage facility was still there, adjacent to a 30-foot greenhouse, just as he'd last seen it eight years ago, except that the wooden roof and corrugated metal sides of the shed were even more dilapidated than they used to be. It was funny how they operated at the National: Anything that might be seen on TV or by the ticket-buyers was kept in pristine condition; stuff set back in the woods, away from the public eye, looked as though it could have belonged to an under-funded municipal golf course.

There were no lights at the 40-by-100-foot shed, and as he'd assumed, no guards watching it. Perfect. He slipped inside and, turning on the flashlight, maneuvered past a flatbed maintenance cart to a cabinet above a workbench. He opened one of the doors on the cabinet and found a small squeeze bottle of herbicide. He slid it into his pants pocket and cast the flashlight's beam around the shed. Yes—everything he would need was right there, free for the taking.

He left the shed and headed toward the golf course. The night air was cooling; Doggett was glad he'd worn the dark blue windbreaker he'd bought earlier in the day at a strip mall on the south end of town. It kept him warm and made him harder to see.

Doggett followed the paved service road through the trees and out to the spot where it crossed in front of the deserted 11th tee. Even in the darkness, the course looked ready for the crush of 40,000 practice-round spectators who would flood the grounds the following morning. The gallery ropes, trash containers, ice coolers, and covered television equipment were all in place. The place was spotless as ever.

An evening breeze blended intoxicating aromas of magnolia and dogwood blossoms, vaguely reminding Doggett of a fragrance his mama had worn long ago. When he thought of her, his hand instinctively went into his jacket pocket and gripped the butt of the Smith & Wesson. She had been so happy that day he'd come home to tell her he got the job on the National's grounds crew. Doggett had liked the job, too—until the day he found out why he'd been hired.

His mama had always told him his real daddy was dead and she didn't want to talk about it. When his own marriage started to go bad, he began to wonder if maybe there was something he'd inherited from his father that caused him to have so much trouble with Renee—in fact, with every woman he'd ever known, except for his mama.

He'd been working for five years on the National grounds crew when he stopped at has mama's house one night after another fight with Renee and asked her to tell him who his father was.

Laverne could see the determination in his eyes—those cold eyes that could only rarely be warmed up by her telling a joke, singing a song, or stroking him as he leaned his head against her on her porch swing. He was not going to leave until she told him. She got them both a beer, sat next to him on the swing, and began to cry.

She told him about Ralph Stanwick. She told him what happened in his cabin. She told him that while she was on maternity leave she'd married Joe Doggett, an unemployed welder she'd met in a bar shortly after learning she was pregnant. That put a stop to most of the talk. Lee grew up knowing that Joe was his stepfather, but if anyone else thought Joe was Lee's daddy—especially at the National—she let them go on thinking that.

When Lee heard the story, he was furious. His mama had been treated like trash, like a whore, by a member of the club he worked for. Until then, he'd simply considered the members to be lucky guys—guys who didn't have to get down in the dirt and transplant seedlings or drag bags of fertilizer around. Now that all changed; at least one of them was a rapist.

That's not how it was, Laverne said, sobbing. It was part my fault, too.

Doggett wished he could cry with his mama, but he felt only rage for the members of the National. They were all the same—do what they want, hurt whoever they want, and buy their way out of anything. All they care about is their goddamn golf club. Stanwick—his father—was rich, and Doggett and his mama lived like dirt.

Laverne continued to cry, but her story had snuffed the last spark of human pity in Doggett's heart. The beatings from his stepfather, the laughter and humiliation from his schoolmates, the bottom rung of the ladder he and his mama had been living on while his daddy jetted in and out of Augusta whenever he wanted—it wasn't fair. It was a crime. Someone had to pay.

Doggett knew who Ralph Stanwick was. He'd seen him from a distance, playing golf and going in and out of the Firestone Cabin during Masters Week. A tall, balding guy, with the confident demeanor of a man who didn't worry about money. Doggett thought about confronting him, but dismissed it as foolishness. He knew Stanwick would deny everything, and would make sure he and his mama were fired. Doggett needed the job. Renee wasn't working, but was spending way more than he was taking home. They had bill collectors calling almost every day. He didn't know where the money was going, or how they were going to get out of debt, but he knew he couldn't afford to lose his job.

Then he thought of a way to hurt the club and help himself at the same time: counterfeit Masters badges. The club tried to stop it, but every year hundreds of badges changed hands for thousands of dollars, and some of them weren't real. You could do it all on a personal computer.

He bought a computer, and Renee hit the roof. Bad enough that he spent so much on beer, she told him. This computer is a waste of money—you're a fucking greenskeeper, for Christ's sake. He told her he could keep up with new developments in golf-course maintenance on the Internet, and the computer would give Lee Jr. a chance to keep up with the other kids in school. She laughed at him, and he hit her. He didn't want Lee Jr. to see that, but maybe that's what a man had to do to get a woman's respect.

He knew he and Renee were through. This was for him now, and for his mama. He found a picture of the previous year's Masters badge in a golf magazine, scanned it, and changed the dates on his copy. He printed one on heavy paper stock, laminated it, and inspected the finished product. It wasn't perfect, but it would fool someone who had never seen a Masters badge before and was desperate to get into the tournament.

He waited until Wednesday of Masters Week before hitting the streets with his forged badges. He assumed the price would go up each day before the tournament began. He sold two badges for $3,000 apiece on Wednesday.

On Thursday he sold another badge—to an undercover cop.

On Friday the cops went to Doggett's house and turned the place upside down. They found the counterfeiting program on his hard drive. They found his printing supplies, and badges. They also found a pound of cocaine.

Lee had never used drugs, and couldn't afford cocaine. It was obviously a plant, and there was no doubt in his mind who was behind it: Ralph Stanwick.

But he had no proof, and he knew that if he even breathed Stanwick's name, his mama would be fired. He couldn't do that to her. That job was all she'd ever had in life.

A year after he went to prison, his mama got cancer. She wrote that she was going to be fine, but she wasn't. He didn't hear from her for several weeks, then he received notification that she had been buried in a county cemetery. Renee sold the house and moved to Florida with Lee Jr. and didn't leave a forwarding address. His life was ruined, all because of one man.

◇◇◇

Doggett kept to the edge of the tree-line as he cautiously made his way up the hill toward the clubhouse and cabins. The half-moon was already beginning its descent in the sky, partly obscured by the 80-foot pines. He didn't need its light; he knew every foot of the property. He knew exactly where the Firestone Cabin was—just below the crest of the hill from the 10th tee, and a short walk from the main clubhouse. The Stanwicks had stayed there during the last couple of Masters before he'd been sent to prison, and he knew that no one gave up the Firestone Cabin once they got it. It was in a prime location for entertaining and watching the tournament.

He stayed in the shadows of the loblolly pines, moving quickly from bush to bush on the pine straw that lined the 10th fairway. The hill was steeper than he'd remembered, probably because he had always used some kind of maintenance vehicle to traverse the course when he worked there. He was panting by the time he neared the Firestone Cabin. He crouched behind the trunk of a pine and rested for a moment. Maybe he should have eaten a little more in prison, but the food was so awful that he'd lost a lot of weight while working out incessantly—and all the weights he'd lifted hadn't prepared him for climbing the hills of the National.

The parties were over for the night, and most of the lights were off in the clubhouse and the cabins. There was a light in a front window of the Firestone Cabin, however. So much the better. If he could lure Stanwick outside, he wouldn't have to kill his wife, too. Not that he would mind killing her. She deserved it, for not giving Stanwick enough sex to keep him in his own bed. But it would be much harder to kill both of them quietly.

To be sure no one else was around, Doggett circled the cabin, moving from the trees to an azalea bush to the black Mercedes S-500 parked in the driveway off the back door. He slipped on the work gloves he'd found at Robey's farmhouse and tested the front door on the Mercedes. It was unlocked, of course. *They live in such a dream world here.* He slid into the car and opened the glove compartment, where he found the rental agreement from an Atlanta agency called LuxuRide. Using the flashlight, he read the signature on the $250-per-day agreement: Ralph Stanwick.

He put the rental agreement back in the glove compartment and got out of the car, closing the door quietly. This was where Stanwick was staying, all right. He'd called the club's main switchboard at about six and asked to speak to Ralph Stanwick in the Firestone Cabin, and they'd put him through. He'd hung up as soon as his wife said, "Ralph, it's for you." The rental agreement cinched it.

He continued his circle of the house, looking into each of the darkened windows on the north side of the cabin—*cabin, hell, this place is big enough to house half my cell block.* Doggett felt his anger rising, as it had so many times in prison whenever he thought about Augusta National. He'd spent the last eight years living in a space that wouldn't even qualify as a closet in Stanwick's "cabin." *They have so much here; me and Mama had so little.*

The north side of the cabin was landscaped by a low hedge and a small flowering tree that brushed the white siding next to a window. He crept along the hedge to the base of the tree and carefully eased up to the edge of the windowsill that looked into the lighted front room. A balding man in a green jacket sat in an armchair watching television. The light was coming from a floor lamp behind the man, whose face was in shadow and turned at an angle toward the TV screen.

It had been eight long years. Doggett was not about to wait any longer.

He walked to the front door of the cabin and knocked just loud enough to be sure the man inside could hear it. Then he ran around the right corner of the house by the pine trees. He heard the door open and saw Stanwick stick his head outside, looking in both directions.

"Help…I'm hurt," Doggett groaned, just loud enough to be heard from the front door. "I need help."

The man in the green jacket hesitated, then called, "Who's there?"

"Bill," Doggett said, pulling a name at random. "Ohh…"

The balding man walked down the steps and toward the dark stand of pines where Doggett crouched. "Bill who? Where are you?" he called.

"Here," Doggett groaned.

When Stanwick was almost on top of him in the darkness, Doggett grabbed his legs and pulled him to the ground, jamming a gloved hand over his mouth and putting his free hand around his neck. Then Doggett pinned Stanwick's arms under his knees and put both hands on the man's throat, squeezing his windpipe so no sound but a desperate gurgle could escape. This was the moment he'd waited for all those years, the moment for which he'd done 20 extra reps at the end of each grueling weight session, working the muscles in his hands and his forearms so one day—*this* day—he could choke the life out of the bastard who'd created and then ruined his own life. Doggett exulted in the satisfaction of killing Ralph Stanwick with his bare hands.

Die, you miserable cocksucker. Die!

Stanwick's eyes rolled up in his head; his arms and legs flailed helplessly, then not at all. When he'd been still for at least a minute, Doggett put his ear to Stanwick's chest, felt his carotid artery and then his wrist. He let Stanwick's arm fall limp to the ground, and stood up, feeling—for one of the few times in his life—proud of himself. For once, he'd done exactly what he'd planned to do. He'd killed his father, for his mama.

He gazed in triumph at the crumpled form in the darkness at his feet: *Not such a big man now, are you?*

He reached down and lifted Stanwick's body over his shoulder. He was lighter than Doggett had expected, but it would still be a difficult task carrying him all the way down the hill. It couldn't be helped, however; he had to get Stanwick's body away from the cabin, away from the clubhouse area in case his wife had awoken or the guards walked by. He needed time to finish his work.

Doggett began descending the hill with cautious steps, trying not to slip on the pine straw, but found the going fairly easy. He stopped to rest behind the 10th green, dumping Stanwick's body to the ground like a bag of laundry. He listened for sounds of alarm from the cabins, but the night air was still. Then he hoisted Stanwick's body over his shoulder again and half-jogged the rest of the way down the 11th fairway to Amen Corner, the lowest part of the club's property, where a wide spot in Rae's Creek formed a pond in front of the 12th green.

When Doggett reached the pond, he threw Stanwick's body into the water. The splash was a jarring sound against the silence of the empty golf course, but Doggett knew no one could hear it. As the ripples slowly stretched across the pond and lapped against the grass bank on the other side, Doggett crossed the Hogan footbridge and walked onto the 12th green.

He pulled the squeeze bottle of herbicide from his pants pocket and began squirting the liquid onto the green, making precise letters that in the morning would spell out a five-word message. When he was finished, he went back across the Hogan Bridge, pausing to take a final look at the body of his father. Stanwick floated face down in the now-calm pool of Rae's Creek, his green jacket spread open around him like a halo.

It feels good that he's dead—that I killed him. But it's not enough.

Doggett headed back up the hill toward the woods, and the maintenance shed.

Chapter Four

Monday, April 7

Sam Skarda's rented Ford Taurus crawled past the gas stations, discount stores, and fast food joints along Washington Road. The speed limit sign said 45; the two lanes of traffic were doing five miles per hour at best. The smell of greasy sausage-and-egg sandwiches mingled with exhaust fumes through his open window.

He reached into the travel bag on the passenger seat for his iPod, inserted the FM audio adapter into the player, and selected the April 1965 playlist—the year Jack Nicklaus won his second Masters.

With the first few notes of the Kinks' "Tired of Waiting for You," Sam felt himself begin to relax. He wondered if The Golden Bear had sat in a traffic jam like this on the way to the 1965 Masters, listening to the Kinks on the radio. Probably not; Nicklaus seemed more like an Andy Williams kind of guy.

"Tired of Waiting" could be the song that would stick in his head today. He always had some song going through his mind on the golf course; listening to old songs on the iPod before a round was the best way to make sure he wasn't stuck with some annoying earworm he'd catch by accident on the radio. He let Dave Davies' languid guitar riff sink in, taking him out of the bumper-to-bumper traffic and off to the America of 1965: astronauts orbiting, British bands invading, Nicklaus winning the green jacket...

He was jolted back into the present by the sound of knuckles rapping on his window. A sweaty man wearing a red polo shirt and a well-worn 2002 U.S. Open cap held a cardboard sign up to the window. It said: NEED A BADGE!!

Sam shrugged with his right shoulder and held up his palm. The man with the sign lowered it and yelled, "I'm paying top dollar!"

"Not to me, you're not," Sam said. The guy with the sign moved down the line to the next car.

He tried to recapture the mood of the Kinks song, but was distracted by the line of people hustling for tickets along Washington Road, waving signs at the passing parade of cars. A dapper couple—the man wearing pressed khakis and a Cutter & Buck wind jacket, the woman in a turquoise cashmere sweater, an expensive pair of Bermuda shorts, sunglasses, and a Masters visor—stood on the curb by an Outback Steakhouse parking lot, waving a sign that said: $$ TWO BADGE$ WANTED $$!

Sam lowered the window on the passenger side and leaned over.

"I'm not selling," he said. "I just wanted to know what badges are going for."

"Four thousand," the man answered. The woman nodded.

"Apiece?"

"Yes," the man said.

"You can see it better on TV," Sam said.

"Oh, you've got to be there in person—we never miss it," the woman said, walking alongside the car. "Do you know anybody with badges to sell?"

"Sorry," Sam said, starting to roll up the window. "Try an online broker."

"We did," the man said. "It's a tough ticket this year. Not many people selling. We'll settle for one."

The woman looked at him sharply. "We will?"

"I hope you two kids work this out," Sam said. The line of cars crept onward.

The Taurus inched past an Olive Garden, a Sinclair station, and a Hooters—not exactly the most picturesque run-up to America's most beautiful golf course. Eventually he came to the water tower at the corner of Berckmans Road, and the shrubbery-covered chain-link fence surrounding the grounds of Augusta National Golf Club.

The cars in front of him were turning right into parking lots marked GATE 5—PATRONS PARKING—NO WALK-INS and GATE 4—PATRONS PARKING—WORKING PRESS—NO WALK-INS. He kept going.

On the opposite side of the street, in a mall parking lot, a dozen women held signs that said *Admit Women NOW!* and *Wake up, Augusta National! It's the 21st Century!*

Sam knew about the protest planned for this year's Masters. Rachel Drucker of the WOFF had announced a huge rally for Tuesday. David Porter, the club chairman, had refused to acknowledge them.

The national media kept trying to fan the flames of the protest story, but the Monday morning picketers were being ignored by the streams of golf fans walking past them—mostly paunchy, middle-aged men wearing caps with golf equipment logos, looking pleased with themselves for being in possession of the practice-round tickets that flapped from elastic strings attached to their caps, collars, or belt loops.

He turned right when he reached the white sign with the green block lettering that said GATE 2—MEMBERS—PLAYERS—HONORARY INVITEES—OFFICIALS—NO WALK-INS—the club's main entrance on Magnolia Lane.

Three cops in flat-brimmed trooper hats stood in front of the driveway near the small brick guardhouse, painted white with one latticed window looking out onto the street. A guard wearing a white shirt with green epaulets, a dark tie, and a black baseball cap bearing a SECURITAS logo emerged from the guardhouse and asked to see his badge.

"Player," Sam said, handing his laminated plastic badge to the guard, who looked at the photo and then ducked to get a better look at him.

"Driver's license," the security guard said.

Sam's license said he was 5-11, 175 pounds, 37 years old. The guard was satisfied that the picture and the statistics matched the man in the car. He handed the license back to Sam.

"Wait here, please," said the guard. He turned and walked inside the guardhouse and picked up a clipboard.

Sam had been aware of sirens approaching from somewhere in the distance, but as he prepared to drive down Magnolia Lane, he looked in his rear-view mirror and saw squad cars converging behind him.

"Excuse me," the guard at the gate said. "Move your car to the side. Emergency vehicles coming through. You can follow them in."

"What's going on?" Sam asked the guard.

"I don't know, sir," he said. "Enjoy your week."

Sam pulled the car to the edge of the lane as five Richmond County Sheriff's squad cars, an ambulance, and a fire department rescue truck drove past him.

He followed the last squad car through the canopy of magnolia trees to the Founders Circle, and got his first look at the famous white manor house with the green shutters, the second-story wrap-around balcony, and the twin white chimneys on either side of the cupola atop the roof. On golf's most recognized front lawn, two maps of the USA made entirely of yellow pansies were laid out on either side of a raised mound in the grass, one map facing the gates to the club, the other facing the clubhouse. A flagstick with a green Masters flag protruded from the lower right corners of the flower beds to mark the location of Augusta National. The not-so-subtle message: This is the capital of American golf.

The emergency vehicles turned left at the circle and took a service road that led past the short-game practice range to the cabins left of the 10th hole. Sam was curious, but whatever was happening, he figured he'd find out soon enough.

He was directed to turn right at the clubhouse, and followed the driveway around the west practice range to the unpaved player's parking lot. As he got out of the car, he was greeted by a valet who took the keys to the Taurus, loaded Sam's clubs and travel bags onto a golf cart, and handed him another set of car keys.

"These are for your courtesy car," the valet said. "It's the first one in that row."

He pointed to a row of identical white Cadillac STS sedans.

The young man, whose green name badge identified him as Darrell, said he'd drop Sam at the registration desk, take his clubs to the bag room, and have his luggage sent up to the Crow's Nest.

"What's with all the cops?" Sam asked Darrell as he was putting the clubs on the golf cart.

"All I know is one of the guys on the grounds crew came running up the 10th fairway this morning just after sunup and went straight into the clubhouse," Darrell said. "Then we started hearing sirens. Something happened down by Amen Corner, I guess."

Darrell drove Sam down the tree-shaded lane to the tournament headquarters building, a green, two-story wooden house that doubled as the club's administration building. Another squad car drove down Magnolia Lane to the Founders Circle, followed by the kind of vehicle Sam had seen too many times—a hearse from the county medical examiner's office.

At the tournament headquarters building Sam handed his player's badge to one of the attendants, a young woman who welcomed him to the club and located his registration packet. She handed him his player I.D. badge—number 55, the same number that would appear on his caddie's uniform.

"Your accommodations are ready in the Crow's Nest," the young woman.

Sam walked up the sidewalk to the main clubhouse entrance, shaded by a green-and-white striped awning. The lobby area was surprisingly simple and unpretentious, with creaky floorboards and a front desk and switchboard where members could check into their rooms, pick up the day's newspapers, or buy a cigar. Sam could feel the layers of history in the 150-year-old building as he looked at the portraits of the founding members that lined the wall of the winding staircase that led to the second floor. Each face seemed to convey the same message: This isn't just another PGA Tour stop, pal—or, as a former Augusta chairman had famously and derisively said, "We will never be the Pizza Hut Masters."

On the second floor, Sam found a guard standing in front of a room labeled *Masters Club Room—Private*. The door swung open, and Tiger Woods walked out, giving Sam a slight smile as he went by. Sam smiled back and nodded. Just a couple of Masters participants exchanging regards.

"This is the champions' locker room," the guard informed him. Sam nodded as though he'd known that all along.

"I'm looking for the Crow's Nest."

The guard told him to walk through the library next door and follow the narrow hallway to the right. He'd find the stairway up to the Crow's Nest.

Sam climbed to the top of the stairs and entered the 30-by-40-foot room, bathed in sunlight that poured through the windows of the 11-foot-square cupola overhead. Cream-colored wood paneling partitioned the room into four sleeping cubicles. The open common area had a card table and four wooden chairs, a leather couch, a garish plaid-patterned armchair, a telephone and lamp on an end table, and a small TV sitting on a stand next to the closets. There was plenty of reading material; the club had placed books on golf history around the room and lined the walls with photos and sketches from the Masters. Off to the side was a full bathroom to be shared by all the residents of the suite.

There was no sign of U.S. Amateur runner-up Brady Compton from Oklahoma State or U.S. Mid-Amateur champ Thomas Wheeling III from Newport, R.I., the two players who would be sharing the room with Sam. His luggage had been put in the first cubicle to the right of the stairway. He unpacked his bags, hung up his clothes, and then went back downstairs. Before stopping at the pro shop to set up his practice round, he thought it would be a good idea to introduce himself to chairman David Porter and thank him for the invitation.

He returned to the tournament headquarters building, went up the stairs, and found Porter's secretary, a woman in her mid-50s wearing a white blouse, a green vest, and a motherly expression. She nodded at him when he introduced himself, but she looked upset.

"I just thought I'd stop by and thank Mr. Porter for inviting me," Sam said.

"I'm sorry," she said in a strong Southern accent. "Mistuh Porter is speaking with a gentleman in his office. He might be busy for a while. We've had some trouble this morning."

"What sort of trouble?"

"I'm afraid one of our members has died," she said in a tremulous voice. She brushed a tear away with the palm of her hand.

"I'm sorry," Sam said. "Maybe I'll stop by later."

He thanked her and went back down the stairs to the pro shop.

Masters Week was getting off to a rough start.

◇◇◇

Richmond County Sheriff Leonard Garver felt like an unwelcome guest, rather than an authority figure, as he sat across the desk from David Porter in the chairman's office. Garver was a wiry man with narrow-set eyes, bushy eyebrows, and short, graying hair that he could feel getting grayer with each day of this year's Masters.

Aside from an occasional trespassing call, Augusta National normally didn't need his department's services. Garver had been invited to play the course several times, but had politely turned down the offers. He didn't have time for golf. Nevertheless, David Porter had made sure to have a bottle of George Dickel, Garver's favorite bourbon, delivered to his office every Christmas—a token gift that Garver politely accepted. In addition, the sheriff was given the opportunity to buy two Masters Badges each year at the face value of $200—just as the mayor, the city council president, the district attorney, and the local judges were offered the same opportunity.

Cordial relations between the club and the local officials were thus maintained. But this quiet enclave of American power-brokers—a source of deep pride for a small city in northern Georgia one week per year, nearly invisible the other 51 weeks—was suddenly becoming a headache.

First it was the women's group causing problems during Masters Week, and now there was a very suspicious death. The body had not yet been taken to the morgue, but the medical examiner had already detected signs of trauma.

"Looks like he was strangled," Garver told Porter. "It could have been one of your members."

Porter, a slightly heavy man with a thick head of short, graying hair, fixed Garver with a stare that contained all of the dignity and authority that the Augusta National chairman could muster.

"That's horseshit, Leonard," Porter replied.

"Now, it's not an accusation, David," Garver said. "How many cabins do you have on the property?"

"Ten. Between the cabins and the residence wings of the clubhouse, we have beds for 105 guests on the grounds."

"You got somebody in each one this week?"

"We're always filled during the Masters."

"How many security guards patrolling overnight?"

"A dozen."

"So you got more than one hundred members, family, players, and employees spending the night here. Could have been any one of them."

"I'm telling you, Leonard, we're looking for an intruder here."

"So tell me how this intruder got on the grounds."

"My guess is he climbed the fence between our 12th hole and the Augusta Country Club. You should be talking to them about their security."

"We're looking at that, David. But we got to eliminate any suspects who were already on your grounds, too. Now, I need you to be dead honest with me here: Do you know of any individual at the club who had a grudge against this guy?"

"Leonard, our members are not killers," Porter said. "For Christ's sake, half the members here are too old to strangle a chicken."

"You know how this looks, David. First Drucker announces she's going to hold another one of her protests. Everybody knows you got members who don't want women, and some who do. Then one of your boys turns up dead in Rae's Creek. My investigators are going to need to talk to your people."

"I don't want you conducting some goddamn witch hunt, Leonard. We're a private club. Our members expect confidentiality when they join, and as chairman, I intend to protect their privacy."

"Hell, David, this ain't a church and you ain't a priest," Garver said.

David Porter paused to form the answer that would most directly address the sheriff's objection. Finally, he said:

"As far as our members are concerned, this is the Vatican, and I am the pope."

Garver rolled his eyes. He'd rather be dealing with an uneducated car thief than these high-and-mighty tycoons.

"I could subpoena you and force you to give me names," Garver said.

"You don't want to do that, Leonard," Porter said. "We want this bastard caught more than you do. But nobody here is a killer."

"It ain't for you to decide who did it," Garver said. "That's our job."

"Then I suggest you do it, Leonard."

"Dammit, how'm I supposed to do my job when you won't cooperate? You think a bottle of George Dickel and a couple of Masters Badges lets you people hold yourselves above the law?"

"I can't stop you from talking to our members," Porter said. "But you'll be wasting your time."

"You're tellin' me," Garver said. "You've got 300 members."

"Now it's two hundred ninety-nine," Porter corrected him. "And I'll vouch for every one of them."

Chapter Five

The assistant pro ran his finger down the day's tee sheet on his clipboard and told Sam that he could get him out with Al Barber in about 45 minutes.

Sam knew his Masters history. Al Barber had won the tournament—and his lifetime exemption—during one of those years when Nicklaus was slumping, Palmer was fading, and Watson had not yet arrived. Playing with him would be an advantage. Even if Barber couldn't hit the shots anymore, he had 40 years of course knowledge, if he were willing to share it.

"Your caddie will be Dwight Wilson," the caddiemaster said to Sam. "He's waiting to meet you in front of the locker room."

Sam walked through the breezeway between the pro shop and the bag room and up the sidewalk to the locker room entrance, where an enormous black man in a white jumpsuit was waiting for him by the door with his golf bag.

The caddie extended his huge hand and shook Sam's with a firm but gentle grip—that of an experienced caddie, who would know that a golfer with crushed fingers wasn't going to earn him any money.

"Morning, Mr. Sam," the caddie said. "Dwight Wilson."

Sam assumed it was standard Masters caddie lingo to address players as "Mr. Phil" or "Mr. Ernie," but this formality made him uncomfortable.

"Please just call me Sam," Sam said. "You're the boss this week."

"Yes, sir," Dwight said. "But I'm here to help you. Ask me anything at all. There's nothing I don't know about this golf course."

Dwight had a clean-shaven baby face, round jowls, and warm, friendly eyes shaded by his green Masters cap. Sam liked his face; he looked like he wouldn't be afraid to tell you what you needed to hear, even if you didn't want to hear it. He must have weighed 300 pounds, but appeared to be very strong. He slung Sam's bag over his shoulder as though it were a school kid's backpack, and they started walking across the parking lot to the practice range.

"I've heard all about you," Dwight said. "You beat those college kids last summer."

"Kind of a fluke," Sam said. "I had a good week."

"We're gonna have another good week right here," Dwight said.

"It's a bad deal for you that amateurs can't accept prize money," Sam said. "Ten percent of my winnings is squat."

"Don't matter to me," Dwight said. "I'm just glad to have a bag."

"How long have you caddied at the Masters?"

"Since 1980. Three years before the club let the pros start bringing their own caddies here. Now, some years I get a bag, some years I don't."

"What about the other caddies here?" Sam asked.

"Some still caddie for the members, like I do. Some quit. They made more at the Masters than they could make caddying the rest of the year."

"Must be tough to get by."

"We do all right. You can get out three, four times a week with the members, except for summer, when they close the place. And a lot of us make money on the side. I'm gettin' too old to do this full-time."

"I'll bet you're named after Dwight Eisenhower, right?" Sam said as they emerged from the roped-off corridor onto the practice range.

"That's right," Dwight said. "My mama met the president many times. She used to clean the cabins at the National. Says he was the nicest man she ever met at this club, except right after a round of golf. Then he could be a little out of sorts. One time when she knew he was kind of low about the way he'd played, she thanked him for winning the war. He cheered right up and said, 'You're welcome, Helen.'"

Green mesh bags of range balls from every major manufacturer were piled up on a table at the right side of the range. Sam grabbed a bag of Pro V1s and found a spot on the range next to a bandy-legged older man wearing green checked pants, a white polo shirt, and a white Hogan-style snap-brim cap. He turned to Sam and introduced himself.

"Al Barber," the man said, his eyes looking Sam up and down as though trying to guess his scoring ability from the way he dressed and carried himself. He took off his hat, revealing a silver crewcut, and extended his hand.

Sam shook the man's firm, knobby, age-spotted hand. He saw a determined glint in Barber's eye, the look of a competitor—even at his advanced age, the look of a champion.

"I saw a film of your Masters win on the Golf Channel."

"I love that film," Barber said. "Especially the ending."

Dwight walked over to Barber's caddie, put an arm around him and gave him a soul handshake.

"This is my cousin, Chipmunk," Dwight said, introducing him to Sam. "How you doin' this morning, Mr. Al?"

"Couldn't be better, Dwight."

"Looks like they've got us playing a practice round together," Sam said.

"Terrific," Barber said. "I hope you brought some money."

Sam began to stretch, holding his sand wedge out in front of him, one hand on the grip end and one hand on the hosel, and twisted slowly around without moving his feet until he could look behind him and see the player who had walked up to the hitting station to his left.

It was Shane Rockingham.

Sam turned all the way around in the opposite direction, still keeping his feet planted, until he could once again see behind him. It wasn't the Rockingham he remembered from college. He still had the same babe-magnet features—the thick dark hair, the two-day growth and the sleepy-looking eyes—but he'd lost weight and added muscle. As he stretched, his chiseled torso and knotted biceps looked as though they were going to rip through the fabric of his golf shirt. No wonder his nickname on tour was "The Rock."

"There he is," Rockingham said when he noticed Sam watching him. "What's new, Sam?"

"Since the last time we saw each other? Pretty much everything."

Rockingham reached over and squeezed Sam's outstretched hand with a grip like a trash compactor.

"You've been working out," Sam said.

"You noticed," Rockingham said. "Yeah, I'm in the Tour fitness trailer five days a week. With all the money to be made out here, the guys who don't use it are idiots."

"I'd rather sit in the shade with a cool drink," Barber said, overhearing their conversation.

"You've earned a rest, Al," Rockingham said. "You got a game this morning?"

"Just me and Skarda here."

"Mind if Cody Menninger and I join you?"

"Your money is as good as anyone else's," Barber said.

"You ever hear from any of the guys?" Rockingham asked Sam, though his tone suggested it was a perfunctory question. The son of a Detroit auto executive, Rockingham never had much in common with his college teammates—like Sam, who was the son of a Minneapolis cop.

"Now and then," Sam said. "We usually talk about seeing you on TV."

Rockingham nodded and continued with his stretching routine. Sam was still astounded by the physical transformation. He'd heard rumors that some guys on the pro tour were experimenting with steroids. Rockingham certainly looked like he might use substances stronger than milk and Wheaties.

"You seem to be taking better care of yourself," Sam said. "I remember you sleeping it off in a Dunkin' Donuts parking lot the night before the Penn Invitational."

"I've grown up since then."

Rockingham bent at the waist and twisted from side to side several times, then straightened up.

"You're a cop now, right?" he said to Sam.

"Yeah."

"What's that like?"

"Pretty much like TV, except for the tidy endings and the hot women."

"So why do it? Can't be for the money."

"No, the money sucks. But I do like sending assholes to prison."

"Somebody else could do it."

"I know. I'm on a leave of absence now. I'm trying to decide whether to go back, or try something else."

"It's tough out here if you don't already have your name on your bag," Rockingham said. "A lot of amateurs qualify for one Masters and think they can go pro. Most of them, you never hear from again."

"I'm not going pro," Sam said. "I know I'm not good enough."

Sam turned back to his pile of balls and tried to concentrate on his warm-up routine. He would have felt self-conscious about hitting balls in front of so many critical eyes, but he realized that the crowd that had gathered in the grandstand behind him was there to watch Rockingham.

Rockingham's caddie was a skinny man with a droopy moustache and tattoos on his neck. The other tour caddies called him Weed, for reasons Sam could guess. Weed knelt next to his pile of range balls while his boss finished his stretching—or posing, as Sam would have described it. Then the floor show began.

After each shot Rockingham hit, Weed picked up a new ball and threw it directly at his boss' head. Rockingham caught each ball in his right hand with a loud smack, dropped it on the grass in front of him and exploded through the shot, grunting at impact like a pro tennis player delivering a 140-mph serve as ball after ball went screaming down the range. Then he stuck out his right hand to catch another fastball from his caddie. The crowds in the bleachers behind the range seemed to enjoy the pitch-and-catch act as much as the long, rifle-crack iron shots. Sam was as entertained as anyone. Weed turned around to look at him

"Everybody stares at first," Weed said with a grin that showed gold and gaps from years of haphazard dental work. "You'll get used to it."

"What do you think, Weed?" Rockingham said. "Should we carry the utility club or the two-iron this week?"

"Let's see how you're hitting them."

Rockingham took the two-iron from his caddie, teed up a ball, and sent it to the base of the fence at the other end of the range, 270 yards away.

"Now the utility," Weed said.

Weed took the two-iron and handed his boss the slim-backed utility club. Weed fired another ball at him, and Rockingham launched it halfway up the 105-foot-high net suspended above the fence to protect the cars and pedestrians on Washington Road.

"Tough call," Weed said with a snicker.

The fans in the bleachers behind them started chanting "Over the net! Over the net!" before being admonished by a marshal. The players knew they were not supposed to hit balls over the net, but Rockingham pulled out his driver and sent one of the range balls disappearing into traffic. He twirled his driver and slammed it back in his bag.

"See you on the tee," he said to Sam as he walked off the range to sustained applause.

Dwight whistled and said, "He ain't human."

"Yes, he is," Sam said.

Sam finished his warm-up shots and spent ten minutes on the lightning-quick practice green on the other side of the clubhouse. When it was time to tee off, he followed in Dwight's massive wake through the throngs of spectators gathered around the first tee. He presented his player ID to the tee marshal, stepped through the ropes, and took a deep breath. He was about to play Augusta National.

Rockingham and Cody Menninger had been pals and running mates on the Nationwide Tour before breaking through to the big show. Menninger had made some decent money, but it was obvious that Rockingham was the star in this pairing. He was being photographed by fans all the way to the first tee.

"You guys want to play us?" Rockingham said to Sam and Barber when he arrived at the starter's table.

"Whattya got in mind?" Barber said. "Whatever it is, we're gonna need strokes from you two gorillas."

"Al, you've forgotten more about Augusta National than I'll ever know," Rockingham said.

"That's the trouble," Barber said. "I forgot it all."

◇◇◇

Sam was so mesmerized by the beauty and perfection of the golf course that he barely noticed he and Barber were losing their match after the front 9. Barber suggested a back nine press, to which Sam reluctantly agreed. The needle on his bank account back home was pointing at "E."

Yellow police tape greeted Sam's foursome when they arrived at the 12th tee. Several squad cars were parked along the service road behind the grandstand, and a canine unit explored the wooded area along the left side of the 12th green. Sam's group was met by a uniformed Richmond County sheriff's deputy and an Augusta National member in a green jacket.

"We're not playing 12 this morning, fellas," said the member, an older man with a dark tan that showed through the wispy white hairs on top of his head. "There's been an accident here."

"What kind of accident?" Rockingham asked.

"Sorry, gentlemen, I can't say any more. Please proceed to the 13th tee."

"Shit," Rockingham said to Menninger as they began walking to a waiting Cadillac Escalade. "They better let us practice here tomorrow. I'm never sure what club to hit on this hole."

Rockingham was so locked into his tournament preparation that he didn't even seem to care why the cops had shut down the hole. But Sam was interested.

"Officer," Sam said quietly to the deputy. "Is this a homicide?"

"You'll have to talk to the investigator, Lieutenant Harwell."

He pointed to a man walking toward the tee from the edge of the pond. He had wiry red hair and wore a white short-sleeve shirt, a red tie, and navy blue pants, with a police radio and a holstered handgun attached to his belt. Sam waited until Harwell reached the tee.

"Lieutenant Harwell, I'm a detective with the Minneapolis Police Department," Sam said.

"What's a Minneapolis cop doing here?" the investigator said to Sam.

"I'm playing in the Masters this year. Sam Skarda."

"Oh…," Harwell said, letting the sound escape from his mouth like a draft through a barn. The idea of a cop playing golf made no sense to him whatsoever. "What can I do for y'all? We're a little busy here."

"What happened here?" Sam asked.

"We don't know. The M.E. will determine that."

There was no body visible. The ambulance and the hearse were gone.

"Why is the hole closed off?"

Harwell looked around, then lifted the police tape.

"C'mere. Have a look."

Sam and Dwight followed the detective to the end of the tee and down the slope to the edge of the pond. Cops and forensic technicians stood around the 12th green, some taking pictures, some on their hands and knees inspecting the grass, and others just standing around enjoying the warm April morning.

"We found a body floating here this morning," Harwell said. "And that writing on the green."

At first Sam couldn't see anything unusual. Then, through a gap between two cops, he spotted some brown grass in the center of the putting surface. That never happened at Augusta. Looking more closely, there appeared to be a pattern to the spots of dead grass.

Someone had burned a message into the green. Sam took a few steps closer until he could make out the words, written in letters a foot high:

THIS IS THE LAST MASTERS

Chapter Six

Sam couldn't get the image of the defaced green out of his mind for the rest of the round. Nor could he imagine why someone was willing to commit murder to end the tournament. Could it have something to do with the protests?

He made a string of distracted swings that led to bogeys and double-bogeys as they played their way back to the clubhouse. The temperature had climbed into the 80s by the time Sam's foursome walked up the 18th fairway, and Dwight was laboring.

"Are you okay, big guy?" Sam asked as they approached the two-tiered green, surrounded by milky white bunkers and hundreds of spectators. Dwight toweled his face and offered a weak grin.

"These hills get steeper and this jumpsuit gets hotter every year," he said. "But I'd feel a whole hell of a lot better if you'd get your mind back on your game."

Sam responded to Dwight's challenge, sinking a 25-foot birdie putt to win the hole and three carry-overs worth $200.

"You just cost me a steak dinner, pards," Rockingham said to Sam as they walked off the 18th green. He was smiling as he compressed Sam's hand, but the force of the handshake convinced Sam that Rockingham wasn't joking.

"Two hundred bucks for a steak dinner? You need to find cheaper restaurants," Sam replied.

"I made four fuckin' point nine million last year," Rockingham said, suddenly not smiling. "What'd you make?"

"Less than you make in a week."

"You need a better job," Rockingham said, and headed for the locker room, whistling an unrecognizable tune.

Can't argue with him there, Sam thought.

Sam told Dwight they'd play another practice round Tuesday morning around ten. Dwight said he'd be there early, but he was walking with a limp as he and Chipmunk headed for the bag room with the clubs. The steep 18th fairway had been hard on both of Sam's knees; he could only imagine how tough it was for Dwight, who had to be at least 10 years older and 100 pounds heavier than Sam.

Sam made his way through the throngs of spectators, hreen jackets, reporters, photographers and club employees milling around the 150-year-old oak tree that shaded the southwest corner of the clubhouse. Its tentacle-like branches extended horizontally at least 40 feet from the trunk and were held aloft by a network of steel cables. There was a buzz in the air that had to be connected to the body that had been found in the 10th fairway.

"Skarda? You Sam Skarda?"

Sam heard a gruff voice call his name through the commotion on the lawn. Sam turned to see a dumpy, sweaty man with thinning, unkempt hair and a press badge hanging around the frayed collar of his beige—or was it supposed to be white?—golf shirt. There was a mustard stain on the lapel of his ratty tan sports jacket and an ink smudge that ran from the cuff of his left sleeve almost up to the elbow. He was wearing baggy jeans and dirty white sneakers.

The name on the badge was R. Daly. Sam recognized him: Russ Daly, sports columnist for the *Los Angeles Times* and a frequent guest commentator on ESPN. He wrote acerbic columns about players, managers, coaches, and owners, and when he was bored with his usual targets, he'd rip cheerleaders and batboys.

"Skarda?" Daly asked again.

"That's me," Sam said.

"Russ Daly, *L.A. Times*. How ya doin'?"

"I didn't play too well this morning. A lot of distractions."

"Yeah, well, nobody expects you to make the cut, so what's the difference?" Daly said. "You were going to be my column for tomorrow—but I guess you could say things have changed a little since they found the stiff."

"What have you heard?" Sam said.

"Press conference in about an hour," Daly said. "David Porter—Chairman Sphinx—is supposed to tell us that a member was found floating in the water at Amen Corner."

"Looks like a homicide investigation to me," Sam said.

"The press guide says you're a cop," Daly said, pulling out a spiral notebook and a pen. "Did you talk to the local boys down there?"

"Yeah, for a minute. They didn't tell me anything."

"What did you see?"

"Somebody wrote THIS IS THE LAST MASTERS in the grass where they found the body."

Daly scribbled that down.

"So, what's your opinion?"

"Off the record?"

"C'mon, you've been interviewed by assholes like me before."

"None with a couple million readers," Sam said.

"Okay, off the record, then."

Sam took off his sweat-stained golf hat and ran his hand through his hair. The sun was high enough now that the huge oak provided some welcome shade.

"Well, one of two things: Either the guy made that message himself and then committed suicide, which isn't likely, or somebody else killed him to make a point."

"You heard that a member came out publicly last week in favor of admitting women to Augusta," Daly said. "Hell of a story."

"I suppose it was your story?"

"I wish," Daly said. "No, it was hers."

He jerked his pen backward, indicating a woman standing over his right shoulder, interviewing Cody Menninger. She didn't look like she attended a lot of golf tournaments. She had short, curly, white-blond hair and her hoop earrings dangled below the collar of the white turtleneck she wore under a beige blazer. She finished off the look with black, spike-heeled boots and skin-tight black pants. She was filling up her notebook with Menninger's recollections of what he'd seen on the golf course that morning.

"Who is she?" Sam asked Daly.

"Deborah Scanlon of the *New York Times*," Daly said. "Pain in the ass. Don't talk to her."

"I heard that, Daly," Scanlon called over her shoulder. She thanked Menninger and moved over to join them.

"Hi," she said with a quick, tight smile that seemed as practiced as it was insincere. She extended her hand to Sam. "Sam Skarda, right?"

"Right," he said. She gave him the kind of dead-fish handshake that made him do all the work.

She pulled out her notebook and flipped through the pages with hyper-kinetic energy. Her eyes darted back and forth between Sam and others in the crowd around him like a flirt at a cocktail party, afraid she might be missing a better opportunity.

"What did you tell Daly?" she said, felt-tipped marker poised to write. "I know you're a cop. You must have noticed something down there. How close did you get?"

"Close enough," Sam said. "I saw that somebody had burned the words THIS IS THE LAST MASTERS into the grass on the fairway."

"Who would do that?" Scanlon demanded. "An Augusta National member?"

"I have no idea," Sam said.

"My sources tell me there are some members here who'd rather shut down the Masters than let women into the club. They figure if the Masters goes away, the protesters go away."

"I don't see it, Debbie," Daly said. "They love their greens more than they hate women."

"Butt out, Daly," she said. "I want to know what Sam thinks."

"I don't know anything about Augusta National's members, except that they invited me to play here," Sam said.

"What else did you see?"

"Medical examiners. Forensics experts. Canine units. The usual crime scene personnel. There's no way I could tell what they were looking for from where I was."

"How many dogs?"

"Two, that I saw."

"What were the dogs doing?"

"Probably taking a whiz on Porter's azaleas," Daly said. "The cops are going to get a bill for that."

"The dogs were sniffing around the trees and bushes on the hillside left of the green," Sam said.

"And what does that tell you?"

"Tells me they're looking for someone's scent."

"Whose scent?"

"If I knew that, I'd be talking to the cops, not you," Sam said, suddenly tired of Scanlon's staccato questions. "Look, if you don't mind, I'd like to take a shower."

"Debbie doesn't mind," Daly said. "She'd be glad to interview you while you take a shower."

"Daly, you're a pig," Scanlon said. "And it's Deborah. Before you go, Sam, I just want you to tell me what you think happened down there. From a cop's perspective."

"I'll tell you the same thing I told Daly—off the record," Sam said. Scanlon didn't indicate any disagreement, so he continued: "It looks like somebody was trying to make some kind of statement. Maybe a warning."

"Who was he trying to warn?"

"You got me."

Scanlon closed up her notebook and walked off.

"I'm just here to play golf," Sam said to Daly. "Why is anyone interested in what I think?"

"Because the local cops aren't saying anything, they've got Amen Corner taped off, and we're talking to anyone who's been down there," Daly said. "But you know how most Tour pros are: If it's not about golf, fishing or fucking, they're not interested. I figured you might have taken a look."

"You might want to talk to the maintenance crew," Sam said.

"Why?"

"It must have been some kind of herbicide used to burn that message. Maybe it was the kind they use here."

Sam was tired and ready to head to the showers. He thought back to the scene in the 10th fairway; if he had been investigating the death, he'd probably try to find the names of club members who opposed admitting women members. That seemed to be the only raging issue around here.

"So they haven't released the name of the guy who was killed?"

"Not yet," Daly said. "But I know who it was."

"How did you find out? The cops aren't saying anything."

"I didn't get it from a cop," Daly said. "I've been covering this tournament for 20 years. Even a fat slob like me can cultivate an Augusta National source or two in that amount of time."

"Okay, so who got killed?"

"A guy named Harmon Ashby."

Chapter Seven

"Harmon Ashby! Who the fuck is Harmon Ashby?"

Lee Doggett shouted those words at the television set in his motel room shortly after turning on CNN at 1:30 p.m.

He'd managed to find a fleabag motel six miles west of Augusta in Grovetown, one that charged only $300 a night for what was normally a $30 room. He'd checked in just after sunrise, drank a six-pack of beer to celebrate his father's death, and then passed out on the bed without taking his clothes off.

When he came to, the morning was gone and he felt groggy, but he instantly recalled being on the grounds of Augusta National the night before, and strangling Ralph Stanwick.

At least, he'd thought it was Ralph Stanwick. Now the TV reporters were saying something else.

He flipped frantically through the channels; the news of the suspected murder was everywhere. Constant headline crawls and half-hour updates on CNN and Fox; bulletins interrupting regular programming on ABC, CBS, and NBC; special reports on ESPN and the Golf Channel. The death of an Augusta National member on the eve of the Masters was the kind of story news organizations could not get enough of.

But the reporters kept saying that the victim was thought to be Masters Rules Committee Chairman Harmon Ashby—not Ralph Stanwick. How could he have made that mistake? Sure, it had been dark outside the cabin, but the guy looked like the

Stanwick he remembered—tall, balding, sixtyish. He had come out of the cabin where the Stanwicks were staying, wearing a green jacket. Stanwick's car was parked in the driveway behind the cabin.

Then NBC put up a picture of Ashby. Bald, probably in his late '60s. There was a superficial resemblance—enough that, in the dark, you could mistake one for the other. And, apparently, that's what he'd done. There were just too damn many old white guys at that club.

Shit—now what?

He came across a live feed of club chairman David Porter's press conference on The Golf Channel.

"All of our hearts go out to Harmon's wife, Annabelle, their son Robbie, and their daughter Cassie," Porter said, as the cameras clicked away in the background.

Porter prattled on about poor Harmon and his family, that there was no new information on the cause of death or the message that had been found on the green near the body. He wouldn't speculate on what THIS IS THE LAST MASTERS could mean, but there would absolutely not be any interruption in this year's tournament. Did he think the killing had anything to do with Harmon Ashby telling the *New York Times* that he favored Augusta National admitting women members? Porter had no idea, and he would not comment on the club's membership policy.

After the press conference, most of the news channels cut to reporters who seemed to focus on the possibility that Ashby had been killed by someone at the club, possibly another member who didn't want women joining, and didn't care if that meant shutting down the Masters. The cops probably thought the same thing.

Doggett had meant the message to scare the shit out of the bastards at Augusta National, but it hadn't occurred to him that somebody would read a political motive into it.

Maybe this hadn't turned out as bad as he thought.

Doggett got up off the bed and went into the bathroom to splash some water on his face. He looked at himself in the mirror, seeing a younger, stronger version of Ralph Stanwick staring back at him. He was probably about as tall as his father, 6-3 or so, and like his father, he was losing his hair. He wished he looked more like his mother. She'd been beautiful, with thick, dark hair—hair that had fallen off her head in the last photo that he'd received from her in prison. The chemo had done that.

The rage began to rise again. Stanwick still had to die. But it didn't have to be today, or tomorrow. Stanwick must have realized that Ashby wasn't the real target, but he'd never tell anybody. He wouldn't dare. Instead, he'd sit in his cabin and piss himself every time he heard a noise, every time the phone rang, and every time a stranger walked by his cabin. He would think it was Doggett coming for him. Meanwhile, Doggett could begin tearing down the club's reputation, piece by piece, while his father had to sit by and watch it all happen, powerless to stop it, praying for his life. Torture, is what it would be—the worst kind of torture, knowing that you were going to die, but having to watch someone or something you loved die first.

Just like Doggett had had to suffer in prison while his mama died.

Best of all, the cops were confused. While they were looking at the club for suspects, it would give Doggett a clear field.

He returned to the bed and clicked through the channels. The police were either clueless or keeping quiet. No details were escaping the National. But the talking heads were indulging in an orgy of speculation.

On Fox, a male attorney was engaged in a heated debate with a female newspaper columnist.

"Look," he said, "if we force Augusta National to admit women, what are we going to do about the women's colleges? You went to Wellesley, didn't you, Deborah? And what about the Girl Scouts? The Junior League? What about sororities?"

"Red herrings," the woman responded. "Those groups don't open their doors to the public one week per year, rake in millions of dollars, then shut half the population out the other 51 weeks of the year while the members make each other even richer with their backroom deals."

Doggett looked closely at the woman columnist. The caption identified her as "Deborah Scanlon—*NYT.* Interviewed Harmon Ashby on women at Augusta National." She wasn't bad-looking—though the short, white-blond hair and the red lipstick were a little too brassy for his tastes.

Her support of Rachel Drucker's campaign against Augusta National was articulate and passionate. Between the column and the network interviews, she was almost as visible a symbol as Drucker herself.

Doggett returned to The Golf Channel, where a male and female anchor were seated at the network's outdoor broadcast desk near the main scoreboard alongside the first hole. A third face was superimposed on a screen behind them.

"We're talking to former PGA Tour pro Danny Milligan, who once broadcast the Masters on CBS before being dropped for making controversial on-air remarks," the male anchor said. "How are you, Danny?"

The face on the screen behind them was framed by thick, wavy gray hair that cascaded to the man's shoulders. He was clean-shaven and deeply tanned except for the age lines at the corners of his blue eyes, which were alive with merriment, in stark contrast to the logo plastered across the bottom of the screen: *Masters Murder?*

"Oh, I've been better," he said, then added: "I've been worse, too."

"We're sure Harmon Ashby's death came as a shock to you, as it did to all of us," said the woman anchor, turning to look at the screen.

"Harmon was a great rules official, and a helluva guy," Milligan said, in a soft southern drawl. "You don't find many like him at the National. They need all the Harmon Ashbys they can get over there."

"Do you think he was murdered?"

"Does a golf ball have dimples?"

"Danny, you live on the outskirts of Augusta," the male anchor said. "You do some golf broadcasting for TBS, and I know you're still very familiar with what goes on here at the Masters, even though you haven't been here for a while. What kind of impact is this going to have on this year's tournament?"

"Honestly?" Milligan said, with a grimace of distaste. "None, probably. You know how they handle things at the National: If they say it's not a problem, it's not a problem. By Thursday, they'll have Harmon Ashby stuffed and mounted in the clubhouse next to Bobby Jones and Clifford Roberts, and everything will be back to normal."

"Let me ask this, then," the woman anchor said. "What should the impact be?"

"If I had anything to say about it, there wouldn't be a Masters this year, or any year, until they open up the club to women," Milligan said.

Doggett fingered the remote, tempted to switch to another channel, but something about Milligan's comments made him pause. He was like Scanlon—a high-profile, big-mouthed critic of the club.

"But Danny, the National is extremely accommodating to women in every other way except membership," the female anchor said. "Women can play the course, they can attend the tournament, they can dine in the clubhouse. There have even been women caddies at the Masters, and David Porter says if a woman can qualify, she's welcome to play in the tournament."

"It would be hard to argue that Augusta National is a hostile environment for women," the male anchor said.

"Sure, they'll kiss their hands and put honey on their grits all week," Milligan said. "But Sunday night the women will be headed home, and everything will be back to normal: 300 men keeping 3.2 billion women at arm's length, as though the entire gender has some kind of rash or something."

"Well, obviously we're not going to resolve this today," the female anchor said. "We'd like to thank Danny Milligan for being our guest. Danny, will we be seeing you here sometime this week?"

"Not unless the National's security has totally broken down," he said. "I'm about as welcome there as the touring company of 'Rent.'"

Fox News had a live shot of a dozen protesters walking on the opposite side of Washington Road from the main gates of the club, carrying signs saying "The Golf Gods Are Angry, Augusta National!" and "NO WOMEN, NO PEACE." The police were trying to move them along, while several reporters were trying to get comments from them.

"It seems abundantly clear to us that Mr. Ashby was silenced for his liberal views," said a round-faced, bespectacled woman, identified on the screen as Rachel Drucker, the president of the Women's Organization for Freedom.

Doggett switched off the TV to think over his options. He wanted to terrorize the Masters, but there was more than one way to do it. Stanwick and the other members would be on their guard now, and harder to get at. But he could kill someone who hated the National, someone everybody knows, like Deborah Scanlon, Danny Milligan or Rachel Drucker. He could leave the same THIS IS THE LAST MASTERS message, and the cops, the media and the public would drive themselves crazy trying to figure out who was doing it, and why. A psycho member of the National killing the club's enemies? A nut-job protester?

Only two people—Doggett and his father—would really know what was going on. And, in a few days, he'd make sure that number was down to one.

He pulled out his wallet and found the scrap of paper on which he'd written the phone number for Augusta National's main switchboard. As he had a day earlier, he dialed the number and asked for Ralph Stanwick in the Firestone Cabin. This time a man answered the phone.

"Hello," the voice said.

"Ralph Stanwick?"

Doggett could sense a fearful pause on the other end of the line.

"Who's calling?" Stanwick finally asked.

"Your son. Enjoy your last Masters, old man."

Doggett hung up.

Chapter Eight

After his practice round, Sam took a long shower in the locker room and then went up to the Crow's Nest. His roommates had arrived and unpacked, but they were apparently out on the course. He settled into an armchair in the common area and turned on the TV.

The coverage of the Masters on Augusta television must have been over the top in a normal year. This year, with the death of Harmon Ashby, it was beyond shrill. He flipped stations and found that the networks and cable news channels were also devoting extensive coverage to the mysterious death. One of the networks had already created a logo for the story: "Murder at Amen Corner?" They were obviously hoping to remove the question mark as soon as possible. He clicked back to one of the locals, where a big-haired female anchor was reporting on the case.

"…Augusta National Chairman David Porter said this afternoon that the club did not know whether Ashby's death was self-inflicted, foul play, accidental or a result of natural causes."

Sam had to laugh at that last possibility. What were the odds that a member of Augusta National would topple into a pond a few feet from a warning message that the Masters was going to end?

The station went to footage shot at the afternoon press conference. The calm, no-nonsense figure of David Porter stood before a bank of microphones and tape recorders, the Masters logo displayed behind him and the sound of automatic cameras squeezing off shot after shot in the background. He looked grim and concerned, but not devastated, as though announcing a failed business deal.

"All of our hearts go out to Harmon's wife, Annabelle, their son Robbie, and their daughter Cassie," Porter said. "He was my friend for more than 20 years…there wasn't a more dedicated member of this club. No one loved Augusta National and this tournament more than Harmon Ashby. We will miss him dearly."

The reporters paused for a respectful instant, and then bombarded Porter with questions.

"No, this will not delay the start of the Masters," Porter said. "We will have a moment of silence for Harmon Thursday morning before our ceremonial first tee shots, and then we will run the tournament as usual. Harmon would have wanted it that way."

Sam always wondered how people knew what a person would have wanted. Maybe Harmon Ashby would have wanted the membership to postpone the tournament for a year and add a dozen women members before starting it up again. Who could know?

"What's that…?" Porter said on the TV, pointing at a reporter to distinguish between the many questions being shouted at him. "No, I have no idea how those words got on the 12th green, or what they mean…No, I won't speculate…

"No, we won't comment on any aspect of the police investigation…No, absolutely not. I will not discuss our membership policies here. That would be totally inappropriate."

But totally relevant. "THIS IS THE LAST MASTERS" certainly suggested that someone was not happy with the way Augusta National was being run. David Porter couldn't dodge that one forever.

"…the damage to the green was not severe," Porter was saying. "We'll have our maintenance crew working on it as soon as the police give us permission to repair it. We think we have a satisfactory way to cosmetically deal with the defaced area, until after the tournament."

Sam had heard the stories that the National put something in the water to make the ponds bluer. If that was true, they could certainly make the grass greener.

The TV coverage switched from the press conference to the small protest across Washington Road from the main gates.

"It seems abundantly clear to us that Mr. Ashby was silenced for his liberal views," said WOFF president Rachel Drucker. Behind her, a dozen protesters shook their signs in the air and yelled their agreement. Drucker didn't look all that threatening—like somebody's plump aunt, with no fashion sense. Sam couldn't understand what good she thought she was doing there. Ashby's death was a tragedy, not a convenient excuse to get TV time to push a political agenda.

"Open your gates to your sisters, Augusta National!" Drucker shouted on camera. "Don't let Herman Ashby die in vain!"

If she's that broken up about it, she could at least get his name right.

Compton and Wheeling eventually returned from their practice rounds; introductions and mutual congratulations were exchanged among the three. Compton was a wiry college kid who had thought of nothing but a professional golf career since the day he was old enough for his dad to buy him his own set of Pings. Wheeling was a little older. After graduating from Duke, he had tried the pro mini-tours for several years before reluctantly accepting the reality that he wasn't quite PGA Tour material, and preferred the comforts of working at his father's yacht brokerage firm in Newport, R.I. He'd reapplied for his amateur status, and once he knew his future didn't depend on each four-footer, he was able to relax enough to play his best golf. After winning last year's Mid-Am, he was thinking of going back to Q-School—but he was putting that off until playing in the Masters.

"I'm hungry," Sam said. "Anyone want some lunch?"

"Already ate," Wheeling said. "I need to work on my putting."

"I gotta call my buddies back home," Compton said. "I promised them I'd give 'em a picture-phone tour of the clubhouse."

Sam walked down to the first floor of the clubhouse and entered the men's grill. He smiled when he saw a sign outside the room that said women were permitted inside during Masters Week. That must chafe at some of the hard-liners.

He sat at the bar and ordered a bowl of seafood chowder and a grilled bacon, tomato, and cheese sandwich with a bottle of Heineken.

"This seat taken?" Sam heard someone ask him as he was finishing his lunch.

He looked up to see an attractive, smiling brunette with shoulder length hair, a black sleeveless top, and black shorts that nicely accented her tanned legs.

"All yours," he said.

She sat down and ordered a gin and tonic.

"I don't recognize you," she said.

"That's because we've never met," Sam said. "I'd remember."

"No, I mean, you're a player, right?"

"How can you tell?"

"I know golfers. You've got that look. The hat tan, for one thing. And your left hand is much whiter than your right, from wearing a glove. Ironed trousers, instead of wrinkled khakis. You're not a pro—I'd know you, if you were—but you're a player. Let me guess. You won last year's Mid Am?"

"No. Publinx."

"Congratulations. First Masters, right?"

"Right. And last."

"You don't know that."

"Let's just call it an educated guess."

"Now I know you're a golfer. You've got that determined streak of pessimism."

Sam looked at the brunette as she took a sip of her drink. No doubt about it—she was gorgeous. Her thick dark hair, glinting in the afternoon sunlight that slanted through the grillroom window, was parted on the left and swept over to the right above her arched black eyebrows. Her flecked blue-green eyes seemed probing and serious, while her full lips and deep smile lines projected a sense of playfulness.

Sam glanced at her left hand, not sure if it was his cop instinct or his libido that made him want to check out whether she was married. She wasn't wearing a ring.

He offered his hand and she took it with the kind of firm, full-palm grip he liked, but didn't often receive, from a woman.

"Sam Skarda," he said.

"Oh, I should have known," she said, a wry smile cracking the corner of her mouth. "Caroline Rockingham."

Sam had no idea what to say next. He'd never seen a photo of Shane Rockingham's wife, but he wasn't surprised she was model-pretty.

"Shane talks about you," she said. "You went to college together."

"We played on the golf team together. I'm not sure Shane actually went to college."

"When you won your tournament last year, he said he'd always wondered what happened to you. So what happened to you?"

"I became a cop," Sam said.

"Now, that I wouldn't have guessed," Caroline said, leaning back and looking him over again.

"Why not?"

"I don't know. Maybe I'm not used to seeing cops with golfer's tans."

"I've been on a leave of absence for almost two years," Sam said. "I got shot."

"Woah," Caroline said, her forehead creasing. "Now that's an occupational hazard. All Shane has to worry about is putting on enough sun block."

Caroline opened her purse and took out a pack of cigarettes and a lighter.

"One thing I like about the South," she said, lighting her cigarette and exhaling a cloud of smoke away from Sam. "Nobody ever tells you that you can't smoke inside."

"What would you do if they did?"

"I don't know," she said. "Put it out, I guess. I'm not like Shane. I don't like trouble in bars."

"He does?"

"Don't all golfers get into trouble in bars?"

"Not me," Sam said. "Not usually, anyway."

"Shane does. Even if they don't know who he is. I think it's his attitude."

"What attitude is that?"

"Oh, you know—'I play golf for a living, and you probably drive a truck.' That kind of thing."

"I don't play for a living," Sam said. "Maybe that's why I don't get in a lot of barroom brawls."

"I'll bet you could break one up."

"I have."

She crossed her legs and leaned back with her right elbow propped on the arm of her chair, the cigarette up in the air. She looked at him with a mischievous smile.

"So you knew Shane in college," she said. "What was he like then?"

"Charming. Reckless. Arrogant. Fun."

"He hasn't changed," Caroline said.

"I know," Sam said. "We played a practice round together this morning."

"Oh, really," she said, surprised. "Did my name come up?"

"No. Shane was too busy showing me how far he hits it."

"Yes," Caroline said, pushing the lime around in her drink with a plastic straw. She seemed far away now. "He can definitely golf his ball."

"So why aren't you together anymore?"

"Because he's charming...reckless...what else did you say?"

"Arrogant and fun."

"Yeah, he's all that," Caroline said, shaking her head and tapping the ash off her cigarette. "We separated right after the Bob Hope. You might have read about our little dust-up in Las Vegas."

"I saw something."

"I can't help it—I still like the guy…at times," she said. "But everything changed after I stopped caddying for him."

"That's when he started making money."

"That had something to do with it. But up until then we were partners. After I went home, I was his wife. He started thinking of me as just another lay."

"Are there kids?"

"No, thank God," Caroline said. "Although that would have given us something in common. Now…"

"Nothing?"

"Pretty much. A lot of memories. Bouncing around airports and train stations in Thailand, Japan, Malaysia…cheap meals, bad golf courses…I miss all that. Now we have money, and that's about it."

Sam finished his beer and signaled to the bartender for another round. What had started out as a promising meeting had suddenly become awkward. Sam wasn't like his old buddy Shane; he didn't make moves on married women. But what about separated women? He was attracted to Caroline, but didn't know what the rules were.

"If you're separated, what are you doing here?" Sam asked her.

"I love the Masters," she said. "It's beautifully antiquated."

"You don't feel like a traitor to your gender when you come through the gates?"

"No," she said, laughing. "Why should I? I can sit in the men's grill and have a drink and a smoke, just like the guys. Besides, Shane made the mistake of requesting a clubhouse pass for me before he moved out. It was mailed to our address in Tucson, in my name. I'm not giving it up."

"What happens when you run into him?"

"I'm expecting a big scene—broken furniture, flying drinks, maybe a punch or two. Nothing that hasn't happened before."

"I think that kind of behavior is outlawed at the National," Sam said.

"Oh, it is. That's the fun of it."

"Where are you staying?"

"A lovely dive called the Southwinds Inn. I've been there before—they gouge you a little less than the places closer to the course."

"And Shane?"

"He's renting a house with his caddie up at Jones Creek. He'll have hot and cold running bimbos all week. What about you? Where are you staying?"

"The Crow's Nest."

"Oh, that's right—amateurs can stay in the clubhouse. I've always wanted to see it."

"I could take you up there sometime this week," Sam said, then realized it sounded like a come-on. "I'm sharing it with two other guys. The Amateur runner-up and the Mid-Am champ. The Amateur winner won't be there. He turned pro."

He was talking fast now; Caroline sensed his unease and smiled at him as if to say, no offense taken.

For the next hour they talked about her background and his.

Caroline was the daughter of an Air Force colonel who had been stationed at U.S. bases around the world, including Germany, Korea, Japan, Saudi Arabia, and Kuwait, as well as Florida, Arizona, and Virginia. She'd played golf in high school and liked watching the pro game. After getting her degree from Georgetown, she visited her parents in Riyadh and took a weekend trip to Doha to attend the Qatar Masters, a European PGA Tour stop. There she met Jorgen Pedersen, a touring pro from Denmark who needed an emergency caddie. She agreed to take his bag on a weekly basis in return for 10 percent of his winnings and travel expenses.

She met Rockingham during the first round of the Indonesian Open in Jakarta. She couldn't take her eyes off him ("That bad-boy look of his was especially appealing compared to all those other golf geeks"); Shane must have noticed her, too. When Pedersen missed the cut, Rockingham asked her if she wanted to caddie for him. He won the tournament, they ended up in bed, and she spent the next two years traveling around the world with him.

By the time they got married, she was beginning to suspect he wasn't the faithful husband type, but they either had to take the next step or end it, so she took a chance. He was winning tournaments by then, and had qualified for the U.S. tour. He bought a big house for her in Tucson and hired a veteran PGA Tour caddie. He'd be gone for weeks at a time; when Caroline did join him at tournaments, she sensed something in the looks that she got from the other tour wives—something that seemed to her like pity.

"The breakup was inevitable," she said. "He was getting laid at famous golf clubs all across America. I'd hear rumors about a girl at Doral, and one at Riviera, and another one at Muirfield Village. But until he ditched me for that cocktail waitress in Vegas, I guess I just didn't want to face it. After that, I didn't have a choice."

"It must have hurt," Sam said.

"To be the publicly humiliated wife of a rock-star golfer?" Caroline said with a tight smile. "Yes, it did."

Sam looked in her eyes and saw they were glistening. Tough, but not bulletproof.

"So how does an Ivy League guy become a cop?" she asked him.

"There are a few of us," Sam said. "The chief of police in St. Paul is a Princeton guy."

"Are you trying to make chief in Minneapolis?"

"Nope. I couldn't stand the politics. My dad was a street cop in Minneapolis for 25 years. He always told me the desk guys and the suits had the worst jobs in the shop. He was right."

It was almost 4 p.m. when Caroline looked at her watch and said she had to get back to her motel. Sam thought about asking her to stay for dinner, but decided that would be pushing things. He'd see her again during the week—he hoped.

She put down a tip, gave him a wave, and walked out of the grillroom. She had the easy but purposeful stride of someone who could go up and down hills with a tour bag on her shoulder and make it look like she wasn't even trying. Smooth yet muscular calves, thighs that rippled gracefully with each stride.

Golf, Sam. Don't forget, you're here to play golf.

Chapter Nine

Tuesday, April 8

The pro shop put Sam in a Tuesday practice round with Luke Bellecourt, the previous year's Canadian Open champ; Buddy Cremmins, a rookie sensation from LSU who had already won twice on the tour; and Clive Cartwright, an Englishman who'd won the Masters in a playoff a dozen years earlier.

Before his warm-up session on the range, he walked into the Trophy Room to get some breakfast. Caroline Rockingham was sitting at a sunny window table with a bagel, a glass of grapefruit juice, a cup of coffee, and the *New York Times*. She looked utterly at home.

"Want company?" he asked.

"Sure," she said, flashing him the smile that he'd thought about until falling asleep the previous night in the Crow's Nest. "Sit down."

She pushed a chair away from the table with her tanned, sandaled foot and kept reading. Sam ordered a plate of bacon and eggs and a cup of decaf. He picked up a copy of the *Augusta Chronicle* and saw the screaming headline: "MASTERS OFFICIAL FOUND DEAD AT AMEN CORNER. Police investigate possible homicide." Several pages of coverage followed, but the reporters didn't seem to have much more information than he'd heard on TV Monday.

Could one of Ashby's fellow members really have done this? And on the eve of the Masters, when the club was obsessed with running an orderly tournament and keeping negative press to an absolute minimum?

"They made an example of him," one of the members of WOFF was quoted in the paper. "He was a martyr for our cause."

Ashby's wife didn't seem to think so. Another story quoted Annabelle Ashby saying that no member of Augusta National would ever do such a thing.

"They were the people he loved most in this world, besides his family," she had told a reporter. "I know they all loved him, too."

Not necessarily. Sam knew how it was at golf clubs. Nobody is universally liked unless he loses all his bets and pays up cheerfully and immediately. When Ashby went public with his opinion on women at Augusta National, he must have made some enemies.

"Read this," Caroline said, handing Sam the sports section of the *Times*, folded open to a column by Deborah Scanlon:

SEE, HEAR AND SPEAK NO EVIL AT AUGUSTA NATIONAL

Poor Annabelle Ashby. Not only did she lose her husband, Harmon, sometime early Monday morning, but she seems to have lost her sense of reason and outrage well before that.

Harmon Ashby was found murdered at Augusta National Golf Club Monday. The Masters Rule Committee Chairman was a wonderful man, according to his friends.

The thing is, Harmon Ashby's friends are a little hard to find at the National these days. You see, he died less than a week after telling this columnist that he believed women should be admitted as members to Augusta National. As everyone, including the widowed Mrs. Ashby, knows all too well, the club bars women from joining. Always has—and, say many of the members, always will.

But here's poor Annabelle, rationalizing in her grief that it couldn't have been—just couldn't have been—one of her husband's golfing buddies who did him in. Oh, no—they loved him too much, she says through her tears.

To that I say, wake up and smell the fertilizer, dear.

Love, trust, friendship and most other decent human emotions are stopped at the National's gates, along with women who'd like to become members there. To many at Augusta National, the issue of keeping women out of the club is even more important than it was to keep blacks out of the club. After all, Augusta National finally broke down and let a black man join in 1990. Now there are five black members, if you trust the unofficial count—David Porter won't comment on his members—but still not a woman to be found.

Keep in mind that this club is located in the heart of the Deep South, where thousands were once willing to die to retain the monstrous evil of slavery. What makes Annabelle Ashby believe that at least one good ol' boy member wouldn't be willing to see her husband die to retain the despicable institution of all-male country clubs?

Sure, it's within the reach of one's imagination to picture an intruder penetrating the maximum-security walls of the club and, finding Harmon Ashby strolling the grounds in the dark, killing him for no particular reason—and then spraying THIS IS THE LAST MASTERS on the adjacent fairway with herbicide.

Isn't it a bit easier to picture an angry Neanderthal in a green jacket—one who has unlimited access to these ultra-private grounds—taking it upon himself to teach Harmon Ashby and the world a lesson?

And what is that lesson? That anyone who speaks out against the virulent sexism of

Augusta National will pay dearly for the indiscretion, and that the Masters itself is expendable if women keep beating at the gates. A lesson of that sort, written in blood, would certainly keep the rest of the members in the fold.

The world is finally closing in on these throwbacks to the antebellum South; the noose—if you will forgive the use of that term in this context—is tightening around the club. It is hardly a leap to picture one of Harmon Ashby's brethren lashing out in response. I believe Ashby paid the ultimate price for crossing over to the enemy when he openly opposed the club's arrogant, misogynist ways.

There is still time for this club to redeem itself. If, as so many suspect, the killer can be found in the club's directory, David Porter must do all he can to help bring him to justice. Then, the next step is clear. Begin to remove this stain by admitting not just one woman, but many. And not next week, or next year.

Now.

Sam put the paper down and started to take a sip of his luke-warm coffee. A waiter appeared before he could even bring it to his lips and asked him if he wanted a refill. The waiter—a white-haired black man wearing a gold jacket—refilled Caroline's cup from the pot of regular coffee he held in his other hand. Most of the clubhouse employees that Sam had seen were black. He assumed the jobs paid well, and judging from their ages, the employees obviously clung to them. But he also knew that many social critics would presume that blacks waiting on whites at Augusta National was a symbolic preservation of plantation life.

"What did you think?" Caroline asked after he put the paper down.

"I disagree."

"With what?" Caroline asked. "That somebody here killed him? That the club should allow women?"

"With her premise that there's something evil about an all-male club. People like Deborah Scanlon always assume the worst. They think exclusion means discrimination. People make choices every day about who they want to be with."

"Would you be a member here—if you could?"

"I wouldn't have much to contribute when the conversation turned to investment portfolios."

"You could be their token middle-class member."

"How about you? Would you join?"

"They don't allow women, remember?"

"You know they will eventually."

"So what are they waiting for?"

"For their members to demand it. It's their club—not ours. And not Rachel Drucker's, either."

Caroline tilted her head, thinking about what Sam had said, then pulled a pack of cigarettes and a lighter out of her purse.

"You mind?" she asked.

"No," Sam said. "I don't mind smokers, just like I don't mind all-male clubs. If I don't like it, I can go somewhere else."

"Seems reasonable," Caroline said, lighting up.

"Have you seen Shane yet?"

"No. I'm not looking for him, either."

"You can see both of us on Thursday. I'm paired with him and Frank Naples in the first round."

"I might have to catch that threesome. Naples is a hunk."

Sam actually felt a slight pang of jealousy. He put his napkin on the table and stood up.

"Time to practice. Maybe we'll see you Thursday."

"Maybe," she said. Then she returned to reading the newspaper in front of her.

◇◇◇

Sam got to the range at 10:45 a.m. He was determined to really study the course today, not gawk at it. With all the commotion

Monday, he had no idea what kind of score he could have posted. He thought he could finish close to par if he kept his concentration and managed to make a few putts. On Monday, Dwight had constantly reminded him to aim a little higher and hit it a little softer with the putter. Maybe today he'd drop a few.

"No distractions today," Dwight said on the first tee, as though reading his mind. "Keep the ball below the hole and inside the treeline, and you'll do fine."

"How are you feeling today?"

"Old and fat," Dwight said.

Sam teamed with Bellecourt, a tall, burly, black-haired man with large teeth and dark moles on his face and arms, against Cremmins and Cartwright in a best-ball match. Cremmins was a cocky young kid with a spiky haircut, wrap-around shades and one of those pretzel finishes to his swing where the club ended up behind his back, pointing all the way around to the target again. It would have put Sam in traction to swing that way, but it was obvious that kids like Cremmins were the new wave. Cartwright, by contrast, was an old-school practitioner of the controlled fade and positioning off the tee. He was rarely in trouble and relied on his short game to compete with the long bombers.

Sam played decently, but he was clearly the least skilled member of his group—and he hadn't had time to listen to music that morning. The song that kept intruding into his thoughts was a mildly irritating commercial jingle he'd heard on the locker room TV while he was changing into his golf shoes. He tried humming "Georgia on My Mind" to cleanse his brain, but the jingle wouldn't leave.

Dwight wasn't doing well, either. His limp got worse on the front nine.

"Hamstring tightenin' up," Dwight said through clenched teeth as they walked up the steep 9th fairway.

"You want to put the bag down?" Sam asked. "I can carry it."

"No, no, I'll get through this. Don't worry about me."

Beyond the occasional sight of a private plane flying overhead or the sound of a train passing somewhere in the distance, there was never a hint of anything existing beyond the shrubbery-covered fences—except that, for Harmon Ashby, the outside world might have gotten inside the cloister just long enough to kill him.

There was no sign of Monday's drama on the 12th green. The police tape was gone, the gallery was in its usual place in the grandstand behind the tee and up the hillside along the 11th fairway, and the grass where the message had been written looked almost unscathed. Augusta's makeup magicians had figured out a way to hide the blemishes. Only the faintest discoloration was visible. CBS—at David Porter's insistence—would find a way to filter their camera shots of the fairway so that the repair work would be invisible to the viewing audience.

Sam's team lost $50 each in the best-ball match, but Bellecourt didn't mind. He was like most pros Sam had met: all business on the course, but once the round was over, it was forgotten. Just another day at the office.

"Good luck this week," Bellecourt said, shaking Sam's hand after the round. "If you don't do anything stupid, you could make the cut."

"Thanks," Sam said. "That's what my caddie thinks, too."

"Listen to him. He's the best thing you got goin' for you."

Dwight had barely been able to make it up the hill to the 18th green, and there was pain and concern etched into the soft folds of his face after the round. Sam didn't want to risk losing him for the rest of the week.

"Let's skip the practice round tomorrow, Dwight," he said. "We'll just do the Par 3 Contest in the afternoon."

The Par 3 Contest had been a Masters tradition since 1960. It was played on the nine-hole par 3 course to the west of the short-game practice range, and behind the cabins. Players often had their wives or children caddie for them on the short course that wrapped around Ike's Pond—named for the former president, who suggested creating it for fishing.

"You want to go another 18 tomorrow, I can make it," Dwight said, but his sweating, pained face told Sam otherwise. He told Dwight to go home and get some rest, and took his own clubs back to the bag room.

He was looking forward to a hot shower and a beer. The temperature had again reached the 80s by the end of the round, and Sam felt drained. His knee was stiff and sore—for all the golf he'd played in the past year, he hadn't played on a course as hilly as Augusta National. He thought about Al Barber and admired him even more. Somehow the old guy managed to get around this golf course in fewer shots than guys half his age.

Sam was about to enter the locker room when one of the Masters officials in a green jacket tapped him on the shoulder.

"Mr. Skarda? You're wanted in the press building."

"I am?" Sam said. "Why?"

"They'd like to interview you."

Sam laughed and said, "Must be a slow news day."

Chapter Ten

Sam walked with the club official down the hill from the clubhouse to the two-story media building, painted Masters green and hidden from view to the right of the first fairway by a row of tea olive trees.

Sam had worked as a volunteer security guard at the PGA Championship at Hazeltine, and knew that the other major tournaments—held at rotating sites—housed journalists in an air-conditioned tent the size of a football field, complete with carpeted floors laid over miles of computer, telephone, and video wiring.

The Masters, of course, was different. The permanent press building at Augusta National replaced an old Quonset hut in 1990. The new building had all the comforts of a luxury suite at a football stadium, combined with the amenities of a modern newsroom. The main press room looked like a concert hall: eight rows of work stations with enough seating for several hundred journalists and their computers, descending to a main floor dominated by a 20-foot-tall replica of the main Masters scoreboard. A half-dozen large-screen TVs were positioned around the walls, allowing reporters on deadline to keep up with every shot of the tournament. Reporters covered most golf tournaments anchored to their laptop computers in the press tent. At the Masters, they were even less likely to venture onto the course, because they were not allowed inside the ropes. With food, 60-inch TV screens, and air-conditioned comfort inside the press building, why fight with 40,000 spectators for sight lines?

The Masters official led Sam to the door of a separate interview room off to one side of the main press area. Clive Cartwright
was just finishing up his interview with several dozen reporters
looking for the second-day spin on Ashby's death. A page stood
near the rows of folding chairs, ready to pass a wireless microphone from one reporter to the next as they raised their hands
to ask a question.

"...so, no, I don't have a position on what Augusta National
should do about its membership policies, to be perfectly honest,"
Cartwright said in his crisp English accent. "I mean, it's really
none of my business, is it? I leave this matter in the good hands
of the membership. I may have a green jacket, but I don't have
a vote. Incidentally, we have men-only clubs in the U.K., you
know. Muirfield, for one. I'd wager some of you have played
there? Well, cheerio, ladies and gents."

Cartwright popped out of his chair, unclipped his collar mic
and exited the room, having put the reporters on the defensive
and then leaving before they could actually make him say something of substance.

Sam slid into the chair Cartwright had just occupied and
pulled a chilled bottle of Mountain Spring Water—with the
Masters logo on the label—from a cooler next to the table.
He opened the bottle and took a drink while a page attached
the mic to his shirt. He was uncomfortable staring at the faces
before him—mostly middle aged men representing the larg
est newspapers, magazines, TV stations, and networks in the
country and around the world. As a cop he'd been interviewed
many times by local newspaper and TV reporters, but there had
rarely been more than two or three reporters present, and they
were usually in a hurry to get back to their newsrooms. This
was going to be different.

"Ladies and gentlemen, this is Sam Skarda," said a man in a
green jacket who was in charge of the interview room. "Sam is the
reigning U.S. Public Links champion. He lives in Minneapolis,
Minnesota. How old are you, Sam?"

"Thirty-seven."

"You're one of the older players to win the Publinx recently, aren't you?"

"Yeah, I think the college kids all felt sorry for me," Sam said. "I was giving up 40 yards off the tee to some of them. I'll feel right at home here this week."

A few of the reporters laughed, but none jumped in with a question.

"Are you married? Have any kids?" the moderator asked.

"No," Sam said.

"Who's got a question?" the moderator asked the room.

Sam stared straight ahead, noticing the TV camera that was taping his interview. After a few awkward moments of silence, a thin man with a round pot belly and a New York accent asked the page for the microphone.

"Sam, now that you played a couple of practice rounds, what are your impressions of Augusta National?" the reporter asked, pressing down the record button on his tape recorder.

"Well, I made a few impressions on the pine trees to the right of the 5th hole this morning," he said, drawing a few laughs. "It's a spectacular place."

"Did you play college golf?" one of the reporters asked.

"Yes—Dartmouth College. I usually played third or fourth spot. But you know Ivy League golf—it's like Ivy squash, without all the glamour."

"Weren't you and Shane Rockingham teammates there?"

"Yes. Amazingly enough, we never made it to the NCAA tournament. I blame myself."

"According to the press guide, you haven't won any other significant amateur tournaments," a reporter said.

"They have managed to elude me," Sam said. "That's because I haven't played in any of them."

"Why not?"

"Too busy making a living."

"You seem pretty straight-arrow," Russ Daly said. "You got a wild side? Tattoos? A motorcycle? Prescription drug addiction?"

"Nope. I guess I'm a by-the-book kind of guy. That's why I like golf. Rules matter to me."

"The press guide says you're a musician," another reporter said.

"My one vice," Sam said. "Aside from a stiff drink now and then."

"What do you play?"

"Guitar and piano—badly. I'm in a band with some other cops."

"What do you call yourselves?"

"Night Beat. We don't play very often—a bar or a party now and then. I haven't had much time since I started practicing for the Masters."

"How was your game today?"

"If you ask my caddie, he'd say I got my bad shots out of the way. He's a positive thinker."

"Sam," said Deborah Scanlon, "what's your opinion on the membership controversy at Augusta National? Should the club invite women to join?"

Sam paused for a moment. Even Tiger Woods didn't criticize Augusta National's membership policies, and no one was in a stronger position to express his opinion than Tiger. Ducking the question would be the safe and smart thing to do—but then again, they couldn't very well dis-invite him now, and chances were he'd never be back here again. Sam might have been the only man in the field who had nothing to lose by speaking his mind.

"I believe in the right of private clubs to make their own rules, whether the rest of us like it or not. Like Clive Cartwright said as I was walking in, it's not my place to tell them what they should do. But personally, I'd rather belong to a club that had women members."

"So you don't think there should be all-male golf clubs?"

"No, I didn't say that," Sam said. "If 300 men want to belong to an all-male club, that's up to them. They should have that right. So should women."

"Why do you suppose they don't want women here?"

"I have no idea," Sam said. "You'd have to ask them."

"Do you think they ever will admit women?" Scanlon asked.

"Someday, sure. I think it's inevitable. Dartmouth had been all-male for 200 years. They finally got around to admitting women before I got there."

"Any thoughts on who ought to be the first woman member now?" Scanlon asked.

"My mother," Sam said. "She might invite me to play here once in a while."

The room broke up—except for Scanlon, who maintained a look of intense resolve. This story was obviously far more important to her than any golf tournament.

Daly raised his hand, and the page carrying the transistor microphone walked back and handed it to him as several reporters were still laughing.

"We know from your bio that you were a cop," Daly said. "Are you still a cop, or what?"

"I'm on a leave of absence," Sam said.

"Why?" Daly said.

"I got shot in the knee."

"How'd it happen?" Daly persisted.

"My partner and I were investigating a shooting in a night club," Sam said, taking another sip on the water bottle. "We had interviewed a suspect whose story didn't sound right, so we decided to take him downtown. On the way out the door he said he had to go to the bathroom. My partner went in with him to keep an eye on him. A minute later I hear them struggling in there, so I go through the door just as a shot is fired. The guy had stuffed a gun down the back of his pants, and was trying to get it out to shoot my partner. He shot himself in the ass instead, but the bullet went through him and hit me in the knee."

Some of the reporters laughed. Others winced.

Sam told them that the bullet had broken his left kneecap, severed a ligament, and taken out some cartilage. The damage was too serious to scope; it took two operations to put the pieces back together.

"I haven't got much cartilage in the left knee now, and I hurt the right one a long time ago playing football," he said.

"You seem to be getting up and down these hills okay," Daly said.

"I took a medical leave to rehab my knee," Sam said. "The doctors said walking would be good for it. I started with three holes a day."

There were a few laughs from the reporters, and Sam continued.

"I worked my way up to 18 holes a day, and then 36 every other day. By the time my knee felt strong enough to go back to light duty, I was playing the best golf of my life. And to tell you the truth, I didn't want to go back to the job. Any cop will tell you that when you don't want to go into work in the morning, you shouldn't be there. So I took an extended leave of absence to figure out what I wanted to do."

There was sympathetic silence for a while, finally broken by a reporter with a British accent: "Are you going to remain an amateur, or are you thinking of turning professional?"

Sam laughed, relieved that the subject had changed.

"Pro? No way. I can't make a living doing this. I'd need to practice non-stop for at least a year to even get to the second round of qualifying school, and I don't have that kind of time or money. I need to earn a living."

"So you're going back to the police force after the Masters?" Daly asked.

"I don't know yet," Sam said. "I have until Monday to make up my mind."

"Any theories about what happened to Harmon Ashby yesterday?" Daly asked. "I mean, from a cop's perspective?"

"I'll leave that one to the locals," Sam said. "They don't need my help."

"Are you staying in the Crow's Nest this week?" a reporter asked.

"Yes. All week, I hope."

"If that's it, ladies and gentlemen, we'll wrap this up," said the moderator. "Thank you, Sam."

"Thank you," Sam replied, rising from his chair.

As he was leaving the interview room, Russ Daly sidled up to him.

"I took your advice," he said.

Sam looked perplexed.

"About talking to the grounds crew. They've already run tests on the herbicide used to write the message on the 12th green."

Daly pulled out his notebook and flipped through the pages until he came to the passage he was looking for.

"It was something called glyphosate."

"Do they use that here?"

"They use it everywhere. It's the basic ingredient in RoundUp. It kills grass, weeds—everything."

"I guess we're not going to solve this one," Sam said. "What's your column for tomorrow?"

"The protest out on Washington Road this afternoon," Daly said. "Rachel Drucker is promising there will be a thousand sign-waving crazies. I'm betting it's closer to 50."

"I don't know," Sam said. "Looks like this murder has given her cause new life."

Chapter Eleven

Augusta National had reached a compromise with the Richmond County Sheriff's office: Rachel Drucker and the WOFF would be allowed to stage their protests at a park across Washington Road, a mile east of the National's main gate. David Porter had argued that the public was inconvenienced enough by the snarled traffic past Magnolia Lane during Masters Week. Why increase the odds of accidents and injuries by letting a group of protesters picket their entrance?

Richmond County Sheriff Leonard Garver saw the wisdom in Porter's position, as he usually did. If the club had a reasonable request, or even an unreasonable one, Garver tried to see things their way. The Masters inconvenienced his city once a year, but it also brought in millions of dollars. The area's hotels and cateries and souvenir shops depended on the income from the free-spending golf fans, and Garver had an obligation to see that they didn't take a financial hit to accommodate a pack of screaming gals at the gates.

Besides, Garver thought the protesters were nitwits. He saw nothing wrong with a men's club. Didn't these women have anything better to complain about?

With Garver's encouragement, the Augusta city council had passed a law requiring prior approval for any public gathering of five or more people. When the WOFF made it known they planned to picket in front of Magnolia Lane, Leonard Garver made it known they'd be arrested, pursuant to the new law.

Rachel Drucker reluctantly accepted an alternative gathering spot away from the course.

"The networks and the newspapers will cover this goddamned protest all out of proportion, no matter where it's held," Porter said to Garver Tuesday afternoon in the chairman's office. "It's not like we're stuffing a gag in their mouths. But we're not going to roll out the red carpet for them either."

Leonard nodded, letting Porter lead the discussion, as usual.

"Have your boys figured out how the intruder got onto our property?" Porter asked.

"Now, David, don't go jumpin' to conclusions," Garver said. "This is a wide-open investigation. Dennis Harwell is a thorough investigator, and he's lookin' at all possibilities. You say it wasn't a member or an employee, but we don't know that yet. If somebody came over your fence and killed Ashby, we'll find him. You might think about adding more guards."

"We think our security is adequate, but I appreciate the suggestion."

"It ain't adequate if somebody can sneak around the course and kill a person."

Porter and Garver locked eyes for a moment. Then Garver got up to go check on the protest.

◇◇◇

Sam had lunch in the men's grill. He'd read that when Jack Nicklaus played in the Masters as an amateur, he had filled up on the National's shrimp cocktail and New York strips, each costing just a dollar at the time. Sam treated himself to the same meal—though the price had certainly kept up with inflation—complemented by a glass of Kenwood cabernet, recommended by the club's wine steward. It was a far better meal than the traditional Masters lunch, sold at the concession tents and served in the press building: pimento cheese sandwiches, consisting of a slice of cheese slathered in mayonnaise between pieces of white bread, wrapped in a green paper baggie. Sam had tried one on Monday. One was enough.

Sam had the afternoon free to get in some extra practice, but at this point he knew it would be nerves, not technique, that would determine how well he played in the tournament. He recalled what Russ Daly had said about covering the WOFF protest, and decided to take a walk in that direction. He was curious to know if Ashby's death would draw more protesters to the demonstration, and what kind of impact that might have on the Masters. It was all part of the show this year, his one year at the Masters. Might as well take it all in.

He left the grounds through the gate near the players' parking lot and walked east on Washington Road. Within ten minutes he heard the sound of chanting: "Hey hey! Ho ho! Sexist Porter, time to go!"

Several police cars and satellite trucks were parked along the street and on the grass of a public park. A large pink inflated pig was tethered to the ground as a backdrop to a speaker's podium, from which Rachel Drucker was addressing a gathering of several hundred protesters carrying anti-Augusta National signs. Drucker was dressed in a blue pants suit and wore her hair in a short razor cut. Sam thought: She looks more like a cop than I do.

A half-dozen video crews were shooting while Drucker worked herself into a pique. There were many more protesters than Russ Daly had predicted—mostly younger women, college age or slightly older, many wearing green T-shirts with the WOFF logo. A woman with a nearly shaved head wore a long white sweatshirt on which she'd written "MEN ONLY" in a red circle with a line through it. Hand-made protest signs read, "Fair Play on the Fair-way," "DIGNITY RESPECT FAIRNESS," "Sexism is a Handicap," and "College: $80,000. Law School: $124,000. Busting up the Old Boy's Club: Priceless."

Sam had worked crowd control at many protests. Before Ashby was killed, the WOFF rallies he'd seen on TV had an air of mock earnestness about them, as though the protesters knew they weren't going to change anything, but enjoyed embarrassing the CEOs with a little street theater. For the first time, the WOFF was beginning to attract and generate real anger.

"You can't silence us like you silenced Harmon Ashby!" Drucker yelled into her microphone.

Somebody must have taught her Ashby's name.

"No more, Mr. Porter!" Drucker yelled. "No more discrimination! No more secrecy! No more lies! No more sacrificing your own members to protect your precious boys club from the outside world! Your time is up, Mr. Porter! Come out from behind your gates, and let your sisters inside!"

Sam scanned the park. Despite the police presence, it wouldn't have been hard for a sniper to get a clear shot at Drucker. Given what happened to Ashby, it took guts for the WOFF leader to stand out in public now.

Among the several dozen cops and reporters on the periphery of the protest, one old man stood under the shade of a sycamore tree, holding a sign over his head that said, "MAKE MY DINNER." Sam laughed when he saw the sign.

"Is that supposed to be funny?" he heard someone say.

Sam turned to see Deborah Scanlon standing a few feet away from him.

"Yeah, if you've got a sense of humor," Sam said.

"It's not funny—it's pathetic. Rachel is right, you know."

They listened to Drucker repeat the same accusations again and again, varying only the order. She paused for chanting whenever she began to lose momentum.

Sam's interest level rose sharply when Drucker demanded that the players refuse to participate in this year's Masters.

"Yes!" Scanlon responded, raising a fist in the air, and turning to give Sam an accusatory look.

"It wouldn't mean squat to David Porter if I pulled out of the tournament," Sam said to Scanlon. "Or if half the field pulled out, for that matter. What we do won't change this club."

"Maybe not, but it's the right thing to do. This tournament has gone from an embarrassment to an abomination since Ashby was murdered."

"Should the members quit, too?"

"They never should have joined in the first place."

"Not many men are going to turn down an invitation to Augusta National."

"You'd really want to be a member of a club that excludes half the world's population because they don't have dicks?" Scanlon replied.

"Augusta National excludes almost all of the world's population, not just half. I've got the same chance to join that you do: none."

"That's not true," she said. "You're a man."

"That wouldn't matter to the membership committee."

Scanlon shook her head in disgust, as if to suggest she was speaking to a moral pygmy. Then she lifted her chin and a smug grin spread across her face.

"Not every golfer worships at the shrine of Augusta National," Scanlon said.

"I don't know one who doesn't," Sam said.

"I'll bet you do," she said. "Danny Milligan."

Since his firing by CBS a decade earlier for making wisecracks about the Masters, Sam had heard and read Milligan's many jabs at the Lords of Augusta.

"My guess is he's still bitter about getting canned," Sam said. "He didn't seem to hate the place all those years he was covering the tournament."

"We'll see. I'm going to his house in Beech Island tomorrow to interview him. He promised me he'd really unload on David and the boys."

"I read your column this morning," Sam said. "You don't need to quote Milligan to get off a cheap shot at Augusta National."

Scanlon's eyes narrowed. She took a step closer to Sam.

"You golfers always stick up for each other, don't you? Your buddies at Augusta National just couldn't have had anything to do with Ashby's murder."

"I didn't say that," Sam said. "I have no idea who killed Ashby. Neither do you. But that didn't stop you from pointing the finger at them this morning."

"I'm a columnist. I get to express my opinion."

"They treat you well here, don't they? Give you the run of the course, keep you comfortable in a nice air-conditioned press building, serve you five-star meals in their dining room. These are monsters?"

"No. I think only one of them is a monster. The rest are just cavemen."

"So why accept their hospitality?"

"Tell me this, Skarda," Scanlon said. "Have you ever had the braised lamb shanks at Augusta National?"

"No."

"Well, I have, and I'm not passing them up no matter who serves them."

"Now that's why you and I get along so well, Debbie," said Russ Daly, who'd been jotting down notes from Rachel Drucker's speech until he spotted Sam and Scanlon and ambled over to join in. "You don't let your scruples get in the way of a good meal, either."

"Oh, lick me, Daly," Scanlon said. "Life's too short to waste it swapping insults with an unarmed man."

"I just wanted to tell you I loved your column today," Daly said to her, mopping sweat from his forehead with the sleeve of his jacket. "Seriously. Even I couldn't have strung David Porter up by the privates the way you did. You dispensed with the trial and went straight to the execution. Any anonymous death threats today?"

Scanlon actually smiled at Daly's question.

"I haven't checked my messages for a few hours," she said. "I'll let you know."

Scanlon turned and made her way through the assembled protesters toward the podium. She was dressed in tight black slacks and a black blazer, dramatically setting off her short, white-blond hair. The total effect made her stand out in the crowd like a rock star at a church social.

"What a piece of work," Daly said, shaking his head. "She almost gives us cheap-shot artists a bad name."

"What do you think of the turnout?" Sam asked.

"I'm stunned," Daly said. "There's a few hundred more misguided souls here than I thought there'd be. I guess a murder is good for ratings in the protest business, too."

A sustained chant of "What do we want? Membership!! When do we want it? Now!!" died away, and then Rachel Drucker revved up again

"Sisters and brothers, did you read the *New York Times* today?" she shouted. Some applauded and yelled their approval. "Their wonderful columnist, Deborah Scanlon, wrote a brilliant piece in today's paper that told it like it is. My good friend Deborah is with us today, and I'd like her permission to quote from her column."

As the crowd cheered, Scanlon's blonde head nodded consent near the podium. Drucker put on a pair of glasses and began to read:

"'...anyone who speaks out against the virulent sexism of Augusta National will pay dearly for the indiscretion...The world is finally closing in on these throwbacks to the antebellum South days; the noose—if you will forgive the use of that term in this context—is tightening around the club...There is still time for this club to redeem itself. If, as so many suspect, the killer can be found in the club's directory, David Porter must do all he can to help bring him to justice. Then, the next step is clear: Begin to remove this stain by admitting not just one woman, but many. And not next week, or next year. Now!'"

The crowed roared.

A few minutes later, Drucker left the podium and the crowd began to disperse. Sam took another look at the perimeter of the field. If someone had wanted to take a shot at Drucker, they'd had their chance.

Chapter Twelve

Deborah Scanlon returned to the Augusta National media center after the WOFF rally, gratified to have heard her own words echoing from the loudspeakers. She watched the coverage at her work station, and was pleased to see that every newscast was devoting several minutes to the protest. What the WOFF lacked in numbers, it was making up for in air time. Scanlon was also pleased to see that her own face was included in most of the reports, as a cut-in when Rachel Drucker was quoting from her column. Maybe there's a book deal in this, she thought as she flipped through the channels.

The *Times* golf beat writer was still working on his feature for the next morning, so Scanlon made the walk from the media center to the clubhouse dining room by herself. The grounds were nearly deserted, as the guards escorted the last spectators through the gates to their cars and shuttle buses in the gathering dusk.

There was something so staged, so cloyingly precious about Augusta National, Scanlon thought as she approached the clubhouse. It was Southern Gothic meets Disney World. Every charming touch that Clifford Roberts and his successors had taken such pains to implement and preserve had a faint aura of artificiality, as though the entire 365 acres was a theme park devoted to a reality that no longer existed anywhere but here. She half expected to see Rhett Butler lighting a cheroot on the porch overlooking the course, or little Bonnie Blue riding around the Founders Circle on her pony.

It was silly, really. Augusta National had been a perfectly good fruit nursery; now it was a nice golf course. It was just a piece of land, after all. Why grown men elevated this place all out of proportion to its importance was a mystery to Scanlon. Then again, as she walked through the main entrance and took in the aromas emanating from the dining room, she was reminded that covering the Masters was the best assignment of the year. Big-name golfers, wonderful weather, heavenly food, and an opportunity to crusade for social justice—what more could a columnist want?

◇◇◇

Sam attended the annual Amateur Dinner with Compton and Wheeling in the clubhouse library that night. They were joined by more than a dozen members, many of the pros who had played in the Masters as amateurs, and David Porter, who made a fourth at the table with Sam and the other two amateurs. Jack Nicklaus spoke informally after dinner, telling stories about his first trip to Augusta National and his memories of conversations with Bobby Jones.

"Someday, I'd like to be talking to the amateurs at this dinner about meeting Jack Nicklaus," Wheeling said.

"Someday, a guy will be talking to the amateurs about meeting me," Compton said. Sam and Wheeling looked at each other and laughed.

"I knew you were a legend the first time I laid eyes on you," Sam said to Compton, who took it as a compliment.

Porter asked Sam to stay for a moment after the dinner ended. Sam hadn't been able to see through Porter's polished veneer at dinner. He was used to making fast first impressions; it was necessary in police work when you often didn't get a second chance to be right about someone. But in this case, his judgment was influenced by all he'd heard and read about the strict leadership at Augusta National. He sensed an iron resolve behind Porter's slick manner, but that was probably a prerequisite to run this club.

"So you're in law enforcement, Sam," the chairman said.

"That's right."

"I have the highest regard for people willing to put their lives on the line for the public good."

"Thanks."

"I understand you told the reporters today you might not return to the Minneapolis police force after the Masters?"

Sam was surprised Porter had time to monitor his press conference, with everything else going on at the National this week. He was a keen, well-informed man. Sam vowed not to underestimate him.

"I'm going to make a decision after the tournament," Sam said.

"What else would you do?"

"Private investigation, I suppose," Sam says. "I'm not qualified for my dream job."

"What would that be?"

"A man of leisure."

Porter laughed. Sam had noticed during Nicklaus' talk that the chairman enjoyed a witty remark, a side of himself that Porter wasn't inclined to let the public see.

"We hire investigators from time to time," Porter said. "Let me know what you decide. I may call on you some day."

Porter's offer seemed genuine—he had a reassuring demeanor that was undoubtedly a big reason why his corporation had chosen him to be its frontman—but why would he want to hire Sam? There had to be plenty of private detectives in Georgia.

"I trust a man who takes the time to become an accomplished golfer as much as I do an officer of the law," Porter said, as though reading Sam's mind. "It's a rare combination—an appealing one. To be honest, I find many of the competitors here a little narrow in their range of interests and accomplishments."

They shook hands and Porter excused himself.

Sam wondered if Caroline Rockingham might have returned to the clubhouse for a drink in the bar. He walked downstairs to the Trophy room, but didn't see Caroline there—but he did see Deborah Scanlon, making good on her promise to enjoy the club's lamb. She was dining with a striking auburn-haired woman who Sam vaguely recognized from one of the evening news broadcasts, and a well-coiffed man who had to be a television executive. Scanlon certainly wasn't the most engaging personality Sam had ever met, but there was no denying the influence of her newspaper. With the exposure the membership issue was getting this week, Scanlon was on the verge of becoming a celebrity—and she looked the part.

Sam sat down at the bar and asked for a list of their single-malt scotches. He ordered a Glenmorangie, still hoping Caroline might show up. Eventually Scanlon got up and left the dining room by herself. Still wearing the form-fitting black pants and spiked heels, Scanlon caught the eye of several old Augusta National green jackets—some approvingly, others not amused.

"She's got a hell of a lot of nerve coming in here, after what she wrote today," one member grumbled to another, loudly enough that Scanlon could have heard it as she walked out. If she did, she gave no sign.

Sam had a second scotch, but Caroline still did not drop by. When he went up to the Crow's Nest, Compton was on his cell phone, calling a string of incredulous buddies back in Oklahoma to tell them how great Augusta National was, how great the Crow's Nest was, how great the weather was, and how great he was. Wheeling called his wife and his father, then began fiddling with his putter, which he'd brought with him to the Crow's Nest. He cleaned nonexistent specks of material from the insert face of the putter, then practiced his putting stroke on the rug.

"Do you think I'm bringing the blade too far to the inside on the takeaway?" he asked Sam, who was lying on his bed reading an autographed copy of Bobby Jones' *Down the Fairway* that he'd pulled from the bookshelf.

"Let me look," Sam said, sitting up on the bed and pretending to study Wheeling's stroke. "Nope. Looks fine to me."

Sam went back to reading. He had no intention of offering any real advice, which could just mess up Wheeling's game. The guy was just looking for reassurance, so he told him what he wanted to hear. Eventually Wheeling tired of fussing with his putting mechanics, called his wife one more time and then went to bed. Compton ran out of people to call and turned in, too. By 10:30, the lights were out in the Crow's Nest.

◇◇◇

Deborah Scanlon left the clubhouse and headed to the parking lot behind the media building. The sky was black and starless; unlike the venues for most major sporting events, the clubhouse area at Augusta National did not have towering light poles to bathe the vicinity in artificial daylight.

"Miss Scanlon?" she heard a man's voice say as she walked across the driveway in front of the pro shop. The man seemed to have emerged from the shadows by a hedge that abutted a pair of 10-foot tea olive trees.

"Yes?" she said, stopping to look at him. He was a tall man wearing a dark jacket, tie, and ball cap.

"Mr. Porter would like to talk to you," the man said.

Scanlon was surprised and excited to know that she'd somehow earned a private audience with the man who ruled Augusta National. She'd penetrated his wall of indifference.

"He's at the Stephens Cabin," the man said. "I can escort you."

"Thank you," Scanlon said. "That would be nice."

It did make her feel better to have an escort after dark, just in case there really was some psycho running around.

A few cars came and went down Magnolia Lane—players heading back to their rented homes after dinner, and members returning to the club from parties in town. Scanlon and her escort walked along the sidewalk in front of the clubhouse as a security guard stopped the incoming cars to talk briefly with each driver.

"Did the club hire more security for the rest of the week?" Scanlon asked her escort as they passed the Founders Circle and walked toward the east practice range.

"Yes, ma'am," the tall man said. "Can't be too careful anymore."

"No, I suppose not," Scanlon said.

They walked down a driveway between the food service building and the practice range, and past the back of the Eisenhower
Cabin, which was lit up like the other cabins east of the clubhouse, with music and laughter drifting from the cocktail parties
inside. The service road took them past the par 3 course—down
a steep hill to their left—with the Tennessee, California, and
Stephens Cabins to the right. Some 20 luxury cars were parked
on the grass outside the cabins.

Scanlon thought "cabin" was such an inadequate word for the
elegant two-story white buildings. In most parts of the world,
they'd be considered mansions.

Scanlon wasn't sure which one was the Stephens Cabin. She
thought it was to the east of the Jones Cabin—and the Firestone
Cabin, which the Ashbys had been sharing with another couple.
The Stanwicks, was it? She'd never been in any of the cabins,
even in the daylight. What little light there was on the service
road was coming from the floodlights that illuminated the steep
back lawns of the cabins.

They seemed to be walking away from the cabins and closer
to the path that led down the dark, shrubbery-dotted hillside
to the par 3 course and Ike's Pond.

"Look, I thought we were…"

Scanlon never finished the sentence. A staggering blow to the
side of her head knocked her to her knees. She was too stunned
to scream, but even if she had, she wouldn't have been heard.
The man had his hand over her mouth, his forearm around her
throat and was dragging her down the hill, out of sight from
the cabins, toward the spring-fed pond below. Panic surged
through Scanlon's body, already rubbery from the pain in her
head. At barely 110 pounds, she was no match for the tall man
dragging her down toward the water. She tried to dig her heels
into the wood chips and pine straw that covered the hillside, but
they merely bounced along the ground as her attacker forced

her forward. She flailed at him with her arms, but the best she could do were weak, glancing blows against his shoulders. As they gained momentum, her attacker fell on his side, still hanging onto Scanlon and covering her mouth. They rolled downhill, bouncing off bushes and scraping away the ground cover. Finally they rolled to a stop, and dread replaced Scanlon's disorientation as she felt her feet splash into the water.

Desperately she managed to work her tongue out of her mouth and between the man's fingers, trying to create enough space to suck his little finger partially into her mouth and bite down on it. The man shifted his grip on her mouth, and she felt his arm tighten around her throat. If she could just make some noise, make noise—make some noise! The thought was racing around wildly in her head like a horse in a barn fire. She couldn't scream, but somehow she had to attract some attention. They were going into the water—maybe someone in the cabins would hear a splash.

She kicked her legs frantically against the water, but then felt his weight on top of her as they both plunged below the surface. She tried to preserve what little air she had left in her lungs, while still fighting her attacker. She tried again to bite one of his fingers. This time the hand came off her mouth, but she was still underwater. With the last of her strength, she twisted to her right and rolled her head downward. Her legs came up out of the water, and she splashed them down as hard as she could against the surface. The motion made the man lose his grip and drop Scanlon into the pond. With her head still underwater, and her last breath nearly gone, she kicked her legs at her attacker and felt the spiked heel on her left foot make hard contact somewhere around his stomach. He recoiled in pain, and Scanlon struggled to get her head above the surface. They were in two feet of water, and she started to push herself up, feeling the water cascade from her forehead as she broke the surface, seeing the stars over the shoulder of the man looming above her, starting to open her mouth to take in enough air to scream…

But he was on her before the air ever reached her lungs, and pushed her back down into the water just as she began her gasp. The chemically treated water from Ike's Pond flooded down Scanlon's windpipe. She continued to thrash as she choked on the water, but less forcefully now. The blackness that was the sky and the water soon overwhelmed everything, and then she stopped moving.

Still Lee Doggett held her head under the water for another minute, as though he feared this hellcat might come back to life. Finally he let her go and pulled himself to the bank of the pond, panting and holding his stomach. He lifted his sopping jacket and shirt; the bitch's heel had punctured the skin. He was bleeding.

Doggett looked back at Scanlon's body in the pond. Her head was still underwater, her feet splayed up onto the bank. He reached over and took off her left shoe. No point in leaving it behind. It would be their only chance to find his DNA.

He put the shoe in his right jacket pocket and stood up carefully, looking up the hill through the pine trees and listening to see if their splashing had attracted any attention. She hadn't been able to scream, and the sound from the parties in the cabins up above would have masked whatever noise they made tumbling down the hill or splashing in the water. He was sure they hadn't been heard.

He pulled the plastic spray bottle from the pocket inside his jacket and popped the protective cap. Then he squeezed herbicide onto the green next to the pond, not 10 feet from the columnist's legs, leaving the words that in the morning would read:

THIS IS THE LAST MASTERS

Chapter Thirteen

Wednesday, April 9

Sam awoke to the sound of raindrops spattering on the windows of the cupola above the Crow's Nest. He'd wanted to sleep until at least eight, but the drumbeat of the raindrops overhead, which normally would have had a soothing effect on him, instead made him feel anxious.

Rain had been in the forecast for several days, and Sam had been looking forward to it. Some of the pros had been saying the greens were getting so firm and crunchy that, unless it rained, no way in hell would their approach shots hold. They'd all get a chance to see if the rain helped later that day during the Par 3 tournament.

Sam got out of bed and went down to the Trophy Room for a light breakfast. He expected to find a few reporters and club members, but the room was deserted except for two gold-jacketed waiters standing next to the buffet line. That's when he heard the sirens. A minute later, two Richmond County squad cars pulled up the rain-slicked circular driveway in front of the clubhouse, followed by an ambulance. Now he was more than curious. Something was going terribly wrong at this year's Masters.

He pulled on his rain jacket and golf hat and walked out the front door to the Founders Circle, where a crowd of employees and green jackets had gathered around the emergency vehicles.

The sheriff's deputies got back in their cars and followed a golf cart, driven by a man in a yellow rain poncho, past the short-game practice range toward the cabins above the par 3 course. Sam walked along behind them, following the police and EMTs as they scrambled down the steep hill toward Ike's Pond. Several grounds crew members stood next to the pond, with a riding lawnmower idling a few feet away, staring at something at the water's edge.

A pair of lifeless legs—clad in tight black pants, one foot bare, the other wearing a spiked heel—protruded from the edge of the pond. The rest of the body was underwater, but Sam knew who the legs belonged to. He'd seen her yesterday, walking away from him and toward the speaker's podium at Rachel Drucker's WOFF rally, and last night leaving the dining room.

Somebody had killed Deborah Scanlon.

It was raining harder now, the drops hissing off the water. The police had already started cordoning off the area with yellow crime scene tape, but Sam was close enough to see that the killer had left the same message on the green near the body.

THIS IS THE LAST MASTERS

Whoever had done this didn't want to leave any confusion about his identity. It was the same killer, for the same reason. First Ashby speaks out about allowing women into Augusta National. Then Deborah Scanlon. Now both of them are dead. But how was the killer getting onto the grounds? How was he moving around without being noticed? It looked more and more like an insider.

The man in the yellow poncho was Bill Woodley, the club manager. He was on his cell phone, while the police radioed back to headquarters, both relating the same message: There's been another murder at the National.

"Anybody know who this is?" one of the cops asked, loud enough for Sam to hear.

"I do," Sam said, over the yellow police tape.

"Who are you?" a cop asked.

"Sam Skarda. I'm playing in the Masters this week."

"So who's that?" he asked, jerking his walkie-talkie over his left shoulder toward the body in the pond.

"Looks like Deborah Scanlon. Columnist for the *New York Times*."

The cop led Sam across the green to the body. He couldn't quite make out her face under the water, but the hair was obviously short and blond.

"I can't tell for sure unless I see her face."

Another cop stepped into the water, put his hand behind the body's head and lifted it out of the water.

"That's her," Sam said.

"How do you know her?" the first cop asked.

"She interviewed me on Monday. I talked to her again yesterday at the WOFF rally."

"I was there," one of the cops said. "I remember her. Didn't that Rachel Drucker read from one of her columns?"

"Yeah," Sam said. "She was criticizing the National for not allowing women members."

The cops looked at each other.

"Harwell will want to talk to him," the first cop said. "Skarda, is it? We need you to stick around."

"Fine," Sam said. "I've got a few hours before the Par 3 tournament starts."

Bill Woodley shook his head, having just put his cell phone back in his pocket.

"The Par 3 tournament is cancelled," Woodley said. "I just talked to Mr. Porter. He'll be here in a few minutes."

David Porter arrived at almost the same time Leonard Garver did. Porter looked ashen; Garver just seemed bewildered, as though a train that came through town at the same time every day had suddenly jumped the tracks. They stood over the body for a few minutes while a crew of crime scene technicians took pictures, gathered grass samples from the killer's message, and scoured the hillside for Scanlon's missing shoe, footprints, or dropped objects that might be tied to the killing. David shook his head and then huddled with Garver and Woodley. The first order of business was to close the grounds and ask those spectators who were waiting at the gates to go back to their cars and buses. The Par 3 tournament would not be played, for the first time since 1960, because Augusta National Golf Club was now a crime scene.

"What should I tell the staff and volunteers?" Woodley asked, at a momentary loss as to how to handle a catastrophe during the Masters, where catastrophes weren't allowed.

"Tell them the truth," Porter said. "There's been an accident, and we need to investigate."

"What about tomorrow?"

"The Masters will go on as scheduled."

"David, do you think that's a good idea?" Garver asked.

"It's the only idea we will accept," said Porter, who glanced at Scanlon's body, still half-submerged in the pond, and quickly looked away. "It breaks my heart to cancel the Par 3 tournament. Mr. Jones and Mr. Roberts loved it. The patrons love it. I understand we have to cancel. But I will not postpone or cancel the Masters. That hasn't happened since World War II, and it will take another World War before I stop this tournament."

Sam was still standing inside the police tape, though several feet away from Porter, Garver, and Woodley. He wondered when Garver was going to bring up the obvious: that it looked like an inside job. It was time to question those who were most likely to be angry with the club's critics: the members. The grounds crew didn't care one way or the other if the club admitted women. The same was likely true of the clubhouse staff and cleaning people. They'd all have to be questioned, of course, but any detective with half a brain would be demanding from Porter a complete accounting for the members who were on the grounds that week—their whereabouts and their gender politics.

Garver was thinking the same way.

"David, we're going to interview your members," he said to the club chairman. "An agent from the Atlanta office of the Georgia Bureau of Investigation is on his way here to help Dennis Harwell with the investigation. You'll need to tell them whatever they want to know."

Porter appeared to be thinking over his options—which in this case were limited. Two dead bodies in three days on the grounds of a private club tended to eliminate the club's wiggle room, no matter how much power they had over the local authorities. This was a scandal in the making, and refusing to cooperate with police would only make matters worse. But Porter had handled potential scandals before.

"Do what you've got to do, Leonard," Porter said, a heavy note of resignation in his voice. He turned and began walking back up the hill, but noticed Sam standing nearby. He paused and said something quietly to Woodley, then continued walking back to the clubhouse, Porter's shoulders slumped in a way that made him seem far less imperious. Woodley watched them go, and then approached Sam.

"Mr. Porter would like to see you in his office when you have a moment," Woodley said.

Bill Woodley was a small, clean-shaven man with thinning, neatly combed hair who exuded efficiency and devotion to the National. He'd been everywhere around the club in the previous two days, fielding members' requests and promptly conveying them to the employees, who listened to Woodley as though hearing from God's messenger. Yet Woodley did nothing to call attention to himself. Like any good manager, he made it his business to eliminate problems before they became problems. It had to be unbearable for Woodley to see the Masters marred by two murders.

"What does he want to see me about?" Sam asked.

"He didn't say."

"The cops want me to stay here until I've talked to the investigators," Sam said.

"Of course," Woodley said. "After that, then."

"I'll be there."

Sam waited with the police until the investigator from the Sheriff's department arrived. Lt. Dennis Harwell, the same detective Sam had talked to at the 12th hole on Monday, slipped and skidded down the steep, soggy hillside, getting mud on his tan raincoat. He looked anxious, and he had reason to be. He was responsible for solving what would be the most talked-about crime in the country, and possibly hanging a murder rap on some big-shot member.

Harwell asked the cops what time the call came in, what they'd seen when they arrived, and whether there were any witnesses. He examined the position of the body, spoke to the technicians, and knelt down to inspect the grass where the THIS IS THE LAST MASTERS message had been left. Eventually he walked over to Sam.

"The officers tell me you know her," Harwell said, motioning to Scanlon's body. "A *New York Times* columnist?"

"That's right," Sam said. "Deborah Scanlon."

"And who are you again?"

Sam didn't like the way Harwell asked the question, as though he wasn't inclined to believe anything Sam told him.

"Sam Skarda. I'm an amateur golfer, playing in the Masters this year. I talked to you on Monday."

Harwell seemed to be struggling to recall their brief conversation at the murder scene on the 12th hole. He looked at Sam suspiciously.

"The Masters is a pro tournament," he said. "How long have they been letting amateurs play?"

"Since 1934," Sam said.

It sounded like a smartass answer, but it was the truth: From the beginning, the Masters had always invited amateurs to play. Bobby Jones himself was an amateur. Sam couldn't help it if this cop didn't know the first thing about the Masters.

"How did you know—Scranton, was it?" Harwell asked.

"Scanlon. I met her Monday when she interviewed me after my practice round," Sam said. "Then I saw her at a press conference on Tuesday, and later at the WOFF rally down the road."

"What were you doing there?" Harwell asked.

"I was curious," Sam said.

"About what?" Harwell said.

"I just wanted to see what was going on."

It was the cop in Sam that had checked out the rally, not the golfer. As far as he knew, he was the only player who'd bothered to go. If Harwell knew anything about golf or golfers, he would have picked up on that. But apparently he'd managed to live in Augusta for some time without ever developing an interest in the city's most important enterprise.

"Did you see her after that?" Harwell asked.

"I saw her having dinner in the clubhouse dining room last night."

"When was that?"

"Around nine o'clock."

"Did you talk to her?"

"No."

"Was she with someone?"

"Yeah, a couple of people I didn't know. They looked like TV types."

"Were they friendly conversations?"

"Looked like it to me," Sam said. "I didn't pay much attention."

"What time did she leave?"

"Around nine, like I said."

"Did she leave alone?"

"I think so."

"Can anyone account for your whereabouts last night?"

Sam wasn't irritated by the line of questioning; it was standard and proper. It was just the tone of Harwell's voice that grated on him. Sam had always tried to make witnesses and suspects feel he was on their side until and unless they started being evasive or confrontational. Sam had been neither, but Harwell still sounded as though he were looking to trip him up somehow. He occasionally jotted Sam's answers in a small spiral-bound notebook.

"Sure," he said. "I was at the Amateur Dinner last night, then at the clubhouse bar for a while. I spent the rest of the night with my two roommates in the Crow's Nest."

"The Crow's Nest?" Harwell asked, cocking his head as though Sam had just revealed himself to be some kind of deviant. "What's that? A bar?"

"It's the bunkroom on the third floor of the clubhouse, under the cupola."

"Cupola?" Now Harwell seemed convinced that Sam was jerking him around.

"The four-sided bump-up on top of the clubhouse roof, with the windows. There's three of us staying there this week—me, Brady Compton and Tom Wheeling. They're probably still up there. Go talk to them."

"Don't worry, we will. So you say you were in the clubhouse all night?"

"Yes."

Harwell wrote something in his notebook, then flipped back through the pages.

"Do you know why somebody would want to kill...uh... Scanlon?"

The rain continued to fall, smearing the ink on the pages. Rain dripped off the brim of Sam's golf hat; Harwell's red, wiry hair was plastered to his head.

"She wrote a column that basically accused Augusta National of killing Harmon Ashby," Sam said, content to get soaked if that's what Harwell wanted.

"When did this column run?"

"Yesterday. She was also the columnist who quoted Ashby saying he would be willing to have women members at Augusta National."

"Yeah, I know about that one," Harwell said. Sam hoped so.

"So I'd be looking at somebody who didn't want to let women into this club," Sam said, hoping Harwell would take the hint and let him go.

"We're already looking at that," Harwell said. "How do you feel about it?"

"About what?"

"About letting women into Augusta National?"

"I don't have an opinion," Sam said. "It's a private club, and I'm not a member. They can do what they want."

Harwell made another note, then closed his book. A team from the medical examiner's office had arrived and was pulling Scanlon's body out of the pond, preparing to bag it and put it on a gurney. Harwell seemed to have lost interest in Sam.

"Can I go?" he asked Harwell.

"Sure, sure," Harwell said, waving him off. "Stay where we can find you."

"I'll be under the cupola."

Harwell looked up at him and started to say something, but turned away to join the ME team.

Chapter Fourteen

David Porter's office looked like it belonged to the CEO of a bank or an insurance firm, rather than the chairman of a world-renowned golf club. It was furnished with an expensive, polished wooden desk—teak or mahogany, Sam guessed—a couple of padded armchairs, a leather sectional couch circling a round coffee table off to the side, and a 35-inch TV in a cabinet in the corner. An oil portrait of Bobby Jones was the only indication that the business done in this room involved the game of golf. The windows did not even face the golf course.

Two men, both wearing green jackets, were seated across the desk from Porter, apparently waiting for Sam to arrive. Porter introduced them as Ralph Stanwick, acting rules chairman and head of the club's media committee, and Robert Brisbane, competition committees chairman.

Sam shook hands with each of them. Brisbane was a vigorous-looking man with thick salt-and-pepper hair, contrasting with the age spots that dotted Stanwick's skin and balding scalp. Brisbane's green jacket fit him perfectly; Stanwick's seemed both too roomy and too short for him.

"Sit down, Sam," Porter said. He had the look of a man whose child was seriously ill.

"So you're with the Minneapolis police," Brisbane said. "Any advice on what we should do about our two murders?"

"Be honest with the cops, and beef up your security," Sam said.

"We've added security," Stanwick said. "It didn't seem to do us any good."

"This is the worst crisis we've experienced here, at least on my watch," Porter said, almost to himself.

"The club almost went broke in the '30s," Stanwick reminded Porter.

"I doubt if the world would have cared back then," Porter said. "Now, everybody seems to have an opinion about how we should run our affairs. Some would like to shut us down completely."

"You'll survive," Sam said.

"I wish I could be so sure," Porter said. "I don't know what we'll do if there's another murder."

"Maybe we need to think about canceling the tournament, David," Stanwick said. "I don't mind telling you that my wife is very upset about these killings. She's frightened, and I don't blame her."

"We're not closing it down," Porter said, staring at Stanwick with an edge of determination in his voice. "I'm surprised you would suggest that, Ralph. We run the risk that no one would come back next year."

"Rachel Drucker might not come back," Stanwick said. "That would be a good thing in my book."

Porter got out of his chair and walked over to the portrait of Bobby Jones, as if seeking divine guidance from the club's sainted founder. When he was invited to join years earlier, he never imagined that one day he'd be calling a press conference to announce that the Par 3 tournament was cancelled, or that he would open up the club's membership information to the police for a murder investigation.

"My sole duty as chairman of this club is to ensure its future," Porter said. "I owe that to Bob Jones. I owe it to Harmon Ashby, too. If we have to shut down the Masters, this club will eventually become irrelevant, and I will have failed. I'm not going to be the first chairman of Augusta National to fail."

Sam glanced at Brisbane and Stanwick to see if they agreed with Porter's opinion that the club needed the Masters to survive. Both seemed content to let the chairman continue.

"Someone is trying to embarrass us and destroy the club," Porter said. "The police seem to think it's a club member. I'm sure that it's not, but we've got to give the police something else to go on."

"David, you don't have to tell the police a damn thing," Stanwick said. "We're still a private club, aren't we? Let them conduct their own investigation. You know these killings weren't done by a member. You know that."

"I believe that, Ralph," Porter said. "But we need to get to the bottom of this before the police crawl all over this club, going through every drawer in the kitchen, through all of my files, through our closets, ransacking the Cabins…"

Porter trailed off, sickened by the loss of privacy his membership was facing. Sam sympathized with him, to a point. Porter had no right to impede a murder investigation simply because he abhorred prying into his club members' private lives—yet such an investigation violated every principle Porter had been entrusted to uphold at Augusta National. These were some of the richest and most powerful businessmen in America, none of whom would have joined the club had they ever imagined that their personal and professional affairs would be pawed over by homicide detectives. On the few occasions when David Porter granted an interview with the national press, the questions invariably came around to the club's members: Who were they, what did they do, and what did it take to get an invitation to join? Porter's answer was always the same: "We don't discuss our membership." Well, the members were going to be discussed now. They were going to undergo an inquisition. No wonder Porter, normally the sunny face of optimism with the press, was so glum now.

Then again, Sam couldn't dismiss the possibility that Porter was taking this especially hard because he believed—or even knew—that the killer was a member. Maybe he was protecting someone.

"We'll cooperate with the police as much as we're forced to," Porter said. "But Sam, we'd like you to conduct your own investigation."

"David seems to think you can be trusted," Stanwick said, not indicating whether he shared Porter's opinion.

"We'll give you access to every document, every record, every phone number, and every address we have," Brisbane said.

"We're hoping you can work faster than the police, and find out who the killer is before they turn this club upside down," Porter said. "We know you came here to play golf. We want you to play in the tournament. But we'll pay you well if you'll help us find this bastard, whoever he is."

"You must have detectives on your payroll," Sam said.

"Not for this sort of work," Porter said.

"What happens when you offer an invitation to a new member? Don't you have someone check him out first?"

"No, we don't," Stanwick said. "If a man is recommended for membership by a member, that's good enough for us. There's no background check. We just vote him up or down."

"If the new member proves to be a problem—and it rarely happens—he'll lose his membership, and the member who recommended him will usually resign," Porter said. "It's an effective screening policy."

"When do you use private eyes?"

"To stop badge scalping and forgery. They mingle with the patrons and read the classifieds. If they find a patron selling a badge, we drop that patron from our ticket list."

Sam had heard that the National aggressively pursued badge sellers and brokers, but there had to be other times when a detective was necessary. He asked Porter if they ever needed outside help to clean up a mess or lean on someone. Porter hesitated, looked at Stanwick and Brisbane, and then told Sam that the club had hired an investigator a few years back to look into allegations against one of their bartenders. Some members suspected that he was eavesdropping on conversations and passing on business information to competitors.

"The investigator was incompetent and indiscreet," Porter said.

"What happened with the bartender?"

"We never did prove he was passing on information, but we fired him anyway," Stanwick said. "Everyone who works here understands the policy: Keep your nose clean and you won't have any trouble. If there's a question about you, you're gone."

"That's the kind of information I'll need if I take this job," Sam said. "Can you think of any ex-employees who might have a grudge against the club?"

"No, not offhand," Porter said. "The police are focusing on the members and current employees."

"They have to," Sam said. "You have to eliminate those closest to the crime first. There might be something obvious there, and if there is, this case will be solved pretty fast. That's what you want, isn't it?"

Sam was willing to work this case only if everyone at the National truly wanted to find the killer, no matter who he was. He didn't want to take part in a sham investigation, where certain conclusions would not be welcome.

"What about Drucker?" Stanwick said, narrowing his eyes at Sam.

"What about her?" Sam asked. He knew where Stanwick was going, but he wanted to hear the man explain it himself.

"Well, Hell's bells, who's been outside our gates all week trying to make us look like the devil incarnate? She's got to be the happiest person in America that we're in this mess."

"I thought about that," Sam said. "But Deborah Scanlon was a friend of hers. I doubt she would knock off one of her most effective supporters."

"We can't be sure of that," Porter said.

"David, before I commit to this, I've got to ask you straight out," Sam said. "Do you have any knowledge of, or any suspicion of, a member being involved in this?"

Porter looked at his fellow club members. Stanwick, seated in a leather armchair near Porter's desk, shook his head in an emphatic indication that, in his opinion, there were no Augusta National members so craven and black-hearted. Brisbane also shook his head. Porter turned back to Sam.

"No," he said simply.

"Then let me ask you this," Sam said. "How dead-set is the club against admitting a woman?"

Porter leaned back in his swivel chair and drummed his fingers on the armrest, trying to decide how much he should reveal with his answer.

"We're not," Porter finally said, moving his weight forward again. "In fact, we had finalized plans to invite a specific woman to join the club. Then Rachel Drucker showed up with her protesters, and now all this. We've decided to wait."

"Who were you going to invite?" Sam said.

Porter glanced at Stanwick, but quickly decided to put his cards on the table.

"Margaret Winship."

Sam was surprised by the name, but he shouldn't have been. The widow of a former President of the United States would make a logical first female member. Her husband, Warren, had played at Augusta National many times, and it was openly understood that a membership was his for the asking once he left the White House. His fatal heart attack a year after his second term ended had prevented him from inheriting Ike's long-vacant role as the National's resident world leader emeritus. But inviting Mrs. Winship to join was a perfect first step for a club that had never before had a woman member. She would not use the golf course; she was unlikely even to use the clubhouse for social purposes. She might attend the Masters, but her impact on the club itself would be so minimal that the members would barely be aware of her inclusion. Yet inducting her would accomplish precisely what the protesters outside the gates seemed to be demanding: that the rich, powerful men of Augusta National allow at least one rich, powerful woman to write an annual check for membership dues.

"I trust you to keep that information confidential," Porter said to Sam, staring straight at him. "We want to wait a few months before making the announcement. You can see how it would look now if we go ahead with the invitation."

"It will look like we caved in to a few screeching harpies," Stanwick finished. "There will be no end to the demands on this club if the public believes a mob at our front gate can dictate our policies to us."

Stanwick's description of the WOFF made it clear to Sam that the decision to admit Margaret Winship had not been unanimous, and that there were still a good number of Augusta National members who would be quite happy to keep her invitation in their pocket indefinitely.

"How many of your members know this?" Sam asked.

"Only the board of governors," Porter said. "Myself, Ralph, Robert—Harmon Ashby—and Johnny Brooks."

"Who's he?"

"An old friend of Bobby Jones," Brisbane said. "He was a fine amateur player in the '40s."

"Is he here?"

"No," Porter said. "He's too ill to attend this week."

There was a knock at the entrance to David Porter's office. Dennis Harwell entered, accompanied by a man wearing a brown sport coat and a brown fedora with a broad hatband. Sam loved fedoras, but didn't think he could pull off the look. The man with Harwell looked good in a fedora. His face looked appropriately hardened, with a pock-marked complexion, dark eyebrows, and a nose that seemed a little large for the space it had to occupy. Yet there was an odd cheerfulness to his manner as he presented his badge for inspection.

"Good morning, Mr. Porter," he said with the smile of a door-to-door salesman. "Mark Boyce, Georgia Bureau of Investigation, Atlanta office. How y'all doin' today?"

"As well as can be expected, Mr. Boyce, under the circumstances," Porter said, rising from his chair. "Would you mind removing your hat?"

"Sure, I understand," Boyce said, casually taking the fedora off as though he were going to do so anyway. "Another murder—shitty deal, with the Masters coming and all. I think you know Mr. Harwell of the Richmond County Sheriff's office?"

It was obvious who was running the investigation now. Sam was glad that the GBI had been called in; Harwell had been in over his head.

"Let me tell you up front, I sympathize with you people," Boyce said. "I love this tournament. Makes me sick that some dickwad is ruining Masters Week for all of us. We'll get him. I promise."

Boyce pulled up a chair from the edge of the office, placed his hat over his knee and pulled out a notebook.

"We're going to need to start interviewing your members," he said. "If you can give me the names and locations of every member who is in town this week, that would be swell. We also need a list of all your employees, their shifts and their home addresses. Who're you?"

Boyce pointed his pen at Ralph Stanwick.

"My name is Ralph Stanwick," he said. "I'm the rules chairman."

"Good, good. Where have you been staying this week?"

"I'm staying in the Firestone Cabin with my wife."

"Now, that's where the Ashbys were staying—right?" Boyce asked. He looked at Stanwick with an innocent, half-lidded glance that indicated he was enjoying the fact that Stanwick found this process degrading.

"Yes," Stanwick said. "It's a large cabin, with room for two couples."

"Let me see if I remember my Masters geography," Boyce mused, theatrically scratching his temple with the pen. "That would be just to the south of the 10th tee, right? Right between where they found Mr. Ashby's body at Amen Corner, and where they found Ms. Scanlon's body this morning in Ike's Pond. That right?"

"Yes," Stanwick said.

"Anybody with you when the murders occurred?"

Stanwick told Boyce that he and his wife were sound asleep in their cabin Sunday night when Ashby was killed. He hadn't heard him go outside. Last night they had early dinner on the porch outside the clubhouse library with Mr. Porter.

"That right?" Boyce asked Porter.

"Yes. I returned to my apartment after dinner."

"And where's that?"

"In the eastern annex to the clubhouse."

"We returned to the Firestone Cabin around 8:30," Stanwick said. "We watched some television and went to bed."

"Your wife with you the whole time?"

"Certainly."

"She'll say so?"

"Why wouldn't she, Mr. Boyce?" Stanwick said. "It's the truth."

"Is she here today?"

"Yes, my wife's at the cabin."

"What about you, Mr. Porter? Your wife around?"

"No," Porter said. "She doesn't attend the tournament. I'm too busy to spend any time with her. She's back home in New York."

"We'll have a talk with your wife," Boyce said to Stanwick. "Just a formality. Seems to me we're looking for somebody who'd enjoy running around at night throwing people into ponds. You don't look like that kind of a guy."

Sam had to suppress a smile. Boyce was the kind of detective he liked to work with: blunt, but not overtly suspicious of everyone. He kept his interviews moving and kept his subjects off-guard without intentionally antagonizing them.

"And who're you?" Boyce said, pointing the pen at Brisbane.

"Robert Brisbane—competition committees chairman," Brisbane said.

"Where're you keeping yourself this week?"

"I've got a room in the East Wing."

"Your wife around?"

"No, she's back in Des Moines, recovering from a tennis injury. She's watching on TV this year."

"And you?" Boyce said, looking at Sam.

"Sam Skarda. I'm a participant in this year's Masters."

"Oh, hell, I've heard of you," Boyce said, squinting at Sam as he turned to shake his hand. "That was some round of golf you played in the finals of the Publinx last year. Showed those college kids a thing or two."

"You follow golf?"

"Hell, yeah. We all do around here—isn't that right, Detective Harwell?"

"Right," Harwell said. Sam thought Boyce winked at him.

"You're a cop, right?" Boyce said to Sam.

"On leave," Sam said.

"We've asked Mr. Skarda to help us look into this situation," Porter said.

"You gonna do some pokin' around?" Boyce asked Sam. "Hell, that's fine. We can use all the help we can get—especially from the inside. Here's my cell phone number. Call anytime. Just keep us informed."

Boyce smiled as he handed Sam a card, but his eyes lost their twinkle with his last directive. Boyce couldn't keep the club from bringing in a private eye—in fact, he must have expected it. But that didn't mean he'd let Sam interfere with his investigation.

"I've already interviewed Skarda," Harwell said. "He was staying in a room called the Crow's Nest last night, with two other golfers."

"That'd be Wheeling and Compton, the other two amateurs," Boyce said, proving he did know his golf. "Say, I've always wanted to get a look at the Crow's Nest. Can you take me up there sometime, Sam?"

"Anytime you want."

David Porter realized he had lost control of the room after Boyce had breezed in, and he wasn't a man used to surrendering control. He didn't let the situation last.

"What can you tell us, Mr. Boyce?" he asked the investigator. "Have your people had a chance to examine the victim today?"

Boyce regained his professional focus just as quickly.

"The body's at the county coroner's office," Boyce said. "The autopsy isn't complete, but the M.E. says it looks like Ms. Scanlon was murdered, same as Ashby. Somebody jumped her, got her in the water, and held her under till she drowned."

"And there are no signs of where the killer came from, or where he went?" Porter said.

"Nope. He's a wily devil."

The room was silent for a moment as everyone contemplated the facts on the table. Someone was moving around the Augusta National grounds after dark with enough freedom to murder victims singled out for their support of women joining the club, and then escaping without a trace. Why wouldn't the finger point at an Augusta member?

"I have to prepare for a press conference," Porter said, breaking the strained silence. "My secretary can help you with the membership information."

With that, Porter stood up. Sam looked at the two cops, then stood up himself.

"I have to call my caddie and tell him he has the day off," Sam said.

Chapter Fifteen

Dwight was disturbed by the news of Deborah Scanlon's murder, but not disappointed to hear that the day's round had been called off.

"I couldn't go today," he said on the phone. "My leg is too sore."

"How about tomorrow, Dwight?"

"You know I want to, but every time I try to move, it tightens up again. Maybe you better talk to the caddiemaster about gettin' someone else."

"Stay off it if you can."

"I can't," Dwight said. "I got a restaurant to run."

"A restaurant?"

"I got a bar and grill downtown called Big D's."

Sam told Dwight he'd call him later to see how he was doing. Then he walked across the clubhouse parking lot to the media center to attend Porter's press conference. He wanted to know what the chairman was willing to tell the public, and what information he wanted to hold back. Porter had said the previous private investigator they'd hired had been "indiscreet." Sam didn't intend to make that mistake.

The press building amphitheater was packed with reporters when Sam walked in. The golf writers and sports columnists who looked forward to covering the Masters as the year's plum assignment had now been joined by dozens of their newsroom colleagues—some sent after the news broke about Ashby, only to learn upon their arrival about their fellow journalist Scanlon being killed. Even the sportswriters who would normally sleep in on a Wednesday morning were elbowing for laptop space at their own assigned work areas.

Sam was trying to find some wall space halfway up the right-hand aisle when he heard a familiar rasp over his shoulder.

"I don't think we've had a turnout this big since Tiger told Fuzzy to go to hell," Russ Daly said to anyone within ten feet of him.

Several of the reporters seated around him frowned at Daly's remark. He adopted a pained expression and said, "Aw, c'mon, I'm just trying to lighten the mood here. Debbie would have laughed…"

"Mr. Sensitivity," Sam said, having worked his way next to the columnist.

"What the hell are you doing here?" Daly said. "Shouldn't you be out practicing your flop shot or something?"

"My flop shot's good," Sam said. "I wanted to hear what Porter had to say about Scanlon's murder."

"Well, that would make you the first player in the Masters since Bobby Jones to give a shit about anything but golf."

"Don't forget fishing and fucking," Sam said.

Robert Brisbane and David Porter took their seats at the table set up in front of the Augusta National logo background. Cameras flashed and whirred even before Porter opened his mouth. He waited several moments, and then began.

"Ladies and gentlemen, I'll make this brief," Porter said. "We are canceling today's Par 3 tournament because of an unfortunate event that occurred on our grounds sometime last night. A body was found in Ike's Pond on the par 3 course this morning. The police have identified the drowning victim as Deborah Scanlon, columnist for the *New York Times*. I'm sure you'll all join me in expressing our deepest sympathies to her family and loved ones."

The cameras clicked and flashed as Porter somewhat theatrically bowed his head. Several reporters began to ask questions, but Porter resumed before they could finish.

"Out of respect for Ms. Scanlon, and in order to cooperate with the police investigation, we felt it best to cancel today's competition. But the Masters will begin tomorrow at 8 a.m. as scheduled. We are cooperating with the Richmond County Sheriff and the Georgia Bureau of Investigation to bring a quick resolution to this matter. I want to assure all of our patrons, our members, the news media, and other guests on the grounds this week that we have added extra security for the remainder of the tournament. You will be safe here at Augusta National. That is my promise to you all."

"Mr. Porter will take a few questions," a page said into a hand-held microphone.

"David, how can you guarantee anyone's safety here after two murders in three days?" a reporter near the front asked loudly.

"We will provide escorts for anyone who remains on our grounds after dark. We have employed a number of extra security personnel who will patrol day and night. We are confident we've addressed the problem."

"We've heard that the same message was sprayed on the grass—THIS IS THE LAST MASTERS," a woman said, speaking clearly yet emotionally. It looked like the woman who'd sat with Scanlon last night, now standing in the front left section next to an NBC cameraman who was taping her while she asked the question. "It appears someone is trying to intimidate Augusta National."

"That won't happen," Porter said.

"The message suggests the killer is an enemy of the club, but so far he—or she—has killed critics of your membership policy," the correspondent said. "How do you explain that?"

"I can't," Porter said. "Next question."

"Are you rethinking your policy of not allowing women members?" another reporter asked.

"There is no such policy," Porter said, doing his usual admirable job of hiding the exasperation he must have been feeling. "Next question."

Porter ended the press conference shortly thereafter, refusing to go into any further details. The reporters grumbled as Porter and Brisbane left the room, but there really wasn't much more to tell them. Somebody was killing people at Augusta National. The police were trying to figure out who it was. In the meantime, the Masters would go on.

Sam took a look around him at the assembled reporters, tapping away at their laptops, talking on the phone, or bouncing ideas off each other. Some of these reporters had been covering the Masters for thirty years or more, and knew anyone worth knowing in Augusta. They wouldn't run to the cops if they knew something that would help the investigation, but they might be willing to talk to a private investigator, if they didn't have to reveal their sources.

Russ Daly might be helpful.

The fat columnist was haranguing the reporter next to him on the merits of the National's barbecue pork vs. barbecue chicken sandwiches when Sam approached.

"Daly, let me buy you a beer," Sam said.

"I'm working," Daly said. "Make it a Diet Coke."

"Fine," Sam said. "Someplace private."

He got up from his seat and followed Sam up the aisle. They walked outside the media building to the deserted concession windows across the bricked plaza. Rain continued to fall, dripping off the trees and cascading off the roof of the souvenir shop next to the media building. Even the Lords of Augusta couldn't control the weather.

Sam bought a Diet Coke for Daly and a beer for himself and explained the situation to the columnist as they took shelter from the rain under the eaves of the concession building. He told the L.A. sportswriter that the club had hired him to investigate the killings. He had access to all the National's records, phone numbers, and membership information.

"Porter's hoping I'll find something before Boyce and Harwell do. He doesn't want them ransacking the club, but the longer we go without finding out who's behind the killings, the more access he has to give them."

"Is Porter trying to find the killer, or protect him?" Daly asked.

"Find him, I think," Sam said. "Another murder might finish off the Masters for this year…maybe longer. Any idea who I should be looking at?"

"You mean, club members?" Daly asked.

"Anybody," Sam said. "Who stands to gain from these killings?"

Daly's first thought was Rachel Drucker. Sam repeated his conclusion that Deborah Scanlon was the best friend the WOFF had.

"If anything, somebody's trying to scare off the WOFF by killing their supporters," Sam said.

"I can think of a dozen members who hate the idea of a woman joining this club," Daly said. "Benton Sinclair…but he's 80, can barely get around in a cart these days…Henry Lockwood…but God, he's gotta be 90, and senile…well, there's Riley Oakes, the retired football coach at Georgia Tech. What he really hates is the University of Georgia, and Georgia's former coach is also a member here—Jerry Jennings. Jennings is an arthritic old fart who hates seeing women on the golf course, so Oakes almost has to be for 'em. Then there's Ralph Stanwick. He's a Wall Street guy from Connecticut."

"I figured as much," Sam said. "I met him in Porter's office this morning. Definitely anti-women."

"I hear he loves women."

"What do you mean?"

"There's rumors that he has girlfriends all over Augusta."

"What about his wife?"

"You ever seen her?"

"No," Sam said.

"Face like an unraked sand trap."

The conversation was heading in a direction Sam had no use for. He didn't care about the personal peccadilloes of the

Augusta National membership if they didn't relate to the killings. Daly finished his Diet Coke with several big gulps and
started swishing the ice cubes around, expectantly. Sam bought
him another one.

"What about Porter?" Sam asked.

"He's not going to do anything Clifford Roberts wouldn't
have done, until he has to. But as soon as he thinks a majority
of the members are for it, he'll let women in here."

Sam thought about telling Daly about Margaret Winship's
near-invitation, but decided he'd keep that piece of information
in reserve.

"What do you know about Ashby?" Sam said. "Did he have
any enemies here?"

"Not that I know of," Daly said. "He was pretty wrapped up
in putting on the tournament."

"Were you surprised when he came out in favor of membership for women?"

"Sure. Nobody here talks on the record, except Porter. It's a
good way to get the boot."

"I wonder why the Ashbys and the Stanwicks were sharing
a cabin," Sam said.

"Usually the Stanwicks and the Brisbanes use the Firestone
Cabin," Daly said. "But Brisbane's wife stayed home this year. I
guess they offered the extra space to the Ashbys, instead."

"What do you know about Robert Brisbane?"

"Not much. He and Stanwick are best buddies. I like
Brisbane—he'll go off the record almost any time, but if you want
a quote, he'll tell you to get it from Porter. Which reminds me   I
got a column to write. Let me know if you turn up some dirt."

Daly waddled back into the media center while Sam headed
around the corner to the administration building, hardly
noticing the steady drizzle except to step around the widening
puddles.

Chapter Sixteen

Sam returned to Porter's office and asked to see the membership records. Porter took him to an unoccupied office and called up the computerized membership directory, which contained personal information about each member: age, marital status and family details, home address (some had many addresses), educational background, employment records, investment holdings, religious affiliation, professional awards and honors, club memberships, charity work, volunteer organizations—even jacket size.

There was far more information about each of the 300 members than Sam could possibly absorb in an afternoon, but he skimmed the list, hoping something would pop out at him.

Ashby was from Atlanta. He had graduated from Georgia Tech—Bobby Jones' alma mater—in 1956, with a degree in chemical engineering. He'd started his own company in Atlanta that produced biodiesel from animal byproducts. He'd joined the USGA in 1962 and become a rules official, working a number of U.S. Opens. He became a member of Augusta National in 1970. In 1993, he became rules chairman at the Masters. He and his wife Annabelle had two children.

Robert Brisbane was a resident of Des Moines, graduate of the Choate School and Yale, Class of 1967, where he'd lettered in basketball; married to the former JoAnne Konieczny, with whom he had three children. He was president and CEO of Iowa Futures, Inc., a commodity-trading company he founded in 1971, and a member of the Chicago Board of Trade for over

30 years. He was on the board of the American Cancer Society and a member of the Des Moines Country Club.

When he got to Ralph Stanwick's entry, Sam quickly learned why he and Brisbane were buddies. Stanwick, a Wall Street stockbroker who lived in Greenwich, Conn., was also Yale '67, where he'd won All-Ivy honors in tennis. The rest of Stanwick's information was pretty standard: married to the former Lorraine Nelford, no children, member of several corporate boards and three golf clubs: Augusta National, Pine Valley, and Connecticut Golf Club. Augusta National and Pine Valley shared at least two important traits: Each was ranked among the top five golf courses in the world, and each was all-male. But Sam knew nothing about Connecticut Golf Club.

He ran a Google search and found CGC's home page, which included four thumbnail photos of the course, the club's logo—an Augusta National-like map of Connecticut, with a flagstick protruding from the club's location—and a mission statement that said the club was founded in 1969 as golf club, not a country club.

There were menu options on the club's home page: Login, Directions, and Weather. Sam clicked on "Login" and found that the club was private. He clicked on "Directions" and found the club was located in Easton, Conn. The page also included a phone number for the clubhouse. He dialed it and asked for the manager, who confirmed for Sam that yes, in fact, Connecticut G.C. was an all-male club.

Sam leaned back in his swivel chair and thought about Stanwick. He was on the tall side, and seemed to be in good shape for his age—probably still a tennis player. But would he be capable of strangling Ashby and dumping his body in Rae's Creek, or dragging Scanlon down a steep hill into Ike's Pond?

One thing was certain: Ralph Stanwick believed passionately in all-male golf clubs.

He picked up the phone, got the clubhouse operator, and asked her to ring the Firestone Cabin. After a minute, a woman's voice answered. It was Stanwick's wife, Lorraine. No, Ralph wasn't at the cabin this afternoon. No, she didn't know when he'd be back. Was there a message? Sam said there wasn't. He'd call back later.

Sam walked down the hall to Ida's desk and asked if she knew where Robert Brisbane was.

"He's out on the golf course with Mr. Porter and Jimmy Fowler," Ida said. "They're checking the drainage."

"Any idea what hole they're on?"

"They were concerned about the lowest holes—11, 12, and 13," Ida said.

Amen Corner. Walk or take a cart? The walk would do him good, give him time to think. But it would take at least 15 minutes to walk that far in the rain, and he didn't want to waste that much time. Sam went to the pro shop and asked for a cart. In less than a minute a young man drove a cart up to the pro shop door, and wiped the seat with a towel before Sam sat down.

By the time he had driven around the sodden putting green, past the deserted 10th tee, and negotiated the steep, rain-slick service road that led down to Amen Corner, he was doubting his own theory. Sure, Stanwick was opposed to women joining the club. He obviously preferred all-male enclaves. But would he kill to keep women out of Augusta National? Sam couldn't answer that. Brisbane was the member who knew him best.

He found Porter and Brisbane, both clad in yellow rain ponchos with the Masters logo over the breast, standing with another man Sam didn't recognize on the Hogan Bridge, which crossed the wide pond in Rae's Creek to the 12th green. Porter looked up at the sky, where the cobalt clouds were moving swiftly to the east, but continuing to leave sheets of rain as they blew past. They didn't notice Sam until he was standing on the bridge next to them.

Porter introduced Sam to Jimmy Fowler, the club's superintendent—a short man who looked like a garden gnome in his oversized poncho.

"Can I have a minute with Robert?" Sam said as the rain beat like little drumsticks on his Gore-Tex bucket hat.

"Must be important, for you to come all the way out here," Porter said.

Brisbane nodded at Sam, and Porter and Fowler walked off the bridge toward the 12th green. Sam could barely see the putting surface under the pooled water.

"Do you have any idea where Ralph Stanwick is?" Sam asked Brisbane. "I'd like to talk to him."

"Ralph's not going to be back till later tonight," Brisbane said. "He said he had some business to attend to."

"What sort of business?" Sam said.

"He didn't say. Why do you ask?"

Brisbane gazed at Sam from underneath the hood of his rain poncho with a look of simple curiosity. Sam plowed ahead.

"I know he's against women joining Augusta National."

"That's no secret. Many of our members still feel that way."

"The way I hear it, he feels more strongly than most."

Brisbane didn't respond, which told Sam he was going in the right direction.

"I know he's a member of Pine Valley and Connecticut Golf Club—both men-only," Sam continued. "And I know you two went to Yale together."

"That's right. We were roommates our junior and senior year."

"Yale wasn't co-ed then, was it?"

"No, it wasn't," Brisbane said. "But we knew it was going to happen soon."

His eyes held Sam's gaze.

"How did Stanwick feel about admitting women to Yale?"

"When Ralph and I were roommates, he was the leader of an anti-coeducation group," Brisbane said, choosing his words carefully as the rain spattered into the creek.

"What about you?"

"I knew it was inevitable. Why fight it? Two years later, Yale began admitting women."

"Does Ralph feel the same way about Rachel Drucker?"

"I'm sure he does," Brisbane said. "But I'm also sure that he didn't kill Harmon Ashby or Deborah Scanlon."

"And how do you know that?"

"Because he's my friend. Ralph and Lorraine are my kids' godparents. I'll admit that to some people he might come off as a little…brusque. But Ralph Stanwick never killed anyone, and never would."

Sam had been lied to a thousand times by people trying to alibi for their friends. He'd been fooled a few times, but he was sure Brisbane wasn't lying. The man was convinced that his friend was not the killer. But a Brisbane testimonial was not going to be enough.

"Why were the Ashbys and Stanwicks staying together this week, if Ralph and Harmon Ashby disagreed so strongly on the women's membership issue?"

"Lodging is always tight during Masters week," Brisbane said. "When my wife hurt her knee and decided not to come, I took a single room this week. Lorraine and Annabelle are good friends, so the Stanwicks invited the Ashbys to stay with them at the Firestone Cabin."

"Did Ralph and Harmon get along?"

"Sure. You don't have to agree with everything another member says or does to be his friend here. Ralph and Harmon were friends."

"Do you know where Stanwick was when the killings took place?" Sam asked.

"I assume he was where he said he was—with his wife in the Firestone Cabin," Brisbane said. "That's what Lorraine told the police."

Brisbane broke eye contact, suggesting that he was less certain of Stanwick's alibi. At that point, Porter and Fowler returned from their inspection of the 12th green.

"Is everything all right?" Porter asked Sam.

"I just had a question about the membership information I was looking at," Sam said.

"Maybe I can help," Porter said. But Sam wasn't sure that he should trust Porter with his suspicions. Not just yet.

"I got what I needed," Sam said. "How's the course?"

"If it stops raining, we'll play tomorrow," Porter said. "It'll be soft, but the course drains beautifully."

Sam looked back up the hill toward the 11th fairway. From the clubhouse, everything rolled downhill to this spot. He looked up at the dismal grey overhead, catching a raindrop in the eye, and thought about that old blues song about the sky crying. In this case, the tears weren't running down the street; they were running down the fairway.

Chapter Seventeen

"Danny Milligan played 20 years on the PGA Tour without ever winning a tournament," the NBC reporter's voice intoned over video of Milligan, wearing a rainsuit and practicing chip shots on his backyard practice green during a steady drizzle. "But he did win the hearts of countless spectators who loved his comic antics at tournaments. He also won the attention of CBS Sports president Rudy Mendenhall, who hired the puckish pro to join his network's golf broadcast team."

Sam had returned to the Crow's Nest and turned on the TV to see if there were any developments in what the networks were now calling The Masters Murders. Tom Wheeling was out practicing on the soggy course in the near-dark, searching for that one final piece of the puzzle that might help him stay inside the cutline. Brady Compton was convinced his game was in great shape. He sat in a lounge chair next to Sam, watching the NBC Nightly News.

The reporter doing the Milligan story was Jane Vincent, the woman who been at Scanlon's table Tuesday night, and the one who had thrown some tough questions at David Porter during that morning's press conference. She must have known that Deborah Scanlon was scheduled to interview Milligan today—the day after she was murdered. Vincent had taped her piece at Milligan's house across the Savannah River in South Carolina, prodding him for his reaction to the latest events at the club he loved to hate. The network was airing it during the last ten minutes of its Wednesday evening newscast, the spot usually reserved for off-beat takes or in-depth analysis of the day's biggest story. The murders at Augusta remained the day's biggest story.

"But after being part of his network's coverage of the Masters for several years, Milligan ran afoul of the Lords of Augusta National," Vincent's voiceover continued. "During a rain delay in 1996, Milligan was asked by fellow CBS broadcaster Nigel Frawley where the pros went during a suspension of play at the Masters. Milligan joked that they went into the locker room, took off their rain-soaked clothes, and quote 'snapped wet towels at each other' unquote."

The video image switched to a close-up of Milligan, seated under an overhang on his deck, that day's rains dripping off the roofline behind him. Milligan's '70s-style gray shag haircut, mischievous eyes, and impish smile were the features of a born clown. Yet it was obvious that Milligan was not quite as jovial as usual.

"Rudy Mendenhall got a letter from David Porter three days after the tournament, telling him my services would not be needed at the next year's tournament," Milligan said, looking off to the right of the camera at Vincent. "He said they were taking that action because of my disgraceful, disparaging, and untrue remarks about behavior in the club's locker room.

"I mean, come on. It was a joke. It's a golf tournament, not a funeral. Oh, I'm sorry—that's probably another touchy word now." Milligan smirked in appreciation of his little jab.

"But that's not the way his superiors at CBS saw it," Vincent's narration resumed, over some stock video of a previous Masters tournament. "The network agreed to Milligan's ban, and he was subsequently dropped from the network's golf crew. He now works for Turner Broadcasting in Atlanta."

The footage switched to that week's WOFF protests on Washington Road, during which the crowd's anti-Augusta National chants could be heard at diminished volume.

"Now Milligan is siding with the protesters who gather daily down the road from the notoriously all-male golf club. Their numbers have been growing each day since the murders of rules chairman Harmon Ashby and *New York Times* columnist Deborah Scanlon, both of whom had been openly critical of the club. Milligan has a message for them: Right on, sisters and brothers."

The video returned to Milligan, sitting on his deck, with Vincent seated across from him.

"So you support the protests against Augusta National?" she asked him.

"Yes, absolutely," Milligan replied, his normally merry eyes now narrowed. "It's a national travesty that Augusta National hasn't admitted a woman member. They must think it's still 1934. Wake up, fellas; we're in a new century. Woman can vote, blacks can drink from public fountains, gays can hold hands in public."

"Do you think someone at the club had anything to do with the murders?"

"They tried to kill my career," Milligan said.

"Couldn't your opinion just be dismissed as sour grapes?" the reporter asked. "After all, they did ban you from their broadcast."

"Believe me, I felt this way long before I made the wet towel remark," Milligan said. "If I'd known that they were going to ban me for that, I would have told the audience what the players really do during a rain delay at Augusta National."

The video cut back to the scene of Milligan chipping in his backyard, as the reporter described Milligan's current life as a part-time broadcaster, part-time senior tour player, and part-time man of leisure at his comfortable home just across the Savannah River in Beech Island, S.C. He'd built the home recently on the site of a former horse ranch, adjacent to a nature preserve. The camera pulled backward and panned the house, a sprawling ranch-style structure with a stand of mature pine trees visible over the rooftop, and a vast field beyond the backyard.

"Perfect for auditioning new drivers," Milligan said.

"I asked Milligan if he were worried about repercussions within the golf world for continuing to criticize Augusta

National," Vincent said, as the image on the screen cut back to a close-up of Milligan's face.

"Nah," Milligan said with a wink. "I'm playing a lot better these days. If TBS dumps me, I'll just enter more senior tournaments. And I'll donate some of my winnings to the WOFF. We'll get a woman into Augusta National if I have to help her shinny up the drainpipe."

◇◇◇

"You want to watch any more of this?" Sam asked Brady Compton.

"Nope," Compton said, taking the remote from Sam. "Do they get the Cartoon Network here?"

Compton flipped through the channels, then got up from his chair and walked into his cubicle to place another call to one of his buddies back home. Sam turned off the TV and glanced at the travel alarm clock by his bed. It was nearly seven. Sam had no plans for dinner, and again found himself thinking about Caroline Rockingham. He looked up the number of for the Southwinds Inn and asked them to ring her room. No answer.

Could she be out with Rockingham? Sam didn't want to think about that.

Tom Wheeling walked up the stairs into the Crow's Nest— soaking wet, with muddy pants cuffs and sweat mingled with bits of grass and dirt in his disheveled hair. He looked as though he'd spent the entire day gouging one soggy divot after another out of the Augusta practice range. Yet there was a big grin on his face.

"I found it," he announced.

Sam said, "You'd better put it back before David Porter finds out."

Sam remembered that he needed to call Dwight to check on his health. He found the number for Big D's in the phone book. An older woman answered and called Dwight to the phone.

"I'm gonna show up," Dwight said when Sam asked him how his leg was feeling.

He didn't sound confident.

Chapter Eighteen

Doggett's high-beam lights cut through the sticky night air as he made a left turn on 13th Street and headed north across the Savannah River into South Carolina. He made sure to hold his speed just below the limit. Now would not be the time to get picked up for a traffic violation. They'd run the plates, and find out the truck was stolen. He had plenty of time to get to where he was going. Plenty of time to think about what he'd done, and what was still left to do.

Killing Ashby had been a fuck-up, but not one he particularly regretted. The cops were no closer to figuring that one out than they were the morning they found the body. Killing the columnist had started out to be nothing more than a necessary task. He bought a practice round ticket from a scalper for $60, and carried a tie, a ballcap, and a windbreaker onto the grounds with him. As the crowds were leaving at the end of the day, he went into a restroom outside the media center and put on his uniform. When he emerged in the dusk, he was indistinguishable from a Securitas guard.

Scanlon had been easy to spot leaving the press building—there weren't many women who looked like her walking around the grounds of the National. She had put up a good fight for someone so light. He had expected to kill her quickly, and his rage had kicked in again as they struggled—especially when she kicked him in the stomach with her sharp heel. When he was squeezing the air out of Scanlon's lungs, it reminded him of the times he'd had the urge to do that to his own wife.

That murder—and the message left next to the body—had received saturation media coverage. Every TV station and newspaper in the country was providing priceless publicity. Now the goal was tantalizingly close at hand: David Porter had cancelled the Par 3 tournament. Maybe after tonight, he'd cancel the Masters. Even if he didn't, it would keep the club on the defensive until the final blow could be administered.

Doggett followed U.S. Highways 1 and 278 through North Augusta, and took 278 east as it became Williston Road. There were very few cars, houses, or buildings along the dark highway. He didn't know the exact location of the house he'd seen on the NBC News story earlier in the day, but he knew he could find it. He'd driven through that part of Beech Island a number of times on his way to go fishing near Aiken. He was certain he'd passed the ranch land with the pine forest across the road.

He turned left off the highway a few miles outside of town and went north. The house he was looking for would be set well back from the road and isolated from other homes among scattered loblolly pines. After several miles, the road dipped into a valley and then rose again to a plateau, where he saw a pine forest on the left side of the road and a long split-rail fence on the right, interrupted by a private driveway. The mailbox at the end of the driveway was shaped like a small golf bag, with a miniature flagstick on the side that could be flipped up to signal outgoing mail.

What a fool. He might as well broadcast where he lives.

Doggett pulled the truck slowly to the shoulder of the road, turned off the lights, and sat in the darkness for 10 minutes. He hadn't seen a car on the road since he'd left the highway. Still, it might draw suspicion if he parked on the road, so he started the engine and backed the truck into the driveway, leaving the lights off. When he was a good 20 feet from the road, he turned off the ignition and waited for another 10 minutes. He couldn't see the house from where he was, and doubted he'd been heard. Nevertheless, there could be a motion-detection system, or even a security camera. He could leave in an instant if someone came out of the house to investigate.

He reached under the passenger seat for his nylon gym bag, unzipped it, and pulled out the hunting knife and the work gloves.

When he stepped onto the driveway and quietly closed the driver-side door, he noticed the full moon in the clearing sky. The night was warm and muggy for April, but it appeared a high-pressure front was coming in. The weather would be spectacular for tomorrow's opening round, assuming they played it.

The driveway, lined with azalea bushes and mature beech trees, curved to the left and opened to a large parking area in front of a four-car tuck-under garage. The house itself was a cedar-and-stone ranch-style structure with a large lawn and field on the other side of the house—probably where the practice green was. There was a floodlight on the parking area in front of the garage and a porch light next to the front door; Doggett kept to the grass and walked around to the back where it was dark.

He crept slowly up to the double doors that led from the living room out to the deck. The lower level of the house was brightly lit; through the glass doors he could see a man with a bald head relaxing in a plush leather couch, facing a big-screen television mounted in the exposed stone chimney above the fireplace. He was watching a report from the rain-soaked Masters on The Golf Channel.

That wasn't Milligan. Milligan had long gray hair. Doggett felt himself getting angry. *Not this again—do I have the wrong fucking house?*

He looked closer at the bald man. The face was right. Then he noticed a long gray wig hanging from a hook near the front door. It was Milligan, after all. The long hair was a rug. *Fucking phony.*

How to do this quickly and efficiently? He could try to lure him out onto the deck, but if Milligan heard a suspicious sound, he might come out with a gun. Then it occurred to him—Why not just ring the doorbell? Milligan would come to the door. That's all he needed.

Doggett walked around to the front of the house, holding the knife behind his back with his right hand, and went up to the front porch. One last run-through: This was the right house, Milligan appeared to be alone inside, and there were no other houses nearby. He rang the bell.

After 30 seconds, the door swung open. Danny Milligan appeared in the entryway—wearing his gray shag hairpiece.

"I don't know how you found this place, but we've got all the Girl Scout cookies we need," Milligan said. "Unless there's something…"

"There is," Doggett said, bringing the knife from behind his back and pushing Milligan backward into the house. Milligan stumbled against a foyer table, but didn't take his eye off the knife, which Doggett held up near his nose while clutching the collar of Milligan's shirt with his other hand. He kicked the door closed behind himself.

"Hey, let's talk about this, bucko," Milligan said. He was breathing heavily, and his eyes danced with fear. Doggett liked that. He enjoyed watching the funny man squirm. *Not so funny now, was he?*

"Was it something I said?" Milligan asked. "Whatever it was, it was a joke. I don't mean any of it. They pay me to say that stuff. They write it for me. What is it? Tell me—come on!"

Milligan was backing into his living room as Doggett pushed forward. This was good. They were in the middle of a very large house. They'd never be seen or heard.

"Don't worry," Doggett said. "It's nothing personal."

He pulled the knife across Milligan's throat, creating an ear-to-ear smile that the clown clutched at with his hands in horror. The blood spurted outward as Milligan collapsed backward, bounced off the plush leather couch he'd been sitting on, hit the large-screen TV, and fell to the floor. As the announcers on The Golf Channel discussed Ernie Els' chances of winning a green jacket, Danny Milligan's blood dripped slowly down the 72-inch screen. The toupee had been dislodged and lay in the spreading pool of red on the hardwood floor of Milligan's great room.

Doggett put the knife under his belt while he looked around the room. He went to the double doors that led to the back deck, pushed them open, and went back into the living room. He lifted Milligan's ankles and dragged his body across the living room floor, leaving a red smear on the floorboards. Milligan's left arm snagged a cotton throw rug as he was pulled toward the door; Doggett kicked it aside and dragged the body out onto the deck. Milligan's head sounded like a bag of apples as it bounced down the steps to the back lawn.

Dew was beginning to form on the grass, making it easy to slide Milligan's body across the lawn to the middle of his own practice green. Doggett dropped Milligan's ankles and pulled out the spray bottle of herbicide. He actually took time to admire the quality of the natural putting surface Milligan had been able to maintain in his back yard. He must have used a professional-grade walk-behind to cut the grass down to 1/8 of an inch. Almost up to Augusta National standards.

Then Doggett defaced the perfect canvas by spraying THIS IS THE LAST MASTERS on the closely cut Bermuda grass.

Doggett walked back into the house and shut the doors behind him. He went into the kitchen, which could be seen through an open archway from the great room. He opened several cupboards until he found ingredients that would do the job: a can of corn niblets and a bottle of vegetable oil. Keeping his work gloves on, he opened and drained the niblets and filled the rest of the can with the oil. He found a potato masher in a drawer by the cooktop and crushed the contents of the can until it was a slimy batter.

He returned to the back yard and poured the oily corn mixture over and around Milligan's body, putting an extra glob on his face. *That should do it. If the blood doesn't attract the fire ants, this stuff definitely will.*

As he drove back to Augusta, Doggett thought about tossing the knife into the Savannah River. Then he dismissed the idea. He would need the knife at least once more.

Chapter Nineteen

Thursday, April 10

Sam was awake when the first rays of dawn streamed into the Crow's Nest. It was not yet six. Wheeling was already up and getting dressed, even though he had an afternoon tee-time. Sam got up, too.

He'd dozed fitfully all night, dreaming that his group had been called to the tee while he was still in the clubhouse looking for something he couldn't name or describe. He'd wake up, realize it was a dream, that he hadn't been disqualified, then fall back to sleep and begin the same dream again.

He was glad that Bobby Jones had started the tradition of pairing the amateurs with past Masters champions. Compton was playing in the morning with Tiger Woods; Wheeling was going out in the afternoon with Vijay Singh. Sam hadn't met Frank Naples yet, but he was a fan favorite and reputed to be one of the friendliest and most easy-going players on tour. He'd make a good buffer between Sam and Rockingham.

Sam didn't usually watch morning TV—he preferred hearing actual conversations on radio, as opposed to two beautiful people exchanging sugary platitudes—but while Wheeling was in the bathroom, he turned the TV on to CNN, with the volume low so as to not wake Compton. The perky anchor was reading a story about an oil spill off the California coast. The news crawl eventually said police had no leads in "The Masters Murders."

Caroline was in the clubhouse dining room when Sam arrived, with coffee and several newspapers on her table. He wasn't sure she wanted his company, but when she saw him, she waved him over.

"Sleep well?" she asked, as he pulled up a chair and sat down.

"No. How about you?"

"The air conditioner unit in my room is really loud," Caroline said. "I finally had to get up and turn it off. After that, I got a good 15 or 20 minutes."

While eating a plate of scrambled eggs and bacon, Sam read Russ Daly's column:

In 96 hours we'll know if Tiger Woods can add yet another jacket to a closet that already contains more green blazers than an Irish tenor's.

Or will this be the year when a lovable old vet like Frank Naples turns back the clock and thrills the customers—sorry, the patrons—with one more major victory, as Jack Nicklaus did in 1986?

We will also know by then whether a young gun like Bobby Cremmins or even Brady Compton can emerge from the Legion of Perfectly Constructed Swings to contend against golf's most elite field—and whether Augusta National remains a bomber's course, with the jacket likely to go once again to a long driver like Tiger Woods or even Shane Rockingham.

And you know what? The suspense isn't killing me.

All I care about, at this point, is making it back to the airport alive on Monday morning.

That's right; I'm worried that I'm going to be the next bloated corpse found bobbing in one of Augusta National's water hazards. And I'm already bloated.

You see, a few years ago (I don't remember exactly what year; the tournaments tend to run together when nobody's getting killed)

I wrote that the Masters would be a more interesting event if they invited me to play in it. I couldn't break 120 on this course if you let me start on the back nine and didn't count my putts, but at least that would give the spectators a true indication of how difficult this golf course is for normal people using normal equipment.

Instead, each year we witness ever-stronger, ever-skinnier pros demolishing Bobby Jones' proud creation with golf clubs made out of materials found only in outer space, and new golf balls cooked up in a mad chemist's lab. The combination makes this 7,500-yard course play—for the pros—like an Oxnard pitch-and-putt.

You don't get to witness the genius of this golf course unless you hang around on Monday after the Masters and see it played by a handful of journalists, selected each year by lottery to humiliate themselves with their golf clubs instead of their keyboards.

We know the Lords of Augusta National aren't happy about how easy the pros are making their course look. That's why they've plowed most of the Masters profits—ungodly as those profits are—back into the golf course year after year, trying to make the course longer and tougher. They can't do longer anymore. They're out of room, unless they invade the Augusta Country Club next door and annex three or four of their holes.

Tougher is still achievable, but only at the risk of ruining the course. They've added rough, and the scores are still ridiculously low. Do we need to turn it into the Springtime U.S. Open, and see caddies get lost in the fescue? They've speeded up the greens, but they were already faster than Jose Canseco driving through a residential neighborhood, and the scores are still going down. Do we need to see the Augusta greens mowed down to the worms?

The course is perfectly adequate if the tournament could just find a way to restrict the golf ball's distance. For several years now, David Porter and the boys have been hinting at going to a Masters ball—a ball that flies about 20% shorter than the ballistic balls the equipment companies are producing now. In my view, that's the only way to save this old beauty of a course from extinction.

I, for one, don't enjoy watching the artillery shots from the likes of Shane Rockingham destroying the strategic genius of this once-great golf course. It's not as much fun to watch, and some day the rubes in the gallery are going to catch on.

And this is exactly why I'm worried about my own safety. People who criticize Augusta National policy have been turning up dead around here. I was critical about them letting the golf ball get out of control, and now I'm accusing them of ruining their own tournament.

And, for the record, I think they ought to knuckle under to the WOOFs and let women in as members.

There. I said it. Now, would someone mind starting my car for me tonight?

Daly may have come off like another freebie-scarfing smartass, but he had guts. Sam had to give him that much.

He finished his breakfast and asked Caroline if she was planning to follow their group.

"All 18 holes," she said. "I even left my sandals back at the hotel."

She extended her right foot and showed Sam that she had on a pair of Nike running shoes. Sam's gaze drifted up her leg to her tanned thigh.

"You'd better keep your mind on your game," she said.

"Then you'd better watch from behind a tree," he said, standing up and putting his napkin on the table.

When Sam got to the bag room. Dwight was standing in the breezeway with Sam's clubs, a mournful expression on his face.

"I can't go, Sam," he said.

"Your leg?"

"I could barely get out of bed today. As soon as I picked up your bag this morning, I felt the hamstring start to knot up. I wouldn't make it up the first fairway. In a day or two, maybe…"

Sam had no idea what to do. He wasn't even sure if he would be allowed to carry his own clubs. Maybe there were still some Augusta National caddies looking for a loop.

"Not today," the caddiemaster told him. "I could have found you another caddie earlier this week, but if those guys don't have a bag by the time the tournament starts, they don't show up. If you know somebody here who has caddie experience, we can find a jumpsuit for him."

Caroline.

She was the only person Sam could think of. But would she be willing to carry his bag in the same group with Rockingham? Only one way to find out.

He wrote a check to Dwight for four rounds plus tip—Dwight told him it was too much, but Sam insisted he take it—and then jogged back to the clubhouse, where he found Caroline sitting at her table drinking coffee.

"Can you still read greens?" he asked her.

"Sure," she said, looking up at him in surprise. "That's my specialty. Why?"

"My caddie blew a tire. How'd you like to loop for me?"

Caroline didn't say anything. Instead, she pulled her cigarettes out of her purse and lit one. She put her hand on her chin and stared down at the table, shifting her mouth from side to side.

"Now. Today."

"I'm thinking," she said. "Shane is going to be a real dick about it. You know that."

"I don't care. This is strictly business. I can't think of anyone else to ask."

"Well, when you flatter a girl like that, how can she say no?" Caroline said, getting up from the table with a sigh. "I suppose I've got to wear one of those horrible white suits."

"The caddiemaster said he could find one for you."

They walked back to the bag room. The caddiemaster took a look at Caroline and scratched his head. He thought they might have something small enough for her, but it would take some makeshift alterations. Sam told her he'd meet her at the first tee and carried his bag to the practice range.

On the way to the range, he put on his iPod earphones over his golf hat. He needed some strong musical interference to ward off all the distractions he was facing today. He selected the play-list from April 1970, the year Billy Casper won the Masters. The first song up was "Bridge Over Troubled Water." The sweeping piano intro seemed appropriate for the grand setting—thousands of golf fans everywhere you looked, most toting plastic bags of souvenirs and carrying folding chairs, binoculars, or periscopes. He could hear the muffled sound of encouragements as he walked down the path to the range, signing a few autographs as he went. The music was doing its job. By the time he got to an open hitting station, he was dialed in on golf. He stretched, hit a number of half-wedges, and then worked through his bag to the driver. He was hitting the ball well.

He tried to keep the image of Billy Casper in his mind, along with the smooth melody Art Garfunkel was singing. Casper had been perhaps the best putter of his time; the ball seemed to flow gently from his putter to the hole, and that was the feel Sam wanted.

Caroline was waiting for him at the first tee, clad in a white jumpsuit with the name SKARDA spelled out in green letters, squeezed into the small space between her shoulder blades, an Augusta National logo over the right breast pocket, and Sam's number 55 over the left breast. The pants cuffs had to be turned up several folds, but otherwise it wasn't a bad fit. He would defi-nitely prefer to look at her legs, but sacrifices had to be made. Caroline had pulled her thick, dark hair back into a ponytail, which now protruded above the adjustable strap on the back of her green Masters cap—part of the standard caddie uniform.

"I feel like Bozo the Clown," Caroline said.

"Just don't caddie like him," Sam said.

"It's hot in this thing."

"What do you have on under there?" Sam asked, putting his index finger inside the neck of the jumpsuit and pulling it toward him. She slapped his hand away.

"You don't need to know."

The leaders were already at 3 under par when he and Caroline made their way through the ropes to the first tee. He introduced himself to Frank Naples, who seemed loose and relaxed.

"Isn't this a special place?" said Naples, a leading-man type with dark, bushy hair and a deep tan. "No matter how many times I play here, I always get goosebumps."

Caroline handed Sam his driver and put her mouth close to his ear.

"Frank Naples gives me goosebumps," she whispered.

Sam wished he had a photo of the look on Rockingham's face when he and Weed emerged from the crowd surrounding the first tee. His public relations smile vanished when he saw Caroline. He walked directly up to her and put his nose a few inches from hers.

"What the hell do you think you're doing?" he hissed at her.

"Making a little extra money," she said, refusing to back away. "You were late with your half of the mortgage payment again this month."

"Uh-oh," Naples said to Sam. "That's Shane's wife, isn't it?"

"Soon to be ex," Sam said. "My caddie pulled his hamstring. Caroline's filling in. This won't be a problem, I promise you."

"Hell, it might be fun," Naples said with a grin.

Rockingham was still fuming when the three players exchanged scorecards and identified their golf balls, but he said nothing to Sam. Instead, he seemed to take his anger out on his ball. His drive down the first fairway must have gone 360 yards.

With "Bridge Over Troubled Water" playing like a tape loop through his mind, Sam managed to make the turn in 38—an acceptable score, considering that he hit only five greens. Even though she had never caddied at Augusta National, Caroline proved to be adept at calculating the speed and the break on the greens. Naples chatted with them from time to time, but Rockingham ignored them. He was four under at the turn, with a look in his eye that said he was only getting started.

Sam's game began to come apart at Amen Corner, beginning with a bogey at 11. He couldn't help but think about Harmon Ashby as he stood on the 12th tee—Where had the killer come from? Where had he gone?—and the lapse in concentration caused him to fly one well over the green. He then three-putted after a poor chip from the downslope. The double-bogey put him five over par, and he followed that with a triple on 13 when his attempt to reach the green in two bounced off the creek bank and back into the water.

"You're taking this well," Caroline said as they walked to the 14th tee.

"I promised myself I'd enjoy this, no matter what I shot," he said.

"Are you enjoying this?"

"Some holes more than others."

"But, in general?"

He stopped walking and looked her in the eye.

"This is the most fun I've ever had on a golf course," he said.

"Then I suppose you've never…"

"Well, not counting that."

With Art Garfunkel's angelic voice once again floating soothingly through his head, he managed to par 14 through 17, and hit his best approach shot of the day into 18. He needed to make a seven-footer for birdie and a 79, but he left the putt an inch short.

The crowd moaned, then gave him a good laugh as he circled the cup to see if the ball had a chance of falling in by itself. It didn't; he tapped in as the crowd applauded.

Rockingham parred 18 for a 65, which gave him the lead. Naples shot an easy 68. When the last putt was holed, Rockingham shook Naples' hand but left the green without acknowledging Sam or Caroline. He wondered what CBS announcer Cameron Myers was saying about that bit of poor sportsmanship in the television tower.

"Never mind him," Naples said, shaking Sam's hand as they walked off the green toward the scorer's hut. "You learned what it's like out here. You'll do better tomorrow."

Another group was coming up the fairway behind them. One of the approach shots—it looked to be that of Bernhard Langer—nicked the flagstick and spun to a stop three feet from the hole as the crowd erupted. The cheers rang across the valley of the old fruit tree nursery, and were answered by a similar roar coming from a distant hole.

"You hit a lot of good shots today," Caroline said, putting her hand on Sam's back at the door of the scorer's hut.

"And you're a great caddie," Sam said. "You should still be out here."

"I wouldn't mind doing it again tomorrow."

"You're on."

"I'll meet you at the bag room after you sign your card," Caroline said. "You can buy me a drink."

"Has to be a quick one. I've got some work to do this afternoon."

"Your swing's okay. You just lost focus a couple of times."

"No, it's something else."

She shrugged and followed Weed toward the clubhouse. Rockingham had already checked his scorecard when Sam entered the scorer's hut, and was waiting for Sam to sign it. Naples went over his own card hole by hole, and so did Sam.

"Can we speed this up?" Rockingham said to Sam. "I want to get out of here."

"I'd think you'd want to savor a 65," Sam said.

"I do," Rockingham said. "In the hot tub, with a bottle of champagne and two naughty houseguests."

He shot a look at Sam that said, I've moved on. You're welcome to my discards.

When all the cards had been signed, Rockingham issued a curt, "See you tomorrow" and left the hut.

Chapter Twenty

Caroline walked past the roped-off clubhouse veranda where the members and their guests sat at tables under green-and-white striped umbrellas eating sandwiches and sipping gin-and-tonics. Above them, on the porch that ringed the second floor of the clubhouse, those with clubhouse badges enjoyed the club's courtly service while watching the players climb the hillside to the 9th and 18th greens. Caroline recognized many of the tour wives, but if they remembered her—or could even identify her in her caddie uniform—no one waved or made eye contact.

A crowd was clustered near the ancient oak at the southwest corner of the clubhouse, shading their eyes with their spectator guides to read the leaderboard. Caroline followed Weed past the oak tree and put Sam's bag down next to Rockingham's at the door to the bag room.

"Nice round today," she said to Weed.

"Hey, thanks," the caddie replied. "Can't wait to get out of here and celebrate."

Weed cleaned the face of his boss' utility club with a damp towel, put it back in the bag and pulled out the two-iron.

"I didn't think Shane ever carried the two and the utility at the same time," Caroline said. "He didn't when I caddied for him."

"He still doesn't," Weed said. "He—uh, oh."

Weed let the two-iron slide back into the bag and pulled up the utility wood. He then quickly tapped the heads of each club in the bag, including the putter, and then did it again, counting silently. The third time, Caroline counted with him.

"Once more," he said, this time counting out loud. The number was the same. Rockingham had played the round with 15 clubs in his bag.

"Shit!" Weed said, smacking himself on the side of the head with his open palm. When Caroline caddied for Shane, he was always going back and forth between carrying the two-iron or the utility wood for his 14th club, depending on the weather and the playing conditions. Maybe it was seeing Caroline in her caddie suit that had caused Shane to forget to take one of the clubs out of his bag, and Weed had forgotten to count.

He grabbed Caroline by the arm and pulled her into the breezeway, where other bags were waiting to be stored. He spoke in an urgent whisper.

"Look, he's leading the Masters. You know what that means— you're still married to him. You'll get a big chunk of the prize money. Don't let this happen."

"I didn't let it happen," Caroline said. "You did. And you're going to report it, or I will."

"He didn't even use the two-iron," Weed whined. "It's a four-shot penalty!"

"Only if you can catch him before he leaves the scorer's hut," Caroline said. "Otherwise, it's DQ."

She knew the rule by heart. Every caddie did. It was a two-stroke penalty for every hole that a player carried more than 14 clubs, up to two holes. After that, it didn't matter; the maximum penalty was four strokes. But if the player signed his scorecard without including the penalty strokes, it was automatic disqualification as soon as he left the scorer's area.

"You're just doing this to get back at Shane," Weed said, glaring at Caroline.

"I'd turn in my own player. And you're going to turn in yours, or I will."

"Don't do this," Weed pleaded. "Your guy doesn't have a chance."

"I have to protect the field—you know that," Caroline said. "And if you ever want to work on the tour again, you'd better come with me."

She turned and headed back to the scorer's hut. Weed waited a moment, then hurried to catch up to her.

"Bitch," he muttered just loud enough for Caroline to hear.

"Weasel," she muttered back.

They ran into Sam as he was about to go into the locker room.

"Where's Shane?" Caroline said.

"Probably in the locker room," Sam said. "He's late for a hot tub party. I think suits are optional, if you want to go."

Caroline put her hand on Sam's arm.

"This is serious."

She explained what happened at the bag room, with Weed reluctantly nodding his head about the 15 clubs. Sam whistled, and told them to wait for him by the oak tree. He found Rockingham getting ready to take a shower, and told him they had to go back to the scorer's hut. He'd had an extra club in his bag.

"Bullshit!" Rockingham yelled, causing the other players in the locker room to look up quickly. He put his pants back on and followed Sam to the oak tree, where Weed confirmed that he'd counted the clubs three times, with Caroline watching.

"This is your doing," Rockingham said, glaring at Caroline.

"If you mean, your caddie wouldn't have turned you in if I hadn't been there, then yes, it's my doing," she said.

"So what am I supposed to do now?"

"The right thing," Sam said.

"You were a lot of things when we were together, but you were never a cheat," Caroline said. "On the golf course, anyway."

"Let's take care of this," Rockingham said, stalking back toward the scorer's hut.

Rockingham told the official scorer that he'd just found out he had played the round with 15 clubs. Caroline and Weed confirmed it. Robert Brisbane and Ralph Stanwick were both summoned to the scorer's hut, and Rockingham explained again what had happened.

"Robert, there's got to be some way that I don't end up DQ'd for this," Rockingham said, but Brisbane shook his head.

"I'm sorry, Shane," he said. "I wish there was something I could do, but the rules are clear. You signed for a lower score than you shot. Then you left the scorer's area. We have no choice."

"But I never left the grounds. I was in the locker room."

"That's not the scorer's area," Stanwick said. He turned to the scorer and said: "Disqualified."

"Fuck!" Rockingham said, slamming his hand on the table. Then he turned to Weed.

"You're fired."

Rockingham stormed out of the scorer's hut, banging the door shut behind him, but a moment later he opened the door again, and said to Caroline, "You're going to wish you'd never come here."

Sam stayed with Caroline until she assured him she was all right, then he followed Rockingham to the locker room. The pro was angrily stuffing his belongings into a travel bag. Sam came up behind him and put a hand on his shoulder.

"Shane, for some reason I thought you had more class than that…"

Rockingham turned quickly and threw a right cross at Sam, who was half-expecting it, and managed to duck away. He used Rockingham's momentum to pull him forward and shove him into a bank of lockers. Rockingham bounced off the lockers and came at Sam again, his eyes blazing and his right hand pulled back to throw another punch. Sam almost felt sorry for him, but sentiment didn't stop him from blocking the punch with his forearm and delivering one hard punch of his own to Rockingham's ribs. The blow dropped Rockingham to the floor, doubled over in pain.

"You might want to call Harbor Town and tell them you're withdrawing next week," Sam said as he turned to leave the locker room. "Those ribs are going to hurt for a while."

◇◇◇

Sam returned to the scoring hut and found Caroline. He didn't tell her about what happened in the locker room. A red "DQ" went up next to Rockingham's name on the scoreboard next to the first fairway just as Sam and Caroline passed by the big oak tree on their way to the caddie building.

"Hey, Skarda! Over here!"

Russ Daly's gruff voice pierced through the crowd noise. He waved them over to the roped-off media area under the oak.

"What the hell happened out there?" Daly asked.

Sam explained that Rockingham discovered after his round that he'd had 15 clubs in his bag. He turned himself in, but he'd already signed for a 65, instead of a 69, and the tournament officials had to disqualify him. Sam looked at Caroline and she nodded; that was going to be her version of the story, too.

"Why didn't he find out until after the round?" another reporter asked.

"His caddie forgot to count them," Caroline said.

"And you are?" a third reporter asked Caroline. She identified herself as Sam's caddie, and spelled her name as more print reporters and TV crews began to swarm around them.

"You're also married to Shane Rockingham," said a reporter whose media badge identified him as a reporter for *Golf World*. "You used to caddie for Shane. You two are separated now, right?"

"That's right, but before you jump to conclusions, this wasn't payback or anything like that," Caroline said. "Weed discovered the mistake. Shane didn't know anything about it until Weed came forward."

The reporters pressed for more details, but Caroline stuck to the story: It was an innocent mistake, and Rockingham and Weed called it on themselves. That was all she knew. A few of the reporters rushed off to try to find Rockingham and Weed before they left the club. Russ Daly and the others lingered.

"Did you hear the other big news?" he asked Sam.

"What news?"

"They just found Danny Milligan at his home," Daly said. "He was murdered."

"That's awful," Caroline said.

"They won't be lowering the flags in the Founders Circle to half-staff," Daly said.

"How was he killed?" Sam asked.

"Last night somebody went to his house and cut his throat," a TV reporter said. "He was left outside for the fire ants to work on him."

"Fire ants?"

"Seems our killer is a bit of a sadist," Daly said. "He spread some kind of bait on Milligan, and the fire ants ate most of his face off."

"Jesus Christ," Caroline said. Despite the heat, she shuddered.

"The same LAST MASTERS message was sprayed next to the body," said a woman reporter with an ABC News I.D. dangling from the chain around her neck.

"What are your thoughts?" said a man with a spiral notebook in his hand, looking at Caroline.

"Why ask me?" she asked.

"You're the only chick on the course," Daly said. "Looks like somebody would rather shut down the Masters than let people of your particular gender join the club."

"That's ridiculous," Caroline said. She glanced away from Daly and noticed that all the TV cameras had clustered around her, waiting for her response.

"What's ridiculous?" one of the reporters prodded.

"That somebody thinks women don't belong here," Caroline said. She was angry now, because of Milligan's murder, because the killer seemed to hate women, because she'd had to help disqualify her husband, because she was tired and sweaty, and because she had been ambushed by a pack of reporters who expected her to speak for womankind everywhere.

"Of course women belong here," she continued. "I mean, look around. There are women everywhere. They're certainly willing to sell us tickets."

"So you think women should be members at Augusta National?" one of the reporters said. The cameras stared back at her.

"Yes," she said. "I didn't really care one way or the other when I got here. I just really like coming here. But maybe allowing a woman to join would put a stop to these killings."

"That's good," said a woman holding a microphone with a CNN logo.

"That's all I have to say," Caroline said, feeling a bit dazed. "I'm very sorry for Danny Milligan's family."

"Please spell your first and last name for us, Miss...?"

"I already..."

"Again, please."

"Rockingham. Like Shane. First name Caroline."

"Usual spelling?"

"C-A-R-O-L-I-N-E."

"And you're caddying for..."

"Sam Skarda," Sam said. "S-K-A-R-D-A."

They walked off together toward the locker room. Behind them they could hear the TV reporters standing in front of their cameras, working on the intros and wraps to their interview. "Here at Augusta National, the only female caddie in the field has become embroiled in controversy..."

"What time tomorrow?" Caroline asked Sam.

"One-fifteen."

"I guess I'll be awake by then."

"I wasn't sure you wanted to loop for me again," Sam said.

"Why not? The only way to get away from people here is to be inside the ropes."

"I have to go," Sam said. "If you'll meet me back here for dinner at seven-thirty, I'm buying."

"I might be hungry by then," Caroline said. "Right now, I need a drink and a nap."

"Take my courtesy car," Sam said, taking the keys out of his pocket and dangling them in front of her. "I won't need it this afternoon."

"Which one is it?"

"The white Cadillac."

"Very funny."

"License number BGH398."

"Okay, thanks."

She took the keys. Sam gave her a quick peck on the cheek, and walked into the locker room.

Caroline just wanted to get into the courtesy car, turn up the air conditioning, and get the hell away from this place for a while.

Chapter Twenty-one

Sam had returned to the locker room when he saw the story about Milligan on TV. Several of the pros gathered in front of the wall-mounted Sony plasma to listen to the details. One of them said a hushed, "Damn"; another muttered, "This is getting weird." They all shook their heads and drifted away after watching for a minute or two. The news of Milligan's murder wasn't going to disrupt their preparation for the Masters.

Sam couldn't help thinking about Ralph Stanwick. The message burned in the grass indicated it must have been the same killer—though the fire-ant bait was an escalation in the level of hostility. Now the killer had struck outside the gates of the club, but the warning was the same: Speak out against the all-male status quo at Augusta National and your life was in danger. The signs still pointed back to a club member—and one member had a history of trying to keep women from getting through the door.

He had called Stanwick's cabin the previous night. His wife had said he couldn't come to the phone, and had hung up. Sam couldn't guess if she was angry with him for calling, or with her husband for not being there.

The warm April breeze had almost dried Sam's hair, still damp from his shower, when he walked up the steps of the administration building to Porter's office. Ida told him Robert Brisbane was in the chairman's office. Sam didn't bother to wait for permission to join them.

Porter and Brisbane were watching clips of Milligan's NBC interview on television; the voiceover stated that yet another critic of the Augusta National membership policy had been "cut down."

"Mr. Skarda," Porter said by way of greeting. His eyes did not have their usual solicitous sparkle. He lowered the volume on the TV. "Hell of a thing about Rockingham today."

"Hell of a thing about Danny Milligan, too."

"We're sorry it happened," Brisbane said.

"This year's tournament seems cursed," Porter said, waving his hand listlessly toward the Milligan interview on the TV screen. Sam took the opening.

"Where was Ralph Stanwick last night?"

Porter picked up the remote control on his desk and shut off the TV.

"In his cabin, I suppose," Porter said. "Why?"

"Did you see him?"

"No. Robert, did you?"

"No," Brisbane said.

"Why are you so interested in Ralph?" Porter asked.

Sam explained his case: The signs still pointed to a club member; Stanwick's wife was the only one who could account for his whereabouts last night when Milligan was being murdered, and even she didn't seem to know where he was; and Stanwick was openly opposed to women joining all-male institutions, going back to his days at Yale.

"Is that true, Robert?" Porter asked.

"He's wrong about Ralph," Brisbane said. "Lieutenant Boyce has already spoken to him—here in your office."

"That wasn't exactly a grilling," Sam said. "The cops have over a hundred interviews to do. If I tell them they should be looking more closely at Stanwick, they will. Tell me why they shouldn't."

Brisbane looked at Porter, then got up from the chair next to Porter's desk and closed the door to the outer office. When he returned to his chair, he looked at Sam.

"Ralph has a girlfriend who lives here in town," he said. "If he wasn't with Lorraine, that's where he was last night."

Now we're getting somewhere, Sam thought. Not necessarily any closer to the killer, but at least the green jackets were giving him something besides the carefully orchestrated bullshit they fed the press.

"He wouldn't want the police—or anyone else—to know that," Brisbane said.

"At this point, he doesn't have much choice," Sam said. "Does his wife know?"

"Lorraine doesn't know who he sees when he leaves the grounds. I don't think she wants to."

"She's willing to look the other way?"

"She loses a lot if she doesn't," Brisbane said.

Sam sighed and rubbed his eyes with his thumb and forefinger. The deaths—and the lies—were piling up. How many questions would he have to ask before he asked the right one? Working as a cop was simpler. He could be as indelicate as he wanted to be when he was trying to find a killer, because the only thing that mattered was getting to the truth. Working as a private investigator got complicated when you had to investigate the people who'd hired you.

He glanced out the window at the colorful mosaic of Masters spectators wandering over the grounds. They didn't care that Danny Milligan was dead. They didn't care that somebody was trying to stop a woman from joining the National, or ruin the Masters, or both. They cheered for Tiger and Phil, they ate their pimento cheese sandwiches, and they thanked their personal deities that they were lucky enough to be standing where they were today. It was golf's finest annual holiday, and Sam was trying to figure out who wanted so desperately to spoil it. He wasn't getting much help.

"What's her name?" Sam said, turning back to Brisbane.

"I can't…"

"Sure you can," Sam interrupted. "If she exists."

Sam knew he was pushing his luck with the Masters poo-bahs, but he didn't care. They'd hired him to find the killer. They'd promised him full access. What was the worst they could do if he pushed too hard—fire him?

Brisbane finally said, "Peggy Francis."

Porter looked at Brisbane with surprise.

"The gal who works in the Golf Shop?"

"That's her," Brisbane said.

"Hmmm," Porter said, the note of disapproval indicating either that he was disappointed in Stanwick's behavior, or that he thought Ralph could do better. He wrote the woman's name on the back of one of his business cards and slid it across the desk to Sam.

"You'll find her in the merchandise shop next to the main entrance," Porter said. "She works with us at every Masters."

"How will I recognize her?" Sam asked.

"Ask any of the clerks. They'll know her."

Sam picked the card up from the desk and put it in his pocket.

"You're wrong about Ralph," Brisbane said again to Sam.

"Without question," Porter said. "I hope you'll stop wasting your time on Ralph. Nobody is more dedicated to this club—not even me."

Porter picked up the remote, turned up the volume and switched channels to the cable broadcast of Thursday afternoon's play. The network put up a picture of a grinning Danny Milligan, and the dates of his birth and death on a black background.

"Did you know that Boyce and Harwell are interviewing our members and employees in the Butler Cabin?" Porter said, as though the subject of Ralph Stanwick had never come up. "The police are hauling our people over there one by one, like a goddamn perp walk. That's where we present the green jacket to our winner on Sunday."

He looked at the screen again, which now displayed a leader-board that showed Padraig Harrington on top at 3 under par.

"If we make it to Sunday," Brisbane said.

◇◇◇

Sam left the clubhouse and walked to the shaded, bricked plaza where most spectators entered the grounds. The Golf Shop was located immediately to the right of the media building—conveniently positioned as the first structure an entering Masters fan would notice. Hundreds of customers waited in line to enter the high-ceilinged, one-story green building, with its multiple check-out lanes that opened out to the plaza. Inside, Sam could see that shoppers were nearly elbow-to-elbow as they selected hats, sweaters, balls, shirts, jackets, visors, towels, and anything else stamped with the famous Augusta National logo.

Sam showed his player's badge to one of the attendants at the head of the line and told her he was there to speak to one of the employees. Inside, the building looked like a country club pro shop crossbred with the clothing aisles at Target: bright lighting, long shelves of cotton, wool, and cashmere, and countless floor racks of shirts, jackets, pants, and sweatshirts.

He stopped a young woman replenishing a shelf with $125 Bobby Jones polo shirts and asked her if she knew where he could find Peggy.

"She's over at Artwork and Collectibles," said the young woman with a pleasant but slightly harried drawl, as she continued to fold and stack.

Sam looked across the room and saw a glass counter containing commemorative plates and jewelry, above which hung framed prints of Augusta National holes. He made his way through the crowd to the counter. He was looking at the photos and paintings when one of the saleswomen asked him, "Do you collect golf course prints?"

She had a wavy auburn perm and a little too much pink lipstick on her thin, smiling lips, and a Masters name badge that said PEGGY. She was wearing the Golf Shop uniform: khaki pants and a pink polo shirt with the green-and-yellow Masters logo over the breast pocket. No great beauty, Sam thought, but her smile seemed sincere, even after dealing with throngs of golf fans who cleaned out her building each day.

"No, I can't afford them," Sam said. "Maybe I'll learn to paint my own someday."

"Oh, you should," Peggy said. "Painting is a wonderful hobby."

"You paint?" Sam asked her.

"Well, no, but I'm told…"

"You're Peggy Francis, right?" Sam said.

"Yes," she said, still smiling. "Have we met?"

Sam told her who he was and why he was there to see her, and the smile disappeared.

"Is there a place we can talk?" he said. "A break room or something?"

"I don't think we have anything to talk about, Mr. Skarda," she said—not coldly, but nervously. She looked around as though hoping to spot a customer who needed her help, but none came to her rescue.

Sam pulled out the business card with *Peggy Francis* handwritten written on the back and showed it to her. The front of the card read *David Porter, Chairman, Augusta National.*

"The boss sent me to see you," he said.

Peggy took the card and looked at it, as though she expected it to tell her what to say. Eventually she handed the card back to Sam.

"Your friend Ralph Stanwick might be in a lot of trouble," Sam said.

"I doubt it," Peggy said, with a tone of almost mirthful bitterness. "Lorraine will never leave him. I'm sure she knows about me. And the others, too."

"Others?"

"I'm not the only girl he sees when he's in town. Ralph's a popular man."

"I don't much care who he sees, or how many," Sam said. "I need to know where he was last night."

"Why does it matter?"

Sam asked her if she'd heard about Danny Milligan's murder. She had. When she realized where Sam was going, she laughed, genuinely.

"Forget it," Peggy said. "He was with me."

"Mrs. Stanwick made it sound like he was with her when I called their cabin last night. I didn't believe her, either."

"She's been lying for him for years."

"Wouldn't you lie for him?"

"No."

"What did you do last night?"

"He came over to my house. I grilled steaks."

"Can anybody else verify that?"

"We don't double-date," Peggy said. "You can probably understand why."

"How late did he stay?"

"Until about five this morning. Then he went back to the National."

Decent of Ralph to go home to his wife, rather than stay out all night. He could check with the guardhouse at Magnolia Lane to see what time Stanwick returned, but that wouldn't prove where he'd been.

"Was he with you Sunday night? And Tuesday night?"

"You don't think he killed Harmon Ashby and that reporter, too? Look, Ralph might not be the nicest man in the world, but he's no killer."

"What makes you so sure?" Sam said in a low voice, looking around to see if they were being overheard. The expensive jewelry and plates continued to deter the shoppers. "You'd be surprised who's capable of murder."

"Not Ralph," Peggy said. "He's a sneak and a cheat, but he doesn't like to muss himself up."

"Sounds like a real catch," Sam said.

"He used to be."

"What do you mean?"

"I mean, he used to be a fun guy, at least. This week he's been, I don't know—spooky or something. The phone rang a couple of times last night and he practically jumped out of his chair."

"Maybe he thought it was his wife calling."

"No, he knows she wouldn't do that. I think these murders have really gotten to him."

As a cop, Sam could have taken Peggy Francis downtown for more questioning and maybe found a hole in her story. But she was going to defend Stanwick no matter what. And she just might be telling the truth.

Sam asked her if she'd ever heard Stanwick complain about the WOFF protests or Rachel Drucker.

"I don't think I'm going to say anything more," she said. "I told you I was with Ralph last night. That's all you need. That's all you're getting."

She walked to the other end of the display case, flashed a smile at a customer and asked him if he was interested in buying a print or a collectible. She glanced quickly at Sam, then back to her customer. Sam walked out of the shop, not sure if he had made any progress.

The clouds above the tops of the shade trees in the plaza were ivory wisps against the brilliant blue—a perfect day for the afternoon pairings. Occasional bursts of applause and cheers rang across the course from distant grandstands. The Masters was unfolding all around him, in its usual orgy of perfection. Sam wished he could get back to work on his own game—it needed it—but his outside job was just beginning. He'd taken his suspicions about Stanwick as far as he could for now. It was time to look in another direction.

He kept going back to something Russ Daly had said to Deborah Scanlon: The Augusta National members love their greens more than they hate women.

Sam suspected that was true. A member of the National might kill someone, but would he deface the golf course by spraying a message on the grass? Maybe that was for the cops to determine. They were doing the right thing, investigating the members. But that didn't mean the killer was wearing a green jacket.

As for the current employees, they had the best jobs in town. All he'd seen from them in three days was an almost fanatic devotion to making sure everything at Augusta National was impeccable. They seemed to take every bit as much pride in the building, the grounds, the golf course, and the club's reputation as the members themselves.

And yet someone was trying to create at least the appearance of a club backlash against the women's membership movement. He'd investigated enough property crimes against businesses to know that pissed-off ex-employees made good suspects. With no better ideas in mind, Sam resigned himself to a long afternoon digging through the National's employee files.

Chapter Twenty-two

Caroline changed out of her jumpsuit in the caddie building and walked out to the players' parking lot, where she found Sam's courtesy car. When she got onto Washington Road, she turned on the radio.

"…have no suspects in the latest Masters murder," the newscaster was saying. "But yesterday's gruesome slaying of CBS golf analyst Danny Milligan—a frequent critic of Augusta National—has upset many here this week. Earlier today, the only woman caddie in this year's field said she was now in favor of women joining the all-male club."

Then Caroline heard her own voice:

"'Of course women belong here. I mean, look around. There are women everywhere. They're certainly willing to sell us tickets.'"

Caroline couldn't believe that anyone really cared what she thought. She switched to a music station.

What a week—and it had all started when she met Sam. He was nothing like Shane on the surface, but in other ways she saw similarities. Both were self-confident—Shane more openly, but Sam had a quiet assurance. He reminded her of the soldiers she'd met growing up around military bases—guys who didn't just talk about what they would do in an emergency, but did it, and without hesitation. Most golfers she'd met were tigers in competition, but off the course they were often helpless little boys. She didn't get that feeling with Sam.

On the other hand, she had an anti-authoritarian streak in her that went back to her years on military bases, where there was always a rank system, where even the commanders had to answer to someone. Caroline had developed an aversion to being told what to do—not a particularly good quality in a caddie, she had to admit. Maybe that's one of the reasons things ultimately went bad with Shane. She wondered if the same thing would happen if she got involved with Sam. He was a cop, used to issuing orders. That wouldn't work with Caroline. Not anymore.

It was fun to carry a bag in a big tournament again, but at the first sign Sam expected her to be subservient outside the ropes, the way Shane had expected her to be, she was gone. Was there any reason to think he'd be that way? Just that he was a cop. Cops were that way.

She found a parking spot near the front entrance to the motel, locked the car and walked through the lobby and up the stairs to her room. The air conditioner was still making its grinding noise, as though a fan inside the unit needed a new bearing or something. She had called down to the front desk and they'd promised to have someone come up and fix it. So much for promises. She called the desk again and said the unit was still making too much noise. Sorry, the clerk said; they'd have someone come up as soon as they could.

Caroline switched on the TV and began taking off her clothes. A shower would feel great—then a glass of wine and a nap before dinner. The Weather Channel anchor was describing the high pressure system that had moved into the southeast, which didn't interest Caroline. Anyone could stick their head out the window and realize it was sunny and warm now, and likely to stay sunny and warm. She picked up the remote and switched to CNN.

The first thing she saw was her own face, with her name superimposed over the picture, identified as "Only Female Caddie at Masters."

"...So you think women should be members at Augusta National?" an off-camera reporter's voice asked.

"Yes," she saw herself answer, as spectators walked behind her and the tips of reporters' hand-held microphones and tape recorders bobbed in front of her mouth. "I didn't really care one way or the other when I got here. I just really like coming here. But maybe allowing a woman to join would put a stop to these killings."

She thought she actually looked pretty good—especially after lugging that bag up and down those hills in that hot uniform. But she sounded stupid. She wished she'd just said, "No comment."

She left her clothes on the floor in front of the TV and went into the bathroom to turn on the shower.

◇◇◇

Sam found Bill Woodley in the clubhouse kitchen, discussing the Béarnaise sauce with one of the cooks.

"Not too much vinegar," Woodley said to the cook, a black man wearing a white double-breasted coat with three-quarter sleeves and a starched white hat that extended from the top of his head like a chimney. "Mr. Sinclair mentioned to me that he'd prefer the Béarnaise a bit lighter."

"Sure thing," the cook said. He dipped a wooden spoon into the sauce pan and held it out for Woodley to taste. The club manager put his lips to the spoon and sampled the sauce.

"That's it," Woodley said, with a nod. He looked up and noticed Sam standing a few feet away. "Can I help you, Mr. Skarda?"

"I need to look at your employee files," Sam said.

The cook took a sip of his own sauce as they left the kitchen.

"Maybe a pinch more pepper," the cook called to Woodley.

"Just a pinch," Woodley said, and then looked at Sam almost apologetically. "Lunch must go on, even at a time like this."

"I'm a big fan of lunch," Sam said.

They left the clubhouse and crossed the parking lot to the administration building, where Woodley had a cramped office with windows facing the driving range. Woodley's office was furnished with a desk and a computer, several beige metal file cabinets, a bulletin board with photos, notes and business cards thumb-tacked to it, a framed painting of the 16th green, and a 17-inch TV sitting on an end table. The TV was tuned to afternoon Masters coverage. Sergio Garcia was now in the lead.

"Which files do you need?" Woodley asked, with the brisk tone of a busy, efficient man.

"Former employees," Sam said. "How far back do you keep those records?"

"1931," Woodley said, with a slight smile that indicated he expected the answer to surprise Sam. "We don't get the kind of turnover here that a lot of clubs have. Some of our current employees have been with us 50 years or more."

"It must take a lot of people to run this club," Sam said. "Cooks, waiters, maids, grounds crew, caddies, security people, golf shop staff—you've got all of them on file, from the beginning?"

"I'm told Mr. Roberts insisted that no club records be thrown away," Woodley said. "We run the club the way Mr. Roberts wanted it run."

"Where do you keep it all?"

"We have an archive."

Woodley led Sam down the hall to a closed door. He selected a key from the chain he carried in his pocket and opened the door to a one-window room that had a desk with a phone and a computer, a fluorescent overhead light, and eight filing cabinets.

Woodley told him the filing cabinets included club expense records, insurance information and legal documents. He pointed out the cabinets that contained the records of past employees, all stored in alphabetical order, rather than by hiring or termination date. Sam knew he'd have to go through every file.

"Would you like some coffee?" Woodley asked.

"Sure," Sam said. "You might as well bring a pot. I'm going to be here for a while."

Woodley unlocked the two file cabinets with another key. Both three-drawer cabinets had a master lock above the top drawer; there would be six drawers to go through. Woodley said he'd be back in an hour or two to see if he needed anything else.

"Thanks," Sam said. "By the way, do you remember the name of the bartender who was fired a few years ago for talking about members' private conversations?"

"Winston Lamar," Woodley said. "It happened just after I started here. He was very popular with the staff and the members. I hated to fire him."

"Then why did you?"

"He couldn't prove he wasn't leaking information about members to outsiders."

"It's supposed to work the other way," Sam said. "You're supposed to prove that he was."

"Not here," Woodley said. "Once the membership loses trust in an employee, he's gone. I know that sounds harsh, but our employees understand that when they come to work here. They're paid very well. They accept the conditions."

"How long have you been the manager?"

"Six years. The previous manager died. He'd been here for 35 years."

"Anyone else you've had to fire since you've been here?"

"Oh, one or two a year, I guess," Woodley said. "Usually for showing up late for work. If they were fired, you'll see the reason why detailed on their separation form."

Sam opened the top drawer of the first filing cabinet and pulled out an armload of folders, stacking them on the desk next to the computer.

"We want you to find who's doing this," Woodley said. "Whoever it is."

Sam looked up at Woodley to see if there was some special intent with that last remark. Woodley held his gaze for a moment, then nodded and walked out of the room. Sam wondered if this was an upstairs-downstairs situation. He got the impression that it wouldn't break Woodley's heart to learn that a club member was behind the killings. Or maybe he simply wanted this to be over as quickly as possible so he could get back to his normal duties—seeing that the flowers were fresh and the Béarnaise was not too acidic.

Chapter Twenty-three

Sam began plowing through the folders. Aaron. Abarro. Abbott. Acheson. Adderley. Each folder a story, a life.

He tried not to get caught up in imagining too much about them. There were too many folders to linger over any of them for too long. If something caught his eye, he put the folder in a separate stack.

Each employee's folder contained one form with personal information, including address, phone number, Social Security number, date of birth, salary information, performance appraisals, and benefits data, including pension plans, health care records, and 401K contributions on the newer forms. Under the performance appraisals, there was a space for warnings, but there were no warnings cited on any of the employees' records. Apparently, you didn't get a warning at Augusta National.

There was also a separation form in each folder, listing payroll processing issues, final expense reporting, benefits notification, security termination procedures, and reason for separation. In most cases, the employee simply retired. Form after form listed the age of the departing employee as 65 or older. Some had died while still employed. It was obvious that jobs at the National were hard to come by, and clung to by those lucky enough to get them.

The oldest forms were faded and yellowing, and a quick glance at the birthdate of the employee allowed Sam to skip past most of those. The first firing he came across was that of a

William Askew, terminated from the grounds crew in 1939 for arguing with the head greenskeeper over how to mow around bunkers. Askew was 39 at the time; he was certainly dead now. Louise Bascombe, a maid, was fired in 1973 for stealing a small sum of cash from one of the cabins—at least, it was alleged that she had stolen the money. Sam kicked her folder into the separate pile to be looked at more closely, but he didn't expect to spend much time on her, either. She had been 51 at the time. She'd be in her 80s now.

He was looking for ex-employees still in their physically active years who might have a grudge against the club. A blue-collar or domestic worker would have a tough time recovering from losing a job at Augusta National. They weren't going to find a similar job that paid as well, assuming that you could find another employer willing to overlook a negative recommendation from the National.

Eventually he came to the folder of Winston Lamar, fired in 2002 for suspicion of discussing members' business with non-members. Lamar had been hired as a busboy at the club when he was 17 years old. His performance evaluations were excellent; he had moved up to waiter and eventually to bartender in 1987. Again, the performance evaluations were glowing: his acumen at handling multiple orders, remembering members' favorite drinks, engaging in conversation when asked, and keeping his accounts straight all were lavishly praised. He was clearly one of the clubhouse stars until his abrupt termination. No specific members were mentioned in the complaint against Lamar, but he was accused of revealing confidential business information that he'd overheard at the bar. His side of the story was not included in the reason for dismissal.

Lamar would now be nearing 50, according to the file. Certainly capable of overpowering a slender woman or an older man. The motive was there. Sam put the folder into the suspects pile.

He stood up to stretch, feeling buzzed from the coffee Woodley had sent to him. From his window he could see the driveway in front of the clubhouse—the last place Deborah Scanlon had been seen alive. Did he have his man already? Not likely. There were still more than 200 folders to look at. But experience told him he was not necessarily wasting his time here, even if it was a long shot that he'd find the killer in one of these folders.

Sam replaced the folders he'd looked at in the filing cabinet, and took out a new stack. He settled back down at the desk and began again. Eddie LePage. Carl Logan. Margaret Lucas. William Masters. Eugene Maxwell. All either retired or dead. No cause for revenge.

Reggie Morton. Another dismissal—in 1988.

According to his file, Morton had been a caddie at the club since the early '70s. He had steady work for 15 years, so he must have caddied at the Masters during those years—up until 1983, when the pros were finally allowed to bring their own caddies to the tournament. The Masters paychecks must have made his year. After 1983, when the Masters checks stopped coming, Morton had grown difficult and sometimes belligerent, according to the termination account. There were complaints about his attitude. Eventually he was told he was no longer welcome on the grounds.

He would be 48 now. Another folder went into the suspect pile.

He came across Dwight Wilson's mother, Helen, who'd been a maid at the club for decades. She'd been retired for eight years.

After more than three hours, Sam came to the final folder. It belonged to Jeff Zimmerman, a summer employee on the grounds crew during his college years in the mid-'90s. He'd quit working at the club after graduating from Emory and taking a job as a stockbroker in Atlanta.

In all, Sam had kicked out seven files of fired employees who'd been born later than 1920, but after going back over each one, only three looked like they were worth further investigation: Winston Lamar, Reggie Morton, and a guy named Bruce Summers.

Summers had been a security guard at Augusta National from 1983 until 1993, when he'd fired a handgun over the heads of some neighborhood kids who had sneaked onto the course in July, when it was closed for play. Summers had found them swimming and fishing in Rae's Creek at Amen Corner and told them to leave immediately. They did—but when Summers returned, they had come back. Or so went his account of the incident, which was included in the reason for termination. He told them to leave again or he'd call the sheriff. When the kids didn't leave, Summers said, he pulled out his revolver and fired a shot into the air. The kids had scattered, but they told their parents what had happened, and the parents contacted the club. Summers was fired, though some members objected to the dismissal.

Sam moved his chair in front of the desktop computer and went to an online obituary search site he'd used as a police detective. He entered the three names from the suspect pile. Two names came back: Lamar and Summers.

According to the *Atlanta Journal-Constitution*, a Winston Jefferson Lamar had died February 12, 2003, in Atlanta; the date of birth and the middle name were the same as they appeared on the former bartender's employment file.

The obit from the *Augusta Chronicle* said that Bruce Wayne Summers had died on September 27, 1996, in Augusta. Again, the first, middle, and last names and the date of birth were a match. The suspect pile was down to one.

He looked up Reggie Morton in the Augusta phone book. No one was listed by that name, or by Reginald Morton. He went back to the computer and brought up a website that did online criminal background checks for $19 a pop. He thought about asking one of his cop pals back in Minneapolis to run Morton's name through the nationwide NCIC computer network, but he didn't want to have to explain what he was doing or who he was doing it for—not if he could get the information himself.

Sam paid for his online search with a credit card, then did a Social Security number trace on Reggie Morton. The information came up immediately.

Name(s) associated with this SSN:
  REGINALD HARRIS MORTON
  REGGIE MORTON
  REGINALD HARRIS
  REGGIE HARRIS
Addresses:
  5361Baker Rd AUGUSTA GA 30909 12/1972
  787 PO Box AUGUSTA GA 30909 04/1976
  11A Locust St AUGUSTA GA 30909 11/1983
  13 Oak Road AUGUSTA GA 30907 10/1984
  156 Riley Dr AUGUSTA GA 30907 02/1992
  2231 Hurst St AUGUSTA GA 30909 11/2000

Then Sam ran a check on Morton's criminal record and came up with two convictions for credit-card fraud, one for writing worthless checks, and one for possession of a controlled substance, all since his termination at Augusta National.

So Reggie Morton hadn't been a model citizen since getting the boot at the club. That didn't prove anything. What it did show, though, was that Morton—if that was the name he was going by now—had been living in town fairly recently, had a criminal background, and had some life experiences that might give him even more reason to hold a grudge against his former employer. Sam tried the name Reggie Harris in the phone book. He found a listing for R. Harris at 2231 Hurst St., the last address on the Social Security search. He dialed the number. It had been disconnected.

At least now Sam had somebody to look for. He thought about taking a drive to the Hurst Street address, asking neighbors if they knew anything about Reggie, but then he had a better idea. He called Dwight Wilson's restaurant.

"Dad, it's for you!" yelled a girl Sam assumed was Dwight's daughter Cammie. In a minute or so, Sam heard the booming voice of the caddie answer on the other end of the line.

"Dwight, it's Sam Skarda," he said. "Did I get you at a busy time?"

"Yeah, but I got a minute. How'd you play today?"

"Not too well," Sam said. "I shot 80."

"Damn," Dwight said. "I wish I'd been there. I'd have at least got you in at 79."

Sam didn't want to keep Dwight from his customers; he told him he was looking for an old caddie he might remember named Reggie Morton, or Reggie Harris.

"Oh, hell, you mean One-eye?"

"One-eye?"

"That's all we ever called him," Dwight said. "They fired him years ago. Yeah, Reggie Morton. That was him."

"Seen him lately?"

"Why—you couldn't find a caddie today?"

"No, I came up with a pretty good one. She's been on the Tour. But I'd still like to find One-eye. Do you know where he is?"

"He's around. He comes in sometimes with some of the old caddies. He was away for a while, too. Got sent to the joint a couple of times."

"Do you think you could help me find him?"

"Well, I don't know," Dwight said slowly. "Why're you looking for him?"

Sam understood the caddie's hesitation. Dwight knew Sam had been a cop, so his interest in One-eye was probably professional. He also knew Sam would be gone by Sunday at the latest, while Dwight would be living in Augusta the rest of his life. If it came to ratting someone out, Dwight would have to live with the repercussions. Sam wouldn't.

"I'm working for the National," Sam said. "I'm trying to help them find the killer before he gets somebody else."

"Oh, man, One-eye didn't kill nobody," Dwight said. "You got the wrong guy."

"I don't know what I've got," Sam said. "I just spent three hours going through the club's personnel files to see if I could find someone with an axe to grind. Only three people looked like they fit the profile, and two of them are dead."

"Well, it ain't One-eye, I'll tell you that," Dwight said.

"How do you know?"

"I just know, that's all. Are the cops looking for him? I mean, about this?"

Sam told Dwight that the GBI had an investigator working the case, but he hadn't given him Morton's name yet. If he could talk to One-eye first, he said, maybe he wouldn't have to. He was just trying to help the club stay in front of the case.

"They paying you a lot?" Dwight asked.

"So they tell me."

There was silence on the other end of the line. Sam had no doubt that Dwight was a straight arrow. He was a business owner, a family man, and a loyal Augusta National employee of long standing. He wanted to do the right thing, but he didn't feel comfortable about getting in the middle of an investigation into one of his acquaintances. Sam would have to find a way to convince Dwight he wasn't doing something slimy by helping the club.

"You think One-eye could use a few bucks?" Sam asked.

"Sure," Dwight said.

"Well, if you can get him to stop by your place tonight, I've got a couple hundred for him, no strings attached," Sam said. "I'm not a cop anymore, Dwight. You can tell him why I want to talk to him. If he's clean, he'll come in for the money."

Dwight was silent for a while longer, then said: "I guess I could put the word out. I don't know if he's around, though. I ain't seen him in a while."

"How long has it been?"

"Two weeks, maybe. I know who he hangs with, though. I'll ask around. No promises."

"No problem. You've got my cell phone number."

After hanging up, Sam put the remaining folders back in the file cabinet, shut down the computer, turned off the overhead light, and closed the door behind him. Who else, he wondered, would remember One-eye Morton?

Chapter Twenty-four

Sam returned to the media building and scanned the sea of reporters' faces for Russ Daly. He spotted him squeezed into his workstation on the right aisle, looking supremely annoyed at the commotion around him. Sam maneuvered his way down the aisle to the bulky columnist's location.

"Hey, that's my Diet Coke," Daly snarled at the reporter sitting to his left as Sam arrived.

"The hell it is, Russ," the reporter shot back. "You finished your last one about 15 minutes ago. This one's mine."

"You sure?"

"Christ, you've drained about a half dozen since I've been sitting here," said the reporter, who tried to move to his left to create more space between him and Daly's flab. "They don't seem to be working, either."

"Yeah, I'm thinking of suing," Daly said. He looked to his right and noticed Sam. "What's the latest, Columbo?"

Sam debated whether he ought to tell Daly anything. But Daly had covered the Masters for years and was plugged into the tournament and its peripheral characters as well as anyone. If he wanted information from Daly, it only seemed fair to give him something in return.

"Porter and Brisbane are backing Stanwick all the way," Sam said in a low voice, kneeling next to Daly in the aisle—though he didn't have to worry about being heard above the drone of conversation and clicking laptops in the cavernous media room. "By the way, you were right about the guy. He's a regular Hugh Hefner—though his playmates are a little older."

He told Daly about his encounter at the merchandise building with Peggy Francis, then got to his point.

"I'm going to tell you something off the record—and I mean off the record. If I see any of this in print, I'll tell every player I meet this week that you burned me. You won't get the time of day from them if that happens."

Daly snorted dismissively, so Sam rose to walk away.

"Hey, hold on," Daly said. "Okay, I'm curious. Off the record."

Sam knelt back down next to Daly, wondering how long he could stay in that position before his knees gave out. He'd have to make it fast.

"I've got another guy to look at. Were you here in 1983, when they started letting the pros bring their own caddies?"

"Nah," Daly said. "That was a few years before I started covering the tournament. But the stink hadn't gone away when I first got here. In fact, I did a feature on the spurned caddies of Augusta. It was in '88 or '89, I think."

"You remember a caddie named One-eye?"

"Sure," Daly said. "He was one of the caddies I interviewed for that story. All of 'em were pissed off about the change, but One-eye was more pissed off about it than anyone."

"What do you mean?"

"He kept caddying for members for a few years, but he never missed a chance to bring up the subject of how much money he lost not caddying at the Masters. He got a third-place check in 1978 or '79 that paid his rent for six months. A guy like One-eye misses that kind of money."

According to Daly, One-eye started taking his resentment out on the members he caddied for. If a guy hit his ball into the trees, One-eye couldn't find it. If his ball got dirty, One-eye didn't wash it. If a guy asked for a yardage, One-eye couldn't remember it. A member even caught One-eye kicking pine straw on top of his ball in the trees. He began deliberately misclubbing players. ("If you hit the club One-eye handed you on 12 or 16, you were looking at a splashdown.") Then he started intentionally misreading greens.

"That's when they showed him the gate," Daly said. "He'd picked up his nickname because he was so good at reading the National's greens."

Daly had the story: One-eye was looping for Sam Snead in a practice round one day when they disagreed on a double-breaker on the eighth green. Snead thought the ball would go right and then left. One-eye said he was wrong; the ball straightened out after breaking right, and then it was going to break right again at the hole. Snead asked him if he was willing to bet half his day's pay, and One-eye said, make it the whole day. Snead putted the ball the way he thought it would break, and missed it right. Then he put another ball down and tried One-eye's line, and made it from 40 feet.

"Old One-eye says, 'I could read putts better with one eye than you can with two!'" Daly cackled. "And the name stuck. So when One-eye started misreading putts for the members, he was done. That's about all he ever brought to the table, anyway. He was quite a character."

"Could he be a killer?" Sam asked.

"Damned if I know. I haven't seen him since."

"He's been in and out of a few lockups," Sam said. "If he hadn't lost his job here, he might have stayed out of jail. That could make a guy bitter."

"I suppose," Daly said. "But how would he get on and off the property?"

"He'd know how to get over the fence," Sam said. "On Tuesday, he could have bought a practice-round ticket from a scalper. Look, I'm not saying he's definitely the guy. It could be Stanwick, or somebody else. But I went through the personnel files looking for somebody who might have a grudge against the club, and Morton's name popped out. I'm trying to find him."

"Good luck. Guys like him are hard to find if they don't want to be found."

Dwight Wilson was probably Sam's only hope, and Dwight hadn't called back. He stood up and slowly flexed both knees until the ache began to recede. It was time to meet Caroline and get something to eat. Night had fallen, and he began to worry about her walking across the clubhouse grounds after dark.

"I'll be around if you hear anything," Sam said. He started up the steps to the exit.

"Hey, your caddie looked good on TV today," Daly yelled after him.

"Did we make the news?" Sam asked.

"All day."

◇◇◇

While Sam waited in the clubhouse for Caroline, he saw Wheeling and Compton coming down the stairs. He'd forgotten to look for their scores in the media building, but their expressions told him how they'd played. Wheeling, who shot 73, was giddy; Compton, who shot a 77, looked like a kid who'd been told he had to wait another year to get his driver's license. They invited Sam to join them for dinner in the men's grill, but he told them he had a date.

There were more security guards around the clubhouse than Sam had noticed the night before. Still, the thought of a lone, unarmed woman walking the grounds of Augusta National suddenly seemed no more prudent than an unaccompanied woman walking through Central Park after dark.

Sam's cell phone rang as he waited. It was Dwight.

"One-eye called," Dwight said, sounding nervous. "He said he'll come in to talk, but no cops. I said you're not a cop—right?"

"That's right," Sam said. "Right now, I'm a private eye. We're on our way over."

"We?"

"I'm bringing Caroline Rockingham," Sam said.

"Shane's wife?"

"Yep."

"What's going on there?"

"She's my caddie now."

"Anything else?"

"Not yet. But she's not a cop, either."

He was relieved when he spotted Caroline walking from the players' parking lot to the clubhouse. Her dark shoulder-length hair shone in the parking lot lighting. She wore a pair of black walking shorts and a pink long-sleeved shirt bunched up at the elbows. Her clubhouse badge hung from a belt-loop.

"So what's for dinner?" she asked him.

"Hamburgers."

"Did somebody murder the chef?"

"We're going into town."

They returned to the courtesy car in the players' parking lot. Sam drove down Magnolia Lane and took a right onto Washington Road. He turned to look at Caroline, whose smooth, tanned face was illuminated by the passing streetlights in the twilight. She sat with her weight leaning slightly against the passenger side door, her left leg bent and pulled up onto the large, plush seat, as though she wanted a better angle from which to examine Sam. They hadn't had much time to get to know each other beyond the time spent together during that day's round.

"Are you going to tell me where we're going, and what this is about?" she asked.

"We're going to Dwight Wilson's restaurant," he said. "He's the caddie you replaced."

"And the food's good there?"

"I don't know. I'm doing some detective work for the National. Dwight arranged for me to meet a guy there who might know about the murders. In fact, he might be the guy."

"Aren't you a fun date."

"If you'd rather not go…"

"No, I don't mind. But why not let the cops handle it?"

"Porter wants to stay ahead of the cops."

"He's probably protecting someone."

"That occurred to me," he said.

"I don't get it," Caroline said. "Why would you stick your neck out for these people? One of them could be the killer."

"That's occurred to me, too."

"Who else cares whether women join their little club?"

"Most of America, apparently," Sam said. "It's in all the papers."

They rode in silence for a while, until Sam dialed up his April 1975 playlist on the iPod. The car's multi-speaker system enveloped them in Bob Dylan's "Tangled Up in Blue."

"You know, I hope they are forced to admit women," Caroline finally said with a slow shake of her head. "It would serve them right."

She pulled her other leg up underneath her and faced him as they drove into downtown Augusta.

Dwight's restaurant was on a wide commercial boulevard with diagonal parking in the center of the street. A group of middle-aged white guys—all in long pants and polo shirts, a few with women companions—were drinking glasses of wine and beer on the sidewalk outside an Italian restaurant with a maroon awning. Masters fans out on the town. Next door to the Italian place was Big D's Bar and Grill, with large plate-glass windows on either side of the open front door. There appeared to be an apartment above the restaurant.

Sam knew they looked as though they belonged at the restaurant next door when they walked into Big D's. The clientele was a mix of black and white faces, couples and groups, sitting in wooden booths eating thick hamburgers and baskets of French fries and drinking oversized mugs of beer. The place smelled deliciously greasy and salty, with the heavy aroma of sizzling onions coming from the grill behind the bar. Dwight was standing at the deep fryer next to the grill, emptying a fresh load of fries into a basket.

It was about 8 p.m., and the dinner crowd had not thinned out yet. Most of the spacious wooden booths were occupied, and all four of the pool tables at the far end of the long, high-ceilinged room were in use. B.B. King's "How Blue Can You Get" was playing on the jukebox in the corner.

Dwight stood behind the bar, watching as a girl of about 12 flipped patties on the grill. He spotted Sam and Caroline and called out to them.

"How ya doin'," Dwight said. "Sam, this is my daughter Cammie. She's a big help around here. Cammie, this is Mr. Skarda and Ms. Rockingham."

Cammie turned and offered a shy smile and a quick wave, then resumed her watch over the grill. She had meticulously braided cornrows and wore a white apron over a red crew-neck shirt and a pair of blue jeans. Sam and Caroline took seats at the bar.

"I thought I'd take Caroline out for a meal at the best restaurant in town," Sam said.

"Where's that at?" Cammie asked.

"He means here, baby girl," Dwight said, smiling at his daughter. "When you finish those burgers, go see if your grandma can come down and help for a while."

Dwight led Sam and Caroline to a booth. He smiled as he presented menus to them, but Sam could tell Dwight was on edge.

"Got time to sit down, Dwight?" Sam asked. Dwight nodded and eased himself into the booth on Sam's side, taking up what was left of the bench seat. He glanced at his watch, then at the door. Sam knew he was worried about One-eye showing up, and what might happen if he did.

"So what's good here?" Sam asked Dwight.

"Burgers, fries and beer," Dwight said. "We keep it simple."

Dwight's mother had come down the stairs and moved behind the cash register to handle the bills of the departing diners. She was a slightly overweight woman with a net over her short, gray Afro. She had a brisk manner and lively eyes, and looked perfectly at home in the role of part-owner, manager, cook, waitress, cashier, and cleanup crew of her son's bar and grill.

After two groups paid their bill and left the restaurant, she came over to the booth. Dwight introduced her as Helen—which

Sam already knew from looking at her Augusta National employment file.

"Can you join us?" Caroline asked.

"Sorry, but somebody's got to run the place," Helen said, giving Dwight a stage glare. She had a rag in her hand and almost reflexively wiped the tabletop in front of them. "But I'm pleased to meet you both. Dwight says you are a fine golfer, Sam, and a good man."

"I would have been clueless if Dwight hadn't helped me with the greens Monday," Sam said. "He's amazing."

"Who picked up your bag?" Helen Wilson asked.

Sam smiled and pointed his thumb at Caroline.

"Now, why do you want to be lugging around a man's golf bag?" Helen said to Caroline with an exaggerated frown. "It's bad enough all the things we have to do for them. Dwight here is a big, strong man. He's made for carrying stuff. You ain't."

"I'm sure she does just fine, Mama," Dwight said.

"And you—you should be ashamed of yourself," Helen said to Sam, enjoying her lecture. "Making a woman carry your bag. That's like Dwight doing a load of laundry."

Everyone at the table laughed.

"And I don't like you asking One-eye Morton to come here," she said, still looking at Sam. "He's been no good his whole life, and worse since he got fired at the club. He's better off in jail."

"Never mind now, Mama," Dwight said. "We're just going to be talking, is all. Can we get a couple of cheeseburger baskets, and two glasses of beer for these people?"

"I'll see if the kitchen's still open," she said with mock indifference, then turned to shoot them a sly smile as she left.

When the hamburgers arrived, Sam and Caroline both devoured the meal as though they hadn't eaten in days. They were finishing their fries when the door opened and a thin black man stepped hesitantly into the restaurant. His mouth was framed by a caterpillar moustache and a scraggly gray soul patch. His graying sideburns extended below his ears from under a light green bucket hat that bore the yellow Masters logo. He wore his frayed blue nylon jacket unzipped and held an open can of Budweiser in one hand and an unlit cigarette in the other.

"D?" the man said, looking around the room.

"Over here," Dwight said from the booth.

"Can I smoke this in here?" the man asked, walking toward them.

"Sure," Dwight said. "Ashtray's on the table there."

The man pulled out a plastic lighter and lit his cigarette, exhaling nervously, and waited for somebody to say something.

"Sam Skarda, Caroline Rockingham," Dwight said. "This is One-eye Morton."

Chapter Twenty-five

One-eye stood five feet from the booth. He took a swig of his beer and came no closer. Sam recognized the look of uncertainty on One-eye's face: He expected that this was some kind of set-up, but couldn't figure out exactly how it would go down, and he didn't want to risk missing out on free money. Sam didn't know whether to feel pleased or disappointed that One-eye had come in. If he had killed Ashby, Scanlon and Milligan, it was unlikely that he'd be here now. On the other hand, there was always the chance that he was greedy and overconfident as well as homicidal.

"Have a seat, Reggie," Sam said, choosing to call him by his given name.

"Might as well call me One-eye," he said. "Everybody does."

"Okay, One-eye, then."

Caroline slid deeper into the booth, glancing back and forth between Sam and One-eye. She did not seem alarmed by the idea of sitting next to a man who might have committed the nation's three most publicized murders.

"Before I say anything, I gotta see the money," One-eye said.

Sam expected as much. He pulled out his wallet and extracted two hundred-dollar bills. He put them on the table and slid them across to One-eye, who picked them up quickly, folded them in two, and stuck them into an inside pocket of his jacket. The private eye business was already getting expensive.

"I don't know nothin' about no killing," One-eye then said. "I was out of town."

"Where?" Sam asked.

"Down in Waycross, seeing my sister."

"You ain't got a sister, One-eye," Dwight said.

"Not one you know about," One-eye said defiantly. Dwight looked at Sam and shook his head. Sam looked back at One-eye, who was exhaling smoke away from Caroline. Quite the gentleman. Caroline took out her own pack and lit one up.

"Look, One-eye, I'm not the cops," Sam said. "You could be telling the truth that you didn't kill anybody. I don't think you'd be here if you did, but that's not my call. If I give your name to the Sheriff and the Georgia Bureau of Investigation, they'll find out soon enough where you were and if you have a sister. I don't have time for all that. I work for the National, and they don't want anybody else getting killed."

"I got no reason to help you or the National," One-eye said. "They never helped me none."

"Now, see, that's just the sort of talk that's going to make Mark Boyce suspicious," Sam said.

"Who's he?"

"A cop with the GBI. He's good. You don't want to get to know him."

"Why would I?"

"Because he needs a suspect," Sam said, as One-eye exhaled again, this time in his direction. Sam waved it away. "You got pissed off at the club and got fired. You know what that makes you?"

"It don't make me no killer."

"It makes you what we call a disgruntled ex-employee. If they can't find the killer right away, cops always start looking for disgruntled ex-employees. I know. I was a cop."

"That how you come up with my name?"

"Yep. So give me something for my two hundred bucks."

"Like what?"

"Like some reason to think you didn't do it."

One-eye stubbed out his cigarette and pulled another one from his pack. Caroline reached over with her lighter and lit it for him. He nodded at her, exhaled and took another sip from his can of beer.

"Sure, I'm pissed off at the National," One-eye finally said. "Wouldn't you be? When they took the Masters away from us, how was we gonna survive on the money we made caddying for club members? That's maybe a couple thousand bucks for eight months' work. And you can't work no other job if you caddie. You got to be there at 6 in the morning, and you might not get out till the afternoon. You might not get out at all, but you gotta be there."

"So why not do something else?" Sam asked.

"What the fuck am I trained for?" One-eye said. "All I did was carry golf clubs till I was 30 years old. It's okay for D here—he got the restaurant. I ain't got shit."

"Hey, man, I worked my ass off to get this place," Dwight said. "Nobody handed me anything. When we lost the Masters, I saved my money and bought this place."

"You own it clear?" Sam asked.

"Still making payments," Dwight said. "It's tough. But it beats passing bad checks to your friends."

He and One-eye locked eyes for a moment. Sam glanced at Caroline, who seemed fascinated by the conversation.

"Yeah, I been in some trouble," One-eye finally said. "Everybody knows that. But I'm trying to go clean. And I didn't kill nobody."

"Somebody did—somebody who knows the course, somebody who's leaving messages."

"What kind of messages?"

Sam looked intently at One-eye. Was he pretending not to know what had already been in the papers and on the news?

"The words THIS IS THE LAST MASTERS."

One-eye thought for a minute, puffing absently on his cigarette.

"Shit, that could be anybody. You went through all them names, and mine's the only one you come up with?"

"No, there were some others who were fired," Sam said. "But they were either too old, or dead."

"Lee Doggett ain't old or dead."

Sam tried to recall if he'd seen a Doggett in the files. If he had, nothing made it worth closer examination.

"Who's Lee Doggett?"

"Big D, you remember that dude?" One-eye asked Dwight.

"Let me see," Dwight said, rubbing his forehead. "Nah, can't say I do."

"He worked on the grounds crew," One-eye said. "I used to see him driving one of them big old mowers. They caught him printing up his own Masters tickets and sellin' 'em. Fired his ass."

Now Sam knew he hadn't seen that file. He'd have pulled it out and looked it over carefully if he'd seen that reason for dismissal.

"Do you know where he is?" Sam asked.

"I seen him just yesterday, or the day before. Over at the Food Lion, buyin' beer."

"Where's that?"

"Right across the street from the National."

"What's he look like?"

"White dude, goin' bald. Tall. You remember him now, D?"

"Oh, yeah…kinda thin?"

"Yeah."

"And you figure he's got a grudge against the club?" Sam asked.

"You ever get fired?" One-eye said.

"Once. Summer job as a janitor where I was in college. I overslept."

"Didn't that piss you off?"

"Not enough to go back and kill somebody," Sam said. "Besides, why would he care whether the National lets in women?"

No one spoke. Doggett was somebody Sam would have to look into, but the pieces didn't fit. If revenge was his motive, why pick out Ashby? Why kill Scanlon? And why spray "THIS IS THE LAST MASTERS" on the grass?

Sam wasn't ready to dismiss One-eye as a suspect, either. The story about his sister in Waycross sounded phony, and it wasn't surprising that he'd come to the restaurant ready to offer up somebody else's name. Somebody had to check out One-eye's alibi.

"I'll try to find Doggett," Sam said to One-eye. "But I need somebody who can vouch for you the last few days. Your sister, or somebody who's seen you since Sunday and knows where you've been."

"I ain't killed nobody," One-eye repeated sullenly.

"Where are you living now?"

"Noplace special," he said. "I ain't really got settled since the last time I got out of the joint."

"Where've you been sleeping the last few nights?"

"With Flat Head."

"Who's that?"

"One of the old caddies," Dwight said. "He's got a place a few blocks from here. He caddies at the Augusta Country Club now. I called Chipmunk, Chipmunk said to call Flat Head, and that's how I found One-eye."

"So Flat Head will say you've been at his place?" Sam asked.

"Sure. Cause I was."

"Not in Waycross?"

"That was before."

Sam asked One-eye to write down Flat Head's address and phone number. He'd leave it up to the police to pin down One-eye's whereabouts Sunday through Tuesday night—if they felt like it. At least One-eye knew he was being looked at, which might be enough to keep him at home nights for the rest of the week.

"Does Flat Head know Lee Doggett?" Sam asked One-eye.

"I don't know," One-eye said, as Dwight's mother arrived at the table with another round of beers.

"What about Lee Doggett?" Helen Wilson asked.

"Do you know him?" Sam asked her.

"I knew his mama," Helen said. "Poor woman. She died while that boy was in prison."

"How did you know her?" Sam asked.

Helen told him she and Laverne Doggett used to clean rooms and cabins at the National. She remembered when Laverne went away for a few months, and then came back with a new baby and a new husband. The husband was no good, Helen said. Died in a bar fight years ago. But the talk was that Joe Doggett wasn't the boy's real daddy.

"She didn't tell me that," Helen said. "But that boy never looked like Joe Doggett. Some folks thought his real daddy might have been a member at the National."

Chapter Twenty-six

Friday, April 11

Sam wasn't thinking about the second round of the tournament when he woke up Friday morning in the Crow's Nest. He was wondering if anyone had been killed while he slept. There were no sirens wailing out on Washington Road—a good sign right there.

He got up and turned on the TV. Nothing new in The Masters Murders, according to CNN. The body count remained at three. They were still running clips of Caroline's interview from Wednesday, and Sam wished they'd find some other tape to run. It worried him that Caroline was becoming such a visible advocate for change at the National. The killer was probably watching, too.

He thought about the employee files. Had he missed something the first time through?

He went downstairs to the dining room, poured some decaf into a Styrofoam cup, and walked down the driveway to Bill Woodley's office.

Woodley gave him the keys to the file room, where Sam carefully went back through the "D" files. Laverne Doggett's file was there. It said she'd died while on medical leave from the club. That squared with Helen Wilson's recollection.

There was no file for Lee Doggett.

Sam went back to Woodley's office and asked him if he knew who Lee Doggett was. By the blank look on Woodley's face, it was apparent that the name meant nothing to him. Sam asked who had access to the file room. Woodley said that any club official or member who needed to consult the records could do so. All he had to do was ask for the key, which Woodley kept with him. Sam asked who had used the key recently.

"Mr. Porter sends Ida to find things in there from time to time," Woodley said. "Jimmy Fowler and Mike Wickoff, our head professional, use the files. Any member of our board of governors can get in there if he needs to—Mr. Stanwick, Mr. Brisbane—Mr. Ashby…"

Sam went straight past Ida into Porter's office.

"Do you remember a Lee Doggett?" Sam asked the chairman, who was cleaning his eyeglasses at his desk. The TV was tuned to ESPN's "SportsCenter." Porter looked surprised to hear Doggett's name, and put his glasses back on.

"Lee Doggett," Porter said, leaning back in his chair. "Let me think…we had a couple of Doggetts working here some years ago. One was a housekeeper. The other—her son, I believe—was…"

"A greenskeeper?" Sam said.

"Yes, that's right. Now I remember. We caught him selling forged badges and we fired him."

That jibed with what One-eye had said.

"I believe the police said he was also dealing drugs," Porter said. "I haven't heard of him in years. I assume he's in prison."

"How long ago was this?"

"I don't remember exactly," Porter said. He thought for a moment. "At least five years ago."

"Why aren't his employment records in your files?" Sam said.

"I have no idea," Porter said. "They should be. We never throw those out."

"Did the police look at them after he was arrested?"

"I'm sure they did, but they wouldn't have taken them. It was a cut-and-dried case. He broke the law, we fired him, and he went to jail. We do have to fire employees now and then. Why are you interested in him?"

"I don't know yet," Sam said. "But I've heard he's out, and I'd like to talk to him."

Porter was quiet for a few moments. He looked at the TV screen, and saw they were showing highlights of Thursday's play. The sports channels, at least, were back to golf. The Masters was enormously powerful—almost a force of nature. It had a way of overcoming almost any obstacle. But he didn't want to find out how much more tragedy it could absorb.

The first-round scores were running in a crawl across the bottom of the screen, including Sam's 80.

"You're not going to make the cut," Porter said. It was a statement of fact, rather than a question, or an insult.

"Not likely," Sam said.

"But you will stay with us through the weekend?"

"Unless you want me to leave," Sam said. "It's your dime."

"We'll make it worth your while to stay," Porter said, turning to face Sam. "I want you to find this maniac, whoever he is, and stop him. I'll see if I can get you some more information about this Lee Doggett."

"Fair enough," Sam said.

Sam left Porter's office and returned to the Crow's Nest, wondering if Porter's willingness to help him find Doggett was a way to divert further attention from Stanwick.

◇◇◇

He started with the Augusta telephone book. No listing for Lee Doggett. All he had to go on was One-eye's account of seeing him at the Food Lion. That wasn't much, but it was a place to start. The Food Lion was just a short walk from the main gate. It would give him a chance to think.

He was moving against the inward surge of pedestrians as he exited the grounds. He crossed the street where a cop was directing traffic at Azalea Drive and headed toward the Food Lion, on the north side of Washington Road.

Sam stopped near a trio of young men holding "Badges Bought and Sold" cardboard signs, and pulled out his wallet to get the card Mark Boyce had given him. One of the young men asked if he wanted to buy a badge.

"Four thousand," the young man said. "It's a good deal for the last three days."

Sam waved him away and dialed the number on his cell phone. Boyce picked up on the first ring.

"Boyce."

"It's Sam Skarda. I've got two names for you. One's a former caddie named Reggie Morton."

He gave Boyce the address and phone number where One-eye was staying. He said the ex-caddie seemed like a stretch, but he did have a grudge against the club.

"I'm going to do some checking on the other guy," Sam said.

"What's the name?"

"Lee Doggett."

"Why do we like him?"

Sam told Boyce what he knew about Doggett. He asked Sam if he knew where Doggett was.

"He's not in the phone book," Sam said. "I'm going to the last place we know he was seen. Can you do an NCIC search on him? I'd like to know where he did his time, how long he was in, the last place he lived."

"Sure, we'll run him."

"How about you? You getting anything from the members?"

"I never met a nicer bunch of fellas in my life," Boyce said. "Wouldn't swat a fly. Devastated by all this violence, and the damage it's done to the tournament, and so forth. Why I'd want to talk to them is a total mystery to these fine gentlemen."

"And you believe them."

"Got no choice. So far, their alibis check out."

"Stanwick's, too?"

"Hell, yes. Seems old Lorraine hasn't left his side since he got to town."

"Well, that's her version," Sam said. He told Boyce about Peggy Francis, and where he could find her. He still wasn't sure he believed her. She was sleeping with somebody else's husband. No saint there.

"We'll check her out," Boyce said. "But I gotta tell ya, even the members who are young enough to kill someone don't seem like the type who'd mess up a nice pair of pants to do it."

Sam gave Boyce his cell-phone number and asked him to call when he got the dope on Doggett. Then he flipped the cell phone closed and headed toward the Food Lion.

"Thirty-five hundred," the young man with the badge called after him.

◇◇◇

"Ever hear of a guy named Lee Doggett?"

Sam was standing in a checkout lane at the Food Lion, talking to a cashier with wavy, unnaturally dark hair who was working her chewing gum hard. Behind him, a woman with a full load of groceries was unloading her cart onto the belt. She placed the dividing stick in front of her stack, even though Sam didn't have any groceries.

"Lee Doggett? No," the cashier said.

"White guy, tall, thin, comes in to buy beer?"

"Ummm...no," she said again, losing what little interest she had in their conversation.

"Thanks," Sam said, moving away from her register and looking at the four other cashiers in the store. Two of them were with customers, while the other two had empty lanes. With the traffic outside on Washington Road, Sam wasn't surprised that business was slow this afternoon. He walked over to the next cashier, a young black woman with her hair in dreads. Her badge read "My Name is SHAREESE, and I'm Here to Help!" She was just finishing with a customer.

"I need some help, Shareese," he said.

"That's why I'm here," she said, pointing at her badge with a bored expression on her face. She looked up at Sam as she handed a receipt to her customer.

"I'm looking for a man named Lee Doggett—white guy. Buys beer here."

"Don't know'm," she said, leaning back against her cash register and folding her arms. "You sure he comes in here?"

"That's what One-eye tells me," Sam said.

"You know One-eye?" the young woman said. "From where?"

"From the National," Sam said. "I'm playing golf over there. He caddied there."

"Not no more," the young woman said. "They fired his no-good ass."

"I know," Sam said. "But I'm looking for another guy who used to work over there—a guy named Doggett. One-eye says he saw him in here a while ago."

"Lotsa folks shop here," the young woman said. "I don't know half of 'em."

"Is there somebody here who does know a lot of the customers?"

"Lois," the young woman said. "Last lane. She's been here 20 years, at least. If she don't know him, he don't come here much."

"Thanks," Sam said.

Lois was a short, squat woman who wore a white headband to hold back her graying perm and used a heavy rouge brush on her cheeks. She smiled when Sam approached.

"Forget where you put your cart, hon?" she said.

"I'm not buying anything," Sam said. "I just wanted to ask you if you know a man named Lee Doggett."

Lois didn't hesitate.

"Sure, I know him," she said.

"Used to work at the National?"

"That's him," she said. Then her smile faded. "Y'all the police?"

"No," Sam said. "Why? Has he been in trouble?"

"A few years ago," Lois said. "He got sent away. I never did know exactly for what."

"How do you know him?"

"Just to see him, I guess," Lois said. "I knew his mama a little bit. But she died. I think it was while Lee was locked up. Poor woman."

"Do you know where I can find Lee?"

"Uh-uh," Lois said. "Wanna leave your name? If I see him, I can tell him y'all wanna talk to him."

"No, I need to find him as soon as possible," Sam said. "Do you know if he has any friends or family in town?"

Lois held her elbow in her palm and stroked her cheek with her index finger. A man with a nearly full cart had pulled up behind Sam. Lois motioned him to the open lane next to her.

"He had a wife, and a little boy...but I think they're divorced," Lois said.

"Are they still around?"

"No...let me think...she left town, I believe..."

"Do you know where she went?" Sam asked.

"I heard, but it's not coming to me now."

"Do you remember her name?" Sam asked.

"Now, hush, I'm trying to think," Lois said. "My first thought was Florida, but for some reason, I want to say Arizona, or New Mexico, someplace like that. Someplace with horses."

Sam gave her some more time, but she couldn't remember where Doggett's wife had gone. He picked up a discarded receipt from the conveyor belt and wrote his name and cell-phone number on it.

"If you remember her name, or where she went, give me a call—anytime," Sam said, handing his number to Lois. "Any hour of the day or night. It's important."

"Sam Skarda?" Lois said, looking at the back of the receipt. "The golfer?"

"You watch the tournament?" he said.

"A gal's got to know what's going on in her own town," she said, giggling. "How'd y'all play yesterday?"

"Like I won't be here tomorrow," Sam said.

"Well, just hang in there, and I'll watch for y'all today when I get home."

"Thanks," Sam said. "Keep trying to think of that name, okay?"

"Gotcha, hon."

Sam left the supermarket and headed back to the National on Washington Road, where the sidewalks were still clogged with vendors, gawkers, and people buying and selling badges. No one recognized Sam. He hadn't played well enough on Thursday to make any of the highlight packages. Just as well; he didn't have time for autographs.

He returned to the National at Gate 3A and walked through the portable metal-detector columns at the main spectator entrance. His player badge didn't grant him any special treatment, and Sam was pleased that the security was tight.

His cell phone rang as he was climbing up the stairs to the Crow's Nest.

"Skarda," he said.

"Boyce here," the GBI detective said. "I got your information on Doggett. He's had his problems."

"What kind?" Sam said.

"Eight years ago he was convicted of grand larceny, forgery and drug possession."

"What kind of drugs?"

"Cocaine. Cops found it when they searched his house for counterfeiting equipment. He was sent to the Georgia State Penitentiary at Reidsville. He just got out last week."

"He did eight years?"

"Yeah, seems kind of stiff to me, too. You'd have to look into the court records to find out why the judge varied from the sentencing guidelines, and I don't have those. But he's out now. Last known address was 2454 Crescent Street, Augusta."

"Where's that?"

"He's not there anymore. I had a couple of officers run over to talk to him. They say the place is vacant—has been since the last family moved out almost a year ago. Neighbors don't even remember a Lee Doggett living there."

"He was married," Sam said. He told Boyce about Lois at the Food Lion.

"We can find her name," Boyce said. "It would help if we knew where she went."

"I'm working on that," Sam said.

"Good luck. Call us."

◇◇◇

Caroline was still in bed when her phone rang at 10 a.m. She muted the sound on the TV, where ESPN was showing another clip of her interview with the reporters outside the clubhouse, and reached over to the nightstand to pick up her cell phone.

It was Sam.

"What, am I late already?" she said. "You don't tee off for almost four hours."

"You're not late," Sam said, sounding tired. "I've been trying to track down Lee Doggett."

"Any luck?"

He told her about the cashier trying to remember where Doggett's wife and kid had gone.

"She said Florida first, but then she thought it might be Arizona or New Mexico—someplace with horses."

"I think I have it," Caroline said. "Southwest Ranches, Florida."

"What's that?"

"A little town northwest of Miami. Shane played a mini-tour event near there a few years back."

"That could be it," Sam said. "I'll call Lois and see if that rings a bell with her."

Sam got the manager of the Food Lion, who told him Lois had gone home for the day. He asked for her home number, but the manager wouldn't give it to him, or her last name. He didn't know who Sam was; he wasn't going to give out that kind of information to a stranger over the phone. Sam said he understood and hung up.

He tried to remember the name of the first cashier he'd talked to. It was different, a name he couldn't remember seeing before. Sharleen, Sherice—Shareese? It was something like that. Yeah, Shareese—he was pretty certain that was it.

He called Caroline again.

"Now what?" she said. "I'm trying to pick out something racy to wear under my jumpsuit."

"This will only take a second," Sam said. "I want you to dial a number for me and ask for Shareese. When they put her on the phone, tell her you need to know Lois' last name so you can look her up in the phone book. Tell her you were going over your receipt when you got back from the store, and you realized she undercharged you by $15. You want to let Lois know her drawer is short, so she won't get in trouble."

"Why don't you do it?" Caroline asked.

"Because I already talked to the manager. He wouldn't give me her name or number. But I think Shareese would give it to you."

"Okay."

Sam gave her the number and asked her to call him back as soon as she could. Less than five minutes later, his phone rang.

"Another satisfied Food Lion shopper," Caroline said. "Got something to write with? Shareese gave me Lois' home number. Says she calls her all the time to swap shifts."

Sam wrote down the number, thanked Caroline, and dialed Lois' number.

"Hi, Lois, this is Sam Skarda," he said when she answered. "We met earlier today at the grocery store."

"Oh, sure," she said. "Say, y'all don't want to miss your tee time."

"I've got a few hours yet," Sam said. "Lois, remember what we were talking about? The town Lee Doggett's wife moved to? Could it have been Southwest Ranches, Florida?"

"That's it!" she said. "Southwest Ranches. I knew I'd think of it."

"You still don't remember her name?"

"Let me think, let me think...It might have started with a B... or was it an R...I'm trying to get a picture of it in my mind."

Sam waited a few moments, until it seemed likely that the picture wasn't going to form.

"But you're sure it was Southwest Ranches?"

"Positive," she said. "No doubt in my mind."

"You're a peach, Lois," Sam said.

"That's what they say to all the gals around here," she giggled. "Now, concentrate on your game, hon, and forget about Lee Doggett for a while."

"I'd like to," Sam said. "Thanks again."

Sam sat in the plaid easy chair in the common area of the Crow's Nest, feeling a shot of the old adrenaline rush he always got when a case took a sudden lurch forward. If they could find Doggett's wife, maybe she could lead them to him.

He called Boyce and gave him the name of the town she had moved to. Then he went to the bag room to meet Caroline.

Chapter Twenty-seven

Ty Chapman was in trouble.

The Senior Vice President of Franchise Operations for the RoadFood convenience-store chain, Chapman was supposed to be inside the gates at Augusta National, enjoying the second round of the Masters. Instead, he was on the sidewalk along Washington Road, looking furtively for someone who might want to buy his Masters badge.

Ty Chapman liked to gamble. Lately, his luck had turned sour. He'd somehow managed to run up a $10,000 debt to several bookmakers back home in Kansas City. He'd put them off as long as he could, but they were threatening to hurt him—and, worse, to tell his wife. Roxanne was going to find out any day. He owed $5,000 to Max, his usual guy, and a couple thousand to two others who took his action when Max cut him off. He'd promised Max he would come back from Augusta with all of it. The other guys could be stalled a little longer with $500 each. Max had called Ty at his Augusta hotel Thursday night and said his deadline was Sunday. The full $5,000, or a couple of Max's associates would be coming over to Ty's house.

Ty's credit cards were tapped out; he'd already borrowed against their house. Things were shaky between him and Roxanne. She had been on him constantly since he was passed over for President of Franchise Operations. Their car was three years old, their house was in the wrong neighborhood, and their kids were going to a public school that Roxanne was embarrassed to mention around the other RoadFood wives. Maybe that's why Ty had found himself spending more and more time at the riverboat casino—time that he told Roxanne he was spending at the office, catching up on work.

Each year since he was named Senior Vice President, Coca-Cola had given Ty a badge to the Masters by Coca Cola—a reward for RoadFood choosing Coke over Pepsi. That was Ty's call—and unless Pepsi came up with tickets to the Super Bowl, the World Series, and the Indy 500, RoadFood was going to continue to pour Coke.

His first couple of years at the Masters, Ty had found it amusing that people would actually sell their badges. Who would pass up a chance to witness the greatest golf tournament in the world? What kind of sad, desperate idiot would trade an experience like that for a few thousand bucks?

Now Ty knew. A sad, desperate idiot like him.

He'd heard that scalpers were getting as much as $5,000 for their badges this year. That wouldn't wipe out his gambling debts, but it would take the heat off. Roxanne wouldn't have to know. He could stay above water. He could keep his life together.

Only one problem: The badge had to be returned to the Coca-Cola hospitality rep when the tournament was over. Coke received a few dozen badges every year, which they offered to favored clients. The badges were renewable, but handed out at Coke's discretion. They wanted them back, so they could hand them out to whoever they chose next year.

Ty had a plan. After selling the badge, he would call his Coke rep in a panic, telling him it had been in his luggage, and the airline had lost his suitcase. He would say he was just sick about losing the badge, but there was nothing he could do. He was going home, without seeing the tournament this year. Would the Coke rep believe him? Doubtful. There would be no badge next year, of course, but at least no one could prove he'd sold it. He'd be out of the woods.

He knew that badges were bought and sold on Washington Road every day of the Masters Scalping was legal in Georgia.

He just had to be careful not to do it in the street—they'd arrest you for blocking traffic. And there were undercover cops on the street looking for counterfeit badges.

Maybe he'd been too cautious on Thursday, or maybe his asking price had been too high. When he hadn't sold the badge by 2 p.m., he decided to use it himself for the rest of the day and to hit the streets again Friday morning. Maybe, by then, the supply of badges would drop and the prices would rise. But after Max called his hotel, Ty knew he had to sell the badge today.

After a couple of hours with no bites, Ty was beginning to feel desperate. He was about to approach a pair of prospects—a couple wearing matching green golf sweaters, each with a hand on a "Need 2" sign, and a short guy in shin-length cargo pants and a red, short-sleeved collared shirt holding a sign that said "$ for MB"—when he felt a hand touch him lightly on the shoulder.

"Got a badge to sell?" said a tall, balding man with a Southern accent.

Ty looked him up and down. He was bare-headed, with deep-set eyes and sunken cheeks. He looked as though he didn't eat very well. Probably not a cop; probably not a golf fan, either, judging by the man's attire. He wore black sneakers, black pants, and a gray T-shirt.

"Are you a cop?" Ty said, staring him in the eyes.

"Do I look like a cop?" Lee Doggett asked, with no humor in his voice. "What're you asking for the badge?"

"First, you gotta tell me you're not a cop."

"I'm not a cop."

"Five thousand," Ty said, expecting the guy to walk away. It was a huge amount, and this guy didn't look like he had it. But Ty had to get his price; he knew, eventually, somebody would want the badge badly enough.

"Sounds fair," Doggett said. "A guy down the street was asking six."

Six thousand, Ty thought. If I could get six...

"But he's been there for a couple hours," Doggett added. "He's not going to get six if he stands there all day. I'll give you five, cash, straight up."

Ty was momentarily tempted to tell the guy he wanted to see what other offers he might get. But this was a bird in hand. He couldn't afford to let this guy get away.

"Deal," Ty said. "Where...uh, how do you want to do this?"

"I don't have the cash here," Doggett said with a harsh laugh. "The National has private dicks on the street, looking for badge sellers. We'll need to go to my place. I'll take you there in my truck, and get you back here in 20 minutes—or anyplace else you want to go."

Doggett said his truck was parked on a side street several blocks north of the course. The noise from the traffic and the hospitality houses on Washington Road began to recede as they walked downhill toward the river on the curbless street with no sidewalks, past small brick homes with neat lawns and occasional boulevard trees. There was no conversation between the two men, and the silence of the quiet neighborhood was making Ty feel anxious. He began to sweat, perhaps more from nervousness than from the heat. He'd never done anything like this—but facing Max's friends and Roxanne's wrath scared him more than selling a hot Masters badge to a stranger.

The light blue Chevy pickup was squeezed into a spot that overhung the entrance to a driveway, a parking ticket stuck on the windshield. Doggett pulled the ticket from under the wiper and tore it up, dropping the pieces in the street. Maybe he's not from around here, Ty thought.

They got into the truck, and Doggett started it with a noisy rumble. He let it idle as he turned to Ty and said, "I need to see the badge first."

Ty reached into his back pocket and pulled out the green laminated badge with "Masters" written diagonally across the front in green letters on a blue holographic background. The dates of the tournament were written in smaller black letters under the diagonal blue strip, the Augusta National logo was in the upper left corner, and a serial number was printed against a white background in the lower right corner. Each year the badge design changed a little, but they were always instantly identifiable.

"Good," Doggett grunted, handing the badge back to Ty. He put the truck in gear and pulled out into the street, heading north.

"How far is it?" Ty asked.

"Just a mile or so," Doggett said. "I've got a place by the river."

"Nice."

They were on Eisenhower Drive, a mostly residential street that passed several cul-de-sacs as it extended northward away from Augusta National. They crossed another neighborhood street and a set of railroad tracks, and came to a complex of deserted baseball fields next to a sign that said "City of Augusta Eisenhower Park." A divided highway was visible in the distance, buffered by a tightly bunched row of conical fir trees. Beyond the highway was the Savannah River.

Doggett turned right once he entered the park and drove down a narrow, cracked, asphalt road past an abandoned baseball backstop that stood in the middle of an overgrown field. He continued forward on a dirt road that paralleled the railroad tracks and led under a highway overpass. There were a couple of houses on the other side of the tracks, set back and secluded by trees.

Doggett stopped the truck under the highway overpass and put the engine in neutral, setting the parking brake.

"I don't see anything here," Ty said loudly, over the rumble of the truck's engine and the traffic noise above them. He looked around for a house or an apartment building, then looked back at Doggett, who had taken a gym bag out from under his seat and was unzipping it.

"What's going on?" Ty said, his heart suddenly pounding.

Doggett pulled a hunting knife out of the gym bag and slid over next to Ty, holding his collar with his right hand and putting the knife to his throat.

"Get out," he said evenly.

"Oh, no," Ty said, whimpering. "Don't do this. Please…"

"Get out," Doggett repeated, more forcefully.

Ty fumbled for the door handle, trying to decide if he should make a run for it. What had he and Roxanne learned in that self-defense class? Run from a gun…? No, that wasn't right. Run from a knife, attack a gun…that was it. If you stay close to him, he can stab you. But he couldn't run. He could barely walk—in fact, he felt like he was going to shit his pants. Maybe the tall man wasn't going to kill him. Maybe he was just going to take his badge and leave him there.

Ty got out of the truck and pulled the badge from his back pocket.

"Look, take the badge," Ty said, his voice quavering. "It's yours. No questions asked. Just don't kill me. I have a wife and kids."

He started to cry.

Doggett had gotten out of the truck on his side and had the knife trained on Ty as he walked around the front bumper. He motioned with the knife for Ty to start walking forward beside the railroad tracks.

"Up that way," Doggett said. "Now."

"Wait, wait," Ty wailed. "Take the badge. You don't want to kill me. Christ, that's murder! To get into a golf tournament? Don't be insane!"

"Shut up," Doggett said. His eyes were cold, businesslike. "I'm not going to kill you. Now get going."

Ty wanted to believe the man. He walked forward, around a bend in the railroad tracks toward a trestle that crossed a canal. He held the badge in his right hand, his arms held out at his waist with his hands up. He kept babbling to Doggett as he shuffled along in the red clay beside the tracks.

"I mean, murder's crazy. They'll find you—you'll get the death penalty. If you just take the badge, you'll never see me again. I'll never tell. Never. It's not mine, anyway. They can't trace it back to me. It's not worth killing someone."

They'd reached the edge of the canal, where a footbridge led to a water-treatment plant on the other side. Doggett looked around. They couldn't be seen from the highway. There were no houses in sight, and no one on the other side of the canal. The rushing Savannah River was visible on the other side of the treatment plant. This would do.

"Come on, just take it," Ty said, extending the hand that held the badge toward Doggett.

"Okay," Doggett said.

He stepped forward quickly and ran the blade of the hunting knife across Ty's throat. Ty's knees buckled and his body collapsed into a sitting position as he grabbed at the blood that spurted out of his neck. He then fell over backward into the weeds at the edge of the canal bank, and in a moment lay still, his shirt soaked with his blood. The badge had dropped from his hand. Doggett picked up the badge, put it in his pocket, and set the knife down. He went through the dead man's pockets and found his wallet, which contained $73 in cash. He took the money, but left the credit cards. He wiped the knife on Ty's pants, then grabbed Ty's legs, dragged the body a few feet closer to the canal and pushed it down the bank. It tumbled easily into the water and began to drift with the current, leaving a muddy blood slick in its wake. Then Doggett picked up the knife and walked back to the truck.

Lee Doggett now had free access to Augusta National for the rest of the week—or until the tournament ended.

Chapter Twenty-eight

Lee Doggett drove the truck through Gate 4, parked in the large public lot, and entered the course through the main spectator gates. He showed his badge and walked undisturbed through the portable metal-detector columns. Now he needed to know where Skarda was—and where that pretty caddie of his was.

Recognizing Caroline Rockingham wouldn't be hard—he'd seen her half a dozen times on television in the past day. The news channels had turned her into the symbol of liberation at Augusta National. Even Rachel Drucker didn't get as much airtime now. No one would doubt that the membership at the club would love to shut her up.

Her murder would be an outrage that could stop the tournament in its tracks.

He picked up a pairing sheet from a green wooden box with a roof like a birdhouse. The schedule said that Sam Skarda had teed off at 1:17. He wouldn't finish his round for several hours.

Doggett had never paid much attention to the Masters when he worked at the National. It was just a week of 18-hour days to him—more money, but a real pain in the ass. He did know that amateurs usually stayed in the clubhouse during Masters Week. They were in a room called the Crow's Nest. Skarda was probably staying there with the other amateurs. Doggett looked down the pairing sheet for the players with the "–a" designation after their names. Tom Wheeling was one; Brady Compton was another. If he could find one of them, they might know where Skarda was. Compton was still on the course, according to the pairings; he'd also gone off late. Wheeling had played in the morning, and should have finished.

He didn't see a caddie with WHEELING on the back of his jumpsuit in the crowded area around the 9th and 18th greens. He walked over to the rope by the bag room and called to one of the employees standing in the breezeway.

"Has Tom Wheeling put his clubs away?"

"Wheeling's still on the range," the man said. He looked at Doggett as though he knew him, but Doggett turned and walked away.

He walked across the driveway to the practice range. The grandstand had begun to empty out, now that all the players were either on the course or through with their rounds. A few players would be working on their game until the range closed down. Some guys never gave up trying to be perfect, and Wheeling was apparently one of them. He'll know where Skarda will be tonight, Doggett thought. I'll just have to wait until he's finished.

There were three players on the range: Wheeling and two pros Doggett had never heard of. Doggett took a seat in the first row of the grandstand and watched with no interest as the three players hit shot after shot down the range. Golf bored him to shit. He could fall asleep watching these pansies if he didn't have to keep an eye on Wheeling. And yet Doggett couldn't help but feel a tingle of anticipation as he waited for Wheeling to finish. The plan he had come up with was working perfectly. He had Stanwick, the National, the cops, the town—hell, the entire country—trying to guess what he'd do next. They'd never figure it out. They couldn't stop him. They were playing his game, by his rules—and he was on the verge of winning. For that, he could force himself to watch a guy hitting golf balls.

The sun was nearing the tops of the magnolias to the west of the range when Wheeling finally called it quits—the last one left. He handed his pitching wedge to Bluejay, his Augusta National caddie; Bluejay was not happy that he'd drawn a player who couldn't accept prize money, and yet practiced more than Vijay Singh. He cleaned the wedge with a towel, put it into the bag, and started walking down the path toward the clubhouse with Wheeling. Doggett got up from his seat in the grandstand and caught up with them at the roped-off path to the locker room. He put on a pair of sunglasses and the bucket hat he had folded up in his pocket. He didn't want Wheeling to be able to describe him, if it came to that.

"Hey, Mr. Wheeling," he said. Wheeling turned around to face him.

"Yeah?"

"I like the way you hit the ball," Doggett said.

"I don't," Wheeling said, with an expression on his face that said he'd like to toss his clubs under a car.

"Can I have your autograph?"

"Why would you want it?" Wheeling asked. "I shot 78 today. I missed the cut."

"It's for my kid," Doggett said.

"Well…sure," Wheeling said. "Bluejay, you can take the clubs back to the bag room. I'll settle up with you there."

"Anything you say," said the weary caddie, who'd been at the club since 7 a.m.

"Make it out to, uh…to Laverne," Doggett said, handing Wheeling the pairing sheet and a pen as Bluejay walked away.

"Your daughter?"

"Yeah. She loves golf. L-A-V-E-R-N-E. How about that Skarda fella? Is he around?"

"He's still on the course."

"You guys hang out together? I mean, the amateurs? You, like, eat together and all that?"

"Not tonight," Wheeling said, handing the pairing sheet back to Doggett. "I'm leaving tonight. Time to go home."

"What about Skarda?"

"I think he's staying through Sunday."

"I'd like to get the guy's autograph."

"He'll be around. Look, I have to go pay my caddie. See you later."

Doggett checked his watch. It was four hours since Skarda had teed off. He should be finishing soon. Doggett walked around the clubhouse to the 18th green to wait.

The biggest names had finished their rounds, and the crowds were beginning to thin out. Doggett had found a place along the roped-off path from the 18th green to the scorer's hut when Sam and Caroline came off the course, following Naples and their caddies. He glanced at the sign held aloft by a man walking behind them: Skarda was 9 over par for the tournament. That wouldn't make the cut; even Doggett knew that. But Skarda seemed happy, and so did his caddie, whom Doggett immediately recognized from the news.

"Nice round, Sam!" some fans shouted as the golfer walked past them.

"Thanks," he said, reaching out to slap a couple of extended palms.

"Seventy-three is a good score here anytime," Naples turned to say to Sam, patting him on the back.

"I'll take it," Sam said.

Sam stopped outside the scorer's hut and told Caroline he'd meet her back at the clubhouse for dinner. He'd make a reservation for a table on the porch. She could take his car.

Doggett heard every word, and saw her give him a pat on the shoulder, then run her hand affectionately down his arm. So they could be more than just player and caddie. He might have to deal with Skarda, too.

Caroline and the other caddie walked past the hut and down the hill to the bag room. A few reporters called to her by name as she walked past the oak tree at the corner of the clubhouse, but she never turned her head. Doggett drifted along behind her after she dropped Sam's clubs with the bag-room attendant and continued on to the caddie building. About 10 minutes later she emerged wearing shorts and polo shirt, with a travel bag in her hand. She walked past the tournament headquarters building and up the service road to the players' parking lot. Doggett waited behind the ropes in the clubhouse driveway until he saw Caroline come back down the road in a white Cadillac STS. She followed the driveway up to the clubhouse and Magnolia Lane. As she drove past, Doggett wrote down the car's license number: BGH398.

Doggett had what he needed. Time to leave. The gates closed 30 minutes after the last group finished, and Doggett didn't want to get hassled by the Securitas guards, along with the other stragglers who'd had too much beer and didn't know when to call it a day.

He had plenty of time to drive his truck around to Washington Road, opposite the main gates—and wait for Caroline Rockingham to return.

◇◇◇

Caroline could have showered and changed into some decent evening clothes at the caddie building, but there wasn't a specific women's shower in the building, and she didn't feel like changing in the bathroom while the other caddies lounged around the common room drinking beer, playing cards, and gossiping about the pros. At this time of night, it wouldn't take her that long to get back to the hotel, shower, change clothes, and meet Sam back at the clubhouse.

She never noticed the man who wrote down her license number as she drove the courtesy car out of the players' parking lot and up the driveway to Magnolia Lane, nor did she notice the same man parked at the hospitality house directly across Washington Road from the National's main gate when she returned an hour and a half later.

"You look great," Sam said, when they met in the main lobby of the clubhouse. Her dark hair was pulled back in a French twist, and she wore a pair of turquoise and silver earrings, nicely complementing her simple white skirt and black sleeveless sweater.

"At least the shower in my room works," she said.

They walked up the winding stairway to the Library—the preferred dining room among Augusta National members and guests. The room featured wooden shelves lined with valuable old golf books, glass cabinets filled with mementos from the lives of Bobby Jones, Clifford Roberts and Dwight Eisenhower, and plaques commemorating members' accomplishments on the course. A waiter led them outside to a table on the porch overlooking the course. As they walked through the small dining area, several of the green-coated members, some dining with their wives, looked up and watched Caroline, almost as though they knew her.

The table on the porch was perfect, with a view through the branches of the old oak tree to the 18th fairway, where a row of seven triplex mowers, headlights gleaming ahead of them, was cutting the grass in a diagonal formation. They'd be done soon, leaving a breathtaking view of the empty golf paradise bathed in moonlight.

They'd just opened their menus when Robert Brisbane came onto the porch and walked over to their table.

"Hello, Sam," he said, extending his hand.

"Hello, Robert," Sam said, standing up.

"Hello, Caroline," Brisbane said, shaking her hand. "Have you heard anything from Shane since yesterday?"

"No. He didn't call last night. Maybe he's gone back to Tucson to trash our house."

"I'm sorry we had to disqualify him."

"Well, he's a big boy. He'll get over it."

"Mind if I sit down for a minute?" Brisbane said.

"Please do," Caroline said.

Brisbane had a neatly groomed yet weathered look; he appeared to spend just enough time in the sun to avoid the boardroom pallor of many of the Augusta members, but not enough time to come off as a member of the idle rich.

"Nice round today," Brisbane said.

"Thanks."

"Any progress on finding our intruder?"

"To be honest, I don't know," Sam said. "I'm going in a couple of directions. I'll know more tomorrow."

"David tells me the police have finished questioning all our employees, and all the members who are here this week," Brisbane said, sliding a butter knife back and forth on the white tablecloth. "They don't have anything yet."

"Where's Ralph Stanwick tonight?" Sam said.

"He told me he had a talk with Peggy Francis—and with David. He'll be staying home tonight with Lorraine."

"Isn't that what he always says?"

"If it will make you feel better, I'll drop by the Firestone Cabin after dinner. Ralph and I need to talk, anyway."

"I think that's a good idea," Sam said. "Whoever the killer is, I don't think he's finished."

"That's what I wanted to talk to you about," Brisbane said. "I've been watching Caroline on TV all day."

"The interview yesterday?"

"Yes," Brisbane said. "I saw it on NBC, CNN, Fox, and the Golf Channel. I'm sure all the networks played it at some point."

"Sorry," Caroline said, pulling a pack of cigarettes and a lighter out of her purse. "I didn't know every reporter in town was going to jump me. I was just talking to that guy from the *L.A. Times*, Russ Daly. Then they all surrounded me."

"They tend to do that," Brisbane said.

"But I'm not backing off what I said," Caroline said, after lighting and exhaling. "You ought to admit a woman member."

"Many of us agree with you."

"You might have put a target on your back," Sam said to Caroline. "Another critic of the club."

"That's what worried me when I saw your interview," Brisbane said. "But let's not panic. I just wanted to make sure you were taking precautions. We can't have another death. Especially not someone as important to us as Caroline."

She smiled gratefully at Brisbane, but felt a cold chill run through her. It hadn't occurred to her until now that the killer could be watching her.

"Where are you staying?" Brisbane asked her.

"At the Southwinds Inn, a few miles from here," she said.

"I'll drive you over there tonight," Sam said. "And I'm staying with you."

"You don't need to do that," Caroline said.

"I think it's a good idea," Brisbane said.

"I really don't need a babysitter," she said. "You can drive me back to the room. I'll be fine from there."

Sam decided not to press the issue now. Once he got to her hotel, he'd look the place over to see how safe it was. If he wasn't satisfied, he'd sleep in the hall outside her door, if he had to.

Chapter Twenty-nine

No one came out from the party at the hospitality house to tell Doggett he couldn't park his truck there. He was able to sit and watch each car that exited from Magnolia Lane onto Washington Road.

He turned the key in the ignition when he saw a white Cadillac exit the grounds, but the driver didn't look like either Caroline or Skarda. He managed to catch a look at the license plate, but it wasn't the one he was looking for. A few minutes later, another white Cadillac exited the club, and then another. Shit—they gave all the pros identical courtesy cars. He'd need to be very careful about reading each license plate, or he'd miss her.

A little after nine, one of the courtesy cars emerged from the driveway and turned left onto Washington Road. A man was driving, with a woman in the passenger seat. He couldn't tell if it was Skarda and his caddie through the tinted window, but the license plate was the one he was looking for: BGH398. It must be them.

Doggett put his truck into gear and pulled out onto Washington Road, staying just close enough to the Cadillac to keep it in sight. He assumed they were going to Caroline Rockingham's motel. Maybe Skarda would stay with her tonight, which would cause problems—though it was nothing he couldn't handle. He could kill two of them almost as easily as one. It made no difference to him, except that it would mess up the story line. If the public believed someone from the club was killing its political enemies, they'd buy Caroline's killing, too. But Skarda? Doggett couldn't recall hearing Skarda say anything about admitting women to the club. Killing the club's critics was one thing, but would anyone believe a club member would murder a player?

Then again, Skarda was the one who'd brought her to the club, who'd let her shoot her mouth off about women members. Someone at the club might be pissed off at him. Or maybe the spin would be even simpler: Skarda died trying to save his caddie—his lover. Yes, that could work. Either way, killing them both might be the end of it. They'd almost have to call off the tournament. Augusta National's reputation would never recover. Then he could kill dear old Dad.

Now that he'd found Caroline, he had to develop a strategy. He had to find out what room she was in. He had to slip past the front desk and somehow get inside her room—preferably after Skarda had left. Then it would be a simple matter of over-powering her and cutting her throat.

The Cadillac was holding steady at 40 miles an hour on Washington, heading west. Doggett found it easy to stay a half block behind them. If they made a turn, he'd have no problem exiting with them. He turned on the radio, wondering whether he was still the lead story.

"…Richmond County police and state investigators are thought to be focusing their investigation on someone with con-nections to Augusta National, though they would not say if there was a suspect. Mark Boyce of the Georgia Bureau of Investigation told reporters late this afternoon that all evidence points to one killer, with a political motivation. Each victim has been an open advocate for a change in the club's membership policies…"

◇◇◇

"Did you hear that?" Caroline asked Sam, who had turned on the radio when they got into the car.

She now wished she had kept walking, instead of stopping to talk to Daly and the other reporters. But she was being paranoid, she told herself as she lowered the passenger side window and lit another cigarette. Nothing was going to happen. No one knew where she was staying.

"Yeah, I heard it," Sam said, turning up the volume on the news station.

"It's creeping me out."

"You shouldn't have talked to those reporters."

"I know. I made a mistake. Let's drop it."

Sam wasn't in the mood for music, so he left the radio on. Rachel Drucker and the WOFF were calling for the cancellation of the tournament, out of respect for the deaths of Ashby, Scanlon, and Milligan. As many as 3,000 protesters were expected to gather on Washington Road Saturday to condemn Augusta National. Sergio Garcia and Phil Mickelson were leading at the halfway point, seven under par. Fair skies and highs in the low 80s forecast for Saturday.

It was all so incongruous. The ideal Masters combination— beautiful weather, great scenery, outstanding golf—was locked in a death struggle with some madman.

Knowing that Brisbane would be hanging out with the Stanwicks in their cabin eased his mind a little. But he couldn't shake the feeling that Caroline had replaced the name on the back of her caddie suit with a big red target. He was going to stay with her tonight, no matter what she said.

The Southwinds Inn parking lot was full when they arrived at about 9:30. Sam circled the lot, finally finding a parking space on the opposite side of the motel from Caroline's room.

There was a gentle breeze in the air as they walked across the parking lot. Sam noticed a truck with a loud engine pull into the lot as they neared the lobby doors. Good luck finding a spot, buddy, he thought. This motel is jammed. This whole town is jammed.

They walked past the front desk and took a left down a hallway with brownish-maroon patterned carpet—the kind intended to disguise the spills and stains made by drunken tourists and their messy children; the kind that always looked dingy, no matter how new the motel. They went up the stairs to the second floor, turned left, and walked almost halfway down the hall. Caroline's room was about 15 feet from the Coke and ice machines, which both gave off a persistent electric hum.

"Docs that noise bother you?" Sam asked, pointing to the machines.

"I can't hear it over my air conditioner," Caroline said. "Five hundred bucks a night doesn't get you much in this town."

She inserted her plastic key in the slot and opened the door to her room, and Sam immediately knew what she meant. The rattle of the air conditioner was instantly irritating.

◇◇◇

As soon as Doggett saw Skarda and Caroline walk into the motel, he parked the truck just beyond sight of the front desk, blocking in two other parked cars, and walked quickly into the lobby. He carried the hunting knife in his gym bag.

The lobby was empty except for the clerk at the front desk. Doggett ignored him and walked straight through to the first-floor hallway, looking each way. At the end of the hallway to the left, he saw Skarda and Caroline turning right and walking up the stairs.

He walked quickly down the hall and up the stairs, opening the fire door at the top of the stairs and peering around it. They were halfway down the hall, stopped in front of a room on the left, with a Coke machine and an ice machine across the hall from the room. As soon as they entered, Doggett hurried down the hall to check the door they'd entered: Room 245.

He wondered what Skarda was going to do. He hadn't brought a bag in with him, so it didn't look like he was planning to stay. He would watch the door for a while to see if Skarda left. There was no reason to kill him if he didn't have to. Besides, Skarda looked like he was in good shape. It would be easier just to do the girl.

Doggett kept walking past the door and went to the far end of the hall. There was another flight of stairs behind a fire door on that side of the motel. He could stand in the stairwell and keep an eye on Room 245 from a safe distance. In a half-hour or so, he'd have to decide what to do next. But he'd wait for a while and give Skarda time to leave.

◇◇◇

"I've asked them twice to come up and fix it," Caroline said. "They must have a lot of stuff to fix in this dump."

Sam bent down and turned the knob to "Off." The noise stopped. He turned it back up to "Low," then "Medium" and "High." The noise returned. He opened the grate and looked at the fan inside, but couldn't see what was causing the problem.

"I tried all that," Caroline said, lying back on the bed and sighing. "I've got two choices: Stay awake listening to it all night, or turn it off and stay awake sweating all night."

Sam closed the grate and stood up.

"There's a third choice," he said. "I'm going to the front desk and get somebody up here."

"Well, maybe they'll listen to you," she said. "I'm going to have a glass of wine."

She got up from the bed and opened the mini-refrigerator. Inside was a bottle of pinot grigio. She got a corkscrew out of her purse, opened the bottle, went into the bathroom, and came back with two glasses wrapped in plastic sanitary wrappers.

"You can have a glass when you come back," she said. "Then you should go."

"We'll talk abut that," Sam said.

He left the room, then glanced behind him to be sure he'd remember the number: 245.

Caroline's room was in the middle of the motel. Sam looked down the hallway in both directions, and decided to take the same stairs they'd come up.

A man and a woman were pleading for a room at the front desk when Sam got to the lobby. They'd driven all the way from Pennsylvania to see the Masters, the woman said. There must be something available.

"I'm sorry, folks," said the desk clerk, a chubby man who didn't look sorry at all. "We've been booked for months."

"Hell, I know how this works," said the man, pulling out his wallet. "What'll it take, $300?"

The desk clerk looked amused.

"Our guests are paying $500 per night this week," the clerk said.

"For this hole?" the man said, stunned. "Let's go, Linda. I'd rather sleep on a park bench."

"You might have to," the clerk said.

Then he turned to Sam.

"Can you imagine?" the clerk said. "Walking into an Augusta motel on Friday night of the Masters and offering $300 for a room?"

"What were they thinking?" Sam said.

"What can I do you for?" the clerk said, still smiling.

"My friend in Rroom 245 paid your ransom, and she'd like her air conditioner to work."

The clerk lost his look of amusement.

"She'll need to call down here and request a repair."

"She's done that twice since Monday. No repairs. Can you imagine?"

"Well, there's nothing we can do tonight."

"Why not?"

"Rafael, our repairman, works from 7 a.m. to 5 p.m."

"And what exactly does Rafael do when he's working?"

"We have a long list of projects for him each day."

"I'm not surprised," Sam said, looking around the charmless lobby. The clerk frowned. "Put the air conditioner in Room 245 at the top of Rafael's list tomorrow."

"Yes, sir," the clerk said.

Sam turned and headed back to the stairs. He could use that glass of wine.

◇◇◇

Doggett had been relieved to see Skarda leave Room 245—until Skarda looked down the hallway in Doggett's direction, as though he were going to take the stairs where he was hiding. Doggett ducked back to the stairs and quietly pulled the fire door closed behind him, then ran down the steps to the first floor. He listened at the bottom of the steps to hear if the fire door above him was being opened. It remained closed. Then he looked down the main floor hallway and saw Skarda turning the corner from the steps on the other end of the hall. He must be leaving, Doggett thought as he walked back up the stairs. Now it was time.

He hurried back up the steps, two at a time, and walked quickly down the hall to Room 245. He slung the bag over his shoulder, unzipped it, and put his hand inside, fingers curled around the knife's smooth wooden handle. Then he knocked twice on the door. He heard a voice inside say something, muffled, which sounded like "Coming."

"You should have taken the extra key," Caroline said, as she opened the door from inside the room. Doggett put his shoulder into the door and rammed it open, knocking Caroline backward onto the bed. He slammed the door shut behind him and pulled the knife out of the bag. Caroline screamed as Doggett advanced toward her.

"Shut up," he ordered, lunging for her. But Caroline rolled sideways off the bed, pulling the bedspread with her. When she hit the floor, she reached out and grabbed the wooden desk chair, throwing it in front of her as she scrambled backward on her hands, not daring to take her eyes off Doggett. She screamed again as Doggett stumbled over the bedspread and the chair, trying to slash her with the knife.

"Shut up, I said!" he yelled.

Caroline was up on her feet again; before he could reach her, she managed to dive into the bathroom. Doggett was right behind her, and thrust his right hand, holding the knife, into the bathroom as Caroline pushed the door shut. She braced her feet on the toilet and put her back to the door, pushing with her legs, with all the strength she had, to keep him from getting the door open.

"Open the fucking door!" Doggett screamed, while Caroline screamed back at him as loud as she could.

Then they both heard a pounding on the door, Sam yelling from the hallway.

"Caroline! Open the door! What's going on?"

"He's in here! He's got a knife!" Caroline screamed.

Doggett stopped pushing on the bathroom door. He'd meant to get in, kill Caroline quickly, and get out. He hadn't counted on Skarda coming back. Half the people in the motel had probably heard the ruckus by now. There was no way he was going to pull this off. He just had to get away, to think. It couldn't end here. He wasn't through yet.

Doggett dropped the knife, squeezed his arm back out, and the bathroom door banged shut, Caroline pushing on it as hard as she could from the other side. Doggett knew she wouldn't be coming out; he just had to get past Skarda.

As Sam pounded on the door, Doggett moved to the hinged side of the door, then reached across it and turned the handle. Sam saw the door begin to open and pushed it aside as he ran in. Caroline screamed "Sam, look out!" when she heard the door open, and Sam ran straight toward the sound of her voice, coming from the bathroom at the far end of the room. Then he heard a noise behind him and turned to see a figure running out of the room and down the hallway to the right.

"Caroline, are you hurt?" he yelled at the bathroom door.

"No! But he tried to stab me!"

"He's gone," Sam said. "It's safe now. I have to go after him."

"No!" Caroline yelled. "Don't!"

"I can't let him go," Sam said. "Call 911."

Sam ran out the door, turned right, and saw that the hallway was empty, though several people had cautiously stuck their heads out of their rooms to see what all the yelling was about. Sam ran down the hallway, down the stairs, and into the lobby.

"What the hell are you people doing?" the desk clerk demanded as Sam ran past him. Sam stopped on the sidewalk and looked down the parking lot to the entrance, where the light blue truck he'd seen earlier was squealing out into the street. Sam's car was at the other end of the lot; he would never catch him. Caroline needed him more now, so he went back inside.

"I'm askin' you again, buddy," the desk clerk said. "What the hell is going on up there?"

Sam walked over to the desk, attempting to calm himself and catch his breath.

"We need to change rooms," he said.

"That's impossible," the clerk said.

"I don't think so," Sam said. "My friend in 245 was nearly murdered by an intruder a couple of minutes ago. Now, we want the room you were going to sell to that couple from Pennsylvania."

"What room?" the clerk demanded.

"The room you would have found if they'd come up with $600."

"What? Why…" the clerk sputtered.

"The cops will be here in five minutes. You'll have to explain to them how you allowed a guy with a knife to trap my friend in her bathroom. In the meantime, we want the other room. Now."

The clerk had beads of perspiration forming on his upper lip and temples. He looked outside; there were sirens in the distance, getting closer.

"Two queens or a king?" he asked Sam.

"We'll take the two queens."

Chapter Thirty

Two uniformed Richmond County officers arrived a couple of minutes after Sam returned to Room 245. They surveyed the mess while Sam sat on the bed with his arm around Caroline. She was shaking, but the terror she had felt was beginning to subside.

"Was that the guy who…?" she said.

"I think so," Sam said. "Unless somebody else in Augusta hates you."

She laughed weakly, and reached across Sam to the night stand for a cigarette.

"I'm just glad you weren't…"

"Killed?" Caroline said.

"Yeah. That."

"My wrist hurts. And my back."

"Did you get a good look at this guy?" Sam asked. She was calm enough now to take her back through the attack, while it was still fresh in her mind.

"Yes," she said. "I'll never forget him."

"Describe him."

"Tall."

"How tall?"

"Six-two, maybe. White guy. Balding. Dark eyebrows. Thin."

"How old?" Sam asked her.

"God, I don't know. Thirty-five, forty maybe."

"Could he have been older?"

"I guess," she said. "He seemed kind of gaunt, you know?"

Sam thought about Stanwick immediately: 6-2, thin, balding, dark eyebrows. He got his cell phone out of his jacket and called the clubhouse. When the operator answered, he asked for the Firestone Cabin. After a couple of rings, Lorraine Stanwick answered.

"Sorry to bother you, Mrs. Stanwick," Sam said. "This is Sam Skarda. I need to talk to your husband."

"I wish you'd stop calling here," she said. Then he heard her put the phone down and call Ralph's name. In another few moments, the unmistakable voice of Ralph Stanwick was on the other end of the line.

"Yes?" he said irritably.

"It's Skarda. My friend Caroline was just attacked in her motel room on Jones Parkway."

Stanwick's impatient tone changed.

"Is she all right?"

"Yes, she's fine."

"Did she get a look at the guy?"

"A good look. From her description—I'll be honest. I called to see if you were with your wife tonight."

"Listen, Skarda, I don't know what you're getting at, but my wife will tell you I've been with her all night," Stanwick said, resuming his defiant tone.

"She tells that story a lot," Sam said. "Is Robert Brisbane there?"

"Yes."

"Put him on."

Brisbane assured Sam that Stanwick had been in the Firestone Cabin all evening.

"Is Caroline all right?" he asked.

"Yes."

"And you've called the police?"

"They're here now."

Sam thanked him and hung up. That theory seemed dead.

While one of the cops inspected the lock on the door, the other emerged from the bathroom.

"There's a hunting knife on the floor in the bathroom," he said. Then he noticed the open bottle of wine on the dresser. He looked around at the overturned chair and the bedspread on the floor.

"Having a little party in here, were we, folks?"

Sam stood up.

"I told you what happened," he said. "A guy barged into the room while I was in the lobby. He pulled that knife on Caroline. This is the same guy who's killing people at Augusta National. Call Detective Harwell."

"We'll decide who to call, and when," the other officer said, closing the door to the room. "No sign of forced entry. Just the two of you in here now. Maybe it's your knife"

"Call Harwell," Sam repeated. "This is the guy you're look-ing for."

"We're supposed to take your word for that?" one of the cops said.

"My name's Skarda. I'm playing in the Masters this week, but I'm a cop, too. I've been trying to help the National find their killer."

One of the officers started to laugh, but the other held up his hand toward his partner. He took a closer look at Sam.

"You're that cop from Minnesota?"

"Yes. I saw the guy pull out of the parking lot, headed east. I couldn't catch the plate number, but it looked like an older pickup, maybe a Ford or a Chevy, light blue, loud engine. No more than 10 minutes before you got here."

"What was he doing here?" the cop asked.

"Trying to kill Caroline," Sam said. "She was on TV, saying Augusta National should admit women members. He must have seen it."

"So what?" the cop said.

"Look, Harwell knows what's going on. He knows me. Get him here. Garver will have your ass if you don't."

Sam would have preferred to talk to Boyce, but he knew this would have to be handled through channels. At this point, a motel break-in and assault was a Richmond County case.

While one of the cops called headquarters, Sam told Caroline that they were moving to another room in the motel.

"I couldn't stay in this room tonight," she said as she packed.

"I know," Sam said.

"And I don't want to stay in this motel alone," she said, turning to look at him.

"I know," he said.

◇◇◇

Harwell showed up about 45 minutes later, looking irritated and perplexed. The fact that it was Skarda who'd asked for him didn't make him any happier. Skarda was supposed to be staying at the Augusta National clubhouse. What was he doing here? And how did he know this supposed attack had anything to do with the killings at the National?

Sam patiently explained it to Harwell as Caroline finished packing: Caroline's caddie status, the TV interview, the truck that must have followed them from the National after dinner, Sam's trip to the lobby to complain about the air conditioner, the knife attack, Sam chasing the attacker out to the parking lot, and the light blue pickup roaring out of the parking lot.

Caroline described her attacker to Harwell.

"What was he wearing?" Harwell asked.

"Dark blue windbreaker," Caroline said. "Black pants. Black shoes, I think."

While Caroline talked to Harwell, Sam thought about her description. Although it sounded like Stanwick, it would have been impossible for him to get back to the Firestone Cabin that quickly. Besides, Sam trusted Brisbane—or, at least, he wanted to. And it wasn't One-eye; Caroline had met him. The attacker was white.

It looked like he was down to his last suspect.

"Do you have access to booking photos tonight?" Sam asked Harwell.

"Sure," Harwell said. "You got somebody in mind?"

"Lee Doggett."

Harwell paused for a beat and then said, "What's he got to do with this?"

Sam recounted his meeting with One-eye and his attempts to find Doggett earlier in the day.

"Yeah, she could look at his photo downtown."

"How about bringing one here?" Sam said. "You don't want to drag Caroline down there tonight. She could use some rest."

"Well…all right," Harwell said.

Half an hour later, another cop was at the motel with a mug shot of Doggett from the file of booking photos at the Sheriff's office. Caroline recognized him immediately. So did Sam, though he'd never seen him before.

He was a younger version of Ralph Stanwick.

"That's him," Caroline said. "That's the son of a bitch who waved the knife in my face."

"Boyce sent some officers over to Doggett's last known address earlier today," Sam told Harwell. "Vacant."

"I know," Harwell said. "I didn't think much of him as a suspect."

"Why not?"

"Honestly? Because he was a name you gave us. We've got good cops on this case, Skarda."

"I know," Sam said. "I'm one of them."

"We've got patrols out looking for a light-colored pickup with a loud engine, but it's not much to go on," Harwell said, folding up his notebook and putting the mug shot of Doggett into the inside pocket of his suit coat. "If we find him tonight, we'll call you."

"We'll be in Room 127," Sam said.

◇◇◇

While Caroline was in the bathroom, Sam made sure the door to Room 127 was locked and the security chain was in place. Then he called Boyce and told him about the attack and Doggett's booking photo.

"Doggett looks like Stanwick, huh?" Boyce said sleepily. "Maybe we better go back and talk to Ralph again."

"I'd do that," Sam said before Boyce hung up.

Sam pulled down the bedspread on the queen-size bed closer to the door, stripped down to his boxers, and got into bed. When Caroline came out of the bathroom, she was wearing a white tank-top and a pair of running shorts.

"I'd rather sleep in the one away from the door," she said.

"That's why I left it for you."

"Think again," she said. "We're sharing a bed tonight."

Sam nodded and rolled out of the bed. Caroline turned down the bed near the bathroom and got in.

"There's still some wine left," Caroline said.

"I'll get some glasses," Sam said.

He found two plastic glasses, got the wine out of the mini-fridge, and got into bed with Caroline. He poured them each a full glass of pinot grigio, and set the rest of the wine on the center nightstand. They each took several sips before either one spoke.

"So," Caroline finally said. "Nice round today."

Sam laughed. He had forgotten about golf. Now he thought back to Caroline's calming presence on the bag, and the ease with which he'd produced his 73. He had Frank Sinatra's "New York, New York"—1986, Nicklaus' last win—going through his head all day, especially the line about how he could make it anywhere if he could make it there. He'd played as though his score didn't matter, and now he realized how true that was. Caroline had nearly been killed.

"He may be a murdering psycho, but I'm grateful to Lee Doggett," Sam said.

"For what?" Caroline said.

"For getting us in bed together," Sam said.

"Look, I didn't want to talk about this before, but maybe I should," Caroline said, holding her wine in her lap. "I don't know about us."

"What do you mean?"

"I mean, I see some things in you that I saw in Shane—good and bad. I think you need control, and I don't want to be controlled."

Sam was silent. He didn't know how to argue with her, or whether he should. She'd just been scared half to death, and she'd invited him into her bed, so she obviously didn't mind the safe feeling of having a cop around. Maybe not all the time, though.

"Did you ever read *The Spy Who Loved Me*?" Sam finally said. "The James Bond novel by Ian Fleming."

"No. I saw the movie, I think."

"Completely different story," Sam said. "In the book, this woman is being terrorized at a country motel by some really evil creeps, and James Bond happens along. Kills the creeps, sleeps with the woman, then one of the creeps turns out not to be dead, and Bond finishes him off. Then they have sex again."

"So you're James Bond, and we should have sex?"

"No," Sam said. "I'm just saying she was glad to have a guy like him around."

"I'm glad to have you around, too," Caroline said. "How did the book end?"

"She woke up the next morning and he was gone."

Sam turned to study her face, and saw that her green-blue eyes were watery. She'd been through a lot this week. Her nearly getting killed was his fault. If he hadn't asked her to caddie for him, Doggett would never have come after her.

She drained her wine and dropped the plastic cup on the floor. Then she put her arm over Sam's chest and buried her face into him. He finished his wine, turned off the light, and put both his arms around her, wishing that were all it would take to keep her safe.

Chapter Thirty-one

Ralph Stanwick hung up the phone after Sam's call and turned to his friend Robert Brisbane.

"Can you believe that?" Stanwick said. "That goddamn Skarda thinks I've had something to do with these killings."

Brisbane and Lorraine Stanwick were seated in the small living room in the Firestone Cabin. With its simple country-getaway furniture and bridge table, the room looked the way it had when the aging, infirm Bobby Jones used to visit friends there from his own cabin next door, sipping bourbon, smoking cigarettes, and playing bridge, until his final years when he couldn't hold his cards in his hand anymore.

The phone rang again, and as he had all week, Stanwick seemed to tense at the sound of the ringtone. He quickly got up and answered it.

"Yes?"

There was silence for a moment, then Stanwick said, "Repeat that."

More silence, as Stanwick wrote something down in his pocket organizer. Then he hung up the phone without saying another word.

"Wrong number," he said, returning to his chair.

Brisbane exchanged glances with Lorraine, then went to the kitchen and poured himself a bourbon and water.

"While you're in there, Robert, pour one for me," Stanwick called to him. "On the rocks."

When he returned, Stanwick was tapping his foot in the living room, glancing at his watch. He took the drink from Brisbane and swallowed half of it in one gulp.

"Ralph, is everything all right?" Lorraine finally asked her husband.

"How the hell could everything be all right?" he replied. "That killer is still out there. This tournament is becoming a disaster."

Stanwick finished his bourbon in two more swallows, then turned to his friend.

"You'd better finish that drink and go, Bob," Stanwick said. "I'm turning in early tonight."

Brisbane glanced again at Lorraine. The look in her eyes said, "Don't leave," but Brisbane knew that Ralph would insist.

"I defended you, Ralph," Brisbane said, taking a large swallow of his bourbon. "You know that, don't you?"

"Of course," Stanwick said. "Why wouldn't you?"

"It's just that…well, I'm glad you were here tonight."

After Brisbane departed, Stanwick turned to his wife and said, "I have to go out for a while. Don't wait up."

"You said you'd stay in tonight," Lorraine Stanwick said, a look of tired reproach in her eyes. She didn't expect to win this one, but she still felt compelled to make the effort.

"Things have come up," Stanwick said. He took off his green jacket, hung it in the closet, and put on a light zip-up jacket. He picked up his car keys from the kitchen counter and turned to look at his wife.

"It's not what you think," he said.

"Do you care what I think?" she replied.

"No. Not really."

She stared at him as he walked to the cabin's rear entrance. He paused before leaving, looking around, and then picked up the pitching wedge he kept by the door for chipping practice.

She listened as he started the Mercedes and drove up the service road to Magnolia Lane. Then the phone rang again.

◇◇◇

Lee Doggett knew he'd been made.

He should have covered his face, but he didn't expect to have trouble killing the caddie in her motel room. She'd been too quick for him to finish the job quickly—and then Skarda came back. That had ruined everything. Now the girl had seen him, and would describe him to the police. He assumed Skarda had seen the truck as he pulled out of the lot. Worst of all, he'd dropped the knife—and this time he hadn't worn the work gloves. His prints would be all over the handle. The cops would have him ID'd by morning.

He could still end the tournament—at this point, the cops couldn't do anything about that. But his chance to kill Stanwick was slipping away. There was only one way left: draw him out.

As soon as Doggett got back to his motel room, he picked up the phone and called the Firestone Cabin.

"Stanwick? It's your long-lost son," he'd said. "I'm giving you a chance to end this. Meet me in an hour at the Curtis Motel in Grovetown. Room 14...Curtis Motel, Grovetown, Room 14. Got that? I swear to God, if you don't come, there's going to be a shit storm at the National like you can't imagine. Come alone."

Doggett knew he didn't need to add that last part. If Stanwick hadn't found the courage to call the cops yet, he wasn't going to do it now.

◇◇◇

Forty-five minutes later, Stanwick drove slowly past Doggett's motel—a single-story, 20-unit building wedged between Wrightsboro Road and the railroad tracks. He parked the Mercedes a half-block down the street. It was almost midnight; no one was on the street or the sidewalk, and the only illumination came from a streetlight on the corner and a half-burned out fluorescent sign above the office of the motel.

The police would find Doggett soon—Caroline Rockingham had gotten a look at him during the attack at her motel. If taken alive, Doggett would talk. This time, Stanwick knew he couldn't keep Lorraine and his fellow club members from finding out he was Doggett's father, or keep Boyce or Skarda from finding out about the planted cocaine. He'd be disgraced, he'd be forced to resign from the National, and he might go to jail. That couldn't happen.

He'd thought about buying a gun after Ashby was killed, but he didn't know anything about guns, except that he'd have to fill out paperwork, and that bullets could be matched back to the guns that fired them. Not so with a golf club. Stanwick's best weapon was a strong forehand, developed through 50 years of playing highly competitive tennis. Swung with power, the heavy iron head of a pitching wedge would do plenty of damage, if he could just get in the first blow…

Doggett wouldn't expect Stanwick to arrive early, to knock on his motel room door, and beat his skull in with the wedge as soon as he got inside the room. He could slip out again, get into his car and drive off. It might be days before someone found Doggett, and when they did, they'd have no way to link Stanwick to a pitching wedge that would be at the bottom of Ike's Pond. In the meantime, the police wouldn't know whether the Masters Murderer was still on the loose and waiting to strike again, but the tournament would go on.

That was the main thing—the Masters had to survive. Stanwick had done some shameful things in his life, but allowing the heart and soul of Augusta National to be destroyed by his own demented offspring was not going to be one of them. He wouldn't have that on his conscience.

He looked once more in his rearview mirror to make sure no one was around. He didn't see anyone on the street. He didn't see Lee Doggett, who had been hiding behind a dumpster at the far end of the motel, waiting for the Mercedes to arrive. He didn't see Doggett slip behind a boulevard tree, then duck behind a parked car, then quickly come up behind the Mercedes and crouch next to the bumper.

Stanwick got out of the car, holding the wedge in his right hand. He closed the door quietly and walked to the dimly lit sidewalk, glancing quickly to his left and right. That's when Doggett stood up from behind the car and grabbed Stanwick by the shoulder, spinning him around. He punched Stanwick in the face, a blow that knocked the older man to the sidewalk. Doggett swiftly patted him down, then saw the golf club lying on boulevard grass and picked it up.

"What…what are you doing?" Stanwick gasped as he staggered to his feet.

"What I was going to do as soon as I got out of prison," Doggett said.

Doggett took a quick step forward and swung the club, slamming the face of the wedge into the side of Stanwick's head. The older man's knees sagged, and he held himself up by grabbing onto the back of his car.

"You must have thought I was stupid," Doggett said, with a look of hatred Stanwick was able to read even in the near-dark. "But who's the stupid one? You thought you were going to come here and kill me—with this?"

"No," Stanwick gasped. "I want…to help you…They fucked you over…"

"You did!" Doggett barked through clenched teeth, trying to keep his voice low enough to avoid being heard. "You sent me to prison! You killed my mama. It was you!"

"No…"

"Shut up! I'm not stupid! I knew you'd try to kill me. I thought you'd have a gun."

Doggett swung the club again and hit Stanwick in the side of the knee. Stanwick started to howl in pain, and Doggett clamped his hand over his father's mouth.

"You know, I might not have been the smartest guy in prison," Doggett said, hissing into the writhing man's ear. "But I spent a lot of time in the prison library. I read everything—books, news-papers, magazines. Even golf magazines, if you can believe it."

Stanwick's head was aching, and he was confused. What the hell was this maniac babbling about?

"I read a story once about a guy who got really pissed off about a bad shot, and smashed his club against his golf cart," Doggett continued. "Can you guess what happened to him?"

Stanwick was too frightened and aching to say anything. Would Doggett really dare club him to death in the middle of the street? He would scream, and someone would surely look out their window or come out of their house to see what all the noise was about.

"No guesses? Then I'll tell you—the shaft broke, and half of it bounced right back at him. It pierced the guy's jugular vein. He bled to death right there on the golf course before anybody could do a thing to save him."

Stanwick's eyes grew wide as he began to realize what was on Doggett's mind.

Doggett raised the wedge over his head and slammed it down onto the curb, snapping off the clubhead just above the hosel and sending it clattering out into the street. Stanwick flinched, and his eyes followed the spinning clubhead until it stopped. Doggett held up the shaft, which now came to a jagged steel point.

"This is for Mama."

He rammed the shaft into Stanwick's neck, knocking the older man backward onto the boulevard grass next to his car. Stanwick's mouth opened in an attempt to scream, but the shaft had pierced his larynx and his throat filled with blood from the severed artery. Stanwick gurgled and clutched at his throat, but no words escaped his mouth. His movements gradually ceased as he bled to death on the ground.

For the second time in a week, Doggett took a moment to savor the triumph of having finally avenged his mother. This time, he knew he'd killed the right man—but to be sure, he took Stanwick's wallet out of his pocket and checked the driver's license and credit cards. He took all of Stanwick's cash, about

$400, and his wristwatch. After all, Doggett told himself, a father always wants to pass something of sentimental value on to his son.

Doggett went around to the driver's seat of the Mercedes and popped the trunk release. He lifted Stanwick's body into the trunk and threw the club shaft in with him.

"Thanks for everything, Dad," Doggett said, almost laughing at the uncomprehending look on Stanwick's face as he closed the trunk lid.

The pool of blood was already seeping into the grass next to the car.

Doggett went back into his motel room and rinsed the blood off his hands and arms. He looked at Stanwick's watch: just after midnight. How long would it take the cops to find this place? Probably not until morning—but he couldn't take that chance. Even the stupid local cops could put this case together now. The girl's description, his fingerprints on the knife, Skarda seeing his truck—that's why he'd parked it several blocks away. By now, the cops might even have his name and photo on TV and radio. They'd find his place by mid-morning at the latest, so he had to clear out now—take what he needed from the room, take the back roads back to Augusta, ditch the truck, and spend the rest of the night on the streets, on foot.

The night wouldn't be a problem. But the cops would be looking for him tomorrow, too. They'd be looking for him at every gate at the National, and there'd be Securitas guards at the fences all night. He'd killed six people, almost a seventh, and still he knew they were going to play the goddamned Masters tomorrow.

But he had two days to work with. He still had his Masters badge. He just needed to get inside the gates one more time.

There were three beers left in the refrigerator. He opened one, took a long gulp and put the other two in the gym bag, along with a pack of Camel straights and four Bic lighters he'd bought the last time he was in the Food Lion. He hadn't eaten much lately, but still had plenty of cash left for the next few days. After that, it wouldn't matter.

He stuffed a few items of clothes and his twin-blade razor into his gym bag. He left the lights and the TV on when he walked out. He could hear the droning of yet another newscaster as he closed the door behind him.

"Still no new leads in the Masters Murders…"

Doggett exhaled in disgust. *The Masters Murders are the least of your worries now, pal.*

Chapter Thirty-two

Saturday, April 12

Sam had already showered when Caroline awoke at six. He'd slept about as well as he expected to, given that he was in an unfamiliar room in an unfamiliar town and a psycho had broken in last night with a knife.

Caroline had fallen asleep as soon as he'd turned off the light, but she jerked and twitched most of the night, as though she were trying to catch herself from falling.

"Are you okay?" he asked her, when he saw that her eyes were open.

"Yeah," she said. "Did that really happen?"

"Yes," he said. "I called Lieutenant Boyce. We're meeting in Porter's office at 7. You coming?"

"You're not leaving me here," Caroline said, throwing off the covers.

Sam told her to pack everything she had, because she was checking out today. Caroline asked where she was staying that night.

"In the Crow's Nest," he said.

◇◇◇

Things were moving at their usual leisurely pace on Washington Road. A mile from the Magnolia Lane gate, they passed dozens of protesters on their way to the field where Rachel Drucker had scheduled another anti-Augusta National demonstration. They carried signs and banners saying "ANGC: You can't kill all your critics!" "Porter = Hitler," and "Green Jackets = Brown Shirts."

The protest could get ugly unless the cops decided to get the word out that they were looking for a psycho unaffiliated with the club—but that would create a climate of fear and panic among the badge-holding spectators. At this point, the public might not even believe the cops. They'd probably think the green jackets had bought off the investigators.

"What do you think they'd say if I went over there and told them what we know?" Caroline asked Sam.

"They'd blow you off," Sam said. "You'd be spoiling their wonderful tantrum."

Theirs was the first courtesy car to arrive in the lot that morning. The field had been cut to the low 44 scores and ties, and with the small number of players on the course during the last two rounds, the tee times began late in the morning. Nobody had to be up early on the weekend.

David Porter's office had enough bodies in it to form a pickup basketball game. Boyce and Harwell were there, along with Leonard Garver; so were Porter, Brisbane, and Woodley. Sam brought Caroline in with him.

"Good morning, Sam," Porter said. "Caroline, I'm David Porter, chairman of Augusta National. I'm very sorry about what happened last night."

He extended his hand to Caroline over his desk. She shook it, then sat down in one of the two available chairs. Boyce was standing in the corner to the left of the door. Everyone else was seated, so Sam took the last spot open on the couch.

Porter remained behind his desk, looking glum with his chin in his hand, and let Boyce take charge of the meeting. The GBI detective's folksy country lawman persona took on a more urgent tone.

"I talked to Ralph Stanwick's wife last night," Boyce said to the group. "He left their cabin right after Robert did. He hasn't been home since then. She's afraid something's happened to him."

"Did you call Peggy Francis?" Sam said.

"Yes," Brisbane said. "She hasn't seen him for two days."

"We think he got a call from Lee Doggett last night," Boyce said. "It came through the clubhouse switchboard. We're working on finding out where it came from."

In the meantime, Boyce said, he'd been working on linking Doggett and Stanwick, after the physical resemblance between Stanwick and Doggett's booking photo became obvious. They'd located Doggett's ex-wife Renee in Florida. She told them Lee's real father was an Augusta National member, though she didn't think Doggett had ever told her the man's name. Lorraine Stanwick had been shocked by the idea that Ralph could have had a bastard son by one of the Augusta maids, but admitted that Stanwick had seemed terribly agitated all week, even before Ashby was murdered. When she saw Doggett's photo, she'd started to cry.

Boyce then brought up Doggett's conviction.

"Renee confirmed the counterfeit Masters badges," Boyce said. "She saw him make the things with a home computer and printer. But she said Doggett never used drugs—hated them, in fact, and she's got no reason to lie for him. She doesn't care what happens to him."

"So what's with the cocaine bust?" Sam said.

"I asked Harwell to get me Doggett's case files, and I think I've pieced together what happened here. I'd say somebody— probably Stanwick—found a willing cop to plant the drugs in Doggett's house. Maybe he got the D.A. to do him a favor, too, in exchange for a few free Masters badges. He was hoping Doggett would go away for a long time. Maybe something would happen to him in prison. Unfortunately for Ralph, Doggett's sentence was reduced and he made it out in one piece."

Harwell said they ran the fingerprints found on the hunting knife in Caroline's room. They were Doggett's.

"Another thing," Boyce said. "The blue pickup truck Sam saw leaving Caroline's motel last night matches the description of a truck stolen from a farmer down in Claxton. The farmer and the truck had been missing since the day Doggett was released at Reidsville. The cops down there dug up the farmer yesterday afternoon in his cornfield, along with the ax that killed him.

"Doggett had to have figured out that Stanwick put him behind bars," Boyce said. "His mother died while he was away. His wife left him and took his son. He lost his house, his family—everything. He must have been one angry boy. My guess is he spent the last eight years planning to come back here and get even."

"Stanwick must have had a hunch it was his son doing the killings," Sam said. "Otherwise he would have told me about Doggett when I asked about ex-employees. I'd bet he went into the employee files and removed Doggett's folder, too."

"And now Ralph's missing," Brisbane said.

Everyone in the room shared the same thought: the twisted father-son relationship that had existed between Stanwick and Doggett had probably ended last night.

"Now what?" Porter asked.

"We find Doggett," Boyce said. "He's out there somewhere."

"He'll come back here," Sam said.

"Why do you say that?" Porter asked.

"He's trying to stop the Masters," Sam said. "That's his ultimate revenge. He doesn't just blame Stanwick for what happened to him. He blames Augusta National."

No one disagreed.

"He's got two more days left to pull it off," Boyce said. "You could still cancel or postpone, David."

"Never."

"We could put his name and photo out to the media."

"No," Porter said, as forcefully as though he were turning down Rachel Drucker's application for membership. "That would be worse than canceling. We can't have it known that a madman may be wandering around the golf course. It would create a panic. We're going to run the Masters as always."

Boyce agreed not to release Doggett's name and photo to the pubic. He couldn't force Porter to stop the tournament, and he agreed that panicking 40,000 people wasn't a good idea. Besides, he said, if Doggett didn't know he'd been I.D.'d, he might get careless. It would be easier to find him if he didn't know that every cop and security guard on the grounds was looking for him.

"Here's what we're going to do," Boyce said. "Mr. Woodley, alert your staff that we're going to keep the gates closed an extra hour this morning. Get a copy of Doggett's mug shot to all security guards, and make sure they study it. We'll open the gates at nine, and I want every spectator eyeballed, patted down, and wanded after they come through the metal-detector columns. Harwell, we're going to need more cops. Ask Sheriff Garver to free up as many as he can spare to work the grounds today and tomorrow."

"We still might not spot him," Woodley said. "He could change his appearance."

"I realize that," Boyce said. "This boy's smart. He's not going to jump into our laps. But if he's trying to stop this tournament, that's going to be tough to do with a few hundred cops and security guards watching for him, and 40,000 fans on the course."

"Patrons," Porter corrected.

"What about the TV cameras?" Sam said.

"What about them?" Boyce asked.

"Look, there's 50 CBS cameras all over the course. Why not use them? We could put someone in the control booth with the producer, watching all the monitors for Doggett. Caroline knows what he looks like better than anyone. She could do it."

Porter spoke up: "Caroline, do you think you'd be able to spot this man from a TV monitor?"

"I'll never forget that son of a bitch as long as I live," she said.

Boyce started to smile.

"I like it," he said. "An entire television network helping us on a stakeout."

"CBS will never agree to it," Brisbane said.

"They'll do what I tell them to do," Porter said.

Sam had been waiting for Porter to start throwing his weight around in a way that would actually do some good. Now he was seeing it. He and Boyce exchanged grins as Porter reached for his intercom button.

"Ida? Call Peter Bukich at CBS headquarters and tell him I want to see him at his office in fifteen minutes."

◇◇◇

David Porter led the delegation out of the administration building like a heavyweight champion leading his entourage to the boxing ring. He got into his personal golf cart, with Robert Brisbane sitting next to him, and headed up the driveway toward the par 3 course. Sam and Caroline tagged along behind them in one cart, with Boyce and Harwell sharing another.

With the day's crowd still waiting at the gates to be allowed inside, the carts made good time past the clubhouse and the cabins to the tree-enclosed TV production compound east of the par 3 course. Peter Bukich's office was in a one-story green cabin flush against the dense stand of trees at the north end of the compound. Porter led his entourage through the screen door and down a hall to a cramped office where the preppie-looking Bukich sat in a padded leather swivel chair behind a desk with a computer, two TV monitors, several telephones, an Emmy, and a cigar humidor.

Porter took the only other comfortable chair in the room. Everyone else stood.

"I'd like you all to meet Peter Bukich, Executive Producer of CBS Sports," Porter said, gesturing toward the man behind the desk. Bukich nodded. His bright blue salesman's eyes attempted to be gracious and winning, but the oddity of the gathering had clearly made him less comfortable in his loafers.

"I've been explaining to Peter what we'd like his crew to do for us this weekend," Porter continued. "Peter, this lovely young woman is Caroline Rockingham, who got a good look at our killer. She will be working with Tony during the broadcast."

Tony Petrakis was the legendary CBS producer/director who'd been in charge of choosing the pictures used during Masters broadcasts for 30 years. His Greek temper was well known to even casual golf fans, earning him the nickname "The God of War." It was said that the headstrong Petrakis had actually thrown the equally imperious Clifford Roberts out of his truck the first year he directed the Masters, and that there wouldn't have been a second year had Roberts not committed suicide. Yet Petrakis told each succeeding Augusta National chairman that the only one he'd been able to work with was Clifford Roberts.

Bukich listened to Porter with a look on his face that suggested he'd eaten a bad breakfast burrito. His hair was fluffed and combed back in a style that would fit in at the board room or an airport sports bar; his green tie with the subtle Augusta National flag logo pattern came from the club's Golf Shop. He tried to maneuver his way between the boss in New York and the one staring sternly at him from a chair in the cramped office.

"Now, David, we want to cooperate with the police, of course, but we can't compromise our broadcast by having people in there looking over our shoulders," Bukich said, with a condescending smile. Sam knew it wouldn't work on Porter; David Porter invented that smile.

"Call Rudy Mendenhall and tell him we're going to have a police officer and a witness working in the truck through the end of the tournament," Porter said, oblivious to Bukich's objections.

"David, I can't do that," Bukich said. "We're an independent network, not your private production company. We always cooperate with you in every way we can, but letting the police get involved in how we cover the tournament is just impossible, on so many levels."

"There's only one level here—mine," Porter said. "Call Rudy."

Bukich sighed, picked up one of the phones on his desk, and punched a button on his speed-dial pad. Within 30 seconds he was talking to Rudy Mendenhall, President of CBS Sports. He explained what Porter wanted, and listened for a moment. Then he handed the phone to Porter.

"He wants to talk to you," Bukich said. Sam thought he saw the slightest glint of satisfaction on Bukich's face, as though he'd gotten a yes from Mom after Dad had said no.

Porter took the receiver and said, "This is David, Rudy." He listened for a minute, then another, without saying anything. Then he spoke.

"I'm sorry you feel that way, Rudy, because we've enjoyed our relationship with CBS over the years. I'll call NBC, ABC, and Fox this morning and tell them you've terminated your option to carry the tournament next year."

Bukich's tan seemed to slide off his face and land in his lap. He pushed his chair away from his desk and put his hand up to his head as though he'd suddenly felt a wasp fly into his neatly coiffed hair. Porter, meanwhile, sat placidly in his chair as he once again listened to the voice coming from the corporate headquarters 667 miles to the north.

Finally David Porter said, "I knew you'd understand, Rudy. Yes, we'll be as unobtrusive as possible. Our goal is the same as yours: We don't want our viewers to even suspect that there's anything different about this year's broadcast. We're trying to avoid a massive panic here, but we're also trying to prevent another killing."

He listened for another moment.

"That's right…I won't be calling the other networks…Yes, I hope so, too. Come down soon, Rudy, and we'll tee it up."

Bukich's breathing seemed to return to normal as he eased his chair back toward his desk. He would not go down in history as the CBS Executive Producer who lost the Masters to another network.

When Porter handed the phone back to Bukich, he gave a quick nod to Boyce. Bukich, meanwhile, listened to his boss for a few moments, then put down the receiver.

"Anything you want, David," he said. "If Tony gives you any trouble, I'll deal with him."

Chapter Thirty-three

Porter and Brisbane left the CBS cabin and drove their cart back to the clubhouse. As Sam and Caroline got in their cart, Boyce got a call on his cell phone. He put a hand over his ear, listened for a minute, then snapped the phone shut.

"Our boys found out where Doggett's been staying," Boyce said. "They traced last night's call to the Curtis Motel in Grovetown. Doggett checked in early Monday morning."

"Right after Ashby was killed," Sam said.

Boyce nodded. "Want to come along?"

"Sure," Sam said, turning to Caroline. "You coming?"

"Of course," she said.

◇◇◇

The white paint was peeling off the siding of the one-story motel building, located next to the railroad tracks in a working-class neighborhood. The trees on the block looked as if they needed water, and the trash cans could have used more frequent collecting. A handful of kids were riding their bikes up and down the cracked sidewalks. Some barefoot young men in jeans and muscle shirts stood in a driveway next door, drinking Miller Genuine Draft and looking under the hood of a 1991 Mercury Sable. No one in this neighborhood would have paid much attention to Lee Doggett as he came and went.

An unmarked squad car was already parked out front of the building when Boyce and Harwell pulled up. Sam parked the Cadillac behind Boyce's car.

"Nice ride," said a shirtless kid wearing a sideways Braves cap as Sam got out of the car.

"It's not mine," he said.

"Yeah, I figured," the kid said. Sam looked at Caroline, who had her hand over her mouth to hide a smile. "You all cops?"

"Some of us," Sam said. "You know a guy named Lee Doggett? Stayed at this motel? Tall, thin white guy, losing his hair?"

"Nope," the kid said, staring blankly at Sam.

"Drove a light blue Chevy pickup…loud engine?"

"Oh, him," the kid said. "Yeah, I know the truck. It ain't around today."

Sam and Caroline went into the crowded motel room. The unit's manager or owner, a dark-skinned man with a Middle Eastern accent wearing a white shirt, black pants, and sandals, stood with Boyce just inside the open door while two uniforms poked around the drawers and closet. Harwell was looking in the small refrigerator that hummed away on a counter back near the bathroom.

"Hey, Lieutenant," one of the uniformed cops said to Boyce. "Take a look at this."

He had lifted the bedspread off the floor and found a white shirt, a black tie, a black baseball cap, and a black stiletto-heeled shoe.

"Deborah Scanlon's," Sam said.

"Manolo Blahnik," Caroline said, looking at the shoe.

"Who?" Boyce said.

"That's the designer," Caroline said.

Boyce picked up the shoe with a gloved hand and held it up to the light coming in through the window. He gripped it by the toe and examined the heel.

"Blood on the heel," Boyce said. "Ten to one it's Doggett's."

"She put up a fight," Sam said. "I'm not surprised."

"Why would he keep the shoe?" asked Caroline. "Souvenir?"

"Maybe because he knew his blood was on it," Boyce said. "But he didn't seem to care whether we found it here."

"He isn't worried about us knowing who he is—not any-more," Sam said.

"Yeah," Boyce said. "That's what worries me."

Boyce had one of the cops put the shoe in an evidence bag. There wasn't much else, as far as Sam could see. It looked like the kind of place you'd expect to find a guy who was fresh out of prison.

Sam noticed a plastic squeeze bottle on the floor next to the dresser. It contained some kind of clear liquid. He called Boyce over and asked him to unscrew the cap. Boyce held up the open bottle with his gloved hand and Sam sniffed it. The sharp smell stung his nostrils.

"RoundUp," Sam said.

Another uniformed officer walked into the room.

"Lieutenant, you know that black Mercedes we've been looking for? The one Stanwick drives?" the cop said. "It's right up the block."

◇◇◇

Lee Doggett had driven the blue truck into Augusta, left it on a side street near the banks of the Savannah River and spent the night under a highway bridge. When he woke up he was in cool shadow, the sunlight hitting the knee high grass on the hillside a few feet away, promising another warm, humid day. He guessed it was at least 9 a.m., judging by the angle of the shadows. The gates at the National would be open by now. The crowds would be filing onto the grounds. Would they be looking for him? Did the media have his name and picture now? He would have to get to a TV—after he shaved.

He picked up his gym bag and walked down the concrete embankment of the overpass to a grassy path that led to the chain-link fence he'd hopped over the night before. He climbed the fence again and went north on a narrow street that connected downtown to a few warehouses along the south side of the river.

Once he reached the river, he found an isolated spot among some rocks and waist-high weeds. He reached into the sluggish water and soaked his face and his hair. He took the twin-blade razor out of his bag and began shaving his head. When he was sure he'd gotten everything, he reached into the water again and rinsed his smooth skull. He caught his blurry reflection in the rippling water. He had achieved the look he wanted: that of a dying man.

He tossed the razor into the river and waited for his shirt to dry, staring at the barges along the far bank. He figured his new look and his Masters badge would get him past the cops and the guards, even if they did have his name and his picture. But once on the grounds, he needed to become even more inconspicuous. Too bad he didn't have one of his uniforms from his days on the grounds crew. That would've provided all the cover he'd need—but the National had taken them all when he was arrested.

He got up from the riverbank and checked the angle of the sun. The first groups would be teeing off soon, and he needed to find a TV. He started walking toward Washington Road.

◇◇◇

The sight of Stanwick's twisted, bloody body inside the trunk of his car had been jarring to Caroline. She turned away, walked back to Sam's car and sat in the front seat until they were ready to return to the club. After a hearse from the M.E.'s office took Stanwick's body away, the police sealed off Doggett's motel room, sent Scanlon's shoe to the GBI lab, and towed Stanwick's car to the impound lot.

"You don't think this is over, do you?" Boyce said to Sam.

"No. Do you?"

"Hell, no."

Sam and Caroline followed Boyce and Harwell on the slow drive back to the club. It was time for Caroline to meet Tony Petrakis and start hunting for the killer. The drive down Magnolia Lane had lost its charm for Sam; a sense of foreboding had replaced the awe and excitement he'd first felt driving through that fabled tunnel of branches.

"Where will you be this afternoon?" Caroline asked Sam as they neared the television compound.

"Walking the grounds, looking for our boy," he said.

"And if you find him?"

"That's up to him," Sam said.

"I know this is your line of work," Caroline said. "But I wish…"

"What?"

"Never mind. Do what you have to do. But be careful, okay?"

The grounds were now teeming with spectators, none of whom had the slightest idea that they were in the middle of the most extensive manhunt in America.

The security guards cleared Caroline and Sam into the TV compound, and Sam asked a young man wearing a CBS polo shirt where they could find Petrakis. He pointed to one of the extended white trailers with "CBS Sports" and the familiar eye logo painted in blue on the side. They went up the metal stairs and opened the door. Inside they saw a bank of two dozen TV monitors against the far side of the truck, positioned above the director's console. The tournament coverage would not begin for another hour, but Tony Petrakis was already swiveling from side to side in his chair, shouting at his camera operators through the microphone attached to his headset.

Petrakis was a short man with a round middle that he chose not to confine by tucking in his pale blue short-sleeved shirt. He had thick, wavy hair that was either dyed or unnaturally black. Everything on his face protruded—his forehead, his eyebrows, his nose, his cheeks, his chin, and an assortment of little lumps and bumps.

Boyce and Harwell were already there. Their presence did not seem to have a calming effect on the director.

"No, Goddammit, I want a close-up of Crenshaw's hands—his hands, for Chrissake, not his crotch! Get me a different angle!" Petrakis yelled. He glanced contemptuously at Boyce and Harwell. "Fuckin' cops breathing on me, when I'm trying to do a golf tournament here!"

Boyce took Sam and Caroline aside. Petrakis, he told them, was dead set against having his cameras used to search for Doggett. Of course, it didn't matter what Petrakis wanted; he could walk out of the trailer, and they'd just replace him with the assistant director. The plan was the same: The camera operators not involved in showing important action would be scanning the crowds slowly, and Caroline was to watch the monitors for anyone who looked like Doggett.

"I don't need this shit," Petrakis muttered. "I don't need this shit at all. Love's looking at eagle on 8. I don't care if he's 10 shots behind! Get that fuckin' camera off the crowd and put it on Love! We're doing golf here, not 'America's Most Wanted'!"

Boyce interrupted Petrakis and introduced him to Caroline.

"So you're the one who almost got sliced up," Petrakis said, glancing at Caroline—then glancing back again for a longer look before turning back to his monitors. "How do you know you'd even recognize this guy?"

"Anybody ever chased you around a motel room with a hunting knife?" Caroline said.

"Not yet," Petrakis said, staring at a shot of the rippling flag on the 12th green.

He shouted more directions into his headset, then turned to face Caroline.

"They've done tests where a guy runs into a classroom and screams at the professor and runs back out again," Petrakis said. "Two minutes later, nobody in the class can agree on what color the guy's fuckin' shirt was."

Petrakis swiveled around in his chair and pulled a cigar out of his shirt pocket.

"You mind?" he said. He bit off the end and spit it into a nearby waste basket.

"Go ahead," Caroline said. "You're the boss."

"If I was, you wouldn't be here," Petrakis said.

He lit a match and puffed on the cigar until the end glowed. He exhaled a cloud of smoke, as though putting up a barrier between himself and his intruders.

"People overestimate television," Petrakis said. "Just because you've seen Oprah or Jay Leno a thousand times on TV doesn't mean you'd recognize them on the street. You probably wouldn't know your next-door neighbor if you saw him on monitor eight."

He exhaled another puff of smoke and spoke through the gathering haze.

"That's what makes me the best at what I do," Petrakis said. "I get the perfect angles, the right shots, the views that tell the story I want to tell. I don't just show pictures of golfers—I show you their souls."

"I thought the camera operators did that," Caroline said.

"I love those guys, but a chimp could do what they do," Petrakis said, with a wave of his hand. "They point and shoot. They could make a perfectly good video of your kid's fuckin' birthday party, but here they'd be helpless if I didn't tell them what to do. If you put one of them in this chair, the Masters would be a fuckin' joke. I tell you, this is the hardest job in television.

"You take that pencil-pusher in the office…" Petrakis gestured with his cigar toward the cabin where Peter Bukich's office was located. "He gets paid twice as much as I do, and for what? Kissing ass and staying out of my way." He looked directly at Caroline through the cigar smoke. "And that's what I want you to do."

"Kiss your ass?"

"Stay out of my way. Sit over there. Look at the monitors. Don't talk to me unless you're abso-fuckin'-lutely sure you see the guy. Otherwise, I don't want to know you're here."

"Don't worry, you won't," Caroline said, looking at Sam with an expression that said: Are you really going to leave me with this asshole?

Boyce handed Sam a radio that clipped onto his belt and a connected earpiece, and told him to monitor the main police frequency.

"If Caroline spots Doggett, you'll know about it as soon as I do. Same goes for you: If you see him, or anything that looks wrong, talk to us on your handset. We can get a dozen cops almost anywhere on this course within two minutes."

"How are you going to take him down if you spot him?" Sam asked.

"As quietly as possible," Boyce said. "He won't be able to get a gun in here. We shouldn't need to use ours. Now, let's find this asshole."

Chapter Thirty-four

No one gave Lee Doggett a second glance as he walked with the crowds on the sidewalk along Washington Road. His shaved head was protected by his blue bucket hat; his eyes were shielded by a pair of cheap sunglasses. He looked, as did hundreds of others around him, singularly focused on getting into the Masters.

He was almost weak with hunger. Some eggs and bacon would taste good, he thought, and maybe a beer or two. Someplace with a TV.

Up ahead he saw the Hooters sign, and four waitresses wearing tight white shirts with the owl logo, waving their arms at passing cars.

"Hi there!" one of the Hooters waitresses said as he approached. She had wispy blonde hair teased into the consistency of cotton candy, average breasts squeezed toward significance by a push-up bra, and a tired, frozen smile on her face.

"You serving breakfast?" Doggett asked.

"Same menu all day," she said. "Wings and sandwiches and all that. The grilled cheese sandwich is good. Are you going to the Masters today?"

"I wouldn't be anywhere near here if I wasn't," Doggett said.

"Oh," the blonde said, her smile slipping. "Yeah, I know what you mean. It's kind of a zoo out here. I'll be glad when the week is over."

"Me, too," Doggett said. He stared at her chest for several seconds longer than was polite, then crossed the Hooters parking lot and went inside.

He chose a booth from which he could see the wide-screen TV over the bar, and set his gym bag down next to him. The tournament coverage hadn't started yet. The Fox News crawl reported: "No new developments in The Masters Murders…" Good. The news media didn't have his name and photo yet. The public wouldn't be looking for him. But the cops and security guards would be.

A waitress came by, with larger breasts than the one he'd talked to out front. He ordered the grilled cheese sandwich and a beer while staring at the double O's on the front of her shirt, and when she left he stared even longer at her tight orange shorts. He drained his beer while he was waiting for his food, waved the waitress over, and ordered another. He never took off the bucket hat or the sunglasses.

As he drank his second beer, he saw a discarded newspaper on the seat of an empty booth. He got up and brought it back to his table. There was a front-page story about police efforts to find the Masters Murderer, but there was nothing new about the investigation. Milligan's funeral would be held Monday, to allow his former CBS colleagues to attend before leaving town. Scanlon's body had been flown back to New York. Ashby had been cremated before a private ceremony on Friday, with speculation that his ashes would be spread somewhere on the golf course; David Porter said the club would have no comment. No indication whether they'd found that guy in the canal. Even if they did, there was nothing to tie him to the Masters Murders. And it was too soon for the papers to have any news about Stanwick.

The WOFF was still demanding the cancellation of the tournament. Rachel Drucker had called the National "a monstrous evil." The mayor and sheriff both expressed hopes that this year's Masters could be concluded without further incident. Security had been greatly increased at and around the golf course. Police were checking out many leads, but still had no suspect they could name.

Just another lie from the cops. They always lie.

Doggett turned to the sports page and found the same kind of banner headline the Masters always got on Saturday: GARCIA, MICKELSON TIED FOR HALFWAY LEAD. As if there was nothing else going on at the National. Well, that would change soon enough.

Paging farther into the sports section, Doggett found a quarter-page ad for a Masters memorabilia sale at the Augusta Antique Market on Washington Road. He'd seen the place many times; it was just a few blocks away, at a strip mall. The ad said the sale had begun on Monday and would run through Sunday. Doggett looked at a clock by the cash register: 1 p.m. He had time to check it out. There might be something he could use.

◇◇◇

Half an hour later, Doggett paid $5 admission to enter the Masters Memorabilia Show and Sale at the Antique Market. Inside were dozens of vendors at display tables, hawking hats, towels, shirts, jackets, beer glasses, pins, and golf balls with the Masters logo.

He wandered through the displays, maneuvering around souvenir shoppers who either didn't have tickets to the tournament or thought they might find better deals here than in the National's merchandise building. No one seemed to be buying anything, and Doggett wasn't surprised. Bunch of junk.

He was about to leave when he spotted a booth with a white drapery behind it, from which hung the usual array of Masters hats, photos, and shirts—and a white Augusta National caddie jumpsuit, with a green "22" over the left breast pocket and the Masters logo over the right. Doggett had seen those suits many times over the years, and this one looked authentic.

The man and woman sitting at the table in the booth were playing cards when Doggett stopped.

"That thing real?" he asked the man, who laid his cards face down on the table so the woman couldn't see what he had. She did the same. They were both about 45, with the same short, frizzy brown hairstyle. Each wore a green Masters sweatshirt and blue jeans.

"What thing?" the man asked.

"That caddie suit," Doggett said. "Where'd you get it?"

"A guy came in this week and sold it to us," the man said. "Said he'd caddied at the Masters himself. It's real, all right."

"Let me see it."

The man got up from his chair, took the caddie suit off the hanger and handed it to Doggett, who turned it over and looked at the back. Perfect—a player's name was still on it.

"How much do you want for it?" Doggett asked.

"Two seventy-five," the woman said. "You don't see many of these for sale."

Doggett said, "I'll give you two hundred."

The man and the woman looked at each other, trying to decide.

"Two fifty," the man said.

"Two," Doggett said, shaking his head.

The man looked at the woman again.

"Cash," Doggett said.

"Sold, mister," the woman said.

Doggett counted out $200. Then he put another $15 on top.

"I'll take that green Masters hat, too," Doggett said, pointing to a solid green baseball cap with the yellow Augusta National logo. The man put the hat on the table and handed him two dollars change. He asked Doggett if he wanted all his purchases in a bag. Doggett said no.

"Is there a bathroom around here?" Doggett asked.

"Down that aisle, all the way to the back. It's on your right."

Doggett picked up the caddie suit and the hat and walked to the back of the hall, where he found the men's room. Inside a man wearing shorts and sandals stood at the urinal. Doggett ignored him as he slipped off his shoes and took his pants and shirt off in the middle of the bathroom. The man at the urinal turned to look at him over his shoulder as Doggett stepped into the caddie suit and zipped it up.

"Oh, man, I saw that suit," the man said, as Doggett put the hat on. "That's so cool. You could pass for a real Masters caddie."

Doggett didn't respond. He pulled his pants on over the caddie suit, then put on his T-shirt and windbreaker. The suit wasn't a bad fit—just a little short in the arms and legs. It would be hot and bulky, but a little sweat didn't bother him.

He put his shoes back on and stared at the other man in the bathroom, who had finished at the urinal and had moved over to the sink, standing with his back to Doggett. Would this guy get suspicious? Would he mention to somebody that he'd seen a guy changing into an Augusta National caddie suit in the men's room? Doggett could strangle the guy with his belt in about ten seconds. Then he wouldn't have to worry about him.

"You going to a costume party or something?" the man at the sink asked, glancing into the mirror at Doggett, who was staring at him.

"Yeah," Doggett said. "A Masters theme party. Lots of laughs."

"I'll bet," the man at the sink said. The water continued to splash as the man pumped away at the nearly empty soap dispenser. He finally managed to get a few drops onto his hands, and lathered up as much as he could. The water was getting too hot, so he turned the spigot on the cold water to balance the temperature as he rinsed the soap off his hands. He heard the guy in the caddie suit doing something with his belt buckle, so he knew he was still there.

"Who do you like this year?" the man at the sink asked as he turned off the water. He pulled a couple of paper towels from the dispenser on the wall to his right. Then he turned around.

The man wearing the caddie suit was gone.

Chapter Thirty-five

Doris Higgins figured she and her husband Jim had rented their last motorized scooter for the day. Spectators had to be off the Augusta National grounds at about 6:30. It was 2:30 now, and nobody wanted to pay a full day's rent for just a few hours.

Jim had walked down the road to talk to some of the other vendors. Doris pulled a paperback crime novel out of her shoulder bag and settled into the folding chair under the awning of their RV, waiting for the rentals to start returning.

The scooter business had been a bonanza for Doris and Jim. They'd tried selling Masters souvenirs at the corner of Berckmans Road and Washington Road, but there was so much competition outside the gates, everyone selling the same stuff, that they'd never made much of a profit.

When they learned that Augusta National would allow scooters onto the grounds during the Masters—to enable elderly, weak, or ill patrons to handle the steep hills—Jim invested in a fleet of 20 scooters. Each had four wheels under a sturdy red platform, with a steering column in front and a gray office-style seat on top of the motor housing. The whole thing weighed less than 150 pounds, but it could easily support a 300-pound person.

Doris and Jim figured they'd take in about $15,000 this Masters Week. They'd seen a slight dip in rentals after those two awful murders Monday and Tuesday, but now that it was Saturday, and the weather was glorious, and the talk of the killings was beginning to fade, the crowds were as good as ever. They'd rented out all but a couple of scooters every day except Wednesday, when it had rained and the course had been closed for the investigation.

Doris was just getting engrossed in her paperback when she heard someone asking about renting a scooter.

She looked up and saw a tall man wearing a bucket hat and sunglasses, looking at the two remaining scooters parked on the grass near the street. He appeared able-bodied, but Doris noticed he had no hair on the sides of his head—and how bundled up he was. The temperature was almost 80, but the man seemed to be wearing two layers of clothing. The poor man must have cancer.

"I can help you," Doris called to him, getting out of her chair.

He didn't seem to mind that he needed to return the scooter in less than four hours. That would be plenty of time, he said. How does it work? Doris sat on the scooter and showed him how to start it, how to accelerate, how to brake, and how to steer.

"It's very much like a riding lawnmower," she said. The man said he was familiar with lawnmowers

"It's going to be $75," she said. "I'm sorry—I know it's getting late in the day, but we can't pro-rate the price."

He said that was all right, and handed her three twenties, a ten and a five.

"We also need to hold your driver's license until you bring it back."

The man hesitated for a moment, then removed his sunglasses and looked her in the eyes. He said his driver's license had expired last year, and he hadn't renewed it because he wasn't expected to live this long. He took off his hat, and she could see that, as she'd guessed, his hair was gone. He looked positively gaunt. She wondered how long he had left.

"We can let it go, sweetie," Doris said. "You just get the scooter back here around 6:30, and everything will be fine."

He thanked her, sat down on the scooter's seat, started the engine again, and drove off toward the spectator entrance.

What a shame, Doris thought, as he disappeared into the crowd. So young. So much to live for.

She hoped he would enjoy his last Masters.

◇◇◇

Caroline sat in the CBS production truck as far away from Tony Petrakis as she could and still keep an eye on the screens. Harwell stood behind her with a police radio, ready to alert Boyce if she saw anything.

There was so much to look at: multiple camera shots of all 18 holes, the clubhouse area, the putting green, and the practice range. The camera operators were doing what they'd been instructed to do, making lingering pans of the crowds at their holes when there wasn't some action to focus on. They went in for close-ups of the galleries, but Caroline knew that she might not get a good look at more than a few hundred people during the course of the afternoon. It was like looking for a golf ball in a field of dandelions going to seed.

"Spot him yet, sweetheart?" Petrakis would sometimes ask her sarcastically during a break, a taped feature or an interview from the Butler Cabin. "What's he look like again? Tall guy? Maybe that's him on camera 2 at 14. The one in the black Callaway visor."

"No," Caroline would say. "Not him."

"You sure? He looks pretty fuckin' creepy to me."

"Look," Caroline said. "I know this is all a big pain in the ass to you, but it's better than sitting around waiting for this asshole to kill somebody else. You want to broadcast a murder scene to 20 million people?"

"Aghh," Petrakis grumbled, waving his hand and taking a drag on his cigar. "The cops have a killer to catch. I've got a tournament to televise. We should stay the hell out of each other's way."

"Have you got a family, Tony?" Caroline asked.

"Sure, sure, I got a family," Petrakis said. Then he paused, and said into the mike, "Coming out of break in 20 seconds.

We'll go with a leaderboard shot over the 16 background and then pick up Singh's eagle putt on 13. Cameron, be ready for a tournament reset after Vijay putts, and then we'll go to tape of Bellows holing his birdie putt on 8."

Cameron Myers was the slick CBS Sports anchor who hosted the coverage from the tower on 18 with lead analyst Nigel Frawley. Petrakis had explained to the on-air talent that the police were monitoring the broadcast cameras, looking for the Masters murderer with the help of an eyewitness. Caroline had not been given an earpiece, so she didn't know how the announcers had reacted.

"So you have kids?" Caroline said.

He held up a hand to her and said into the mic: "Keep it on Vijay at 13…dammit, the caddie's in the way of the hole, and Vijay's blocking the hole on camera 2. Go with camera 1. Maybe the caddie will move…Godammit! Those guys all know where the cameras are. Why do they fuck us like that?

"Yeah, a boy, 27, and a girl, 24," he said, turning to Caroline. "I didn't get to see them much when they were growing up. In this job, you travel all the time."

"So how do you think you'd feel if one of them was murdered?" Caroline asked. "You'd do anything to catch the guy who did it—wouldn't you?"

Petrakis didn't answer. He was looking at the bank of monitors and telling Myers that he wanted him to run down the leaderboard with Frawley after Singh putted out on 13. They would go four pages deep, he said, to get the viewers caught up on the remaining contenders. Singh missed his eagle putt and tapped in for birdie, and Cameron Myers began his exchange with Frawley. Petrakis turned back to Caroline. There was a new look in his eyes. She'd stirred up some emotions that he didn't usually examine.

"If some sonofabitch laid a hand on one of my kids, I'd spend the rest of my life tracking him down," Petrakis said.

Caroline thought Petrakis' eyes were beginning to glisten. The God of War was human after all.

"When Doggett was slashing at me with that knife, I flashed on my parents," Caroline said. "I could see them getting the news: Your daughter has been stabbed to death in an Augusta motel room. Can you imagine how that would feel?"

"Horseshit," Petrakis said. "Going to eight green. Garcia putting to save par."

"What about Danny Milligan?" Caroline said. "He was on your staff for years. Then Doggett walks into his house and cuts his throat. Doesn't that make you furious? Don't you want to get this guy?"

"Of course I do," Petrakis almost shouted. "Danny Milligan was a good guy. He couldn't keep from saying any stupid fuckin' thing that jumped into his head, but he didn't deserve to be butchered like that."

"Nobody does," Caroline said. "That's all we're trying to do here. Keep Doggett from killing somebody else."

Petrakis seemed not to have heard her. Staring at the monitors, he leaned into his microphone to tell Cameron Myers that they were going to a shot of Mickelson looking for his tee shot in the trees left of the creek on 13.

"Everybody else, keep panning the patrons," Petrakis said. "Give me faces. The guy who killed Danny might be out there. If he is, we're gonna find that sonofabitch."

He looked back at Caroline and winked.

◇◇◇

Doggett drove the scooter through Gate 3A on Washington Road, the walk-in gate through which a few patrons were already exiting. Doggett was the only spectator going in.

He drove the scooter slowly past the rows of parked cars to the course entrance, where three security guards sat on tables talking to each other. He was ready to run if they recognized him; he could beat them to the Washington Road exit, and maybe lose himself in the crowd and the traffic once he was on the street. But if they were looking for him, they would be looking for a tall man who was partially bald—not a cancer patient of indeterminate height sitting on a scooter.

As Doggett approached, one of the guards picked up a detection wand and motioned for him to come through the portable metal-detector columns in his aisle. Doggett held up Ty Chapman's Masters badge and showed it to the security guard, a paunchy black man with a goatee, who nodded.

"A little late, aren't you?" the guard said.

"I had a chemo treatment this morning," Doggett said, not getting off the scooter.

"Oh. Sorry to hear that," the guard said. "Well, you still got a couple hours of play left. You'll want to go out to the back nine."

He wanded Doggett from head to toe.

"Any cameras, cell phones, weapons, or folding chairs?" the guard asked.

"No," Doggett said. "I know the rules."

"You'd be surprised how many don't," the guard said, with a weary chuckle. "Look in this box here. I must have taken 300 cell phones and cameras from patrons today. They all said they didn't know, or they forgot."

"Stupid people," Doggett said, shaking his head.

"You got that right."

"Cigarettes and lighters are okay, right?"

Doggett pulled the pack of Camel straights and one of the plastic lighters from his shirt pocket.

"No problem," the guard said. "But maybe you ought to…you know, cut down or something."

"No point now," Doggett said. "Might as well enjoy the time I've got, right?"

"I guess," the guard said. "Well, you better get in there if you're going to see some golf today."

"Thanks," Doggett said. He engaged the motor and drove through the entrance.

◇◇◇

After walking the course for several hours without seeing anything suspicious or hearing anything through his earpiece, Sam found a place on the hillside next to the 18th green and tried to imagine what Doggett would do next. He didn't seem like the type to give up, but if he was trying to stop the Masters, he was running out of time.

Sam spotted Al Barber walking up the 18th fairway. Barber had made the cut Friday, right on the number, shooting 75-74 to get in at 5 over par. It was the first time he'd made the cut in six years. The scorer's standard said "+12" next to Barber's name. He was running out of gas—but from the smile on his face, Sam could tell Barber was enjoying his rare Saturday round at the Masters. When Al sank his par putt on 18 for a 79, the gallery applauded warmly. He flipped his ball to Chipmunk, took off his hat, and shook hands with Clive Cartwright, his playing partner. As Barber headed up the hill to the scorer's hut behind the 18th green, Sam saw Dwight Wilson standing behind the ropes that led to the clubhouse. Dwight was wiping his face with a white caddie towel.

"Hey, Dwight," Sam called to him. "How's the leg?"

Dwight smiled when he saw Sam.

"Oh, not so bad when I stand in one spot."

When the marshals gathered up the ropes behind the players exiting the 18th green, Sam crossed over to talk to Dwight.

"Did you bring your daughter with you?"

"Nah, they don't give us caddies but one ticket." Then Dwight lowered his voice: "You find that killer yet?"

"Not yet," Sam said. "But we know it's Doggett. He tried to kill Caroline last night. At her motel."

"She all right?" Dwight asked.

"Yeah, she's fine. I was there."

"He's a dead man if I catch him," Dwight said, his eyebrows lowering.

"You might get your chance," Sam said. "We think he'll try to get on the course again. If you think you see him, tell the nearest security guard. They know who we're looking for."

Dwight ran the towel over the back of his neck and wiped his face again.

"I'll be watching for him," he said.

◇◇◇

Lee Doggett parked the scooter next to the Golf Shop in the main entrance plaza.

"Could you watch that for me?" he asked one of the young women in pink polo shirts who greeted shoppers as they entered.

"Of course," she said. "You don't mind if I take it for a little ride while you're shopping, do you?"

"Yeah, I do," Doggett said, not smiling. The perky young woman lost her smile, too.

"It will be here when you get back," she said, turning to the next customer.

There was no longer a line to get into the Golf Shop. Most of the spectators were either out on the course or had started for home, and most of the clerks were idle in the check-out lines. Doggett was familiar with the merchandise. Years ago he had gone into the building during the Masters to buy a T-shirt for Lee Jr. He knew exactly what he was looking for.

He found it hanging on the wall just inside the entrance: a black golf bag that said "Masters" in green stitching on the pouch. The price tag said $125. He brought the bag and a white Masters towel to the checkout counter and paid for them with cash. The clerk put the towel in a clear plastic Masters shopping bag.

"Hey, you'll like playing with that bag," a man said to Doggett as he walked to his scooter with the golf bag over his shoulder and the shopping bag in his hand. "I bought one a couple of years ago. Everybody asks me about it."

"I don't play golf," Doggett said, stopping to stare at the man. "It's a stupid game."

Doggett kept the bag slung over his shoulder and sat down on his scooter. As he drove off toward the course, the man muttered, "Cancer's no excuse for being an asshole, buddy."

Chapter Thirty-six

Sam walked past the umbrella tables in front of the clubhouse on his way to meet Boyce in Porter's office. For the first time, he felt envious of the privileged and carefree spectators sitting there in the shade with a cool drink in hand, oblivious to the fact that a killer could be walking right past them. It was also business as usual for the reporters clustered under the big oak; they, too, were unaware that the cops and security guards were trying to spot Lee Doggett before he had a chance to become the biggest story of their careers.

A few spectators were walking to the main exit or staring up at the leaderboard to the right of the first fairway; the rest of the crowd was packed into the viewing areas on the back nine. When Sam approached the tournament headquarters, he saw some of the players and their families leaving the grounds in their courtesy cars. If Doggett was somewhere on the course, he was letting the day slip away from him without making his move.

The chairman and the GBI investigator were watching the tournament in Porter's office. Frank Naples had a one-shot lead over Garcia, two over Perry Bellows, and three over Woods, Singh, and Bellecourt.

"Nothing?" Boyce asked.

"Nothing," Sam said. "You?"

"Five hundred cops and security guards on the grounds, and nobody has seen a goddamn thing."

"What about Caroline?"

"She and Petrakis are starting to hit it off, but that's about it," Boyce said.

"Well, that's something."

The three men stared at the TV for a few minutes without saying a word. Cameron Myers was recapping the day's action as the screen displayed the leaderboard, superimposed over a background shot of wisteria hanging from the loblolly pines along the 10th hole. Syrupy acoustic-guitar music completed the ambiance of calm and serenity. Sam was wound so tight that he would have flinched at the sound of a staple hitting Porter's carpet, but CBS continued to send out the signal that all was well in Augusta. Finally, David Porter spoke.

"Maybe we're out of the woods, boys. Maybe Doggett couldn't get in. Or maybe he's satisfied with killing Ralph."

"Maybe," Sam said. "But I think his real target has always been the Masters."

"He might be saving the dramatics for Sunday afternoon," Boyce said.

"A bomb wouldn't get past those metal detectors, right?" Sam said to Boyce.

"Nope," Boyce said.

"A bomb?" Porter said. "Oh, for God's sake, is that what you're thinking now?"

"I've been thinking about that since Tuesday," Boyce said. "But there's no way he could get a device through the x-ray machines and metal detectors, and we've had guards watching the fertilizer supplies in both of your maintenance facilities since I got here. This isn't the '96 Olympics. This time we're ready."

"You worked that case?" Sam asked.

Boyce nodded. Sam remembered the story well. Everyone did. The Atlanta police had received a warning phone call saying that a knapsack bomb was going to explode in Centennial Park during a concert at the summer Olympics of 1996. They had tried to clear the area—but the bomb had still killed one person and injured 100 more. Then suspicion had wrongly fallen on a security guard who had been trying to clear the area.

"We were embarrassed," Boyce said. "We couldn't get the people out fast enough."

"Doggett isn't going to give us a phone call," Sam said.

"No, but that park wasn't secure. There were no metal detectors or x-rays for people going in and out. It was an open-air rock concert in a public space, with no fence or gates, and it happened at 1:20 in the morning. We've got more control here. And we know who we're looking for."

"I used to think we had control here," Porter said. "Now, I'm not so sure."

◇◇◇

Doggett drove his scooter onto the grass beside the first fairway. The mowers were already at work on the front nine. Maintenance workers and club members walked the first and 9th fairways with buckets of green-dyed sand, filling in the divot holes from that day's play, while others used hoses to wet down the rough under pine trees and around bunkers. He recognized some of them. They paid no attention to him.

He took the crosswalk that traversed the first and 9th fairways and drove up the hill toward the 18th green, where thousands of spectators were clustered, waiting for the leaders to finish their third round. He circled around behind the green and stopped the scooter behind the throngs who had staked out their spots left of the finishing hole hours earlier. Many were seated in folding Masters chairs, the kind Doggett had seen customers buying in the Golf Shop. The chairs compacted into a narrow shape that fit into a nylon stuff sack with a drawstring.

Doggett wanted one of those sacks.

He parked the scooter, left his purchases leaning on the handlebars, and worked his way into the crowd that was watching Ryan Moore and Davis Love III play their approach shots into 18. He stopped behind an elderly couple, both seated in folding Masters chairs, probably holding down the same spot they'd occupied since Arnie won his last Masters. The woman, who wore a wide-brimmed straw hat with old Masters badges tucked into the green hatband, was absorbed in watching Moore execute his swing. The man wore a checkered snap-brimmed Hogan-style cap and sunglasses, and appeared to be dozing.

All eyes watched Moore's shot arch through the air, half of the ball catching the brilliant late-afternoon sunlight, and descend toward the green. As it fell, Doggett pulled the nylon stuff sack out from under the woman's folding chair with his foot. He bent down to untie his shoe and, while kneeling over the sack, picked it up quickly and tucked it up his pants leg. Then he tied his shoe, got up, and walked back to his scooter while the crowd applauded the shot, which nestled 5 feet from the hole.

He now had everything he needed.

He pulled the chair sack out of his pants and put it into the golf bag, slung the bag over his shoulder, and drove the scooter down the hill to the concession area in the grove of trees by the 18th tee. A Richmond County Sheriff's squad car was parked 30 feet from the entrance to the men's bathroom; a deputy wearing a flat-brimmed trooper's hat and sunglasses leaned on the front headlight with his arms crossed, looking around at the spectators milling through the area. The deputy turned his head briefly toward Doggett as he motored slowly past, then resumed gazing up the 18th fairway.

Doggett parked the scooter next to the bathroom entrance and got into line. In less than two hours, the last groups would have gone through, the concession area would be cleared, and the deputy would realize that the scooter was still parked there, unclaimed. By that time, Doggett would be long gone.

The line moved quickly. Once inside the bathroom, Doggett claimed an open stall and closed the door behind him, leaning the golf bag against the stall door. He pulled the green hat he'd bought at the memorabilia show out of the back pocket of the caddie jumpsuit, put it in the clear plastic shopping bag, and set it on the floor. He took off his windbreaker and T-shirt, pulled down the jumpsuit and his underwear, and sat on the toilet. This was a good place to think, to go over the details one more time. Besides, he didn't want to have to take a crap in the woods later on. It might attract animals.

He lit a cigarette. He never was much of a smoker, though he had smoked in prison—like everyone else—for something to do. He would need just two of the 20 cigarettes in the pack; smoking one of them now might help him think a little more clearly. He went over the plan in his head, and concluded that he'd done everything he needed to do. Rain would be a problem, but there were just a few wispy clouds in the increasingly orange western sky. After all these years, he could still tell when it was going to rain the next morning. Nothing mattered more to a greenskeeper than the morning weather, since the important work had to be done before the golfers got on the course. He was sure there would be no rain tonight or tomorrow. Some things, even eight years of prison can't beat out of you.

He dropped the butt in the toilet, and put the cigarettes and the lighter into the pouch of the golf bag. He flushed the toilet and pulled his clothes back on. Time to go.

He walked out the exit at the opposite end of the men's room and circled around the back of the 10th green, carrying his golf bag over his shoulder and his clear plastic Masters bag in his hand like any other souvenir shopper.

The final pair—Garcia and Bellows—was just heading up the hill to the isolated 11th tee, stuck back in the woods. Doggett walked up the hill with a few dozen spectators. He stood about 15 feet away from the roped-off tee as Bellows and Garcia launched their drives down the sloping fairway. The sun was descending toward the tips of the pines to the west, throwing shadows across the 11th tee. Four security guards were positioned around the tee, along with half a dozen marshals wearing yellow hardhats with the number "11" stamped in green numerals on both sides. One of the marshals wore a white jumpsuit with no lettering on the front or back. When the last drive had been struck, he lifted a flagstick with a yellow flag on the end and began waving it to the marshals positioned farther down the fairway, to indicate that Garcia and Bellows were on their way.

The players, their caddies, the standard bearer, and the rules official all began striding down the hill from the tee, and the gallery went with them—except for Doggett, who began walking back between the trees toward the 10th green. The nearest security guard on 10 was almost 50 yards away, and not looking in his direction. Doggett slipped quickly behind a pine tree, then ducked next to a flowering white dogwood bush and crouched as low as he could. No one called to him. The security guard farther up the hill was watching the handful of spectators who had chosen to walk back up to the clubhouse on that side of the 10th fairway. He looked back at the security guards at the 11th tee. They couldn't see him through the trees and bushes. He was safe where he was.

There was another blossoming dogwood bush about 20 feet deeper into the trees. He waited for several minutes as the shadows continued to descend over the course, then quietly crept back to the next bush. Again he peered through the branches to see if he'd been noticed, but the guards were unaware that he was there. The underbrush was even more dense another 15 feet behind him; he carefully crawled into the thicket, then down a ridge that put him in the middle of the woods. From there he couldn't see the golf course—or anyone.

He laid his bags down and sat on the pine-needled forest floor to wait for dark.

Chapter Thirty-seven

Sam and Mark Boyce stood on the clubhouse balcony, over-looking perhaps 20,000 Masters patrons trying to get a look at Garcia and Bellows, now tied for the lead as they finished their third round on 18. No one had seen Doggett. There had been several reports of men who resembled the eight-year-old booking photo, but after their IDs were checked, the patrons were allowed to go on watching the tournament—with an apology for the inconvenience. It had all been done quietly, without anyone becoming alarmed.

"When this group finishes putting out, we'll do a sweep," Boyce said to Sam. "We'll start from the bottom of the course, at Amen Corner, and move everyone back up the hill to the exits. Standard stuff. They do it every night at the end of play. Only this time, we'll have ten times as many people, and they'll all be looking for one particular man."

"Did CBS agree to keep their cameras on the crowd until everyone is gone?" Sam asked.

"Yep," Boyce said. "Not that it's done us any good so far."

"You never know," Sam said.

"I called the lab, by the way. They I.D.'d the shoe—it was Scanlon's, like we thought. They'll do a DNA test on the blood on the heel, and compare it to hairs we found in the sink at Doggett's motel room, but everything's backed up, as usual. We won't get the results for a week."

"It won't matter by then," Sam said.

"Probably not," Boyce said. "But once we get him, we'll need the evidence."

Sam nodded. In another day, Doggett would either have failed to ruin the Masters, or he would have pulled off some terrible mayhem that would make news around the world. Sam had been hired to prevent that, but he wasn't earning his money. If a thousand cops, security guards, and club employees—not to mention dozens of TV cameras—couldn't find the guy, what else could be done? As he gazed across the golf course from the porch, he felt as though he were standing on the bow of a ship, steering it through a calm ocean, all the while knowing that a submarine lurked somewhere out there, preparing to put a torpedo through the hull.

He told Boyce he was going to the CBS trailer to meet Caroline. It was getting dark, and he didn't want her walking back to the clubhouse by herself.

"If anything breaks, I'll call you," Boyce said. "Otherwise, we'll meet in Porter's office tomorrow morning at nine, and we'll start all over again."

Sam first went up the stairs to the Crow's Nest and opened his suitcase. He took out the Glock and the shoulder holster and put it on under his jacket. He hadn't been asked to go through a metal detector when he first arrived at the course. If you were privileged enough to enter through the main gate, you could bring in an arsenal.

When he walked into the CBS trailer, Sam was surprised to hear the sound of Caroline's laughter, coming from the director's suite. The broadcast had gone off the air for the day; the monitors now displayed pictures of spectators shuffling off the property. Dennis Harwell stood behind Caroline and Petrakis, who were still watching the monitors.

He had expected to see Petrakis blowing cigar smoke at Caroline as she leaned away from him with folded arms; instead, they were looking at a man in a red-yellow-and-white striped shirt stretched so tight across his beer belly that he looked like a walking beach ball.

"Get a load of that guy," Petrakis said. "How does a fat fuck like that even fit through the metal detectors?"

"Come on, Tony," Caroline said. "He probably has a gland disorder."

"Gland, my ass. He never gets five feet from the concession tent."

Caroline laughed. "We're supposed to be looking for Lee Doggett," she said.

"I am, believe me," Petrakis said. "I'd love to find him right now, so we don't have to go through this bullshit tomorrow."

Harwell stood in the background, occasionally glancing at the folded printout of the Doggett booking photo, then back at the monitors. There was another copy of the photo on the console between Caroline and Petrakis, but she never looked at it. Throughout the banter with Petrakis, Caroline remained intently focused on spotting the man who'd tried to kill her. Sam decided not to break her concentration. He stood next to Harwell and watched the exiting fans until Petrakis began talking into his microphone.

"Too dark to see, boys," he said. "Shut 'em down. I want everyone back in their places for rehearsal tomorrow at 9 a.m... aw, quit griping. We didn't find the guy today, so we start looking first thing tomorrow...Yeah, it's overtime. Bukich already cleared it with your shop steward. Now get some rest. And keep this quiet. Anyone shoots off their mouth about what we're up to, he's fired. And I don't have to clear that with the union."

Petrakis took off his headset, stood up and stretched. He flipped a couple of switches on the console, then pulled on a sweater vest that hung on the back of his swivel chair.

"Weirdest fuckin' day I've ever spent at Augusta," he said, to no one in particular. "See ya tomorrow, toots."

He gave Caroline a quick squeeze on the shoulder and walked out of the trailer into the cooling night air, as a couple of network technicians moved in to shut things down.

Sam watched the God of War swagger out, then turned to Caroline, who was slumped back in her chair.

"What did you do to him?" he asked.

"He's not so bad, once you get to know him," Caroline said. "Did you know he won his first Emmy in 1967 for directing a kiddie show?"

"I bet those kids are still in therapy."

As they walked down the metal stairs from the CBS trailer, Harwell asked Sam and Caroline if they wanted a ride back to the clubhouse. Sam preferred to walk off some nervous energy. The gravel road through the trees to the par 3 course was no more than a few hundred feet long, and from there they'd be at the edge of Ike's Pond, within sight of the cabins on the hillside east of the clubhouse. He couldn't shake the thought that Doggett had come out of the same shadows that now surrounded them to drown Deborah Scanlon.

"Thanks, but we'll pass on the ride," Sam said. "I'm carrying my Glock tonight."

"I don't think that's such a good idea," Harwell said.

"Look, I'm still technically a cop, and I'm still licensed to carry," Sam said.

"Well…don't get trigger-happy," Harwell finally said. "You see something, call us."

Harwell got in his car and drove up the dirt road that led to the broadcast media gate on Washington Road.

Sam felt better walking through the woods with the bulge of the gun under his left arm. Even with the moon reflecting off Ike's Pond, and the sounds of music and laughter floating through the balmy night air from the cabins above the par 3 course, Sam saw how completely a man could disappear into the trees that surrounded the National. It was so dark now that he couldn't see five feet into the woods.

Caroline walked next to him with both of her arms wrapped around his bicep. She didn't seem to mind that she could feel the shoulder holster under his jacket.

"Is it going to be a problem bringing me up to the Crow's Nest?" Caroline asked as they walked up the service road that led behind the cabins to the clubhouse.

"No," Sam said. "Wheeling and Compton both missed the cut and went home. I've got the place to myself."

"What's David Porter going to think?" Caroline said.

"I didn't ask."

◇◇◇

They ate dinner on the porch again, watching the half-moon rise peacefully above the course and talking about anything they could think of besides Lee Doggett. The New York strips were grilled and seasoned just the way Sam liked them; the Silver Oak cabernet was the perfect complement. At odd moments Sam still felt at ease at the National. But he couldn't forget that there was something out there in that ocean, under those waves. The police and security guards who were stationed at the clubhouse tried not to make themselves too conspicuous—no doubt at the request of David Porter, who was still trying to complete this Masters in as normal an atmosphere as possible. But every few minutes another man in a black windbreaker, black pants, white shirt, and a black ballcap would walk across the grass below them, past the tables with their drawn-in umbrellas, his gaze sweeping left and right. Sam didn't find their increased presence comforting; with each pass of a security guard, he thought of a new way Doggett might get around them.

They finished the wine, and Caroline yawned.

"I'm sorry," she said, covering her mouth. "It's been a long day—and I didn't sleep real well last night. Mind if I go to bed?"

"I'll walk you up," Sam said.

As they stood up from the table, Caroline took his hand and looked him in the eye.

"I'm starting to feel safe again," she said. "Thanks."

"Least I can do for getting you into this," Sam said.

They walked into the library together and turned down the narrow hallway that led to the champions' locker room.

Halfway down the hall, they turned and went up the staircase to the Crow's Nest.

Sam had brought her bags up that morning and set them on one of the beds. He took off his clothes and hung the shoulder holster on the desk chair in his cubicle. He put on a pair of shorts, brushed his teeth, and got into his bed, turning out his light and listening as Caroline unzipped her bags in the adjoining cubicle. She eventually clicked off the light in the common area, and the moonlight streaming through the cupola made a slanted windowpane pattern on the wall at the foot of Sam's bed.

"I think you're going to like my pajamas," he heard her say.

The shadow of a figure standing in his doorway was now superimposed over the windowpane pattern on the wall. Sam propped himself on his elbow and looked at Caroline, leaning up against the doorframe, backlit by the moon. Her dark hair hung to her shoulders, spreading out across the white of the caddie jumpsuit she was wearing. The zipper on the front of the jumpsuit was pulled halfway down to her waist.

"Now you get to find out what I have on under here," she said, walking slowly over to his bed.

She sat on the edge of his bed, leaned over, and kissed him. He reached up and put his hands on her shoulders, then caressed her hair as it hung down near his face. He kissed her, and with his left hand he found the zipper and pulled it slowly downward. He put his hand inside the jumpsuit. All he felt was her smooth, soft skin. He kissed her again, then put both hands on the zippered edges of the open jumpsuit. He drew the two sides gently apart, and in the moonlight he saw her breasts spill out of the caddie suit.

"You're going to get an incredible tip this week," he said as he pulled her down to him.

Chapter Thirty-eight

Sunday, April 13

The songbirds were chirping with purpose and the eastern sky was beginning to show signs of pink between the trunks of the pine trees as Doggett awoke. The air was crisp; Doggett could see his breath as he rolled onto his back to look up at the sky, but the lack of cloud cover promised a quickly warming morning.

He had used leaves and branches to cover himself on his bed of pine needles. The exposed surfaces of his pants and windbreaker were covered with a light film of dew. He had slept with no fear of being discovered; when darkness had fallen, he'd walked deep into the center of the 55-acre nature preserve, far from the service roads that bisected the forest of pines, hardwoods, and bushes at the eastern edge of the club's property. Now that the first light of dawn was beginning to penetrate the canopy above him, he would be able to find the spot where he'd buried his supplies.

Somehow he'd always known it would come to this. Two murders on the golf club grounds—and several more easily tied to the same killer—might have stopped any other tournament, but the stubborn old men of Augusta National simply wouldn't yield to reality. Doggett knew these men too well. He'd taken orders from them. He'd been discarded and imprisoned by them. He'd lost everything to them—and meanwhile they continued with their single-minded obsession to let nothing get in the way of their annual orgy of self-congratulation. That's why he'd prepared for this day even before he'd been released from prison.

It had begun with his conversations with Bernard Pettibone, and solidified with his trial run at the football field in Statesboro.

After he killed Ashby and dumped his body in the pond at Amen Corner, Doggett had gone back to the open-sided maintenance shed east of the 11th hole and hoisted two sacks of high-nitrogen-content fertilizer over his shoulder. He carried them deep into the woods and buried them under a trio of pine trees that stood taller than any of the other trees around them. He expected the entire course, its fences, and all its facilities to be in lockdown after the body was found floating in the pond, but that wouldn't matter. He could find his way back to those trees again, if and when he needed to.

Along with the fertilizer, he'd buried the farmer's revolver. He knew he'd be back, and he'd never be able to get a gun through the metal detectors at the spectator entrances.

Now he had to find that hole.

Doggett stood up, brushed the debris off his pants and windbreaker, and looked up at the tops of the nearby pines. He didn't see the trees he was looking for, which meant he had to go still farther east. The sun would be spreading beams of light through the woods in a matter of minutes, and he could already hear the sound of motorized vehicles moving around the grounds. The golf bag he carried made it slow going through the underbrush, but it was the density of the forest that made his hiding place so effective. The only living things back here were the squirrels, chipmunks, foxes, birds, and insects.

He came to the top of a steep hillside and again peered toward the east. The maintenance shed was probably a quarter-mile to the north; he'd crossed the service road that led from the 11th fairway to the shed the night before as he went deeper into the trees. The three pines ought to be visible if he went a little farther south, toward Amen Corner. After another five minutes of struggling through the underbrush, he looked up and saw the tops of the three pine trees towering ahead of him, just as he remembered them. His buried treasure was no more than 200 feet away.

He found the raised mound he'd left in the earth at the base of the center tree, undisturbed over the past week. He laid the golf bag down and found a flat rock, which he used as a trowel to scrape away the dirt. When he got down to the fertilizer sacks, he lifted each one carefully out of the hole, brushed the dirt off, and set it aside. Then he took the handgun from the hole and tucked it inside his pants.

He would have to wait until spectators lined the gallery ropes along the 10th and 11th holes. That would be at least another three or four hours. But he might as well get ready now.

He leaned the golf bag upright against the center pine tree, cut open the first sack of fertilizer, and began pouring the contents into the golf bag.

◇◇◇

Sam awoke to the sound of footsteps coming up the creaky stairway to the Crow's Nest. He glanced at the clock next to his bed: 8:45 a.m. He hadn't meant to sleep that late. His knees were stiff from walking the grounds all day Saturday, looking for Doggett. Then he glanced at Caroline, whose naked body was pressed up against his back, her right arm outside the blanket and draped across his waist. Her caddie jumpsuit was on the floor, with the SKARDA name patch facing the ceiling.

He looked back toward the stairs and saw Mark Boyce enter the common room.

"Well, this might be a first," Boyce said, looking through the open entryway into Sam's cubicle. "I can see it in the Masters record book: First participant to sleep with his caddie in the Crow's Nest."

"I'm sure somebody like Dow Finsterwald has already done it," Sam said sleepily. "What are you doing here?"

"I told you I always wanted to see the Crow's Nest, and you said come up any time."

"That's right, I did," Sam said, lying back on his pillow and covering his face with his arm. Caroline opened her eyes, saw Boyce in the outer room, and gave him a wave.

"There's news," Boyce said, suddenly turning serious. "We've been interviewing the prisoners who knew Doggett in Reidsville. There's a guy named Pettibone who's in for blowing up a judge. He said Doggett made him explain how to make a fertilizer bomb."

"The same kind as Oklahoma City?"

"Basically. Doggett isn't going to get a van full of explosives in here. But even 25 pounds of that stuff could kill dozens of people in a tightly packed crowd."

"And he doesn't have to bring it in," Sam said, now grasping the scope of the problem. "It's already here."

"They've got tons of it," Boyce said. "There's something else. A Richmond County deputy reported an abandoned handicap scooter outside the men's bathroom by the 18th tee. He doesn't remember who rode it there, but it was sometime yesterday afternoon. Whoever was on it went into the bathroom and never came back for it."

"Doggett?"

"Yeah. The scooter came from a rental place out on Berckmans Road. We talked to the woman who runs the place. She remembered the guy who rented it. Said he looked sick, like he had cancer. Totally bald head—but kind of tall. She called the club at about 7 last night when the guy didn't bring the scooter back."

"Did he leave an I.D.? Some kind of deposit?" Sam asked.

"No. The lady said he didn't have his license with him. She felt sorry for him and let him have the scooter anyway. We showed her Doggett's picture, and she said she thought it could be the same guy."

"So Doggett might have been here overnight?"

"Yeah. We were going to bring a couple of K-9 units in this morning to start sniffing for him, but Porter said no. He's still worried about a panic."

"He'd rather let a killer run loose?" Caroline said, raising her head to look over Sam's shoulder.

"I called the Atlanta office," Boyce said, averting his eyes. "They told me to let Porter call the shots, unless I've got a definite sighting."

"I guess Porter has a little pull with the state," Sam said.

"You think? Hell, the governor plays here more than most of the members."

"Maybe Porter's got a point," Sam said. "The gates are already open. You get a bunch of cops and dogs running around here with 40,000 people on the grounds, and you're going to have chaos. It could make it that much easier for Doggett."

Boyce said the cops and security guards were being given a new description of Doggett: a gaunt man with a shaved head, about 6-foot-3, wearing a bucket hat and sunglasses, dark blue windbreaker, black pants. They were also being told that Doggett might be looking to plant a bomb somewhere. Anyone even remotely matching that description carrying something heavier than an umbrella should be stopped and searched.

"Meeting's in Porter's office in a few minutes," Boyce said as he turned toward the stairway. "Caroline, I think Tony Petrakis has coffee and croissants waiting for you over at the CBS trailer."

Sam and Caroline got out of bed and dressed quickly. Sam put the shoulder holster on under his jacket. At some point in the afternoon it would be too warm for the jacket; hopefully they'd have caught Doggett by then.

Caroline dressed in shorts and a pullover jersey. Sam watched her brush her thick black hair in the bathroom that he'd shared with Wheeling and Compton. He much preferred the current company.

They went down the Crow's Nest stairs together and saw Clive Cartwright on his way into the Champions' locker room. He glanced at them and raised his eyebrows.

"The club is getting rather broadminded these days," Cartwright said.

On their way down the main stairway to the lobby, they passed one of the club's oldest members, Henry Lockwood, arduously lifting his legs one step after the other up to the second floor. Sam expected a disdainful glare from the real-estate billionaire, but Lockwood merely glanced downward at Caroline's legs, then back up at Sam, and gave him an approving nod.

In the parking lot outside the main entrance, Sam kissed Caroline. He wasn't sure what kind of reception he'd receive, but she kissed him back with feeling.

"Come by the trailer when you can," Caroline said.

"I'll have my earpiece in all day," Sam said. "If you spot him, I'll know right away. Besides, Harwell can protect you from Tony."

"It's not that," she said seriously. "I just want to know you're all right."

They kissed again and then went in separate directions, Sam toward the administration building and Caroline toward the par 3 course and the television compound beyond.

The gun under Sam's arm reminded him that last night was already a long time ago.

◇◇◇

"David, if a man were going to hide overnight on your grounds, where would he do it?" Sam asked.

Leonard Garver and Dennis Harwell sat on one side of David Porter's office with a sober-faced man wearing a neatly trimmed moustache who had identified himself as Curtis T. Dunn, head of the regional office of Securitas. On the other side of the room, Sam sat with Boyce and Robert Brisbane. They'd gone over the information about the bomb-making instructions, the scooter and the new description of Doggett.

Porter swiveled in his chair to face Sam.

"There are wooded areas along Berckmans Road south of the maintenance building, and south of the 16th and 13th holes," he said, as though going over a topographical map in his head. "Then there are the woods around the par 3 course and back by the TV production area. There's 55 acres of forest beside the 10th and 11th holes."

"What's back there?"

"Lots and lots of trees," Porter said.

"Anything else?"

Porter told him about the auxiliary maintenance facility in the woods between the TV compound and the 11th fairway, where the club stored some vehicles, tools and supplies.

"Did anyone look around that area after Ashby and Scanlon were murdered?" Sam asked.

Harwell said the cops had done a walk-through in the woods from the 12th green up to the 10th tee after Ashby's body was found and hadn't seen anything. There were cops at the shed and greenhouse now, making sure the fertilizer didn't go anywhere.

"There's a lot of cover around here," Boyce said. "Doggett could have stayed on the grounds last night, and we'd never know."

"Our people are trained to keep patrons out of the woods," Dunn said.

"Unless you've got agents every 10 feet, somebody could slip in there without being seen," Sam said. "He could detonate a bomb within 50 feet of the gallery and no one would see him."

"Should we send some people into the woods to look for him?" Dunn said.

"Your guys aren't trained for that," Boyce said. "We need all the cops and guards we have watching the spectator areas."

◇◇◇

The first sack of fertilizer filled three-quarters of the golf bag. Doggett cut open the second sack and poured in more fertilizer until there was about five inches of space left unfilled.

He opened the nylon chair sack he'd stolen from the women by the 18th green. *Your container*, he said to himself, remembering Pettibone's tutorial. He poured the remaining fertilizer into the sack. *Your fuel.* Then he took the Masters towel he'd bought at the gift shop and tore it into two pieces, placing the bigger piece on top of the fertilizer in the golf bag, and the smaller piece inside the chair bag. He broke open the plastic shells of the cigarette lighters and poured the fluid onto the pieces of towel in the bags. *Your accelerant.*

He estimated that he was about a third of a mile from the point where he'd entered the woods the afternoon before. Given the rough, overgrown terrain—and the possibility of cops looking for him—it would take him about an hour to carefully return to the golf course. He started walking in the direction of the 11th fairway.

◇◇◇

Sam left Porter's office and walked out to the parking lot behind the clubhouse. The players on the range were banging out their warm-up shots on the other side of the grandstand. Heads protruded above the railing along the entire length of the top row of the practice range grandstand. Full house today, as usual.

Porter was right—a man trying to avoid being seen overnight had almost limitless hiding places to choose from inside the fences of Augusta National. But Sam would have chosen the 55 acres east of the 10th and 11th holes. If you were looking for cover, why not choose the biggest forest on the property?

Sam began walking east, toward the woods.

Chapter Thirty-nine

Sam walked past the short-game practice area, where several players with early tee times were lofting wedges over a white-sand bunker to the chipping green. He saw Dwight Wilson talking to his cousin Chipmunk, who was cleaning Al Barber's clubs with a towel as the former champion hit lob shots. Dwight spotted Sam and gave him the thumbs-up sign, which Sam returned.

He decided to go back into the woods through the television compound, which would give him a chance to stop and see Caroline.

He showed his I.D. badge to the two security guards at the entrance to the TV production parking lot. It was still early; CBS wouldn't be on the air for another four hours. A few technicians were walking around with clipboards, spools of TV cable, and Styrofoam cups of coffee. Harwell was already there; his unmarked squad car was parked where it had been on Saturday, near the cart shed. Inside the CBS trailer, he heard Petrakis' piercing voice putting his announcers and camera operators through their rehearsal. He called out each hole number and listened to the responses through the console speakers as he watched his main monitor.

"Collins, 11 and 12—you're up," Petrakis said.

"Maybe...Yes, sir!" said the voice of CBS hole announcer Ted Collins, a former PGA Tour player. The call was the one made famous by Verne Lundquist two decades earlier, when

Jack Nicklaus birdied the 17th hole en route to winning his final Masters at age 46.

"Good," Petrakis said. "Timmerman, 13—go."

"Maybe...Yes, sir!" the voice of teaching pro Buddy Timmerman repeated from the tower that overlooked the 13th hole.

Each announcer repeated the same phrase as Petrakis switched to shots from each of the closing holes. Though the grandstands had not yet filled on the back nine, Caroline studied the camera shots as they appeared on the monitors. Harwell was where he had been Saturday, standing behind Caroline with a cup of coffee in his hand, looking restless.

"How's it going?" Sam asked.

Caroline turned and smiled.

"Nothing yet—but I'm starting to get the hang of this," she said. "If Tony needs a break, I think I could fill in."

"In your dreams, sweetheart," Petrakis said.

Sam told Caroline he was going out into the woods to look around.

"What do you mean, look around?" she said. "You're going try to find Doggett, aren't you?"

"Yes."

Caroline got up from her chair and took Sam to a corner of the trailer.

"You can't control this one," she said, staring into his eyes. "You understand that, don't you? There's a thousand cops looking for Doggett. You don't have to be the guy that finds him. You don't have to get killed over this."

"It's my job."

"Don't be so goddamn stubborn. You've done your job. You found out who the killer was. Let the cops do the rest."

"I am a cop," Sam said.

Caroline had a grip on Sam's arm, but the grip loosened. She realized who she was talking to—not Sam Skarda, the golfer, but Detective Skarda of the Minneapolis Police Department. It was like trying to talk to Shane. When his mind was made up, nothing could change it. No alternative points of view could penetrate. Why waste her breath?

"You can't go in there alone."

"She's right," Harwell said. "I'll go with you."

Sam preferred to have backup, but Harwell wouldn't have been his first choice. Harwell had yet to impress him.

"Somebody's got to get the word out if Caroline spots Doggett," he said to the Richmond County detective.

"I'll get a deputy over here," Harwell said. "I was bored out of my mind yesterday. I need to get out of this trailer."

"You don't appreciate genius when you see it," Petrakis said.

Harwell got on his radio and requested that a deputy be sent over to the CBS trailer to replace him. He told Caroline to alert the officer immediately if she spotted Doggett on camera; the officer would then radio Boyce and Dunn. Petrakis was to keep a camera on Doggett until the on-course security could converge on him.

"Maybe we'll flush him out of the woods," Harwell said to Sam. "Like a quail hunt."

Caroline held Sam's gaze for a moment before he left the trailer with Harwell. His thoughts flashed back to the previous night. He wanted more nights like that. Did Caroline?

Sam and Harwell walked across the lot to the security checkpoint and kept going south on a gravel service road that led down a hill through the woods and across a wooden bridge over a stream. The road swung back uphill and turned to pavement as they emerged into a clearing. There they saw the maintenance shed and greenhouse, which were being guarded by several Securitas agents and Richmond County deputies. Harwell nodded to the cops he knew as he and Sam walked past. The paved road now led downhill again, toward the 11th fairway.

"This is where we go into the woods," Sam said. "Everything east of here to the fence line is nature preserve."

"You don't have to do this," Harwell said to Sam.

"Neither do you."

"It's my job."

"You could have stayed in the trailer."

Harwell shook his head.

"No, I couldn't."

"What do you mean?"

Harwell looked at the tops of the trees, took a deep breath, and let it out with a heavy sigh. Then he looked back at Sam.

"I helped send the poor dumb bastard to prison. I thought if I did Stanwick a favor, it could help my career. Maybe it did. I made detective a year later."

"You planted the dope?"

Harwell nodded, looking down again.

"Stanwick said the D.A. was sure Doggett would walk if we didn't have a stronger case. Stanwick said he wanted to use Doggett as an example that you can't fuck with the National. I figured in the long run it would make all our jobs easier. Besides, Doggett wasn't an innocent man. He was a crook."

"I know," Sam said. "Now he's a murderer."

"It was wrong," Harwell said. "I've been sorry ever since I did it. But I didn't think it would turn out this way."

"You never do," Sam said, shaking his head.

What else could he say? There was no point in beating up Harwell over a mistake he'd made eight years ago. At least he was trying to make up for it now.

"You gonna tell Garver?" Harwell asked.

"That's your business," Sam said. "What happened back then doesn't concern me. Let's just find Doggett."

Harwell nodded and drew his Heckler and Koch USP, holding it down at his side. Sam drew the Glock from inside his jacket.

"I'll take the left," Harwell said. "You move straight ahead. Let's try to keep visual contact with each other."

Sam watched as Harwell moved into the trees toward the east. The detective wore a dark brown jacket that was barely visible through the underbrush—difficult for Doggett to spot, but difficult for Sam to keep track of, too.

Sam left the pavement where the service road veered westward toward the course. The first 20 or 30 feet into the pine forest was not tough going, but after that, Sam had to push aside sharp branches and step over rocks as he penetrated deeper into the bushes and trees. He snagged his jacket several times; he had to make sure he didn't let a stray twig get inside the trigger guard of his gun. An accidental gunshot would be a disaster—it would be heard by thousands of spectators and send an army of cops and security guards scrambling into the woods. Worse, it would alert Doggett that they were approaching—if, in fact, he was there at all.

The forest was unnervingly silent, except for the sound of his own footsteps crunching on fallen leaves and pine needles, and the singing of the birds overhead. Far in the distance, Sam heard occasional bursts of applause—probably from the 7th green, the closest front nine hole to where he was now. He kept glancing to his left, trying to see Harwell's red hair bobbing slowly up and down through the underbrush. Sometimes Harwell was not visible, but when Sam adjusted his course to the left, he picked him up again.

It was slow going. After nearly an hour, he figured they must be getting close to the 11th green, although they were deep enough into the woods that they wouldn't be able to see it. The first groups of the day would not be arriving at 11 for almost an hour, but he knew the grandstand that overlooked the 11th green, the 12th hole and the 13th tee—the heart of Amen Corner—would already be filled. There was no better place to have a chance at witnessing Masters history.

Sam heard a rustling ahead of him and dropped to his knees. It wasn't Harwell; he was a good 75 yards to the left. It wasn't a falling pine cone—it was something, or someone, moving in the bushes ahead.

Sam crouched as low as he could and tried to control his breathing. He held the Glock in front of him, bracing it with his left hand and listening for a repeat of the sound he'd heard. In the stillness of the woods, he felt as though even his shallow breathing was deafening. Sweat trickled down the side of his face. The grip on the gun felt slick.

He heard the sound again—now more to his right. But he still couldn't see anything through the dense bushes ahead.

Whatever it was, it was moving cautiously toward the west…toward the golf course. Sam leaned slowly to his right, to get a better look through the bush ahead of him, and he saw a quick movement along the ground, streaking between two loblolly pines. He stood up quickly, extending the gun in front of him with both hands, and started to yell "Freeze!" when he realized it was a fox that had run past him.

Sam sat back against a tree and took his finger off the trigger of the Glock, letting out a sigh. He would have felt more comfortable hunting for a fugitive in an alley or a warehouse than skulking around in this forest. He wasn't trained to distinguish the sounds made by animals from the sounds made by psychopaths.

That's when he heard the gunshot.

It echoed through the pines, coming from at least 100 yards to his left. It sounded like a handgun. Had Harwell shot Doggett? If he had, he would be yelling for Sam as soon as he was sure Doggett was down—or he'd be on his radio. But there was no further sound after the gunshot. Did Doggett shoot Harwell? If he did, how did he get a gun onto the National grounds?

Sam's mind raced as he pushed through the bushes. He couldn't presume who had fired the shot, or what he'd find; there was a chance Harwell was dead and Doggett was waiting with a loaded gun for whoever responded to the sound. He used the thick pine trees for cover, sliding from one trunk to the next with his gun in his right hand. He'd peer around the corner and then quickly move to the next pine, hoping he was keeping the tree between himself and the shooter—if the shooter had not been Harwell.

It took Sam 10 minutes to cover the ground to the spot where he thought the shot had come from. His concern continued to increase the longer the silence lasted. Harwell must have been hit—otherwise, why wasn't he giving out his location?

Sam saw three tall pines standing in a row about 50 feet ahead of him. With no other pines nearby for cover, he knelt behind some bushes and crept forward until he saw a freshly dug hole at the base of the center tree.

"Harwell!" he called out, but heard nothing in response. He inched forward and saw two plastic sacks lying on the ground near the hole, ripped open and empty. Even without looking, he knew what had been in the bags. He called Harwell's name again. Nothing. Sam scrambled over to the hole, looked at the empty fertilizer sacks, and found four cracked cigarette-lighter shells scattered nearby. Shit. This was bad.

Doggett could be hiding behind a tree nearby with a gun aimed at his head. But Harwell was down somewhere nearby. Sam had to find him—and radio for help.

Staying as low to the ground as possible, Sam crawled back in the direction Harwell would have been coming from. He guessed that Doggett wouldn't have been able to make a good hit from farther than 50 feet. With the Glock still in his right hand, Sam swept the bushes to the north of the three pines, first moving to his right, then back to his left. On his second pass back to the left, he saw a pair of brown boots with deep treads extending from behind a pine tree. Sam recognized the boots.

Harwell's.

He scrambled along the ground to the other side of the tree and saw Harwell lying on his back with a bullet hole under his left eye. The only thing moving was the blood seeping down the detective's face and pooling under his head in the dirt. Sam checked Harwell's carotid artery with his index and middle finger, and knew instantly that he was dead. The Heckler and Koch was still in Harwell's right hand. Sam smelled the barrel. It had not been fired.

This is bad, Sam repeated. He's made a bomb, and he's heading for the golf course. And I can't just stand up and go running after Doggett, wherever he might have gone. The guy's armed and knows we're after him.

Sam took the radio handset from his belt, depressed the thumb switch, and said in a low but urgent voice, "Officer down in the woods…east of the 11th fairway. Repeat, officer down. The suspect has bomb materials. I don't know his location, but he's not far from the golf course."

Sam listened through his earpiece for the response. Boyce came on the frequency within seconds.

"Sam? That you? We're getting reports of something that sounded like a gunshot."

"Yeah," Sam said. "We're in the woods on the east side of the 11th fairway. Harwell's dead. Doggett got him with one shot. I never saw him, but I found two empty fertilizer sacks. He's got to be heading for the course."

"Goddammit," Boyce said. "Try to find him before he gets out of the woods. We'll send all the officers in the area over there. You didn't see him?"

"He was gone when I found Harwell."

"We're coming," Boyce said. "Find him."

Sam put the radio back in its belt holder and stood up, in pain from kneeling so long. He looked back at Harwell's body and knew it was mere luck—very bad luck for Harwell—that he was standing and Harwell was on the ground with a bullet in his head.

Let's hope my luck holds out, he thought as he began walking through the pines toward the golf course. A song from one of the April playlists popped into his head—Tom Petty's "Refugee," from 1980. Seve Ballesteros won that year. Seve was always good at getting out of the woods.

◇◇◇

At 12 over par, Al Barber was in the first group to tee off Sunday, along with former champion Clive Cartwright, who would be old enough to join the senior tour in July. They had played quickly, as the first group out on Sunday is expected to do. Neither had to worry about being invited back the following year; past Masters champions were always welcomed back until they reached such physical decline that they could no longer play 18 holes of acceptable golf.

Al Barber was trying to prove that he was still several years away from reaching that point. Despite his aching back and legs, he was fashioning another respectable round at four over par, giving Cartwright a spirited battle to stay out of last place.

Barber had the honor on the 12th tee. At least 5,000 people were now clustered in and around the packed grandstand behind him. He took off his snap-brimmed cap and wiped his face with the towel his caddie handed to him. Sweat from the late-morning sun was beading on his scalp between the thinning hairs of his crewcut. Hot, sweaty, tired, aching—God, he still loved tournament golf.

"Seven or an eight?" he asked Chipmunk, surveying the dangerous 155-yard shot over Rae's Creek to the narrow 12th green.

"Smooth seven today, Al," the caddie said. "Flag on 11 is with us."

Barber liked the smooth seven. He took the club from Chipmunk, teed up his Callaway, and prepared to take his stance, glancing again at the Sunday pin placement at the far right of the skinny green. He addressed the ball, looked back at the target one more time, and drew the club back.

At that moment, a noise that could only have been an explosion reverberated from somewhere up the 11th fairway. The gallery snapped their heads to the left, trying to see where the awful sound was coming from, as Barber continued with his swing and sent his ball soaring into the sky above the 12th green. Few saw his ball carry the front bunker and come to rest 10 feet left of the flag; in fact, Al Barber himself stopped watching his shot as soon as he realized that something had gone terribly wrong nearby.

Dwight Wilson was sitting in the grandstand behind the 12th tee when Barber hit his tee shot, followed immediately by the explosion. He stood up and looked to his right as security guards from the 13th hole came running across the grass toward the grandstand at 12, joining the guards at that hole in holding up their hands and pleading with the spectators to remain seated. On the top rows of the grandstand, people were standing and looking back up the hill at the 11th fairway. Dwight heard the word "bomb" filter down from the top of the grandstand to the people seated immediately behind the tee. Now he could see a cloud of white smoke rising in the distance above the grandstand. There was fear in the faces of the spectators around him, but the Securitas agents continued to assure the patrons that everything was under control. Most remained in their seats, not sure where else to go, but Dwight got up and headed for the exit.

"Doggett," Dwight muttered. "Motherfucker got past every-body."

Chapter Forty

When Sam heard the explosion, he started running. No reason to be cautious now—Doggett had detonated the bomb.

He ran through the woods toward the cloud of smoke ahead of him. This was all going to shit. Harwell was dead and Doggett had bombed Augusta National. How the hell had he managed to get the bomb onto the course and set it off without the security guards and cops stopping him? They were all watching for him—how had he gotten away with it?

He pulled out the radio handset and held down the transmitter.

"Boyce! This is Skarda! What's going on?"

"We don't know," Boyce said. "Securitas is reporting some kind of explosion near the 11th tee. I'm heading there now on the service road."

"Can they see anything on the TV monitors?" Sam said.

"Culver!" Boyce said. "Do you read this? Let us know what you're seeing!"

Culver must have been the officer who'd taken Harwell's place in the CBS trailer. An unfamiliar voice came on and said they were seeing a lot of smoke and some downed trees in the woods east of the 10th green and the 11th tee.

"Any bodies?" Boyce demanded.

"Can't tell," Culver said. "Smoke's too thick. But I gotta say, it looks like maybe we got lucky. Not many people over there, from what I can see."

Sam ran as fast as he could through the tangled forest, nearing the emergency personnel hovering around the smoking crater. The lumberyard smell of freshly cut wood and pine sap blended with the acrid odor of burning chemicals. Through the haze Sam could see that Culver's report was accurate: Some 100 feet off the golf course, well away from the gallery, a dozen trees had been knocked down or damaged, some of them snapped off just a few feet above the ground. A black hole still smoldered in the center of the destruction. Police, Securitas agents, and paramedics were converging on the spot, some attending to the terrified patrons nearby, the rest gawking at the damage.

Sam couldn't figure out what had happened. There were no injuries here. Had the bomb gone off prematurely?

One of the officers began stringing police tape from pine tree to pine tree in a wide circle around the bomb site.

"Anybody see who did this, or how big the bomb was?" Sam asked the cop with the police tape.

"Nope," the cop said. "But there are bits of nylon everywhere. I got a piece of it here."

The cop pointed to the ground, where Sam saw a piece of ragged, blackened nylon bearing part of a Masters logo. Sam had seen something like that many times as he'd walked among the spectators looking for Doggett. It was from a stuff sack for those folding Masters chairs. That wasn't big enough. Doggett had much more fertilizer than that. Where was he now?

There was no sign of a body—Doggett hadn't been killed in the explosion. He was still somewhere on the grounds. This wasn't over.

Sam turned on the radio and said, "Culver, this is Sam. Let me talk to Caroline."

"Sam?" He heard Caroline's voice. "Where are you?"

"Near where the bomb went off. Caroline, tell Petrakis not to stop scanning the crowd. We haven't found Doggett yet. He's still loose out here somewhere."

"Are you hurt?"

"No. I don't think anyone got hurt. But something feels wrong about this. Keep looking for him."

"We will. Don't be a hero."

◇◇◇

After a quick consultation in David Porter's office, Robert Brisbane had gone to the media building and announced a suspension of play. It was only temporary, he insisted, until the security forces could assess the damage in the woods by the 11th tee. Play would resume then. It appeared that no one had been injured. Spectators were being encouraged to remain in their grandstand seats; that would make it much easier for the police and security guards to do their jobs, which in turn would allow play to resume that much faster.

The warning horn used for lighting sounded two long blasts. Word went out across the course to the rules official with each twosome: Play was suspended immediately. Players could not finish the hole they were on. No one knew how long it would take to get the all-clear, so players could return to the clubhouse if they wished.

When the official with the Barber-Cartwright pairing gave the two ex-champs the news, both decided to go back up to the clubhouse to wait out the delay. A courtesy SUV parked behind the grandstand at 12 would take them up the hill. Most of the spectators chose to stay in the grandstand and on the hillside overlooking Amen Corner, rather than risk losing their seats when play resumed.

Dwight Wilson couldn't sit still, however. He left the grandstand and walked behind it to the concession area, where confused spectators and employees were creating a scene of near-chaos. He spotted the caddies for Barber and Cartwright loading their clubs into the SUV. He asked Chipmunk if he saw what happened.

"No, we was trying to play golf," Chipmunk said.

"Sounded like a plane crashed in the woods," Barber said.

"No, it was a bomb," the shuttle driver said. "They're saying nobody was hurt. Whoever did it might have blown himself up—dumb shit. Good riddance. Anyways, we might be playing again in an hour or so."

"Well, they'd better catch the bugger first," Cartwright said. "It's difficult to concentrate with explosions in one's backswing."

"We're heading back up to the clubhouse, Dwight," Barber said. "Want a lift?"

"Sure thing."

The driver inched the Cadillac Escalade through the crowd between the bathrooms and the concession tent. Dwight looked out at the people they were passing. Some still looked frightened and confused. Others seemed almost giddy that they'd narrowly avoided a disaster, and now had a story they could tell the folks back in Knoxville or Spartanburg.

Dwight expected all of the pros and their caddies to take the shuttles back to the clubhouse. There was really no place to wait on the course. Then he noticed a caddie, golf bag over his shoulder, walking through the crowd along the ropes behind the 10th green, headed down the hill toward the 11th hole. This was strange. Why would this guy be moving against the flow of security guards, all of whom seemed to be headed up the 11th fairway to the site of the explosion?

Dwight didn't recognize him. Who was he looping for? Dwight shifted his weight and turned his head as far to the rear as he could, looking out the rear window of the SUV, to get a look at the back of the caddie's jumpsuit as he walked through the crowd.

"Chipmunk, you recognize that caddie?" Dwight said to his cousin.

Chipmunk turned to look at the receding caddie. They couldn't read the name on the back of the suit through the crowd. They watched as the caddie kept walking, finally emerging into an open space where they could get a clear look:

ROCKINGHAM

"What the hell? That's not Shane Rockingham's caddie," Dwight said.

"Weed's shorter. Got long hair," Chipmunk agreed.

"He wouldn't be here anyway," Dwight said. "Rockingham left town Tuesday morning. That's Weed's jumpsuit—but that sure as hell ain't Weed."

"No, it sure ain't," Chipmunk agreed.

"You mind if we stop a minute, Al?" Dwight said.

"What's up?" Barber asked.

"I gotta find a security guard."

The driver came to a stop, and Dwight got out of the SUV. The guy with ROCKINGHAM on his jumpsuit had vanished into the crowd. The only security guards and cops Dwight could see were running across the 11th fairway to see if they could lend a hand at the explosion site. Dwight went back to the SUV and asked the driver if he could contact the clubhouse.

"I can call tournament headquarters," the driver said.

"Tell them I need to talk to a guy named Sam Skarda," Dwight said. "Right now."

◇◇◇

Sam had moved out of the smoky woods into the 11th fairway, covered now by a small army of security and emergency people. Photographers who had been following the players were now focusing their lenses on the chaotic scene. A few spectators near the 11th tee had been nicked by flying wood chips and rocks from the explosion, but there'd been no damage to the course, and no serious injuries—just a lot of noise, smoke, and confusion.

Sam had no doubt now. That was just the first bomb—a diversion.

He heard his radio crackle.

"Skarda? It's Boyce."

Sam switched on his transmitter: "What is it?"

"A man named Dwight Wilson called in for you. Says he saw a guy in a caddie suit with the name Rockingham on the back, walking through the crowd with a golf bag. What's the story? Rockingham's out of the tournament, right?"

"He's been gone since Tuesday," Sam said, almost shouting into the radio. "Where was this guy?"

"Somewhere in the crowd between the 10th green and the 12th hole," Boyce said.

"It could be Doggett!" Sam said, starting to run across the fairway. "Call Petrakis! Get the cameras on that crowd. Find the guy in the Rockingham suit!"

His breath was coming in gasps as he ran toward the grandstand behind the 12th tee. If Doggett had gotten his hands on Weed's jumpsuit, he could walk through the crowd unnoticed—with a golf bag full of explosives.

"Where are you?" Boyce asked.

"11th fairway," Sam panted. "Where are you?"

"Halfway down 10. I'm headed for the bomb site."

"There's no way Doggett used two bags of fertilizer on that bomb in the woods!" Sam said. "He's still got a golf bag full of the stuff!"

Sam's left knee was stiffening up on him. He wasn't moving fast enough. He scanned the throngs of people in the pines to the right of 11 and couldn't see anyone in a caddie suit.

"Culver," Sam said into his radio. "This is Skarda. Can you hear me? Put Caroline on."

"Sam, it's me." It was Caroline's voice. "We're looking for that caddie, but we're not seeing anything."

"Are there any hand-held cameras by the 12th hole?"

Caroline was silent a moment. Sam wondered what they were seeing. He needed to go somewhere, do something—but what? Where?

"No," she finally said. "The portable crews in that area went up the hill to where the explosion was. We're looking at a shot from the camera behind the 12th green. Going tight on the crowd. Nothing…I don't see him…"

Sam began running faster, his knee screaming. He crossed the gallery ropes and ran to the concession area behind the grandstand on 12. He looked at the spectators under the tent and standing in front of the souvenir stand. He ran through the men's bathroom. Nothing.

He was about to call back to Caroline when he noticed a gate-like doorway in the green mesh material that covered the backside of the grandstand. The gate was covered by the same material, but Sam could see movement behind it. He pulled the Glock from his shoulder holster, held it at his side, and walked carefully up to the back of the grandstand. He could still see a figure through the tight green mesh. Could the figure inside see him? The backdrop of sunlight would make his image visible through the material. Even though he wasn't wearing a police uniform, Sam couldn't risk that Doggett wouldn't shoot him through the mesh anyway.

He dropped to a crouch, reached for the latch on the gate, swung the door open, and thrust the Glock into the opening.

"Put down the gun!" he yelled.

Inside, three terrified teenagers in yellow jumpsuits—members of the club's litter detail—threw their hands up. The playing cards they were holding fell from their hands and scattered on the makeshift card table between them.

"Don't shoot, man," one of them stammered. "We're just playing poker!"

Sam let out his breath, stood up, and put the Glock back in the holster. He'd been ready to put a bullet into whoever was under that grandstand. Finding Doggett was going to be hard enough; stopping him without hurting anybody else was going to be harder.

He apologized to the wide-eyed litter crew, closed the gate, and suddenly wondered why he was doing this. Why was he risking his life, and the life of anyone who might come between him and Doggett? He could hear Caroline's voice in his head: David Porter had hired him to find out who the killer was. Now they knew—why not let the cops take over?

The question answered itself, and Sam knew it: It wasn't about working for Augusta National. It was about saving lives.

He'd almost been too late to save Caroline; everyone in this crowd meant as much to someone else as Caroline was beginning to mean to him. He had to keep anyone else from dying, if he could.

And maybe Doug Stensrud was right about him, too—once a cop, you're a cop. Maybe a part of him needed this.

Sam walked quickly around the grandstand to the sloping hillside between the front of the grandstand and 12th tee, where hundreds of spectators sat and stood in the grass, waiting for play to resume. He turned to scan the seats behind them—nearly full, with those in the top rows standing and looking up the 11th fairway toward the scene of the explosion.

"I've swept the grandstand at 12 and the concession area behind the grandstand," Sam said into the radio. "I don't see him."

"We're still scanning the pines between 11 and 13," Caroline said into Culver's radio. "Lots of people still there, but I don't... wait."

"What?"

"There's a caddie! Tony, can we get a close-up with the fairway camera on 11?"

Silence for a few moments.

"Tighter!" Sam heard Petrakis yell in the background. Then Caroline said, "It's him! That's the bastard who tried to kill me! I know it! He's got a golf bag over his shoulder, but no clubs. Yeah, it says ROCKINGHAM on his jumpsuit. He's in the trees...between the 11th and 13th fairways...It looks like he's headed toward the 12th hole."

Sam ran around the right corner of the grandstand. There were still too many people milling around the concession area. Did every spectator on the course come running over here when they heard the explosion? And where were the cops?

"Keep a camera on him," Sam said. "If he changes direction, let me know. Boyce, are you listening?"

"Yeah. We're trying to get the security guards back from the explosion site."

"Well, make it quick, or there's going to be another one," Sam said.

Sam ran into the pine trees that guarded the high side of the dogleg on 13, hoping to intercept Doggett before he got to the densely packed Amen Corner. He pushed past knots of spectators until he'd almost reached the 14th fairway. Nothing. He asked a marshal in a yellow plastic hardhat if he'd seen a caddie go by. The marshal nodded and pointed back into the trees, toward the 12th hole.

Sam dodged spectators as he ran back along the paved path through the trees to the concessions area behind the grandstand on 12. No security guards or cops yet—and no sign of Doggett, either. There couldn't be a better spot to kill hundreds of people. Where the hell was he?

"Sam!" Caroline yelled in his earpiece. "We've got a close-up of him from the camera behind the 12th green. He's kneeling beside the grandstand! He's leaning the bag against the grandstand and lighting a cigarette...Now he's putting the cigarette into the golf bag!"

"Which side?" Sam yelled. "Left or right? You gotta tell me which side!"

"Right side—looking from behind the green!"

He pushed his way through the people clustered around him and ran around the corner of the grandstand.

There was Doggett—the sides and back of his head shaved under the green Masters cap, ROCKINGHAM written across the back of his jumpsuit—stepping over the rope next to the 12th tee and walking toward the Hogan Bridge, away from the crowd and away from the golf bag he'd left leaning against the grandstand. A wisp of smoke curled up from the smoldering cigarette that he had placed on top of the fluid-soaked towel and the fertilizer.

Sam pulled the Glock from its holster. He couldn't stop both Doggett and the bomb. He ran to the golf bag.

Doggett looked over his shoulder and yelled, "Hey—get away from there!"

Doggett reached inside his jumpsuit for the gun he'd used to kill Harwell. With Rae's Creek and the 12th green behind Doggett, Sam had a safe shot.

"Police! Put it down!" Sam screamed as he aimed the Glock. Doggett's hand emerged from the jumpsuit, holding a gun.

The shot wasn't perfect, but it was good enough. It hit Doggett in the neck, spun him around, and dropped him onto the fairway.

Sam picked the cigarette fuse off the top of the golf bag and threw it onto the grass. The gunshot still echoed across Rae's Creek as Doggett's blood oozed onto the immaculate turf. People in the grandstand were screaming, stunned to have witnessed a Masters caddie gunned down before their eyes. Who was the madman who shot him? Who would he shoot next?

"Everybody get back!" Sam yelled to those standing nearby. "I'm a cop!"

He picked up the golf bag, one hand on the handle and the other on the bottom of the bag, ran to the edge of Rae's Creek, and threw the bag as far as he could. It landed in the still pond with a splash, bobbed briefly, then sank silently to the bottom.

Sam returned to Doggett, lying on his back in the middle of the tightly mown slope that led down to the Hogan Bridge. He was still alive, but blood poured from the wound in his neck. His eyes were wide open, staring at nothing but conveying an unquenched fury.

"Doggett," Sam said, kneeling next to him. "What the hell were you trying to do?"

"Kill it," Doggett said, gasping. There was blood in his throat, bubbling into his mouth and running down his chin.

"Kill what?" Sam asked.

The lids of Doggett's eyes were beginning to droop, and the blood from his wound was turning the front of the jumpsuit from brilliant white to a deep cherry.

"The goddam...Masters..."

His eyelids fluttered and closed.

Sam stood up. Every eye in the grandstand was riveted on the lifeless Doggett. His green hat lay a few feet away, and the blazing sunlight glinted off his shaved, sweaty head.

Sam switched on his radio and called Boyce.

"It's Skarda. Doggett's dead. Tell Porter he'll get his final round in."

Chapter Forty-one

At the post-tournament press conference, the questions centered on Lee Doggett. Who was he, the reporters wanted to know. Was he responsible for all of the killings that week? How had he gotten onto the course? Why was he trying to bomb the Masters?

Mark Boyce of the Georgia Bureau of Investigation joined David Porter at the front table in the media center, giving the same sort of circumspect answers that Porter usually gave to questions about club matters.

"We don't know whether or why Mr. Doggett may have committed the series of murders this week," Boyce said in an authoritative monotone, as he faced the tiers of reporters and cameras. "That will have to wait until we complete our investigations. He's our prime suspect, obviously, but we can't say more than that now."

Sam stood off to the side with Caroline, watching the spectacle. Boyce had told him that he shouldn't answer any questions. But Sam wanted to be at the press conference, if only to prepare himself for whatever spin the media would put on the story.

The question foremost in every reporter's mind was asked by Russ Daly of the *L.A. Times*.

"David, can you tell us why you went ahead and completed play today?" Daly asked. "You had a cop shot and killed, a bomb go off on the grounds, and an alleged murderer gunned down in front of your customers. Didn't you even think about calling it off?"

Porter cleared his throat, adjusted his microphone and assumed the calm, controlled manner he'd always exhibited in front of the assembled media.

"Our weather radar indicated a series of thunderstorms moving in this evening, which we were told would last through most of the day tomorrow," Porter said. "We felt we owed it to our patrons to do everything we could to complete the tournament on schedule. We understand that today's events were shocking, but after order was restored, we believed everyone preferred to see the golf tournament resume. CBS did a wonderful job of keeping our millions of viewers informed throughout the afternoon, and I would particularly like to compliment Cameron Myers for his professionalism during the...disturbance, and afterward.

"The players put on a wonderful display of shotmaking today. Frank Naples' chip-in to win on the 18th hole will be remembered as one of the greatest shots in Masters history."

Sam looked at Caroline in disbelief. Everyone else in the world would remember this Masters as the year a murderer ran amok on the course—but to David Porter, the crisis had been handled, and all was right again on Magnolia Lane.

Even Robert Brisbane, seated to the side near Sam and Caroline, had to cover his chin with the palm of his hand to suppress a smile.

Brisbane had advised Porter to postpone the tournament's conclusion, but Porter had insisted on trying for a Sunday finish. It had taken the police and EMTs about two hours to complete their crime-scene investigation and remove Doggett's body from Amen Corner. Play then resumed with Barber and Cartwright—the first group out—finishing their 12th hole.

When the cops had taken Sam's statement, Boyce brought him up to the Butler Cabin, where Caroline was waiting for him in the basement studio CBS used for the televised presentation of the green jacket. She put her arms around Sam and held him tightly for a moment, then pulled away. She told him she'd watched him shoot Doggett on the CBS monitor. It hadn't gone out over the air, but it was an image that would never leave her.

"You didn't hesitate," she said. "You were trying to kill him."

Her tone was not accusatory, but matter-of-fact. She was still trying to process the violence she'd witnessed.

"I had a clear shot," Sam said. "And I was only going to get one."

"I'm glad he's dead," Caroline said quietly. "I'm just sorry it was you that had to do it."

"So am I."

They had stayed in the cabin to watch Frank Naples compete with Sergio Garcia and the dwindling sunlight, finally winning his second green jacket with his 70-foot chip-in from the back of the 18th green, down to the first tier and into the hole, cut in its usual front left Sunday location. When Naples was brought to the Butler Cabin, Cameron Myers used his most soothing voice to conduct a bland, content-free interview prior to the jacket ceremony. He referred to the explosion and the shooting of Doggett only once—indirectly—in a question about how Naples had managed to keep his concentration during the interruption of play.

"I'll never watch a golf tournament the same way again," Caroline said, as they watched Naples slip on the green jacket in the small basement studio. "I'm always going to be staring at the faces in the crowd, instead of at the players."

"I put you through a lot this weekend," Sam said.

"Damn right you did," she agreed. She stared intently at him with her piercing blue-green eyes.

"I'm sorry," he said.

"I know you are. But it's what you do. It's who you are. I should have realized that."

When the reporters asked Boyce at the press conference how Sam Skarda happened to be the one to shoot Doggett, he told them Sam had been working as a private investigator for the club. Porter was asked how long that arrangement had been in effect.

"We don't discuss the club's private business," Porter said.

"How much is he being paid?" someone asked.

"As I said: We don't discuss the club's private business," Porter replied. "But rest assured, we are very grateful for what Sam has done for this club."

"David, now that this is over, will Augusta National be rethinking its position on women members?" asked Jane Vincent of NBC.

Sam saw her question as the perfect opening for Porter to announce to the world that Margaret Winship would be asked to join. The National had stood firm through a vicious character assassination, proving its hands were clean in the killings and making a convincing case that private clubs should not allow themselves to be bullied or blackmailed. And with Rachel Drucker and the WOFF now being forced to retract their accusations, the National could play the perfect grace note by admitting Margaret Winship—not as a result of coercion, but simply because the club had chosen to, for its own reasons.

"We've had no discussions about that, and I don't believe we will in the immediate future," Porter said. "We'd prefer to focus on the golf tournament."

Business as usual. Never give an inch, until you're ready. Why should Sam have been surprised?

When the press conference ended and the reporters began working on their stories, Boyce accompanied Porter, Brisbane, Sam, and Caroline out of the media building.

"Well, I've got reports to file," Boyce said, looking at Sam. "Will you be staying here at the club? We'll need to reach you."

Sam looked at Porter, who nodded.

"I guess they'll let me hang around a little longer."

"Good," Boyce said. "That was outstanding police work today. You ought to reconsider quitting."

"Thanks," Sam said, shaking Boyce's outstretched hand. "I'm just sorry about Harwell."

"I know. We all are."

Boyce turned and walked to the parking lot. Porter asked Sam to accompany him to his office.

"I've got to pack," Caroline said. "I'm catching the red-eye back to Tucson tonight at 11:45."

"We could find a nicer room for you," Brisbane said with a smile.

"It's not the accommodations," Caroline said. "I really do have to get home."

"I'll drive you to the airport," Sam said.

"All right. See you in a while."

He watched her walk toward the clubhouse. She could have stayed if she really wanted to—but too much had happened here. Blood had stained the surreal beauty of Augusta National. A trip that was supposed to be purely for pleasure had turned into a nightmare. She'd almost been killed, and she'd watched Sam kill a man.

He wished he could be on the plane to Tucson, talking her through it.

◇◇◇

It was raining by the time Sam drove Caroline to the Augusta airport in the rented Taurus. He'd had to give the keys to the courtesy car back to the valet—another sign that Masters Week really was over.

He dialed the iPod to the April 1973 playlist—the year that Georgia native Tommy Aaron won his only Masters. There had been some great soul music on the air that spring. The first song was the O'Jays' "Love Train," followed by the Four Tops' "Ain't No Woman Like the One I Got."

Sam turned to look at Caroline in the illumination from the passing streetlights. There was no woman like her, but he didn't have her. Sunday had wiped away what had been a great beginning on Saturday night. Caroline had trouble accepting what he did for a living, and he couldn't tell her he was through doing it.

She had been quiet during the drive. He didn't know what he could say to her that wouldn't sound like he was just making conversation. He wasn't going to bring up anything about Doggett or the murders.

Then she did.

"How much did they pay you?"

She might have been stunned by the answer.

When Sam had gone back to the tournament headquarters with Porter and Brisbane, he was expecting a warm thank-you and a check for, what—$20,000? Maybe as much as $50,000. After all, these guys were rich, he'd helped save the tournament for them, and there had been bombs and bullets flying.

The check Porter wrote was for $250,000.

Sam started to ask if they could afford it, then almost laughed at himself. They'd probably spent more on shrimp this week.

"That's a lot of money," was all Sam managed to say.

"That's a fraction of what we paid Frank Naples today for winning," Porter said, with the first genuinely friendly smile Sam had seen from him all week. "Naples is a great guy and a hell of a golfer, but if he'd stayed in Texas, we'd still have had a Masters."

"You deserve that check as much as Naples deserves his," Brisbane said. "More, really."

Yet Sam couldn't bring himself to tell Caroline what he'd been paid. He wanted to see her again, but he didn't want money, or his job, to influence whether she wanted to see him again.

"They paid me enough," he finally answered her.

Enough to quit the cops. Enough to do something else. Maybe open his own investigations office, taking only the work that interested him. Maybe spend some time in Arizona...

That's what he wanted to tell her, but it would have to wait. Wait until Caroline made up her mind about him, and about who and what she wanted now that she was through with Shane Rockingham.

Gladys Knight and the Pips were singing "Neither One of Us Wants to Be the First to Say Goodbye" as the car pulled up to the curb in front of the terminal. The sob in Gladys' voice over the end of a love affair had never sounded more sincere.

"You timed that," Caroline said.

"If my timing were only that good," Sam said.

He helped her take her suitcase out of the trunk. They kissed, and Caroline walked into the terminal.

Neither one of them said goodbye.

To receive a free catalog of Poisoned Pen Press titles, please contact us in one of the following ways:

Phone: 1-800-421-3976
Facsimile: 1-480-949-1707
Email: info@poisonedpenpress.com
Website: www.poisonedpenpress.com

Poisoned Pen Press
6962 E. First Ave. Ste. 103
Scottsdale, AZ 85251